VALKYRIES RISING

VALKYRIE RENEWED

USA TODAY BESTSELLING AUTHOR

SHANNON PEMRICK

Valkyrie Renewed
Valkyries Rising | Book Four

Copyright © 2025 Shannon Pemrick
www.shannonpemrick.com

Cover Design by Covers by Combs
Editing by Sandra Nguyen
Chapter art by BRoseDesignz

First Edition © 2023

Print paperback ISBN 978-1-950128-30-3
Print hardcover ISBN 978-1-950128-29-7

BOOKS BY SHANNON PEMRICK

VALKYRIES RISING

Valkyrie Lost
Valkyrie Unknown
Valkyrie Destined
Valkyrie Renewed
Valkyrie Restored
Valkyrie Confused
Valkyrie Condemned
Valkyrie Freed
Valkyrie Shattered
Valkyrie Transformed

LOOKING FOR GROUP

Spellbinding His Ranger
Protecting His Priestess
Summoning Their Elementalist
Binding Their Elementalist

EXPERIMENTAL HEART

Destiny
Pieces
Secrets
Exposed
Surrendered
Reborn

ORACLE'S PATH

Prophecy of Convergence
Prophecy of Unbroken Oaths

See all books and learn more at
www.shannonpemrick.com

For those who would go to the end of eternity for those they love.

CONTENT WARNING

VALKRIE RENEWED contains mentions, discussions, and depictions of content some readers may find distressing. Reader discretion is advised. Please review the listed topics below and proceed with caution if needed. Your mental health is important.

Consensual non-monogamy	rough sex, swallowing
Child abuse/trauma (recovery from)	Hostage situation
Discussions of death & the afterlife	Magical prosthetics/limb regrowth
Domestic violence (mention only, not main characters)	Nudity
	Profanity
Familial, parental, & spousal death	PTSD & mental illness
Graphic (consensual) sexual content including: degradation & praise, DP, impact play, multiple partners, oral,	Resurrection & reincarnation
	Toxic familial relationships
	Violence, gore, & death

ONE

ASTRID

*H**ealing isn't easy. You must first accept you need it before you can begin your path to become a stronger, more whole person.*

This fake philosophical statement was just one of many my mind decided to concoct while I made breakfast.

Bacon sizzled and popped in the cast iron pan on the stove. The warm, caramelized, almost nutty scent of brewing coffee filled the spacious kitchen. Birds chirped and bees buzzed around some hanging plants beyond the open windows of the breakfast nook overlooking the deck, a refreshing summer mountain breeze drifting in.

I cracked another egg into the almost-full bowl, and grabbed my fork to whisk. My mind wandered, thinking of things I needed to do around the retreat today, which wasn't as much as I was used to.

We had the lowest number of residents living here that I could remember since Dad and I arrived when I was seven. Even when my best friend Diego and I went off to college, this place was insanely busy with activity and people needing counseling. But today, it was just me and Diego and three residents. Even Dad had gone off on a guys' hunting and fishing trip with Diego's dad, Xavier.

Of course, they deserved it. They'd worked so hard to keep this place running over the years, I wanted them to get out there and worry about just themselves for once.

And I didn't mind the lull. It allowed me to really focus on those who were left here, and even on myself. I'd come a long way since my traumatic past that brought Dad and me here, but I still needed to work on a few things.

I gasped when something cold and wet poked my arm. I whirled, and my heart rate kicked up when I came face-to-face with a black and brown furry face with light brown eyes. Closing my eyes, I sucked in a deep breath. I exhaled and looked at the sable German shepherd wagging her tail at my feet. "Angel…"

She whined and nudged my arm again. I stroked her head, noting the slight shake in my hands. I couldn't ignore the prickle of disappointment in myself. I'd worked so hard to face this fear. I'd gotten to the point where I could raise Angel myself, and I had for the last two years, ever since she was a puppy. And yet, I still had these reactions with her too often.

"Do you want to go outside?" I asked her in a cute voice.

Angel cocked her head and then spun around excitedly. I chuckled, the tension in my shoulders lessening.

When I opened the front door, she bolted out and ran into the yard, toward the surrounding forest. I went back to scrambling my eggs.

My vigorous hand motions paused when a large presence loomed over me. "Yes, Diego?"

"Damn, almost had you that time," he said, his voice smooth and warm. The sound wrapped around me like a comforting embrace, while also sending a prickle down my spine.

He pulled away, including his hands, which had hovered dangerously close to tickling my sides. "What's for breakfast?"

"I'm having eggs and bacon. Not sure what you're having."

He snagged the tongs from the counter to handle the bacon. "Seeing as it looks like you've prepared enough for an army, I'd say you're feeding post-workout me."

I turned to face him and was hit with a six-foot tall wall of hotness.

Fit, with tousled dark brown hair, a strong profile and prominent cheekbones accentuated by a delicious amount of stubble, and dusky brown skin, his exotic looks turned heads everywhere he went. He had a charming personality that won most over to boot, and I swore I was the only one who didn't ogle him, or the ripped abs he was showing off in his current shirtless state.

"You know the rules. You need to wear clothes outside your room."

He turned warm brown eyes on me and I had to stifle a sharp inhale. "I'm only missing a shirt, Astrid."

Okay, so maybe my lack of attraction to him was a lie. I did ogle when he wasn't looking. But only when he wasn't looking, because he was my best friend and life wasn't a romance book. You didn't fuck your best friend, no matter how hot, and magically everything turned out perfect and you two lived happily-ever-after.

"Yeah, and do you remember the last time you did that around a bunch of hormonal teenage girls?"

He laughed and gestured to the empty house. "We're alone. So, unless you've got a personal issue with me half-naked…"

Diego added a smirk to his implication, and I had to fight my insides from melting. "Why would I have any personal issue with it?"

He turned to face me, providing a tantalizing view of his broad shoulders and lean, yet well-muscled physique. His low-slung pants accentuated cuts of muscle, especially the deep V where his hips and torso met and disappeared into his sweats, tempting me to appreciate lower. *Don't look, Astrid. Don't you dare look at what those gray sweats try to tease.* "Hmm, maybe because you're one of the few who seem so unaffected by me, that it's almost like you're trying too hard."

I rolled my eyes. "Ah, yes, says the guy who, upon meeting me when we were seven, declared openly we were going to be best friends forever right then and there. It's almost like I took that declaration to heart or something."

And yet, when we hit our teen years, things changed for me. I saw him differently. The way he made me laugh was different. The way he treated me made me feel things I shouldn't. And my desire to be with him all the time like some clingy, horny—

I cursed my hormones ever since then as I fought attraction for the guy who clearly only saw me as his best friend, regardless of all the teasing between us. It was always just friendly banter—like now.

Diego slid his hand along his chest and down his delicious-looking abs I'd dreamed of touching intimately on a number of occasions. My eyes followed the motion without my say-so. The trail of dark hair dipping beneath the band of his sweats taunted me to look even lower. "You sure you're not just lying to yourself, *mi amor?*"

I leaned against the counter and pointed my egg-coated fork at him. "I think I'm quite certain I appreciate the hard work you put into yourself, but it's not doing anything to melt my panties."

Liar, liar, panties on fire.

His stupid grin didn't go away. "Touch me and prove it."

I bit back the urge to allow the challenge to rile me up. He knew I couldn't back down from a challenge he made. My pride wouldn't allow me to be so cowardly in front of him, and he was the same. It'd gotten us into so much trouble over the years.

And sure, I'd touched him as a friend all the time, which gave me a base idea of what I'd feel. But this was different. This was… it was outright feeling up my best friend's spectacular abs per his invitation and that caused all sorts of conflicting feelings in me. *One quick feel couldn't hurt, right?*

Diego patted his stomach. "C'mon, Astrid, just one appreciative touch."

I rolled my eyes. "Fine."

I'd prove to him I could do this and not react in the way he thought I would.

I reached out and pressed my hands against the hard muscles of his abdomen. A jolt shot through me from the contact. *Oh, gods, why?* They felt incredible, and it took everything in me to not react externally or internally.

Diego grasped my elbows and pulled me closer. His heat teased my skin, almost begging me to press against him. He towered over me, his attention strong and snaring. I wasn't short; I was a respectable height of five-two. It was just that most of the men in my life were giants. Xavier was the only rare exception at five-eight.

But the way Diego's height overtook me, mixed with our closeness, and me copping a feel—it did something to me, weakening my usually stiff backbone, and threatened my resolve. I squeezed my thighs together, desperate to fight back the sensations building in me.

Diego's hands slid down my arms, heating my skin, until he reached my hands. Grasping them, he glided my hands along his hot skin, allowing me to feel every peak and tantalizing valley of his hard abs.

Heat rushed toward my face, and I fought so damned hard to not let it show how this affected me. "What the hell are you doing?"

He grinned. "I don't think you're appreciating them enough."

I opened my mouth, but nothing came out. *Is he serious right now? He has to be messing with me.*

"Um, Astrid, what are you doing?" a young voice said.

I choked, all my building desire snuffing out in an instant, and Diego froze. He stared at the person standing just beyond the foyer. I turned to look at the teen girl with tightly braided, long black hair and dark umber skin. "Raeni, hi. Um, what are you doing?"

She was one of our residents at the retreat. She and her mom, Carrie, had shown up a number of years back after a rough life situation. Like Diego and me, she had grown up here most of her life.

Raeni's eyebrow rose. "That was my question to you. Why are you feeling Diego's abs?"

"Uh… well… I was…" I wracked my brain through several reasons to get me out of this jam. "Diego was feeling a bit insecure."

Diego fixed me with a disbelieving stare. I didn't care. This was his fault.

Raeni's expression didn't change. "Insecure?"

"Yeah," Diego said, forced to work with this. He leaned against the counter. "I've been working hard on my physique, but since I've been struggling to secure a long-term partner, I've been feeling down. I just need some reassurance."

"And as his BFF, he asked me," I said.

The girl tipped her chin down. "You? Insecure? But you're hot."

Diego and I passed each other a look. "Uh, Raeni, does your mom know you say that about people?"

She snorted. "You're kidding, right? I'm fifteen. Besides, she calls Idris Elba a beefcake all the time around me."

Well, she wasn't wrong. I drooled over that man too, especially in the MCU movies.

"But anyways, you didn't answer my question."

Diego shrugged. "Anyone can be insecure. Doesn't matter how good they look. Astrid and I have helped many people through those emotional boundaries."

Raeni shook her head. "Then you should work on that for yourself, 'cause you're seriously hot. Right, Astrid?"

Fuck. Why did this have to circle back to me every time someone brought up his looks in conversation? My other best friend, Aya, did it to me all the damned time.

"Yeah, he's hot," I said in the most nonchalant tone I could attempt.

Raeni held out her hands. "See."

Diego shook his head. "Go hang out with your *amigas* or something, Raeni."

She whipped out her phone, and her gaze flicked down to his abs. "Are you going to be walking around today like that?"

"No."

She huffed. "Fine. I'll go to a friend's instead of them hanging out here."

I bit back a laugh. *Called it.*

Diego turned back to face me when Raeni walked off. "You owe me."

I grunted and scooped my bacon onto a paper-towel-lined plate. "Your fault for putting me in that position."

He came up behind me again and his lips hovered close to my ear, puffing his hot breath against my skin, and sending a shiver down my spine. "Position? You say that like you didn't enjoy providing me a little appreciation. You even said you find me hot."

"Yes, and?" I really wanted this conversation to end. "As your friend, I can still find you objectively hot."

"Objectively."

Why did he sound so offended by that word?

My cell phone pinged with a new text and I took that as my way out of this awkward situation.

Slipping around Diego, I snatched my phone off the counter. I cocked my head at the notification.

"What's up?" Diego asked as he threw more bacon into the pan.

"It's a text from Officer Rory," I mumbled. I closed the open text conversation I'd had with Aya and pulled up the new text. "Looks like he had contact with someone who may need the retreat. He sent the guy our way and was checking to see if he arrived."

I texted Rory back to let him know we hadn't had any new arrivals yet, but we'd keep an eye out. "If he shows up, he'll be driving a blue pickup."

"Well, Rory hasn't been wrong yet with the people he's sent to us, so let's hope he does show," Diego said. "Have you heard from Aya?"

I nodded and put the phone down. "I was texting her this morning."

His brow spiked. "Isn't she in Chicago right now visiting her brother? It's a bit early for her to be up."

Given it was only eight A.M. here, he had a decent point. "You know she's always been an early riser, if she even slept at all."

Only whatever gods who were out there knew whether she did or not. I swore I could wake up at any time of night for whatever reason, and there she'd be, awake herself. Maybe her brother was like that, too. The way she talked about her twin, I didn't doubt it. "Plus, I think she's still working on Norwegian time."

After college, Aya had joined the retreat's staff to help run, and even improve, the technical infrastructure we had. But she also enjoyed seeing her family, who were split between Norway and Chicago, so she took time off periodically for visits. She came from a well-off family and did her own freelance gigs, all of which paid for the expenses, which was nice. Running a non-profit made it impossible to pay my friend enough of a wage to support her free-spirit ways.

"Did she say when she'll be back?" Diego asked.

I joined him by his side and poured the scrambled eggs in a waiting pan. "She's aiming for the next few days."

Diego scooped the finished bacon from the cast iron pan. "Tell her to text me back. She's the one who picked the Viking-age Norway theme for this year's cultural event. I still need her to approve a bunch of activities."

I laughed. I knew she was doing it on purpose to rile him up; she'd said so in her text.

The two of us finished making breakfast and fell into casual conversion while we ate in the breakfast nook. Around the time we finished, Angel was bouncing around the windows by the front door, begging for someone to play with her. Diego had a session this morning with Carrie, so Angel would only get one of us as a playmate.

"Good luck," I said. "And you know to call out if you need me to step in."

I was Carrie's main therapist, but for the last year, Diego had been sitting in on her sessions to help with her healing. Today would be her first session with just him.

Diego nodded. "She's been doing amazing lately. I think she can handle this."

Angel barked, and I rolled my eyes. "Impatient."

Diego laughed and went off to dress for his session while I snagged one of Angel's many balls she had around the house. The moment I stepped outside with her ball, Angel barked and spun in circles. I laughed and tossed her toy.

We played fetch until the sound of an approaching truck distracted us. I turned to face the winding driveway that disappeared into the forest and soon enough, the front end of a blue pickup truck appeared. *This must be the guy Rory mentioned.*

Angel, on full alert and ball still in her mouth, huffed at the approaching vehicle. I commanded her to heel and she tucked up to my left side. Whomever this was, I couldn't be sure they were comfortable with dogs. We'd never had anyone come here with cynophobia—my particular fear was the worst we'd had to work with—but I made sure I trained Angel appropriately to ensure all introductions to new people were as positive as possible.

I walked up to the porch, watching the truck park in the expansive driveway, facing the house. Commanding Angel to sit and stay where she was, I approached the edge of the porch.

The driver-side truck door flung open and a broad-shouldered man with an impressive musculature climbed out. *He's huge.* He had to be at least six-five, and appeared to be in his mid-to-late thirties, making him maybe five or so years older than me.

His chestnut brown hair was shaved on both sides, and the rest swept to one side past his high cheekbones, down to his prominent jawline of his angular face. His well-kept beard added to his rugged features. Scars littered his tan skin, and he had a few tattoos banding his arms and lower neck onto his chest under his shirt that hugged his body everywhere just right.

He leaned against his open door and looked up at me with unreadable blue eyes. *Hot damn, this guy is hot.*

Not only did this guy check off a hell of a lot of sex-appeal boxes, but the strangest sensation of familiarity washed over me. Yet, I'd never met this man before, I was sure of it.

"Hey there. Name's Astrid Erikson. Welcome to Valkyrie's Reach."

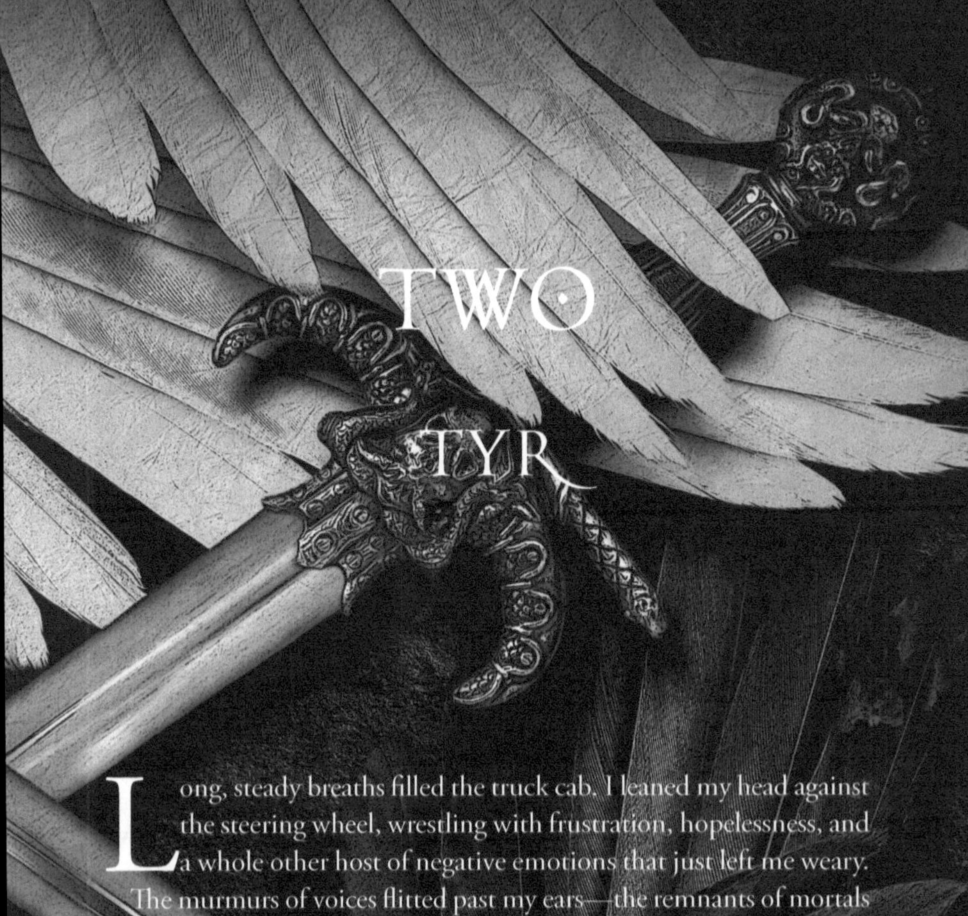

TWO ·

TYR

Long, steady breaths filled the truck cab. I leaned my head against
the steering wheel, wrestling with frustration, hopelessness, and
a whole other host of negative emotions that just left me weary.
The murmurs of voices flitted past my ears—the remnants of mortals
and immortals who still valued my name and power after these long
centuries. A few, I acknowledged on instinct, pushing power toward
them. Most, though, were left unanswered, my heart not in it to
properly listen to them.

I lifted my head and gazed at the set of old, worn gold rings hanging
on a chain from my rear-view mirror. They glinted in the early morning sun peeking through the thick tree canopy sheltering this worn
mountain road I parked on the side of. I reached out and touched
them with the healed-over stub where I'd lost my hand in an attack
by my former close friend, now mortal enemy, Fenrir.

Millenia had passed since that fateful day, the day he took my
Valkyrie from me. I'd searched endlessly, trying to find her after I
forced Freya into a binding oath to bring her back to life. The resulting spell reincarnated her, sending me on this search.

I gazed at the rings, longing aching in my chest. *I'm not giving up, Astrid. I promised I'd never rest until I found you.*

Technically, I had in the past—a few times, in fact. But I was… too late, each time.

Just like that fateful day, we found her mangled, bloody body. Each time a different age, but never older than a child. The only reason we knew it was her was because Freya detected her magic around the girl—and her unmistakable, flaming-red hair.

And then my binding oath on the goddess forced her to try the process all over again. Why Astrid continued to die, and what had killed her each time, was a mystery even to this day. But I was determined to have my Astrid back.

Maybe it was wrong of me to do this. Maybe I should let Astrid rest finally and release Freya from her oath. But a part of me wasn't ready for that yet. I was selfish enough to want to try, just one more time.

My gaze flicked to the rearview mirror when a car door slammed shut. A police car parked behind me, its lights flashing. *Shit.* I probably wasn't supposed to park here.

An older man in what I guessed was his mid-fifties, with rich brown skin and dressed in a blue uniform, approached the driver's side of my truck. I rolled my window down.

"Morning, Officer," I greeted. I'd play nice to ensure this ended quickly, so I could get on my way.

"Morning," he said in a gruff, low voice. "You broken down?"

I shook my head. "No. I was taking a break. I've been driving for a while. I thought this was the safest place on this road to pull over."

The officer nodded. "It's one of the safer spots, but we still don't like it on account of safety."

"I apologize. I'll get moving right away."

The officer glanced into the cab of the truck. "Anyone in here with you?"

My gaze flicked to the passenger seat, where paper maps sprawled instead of where Baldur should have been sitting.

"No, just me," I mumbled. It was always only me. My one goal kept me focused. I needed no distractions from other gods, immortals, or even mortals. I'd lost track of most of those I knew. I didn't keep in contact with anyone, not even Freya these days. She would be bound by the oath, and since she could sense out most immortals, she'd come find me if she located Astrid. So, these days, I was a lone wolf, so to speak.

No, that's not quite right. I'd also had contact with Davyn, a Berserker who was loyal to me and was a good friend to both Astrid and me. We'd rekindled that bond a few years ago when he sought me out after centuries of silence. It'd been good for me, at least when he was around. I fell back into the darkness soon after he'd leave.

The officer nodded, his eyes sympathetic. "I know that feeling, son."

I doubted he did, but I didn't voice it.

"Where you headed?" he asked.

I shrugged. "Don't know. Just wandering, really. I'm nomadic these days."

Wasn't a stretch from the truth. I couldn't remember the last time I'd gone home to Norway. Too many memories. Too much pain. It made more sense to follow the feel of battle, however that conflict manifested itself and in whichever country, and then drive from there.

But that wasn't the exact reason I'd come this way. Davyn was.

His woman, Azzie, prayed to me—not to me specifically, but her original open prayers resonated with my domain enough for me to take them on, so I'd accepted her as one of mine. As a result, recently she'd prayed for safety for another man of hers, Zeke.

It was a strange prayer to come to me. Davyn offhandedly mentioned that Zeke was heading to New York to visit with some friends. He did that on occasion. Normally I wouldn't have cared, but Davyn had mentioned the name of one of these friends—Astrid.

We'd learned that whatever magic Freya had used in her ritual had resulted in Astrid always being bestowed the same name, much like Kirby with her curse. However, it also wasn't that uncommon of a name.

I'd run across it many times, but it was never my Astrid. Its common occurrence was why Davyn had been so casual about it. But I couldn't shake the idea it might be a lead; it was too much of a coincidence to ignore.

So, I used my abilities as a war god to teleport as close as I could, latching onto some trouble in Albany and then traveled from there. Davyn didn't know exactly where in New York Zeke had gone, as he'd never bothered to inquire. That put me at a disadvantage considering the state's size, leaving me to do what I did best—wander until I felt a tug in my gut to change directions. As far as my map said, or when I last checked, I was somewhere in the Adirondacks now.

"You lost?"

I shook my head. "No."

He gazed at me for a moment. "Sure seem it to me."

My lips pressed into a thin line. "I know where I am on this map."

The officer shook his head. "That's not what I mean."

Then what did he mean? What other kind of lost could I be?

The gentleman pointed up the road. "Five miles up this road on the left is a secluded drive. I recommend following that path."

My eyebrow raised. Miles. Americans and their archaic measurement system. "What's there?"

"We call it the Retreat. That's not the name of it anymore, but we locals are used to calling it that. Good place for people who are lost like yourself. Astrid will take good care of you."

Everything in me froze. "What was that name again?"

"Astrid. Nice gal." The officer smiled, something warm and affectionate, like a father or good friend. "She's got a good heart, always doing what she can to help others. She and that family have done a lot of good here."

Something tugged in me. Like rope yanking me toward his words. Had I finally found the Astrid Zeke knew? *Could she be...* "You said five miles?"

The officer nodded. "It'll be the first left you can take. They put up a big sign recently, so it shouldn't be too hard to tell if you've taken a wrong turn."

"Alright, I'll check this place out." I didn't care what the purpose of the place was. I just needed to check.

"Drive safe, and keep your eyes peeled," the officer said. "People hike and ride horses along these roads."

The officer walked back to his car, and after waiting for him to enter the vehicle, I started my truck and drove off. I took in every landmark possible along the eight-kilometer drive. If this wasn't a dead-end lead, I'd need to familiarize myself with this area.

My thoughts also went to Astrid. What did she look like? How old was she? What was she like?

The officer made it seem she was a fairly prominent member of the community here. That was on track for how she was in the past. But what was this retreat? Some sort of resort? That couldn't be. My Astrid was a healer. *Remember what Freya warned you.*

I took a controlled breath. I couldn't go into this thinking she was the same woman I loved. Maybe there would be similarities, but she would be a new Astrid. I had to treat her as she was now.

A tingling sensation prickled my nerves where I was missing my hand. I also had to prepare for the real possibility that she'd want nothing to do with me.

I had tried to ignore those thoughts ever since I began my journey. I didn't want to face that consequence after everything I'd done to have her again.

The road curved, and then on my left opened to an offshoot dirt road. I slowed the truck. *This has to be the turnoff.* I didn't see the sign the officer mentioned, but it could be farther up.

Taking the left, I drove for several meters before finding the sign the officer mentioned. The truck lurched to a halt. *It can't be…*

Numbness fell over my body. The ornate wood and metal sign read:

Valkyrie's Reach
Where the lost are found

My hand gripped the steering wheel tighter. It creaked under my massive strength.

I sat there for… I wasn't sure how long… struggling to breathe and sort out my racing thoughts. *Does she know? If she does, why is she here? Why didn't she seek any of us out? Maybe she's tapping into ancestral memories without knowing. Could this be a coincidence? Is there something else at play here?*

My mind raced and looped, trying to make sense of this all, one thought after another.

Until they stopped.

Nothing. Nothing swam around in my head. I shifted the truck into drive and drove up the road, as if compelled.

This was the only way to know for certain. I had to see with my own eyes.

The drive was longer than I expected. I would have guessed a retreat of sorts would want to be closer to the main road for access, given we were so far from the main town as it was, but maybe the appeal was the seclusion.

Eventually, the sheltering trees thinned into a clearing where a sizable house of timber and stone stood. The road, now I saw, was one long driveway, widened, spanning in front of the house and leading up to a two-car garage. Two cars were parked at the far end of the driveway.

My pulse picked up. A woman with flaming-red hair played with a dog out front. Her back was turned to me, but I couldn't stop myself from believing my search might have finally come to an end.

My truck's engine roared when I hit a slight incline on the driveway. The woman and dog, a German shepherd from the looks of it, turned my way. Everything slowed. *It's her.*

Hair vibrant as wildfire, and skin as pale as the moon, with freckles splattering her like stars in the sky.

I threw the truck into park in front of the house. She stood on the porch with the dog now, gazing back at me with those same piercing green eyes framed by thick lashes I remembered.

My movements to get out of the truck were slow. It was as if, just like my mind, my body couldn't process this moment I'd longed for. I leaned on the open truck door, mostly using it for balance, as Midgard had been thrown off-kilter.

"Hey there," she said, her voice a light alto, just like back then. "Name's Astrid Erikson. Welcome to Valkyrie's Reach."

Her body was a little different. While the same height I remembered, her proportions weren't the same. She had toned muscle in all the right places, however her leaner figure of the past was replaced by eye-catching wide hips and large breasts.

She had minimal jewelry. A few earrings to accentuate her elegant face with tapered jawline and high cheekbones, a ring, and a septum piercing in her petite nose were the only things to adorn her.

The most notable feature about her, though, was the unmistakable long scar that cut diagonally on her face from her right eyebrow to left cheek. It was the spitting image of the one she had in the past.

She's as stunning as the day I lost her.

Astrid cocked her head. "You okay?"

"Uh, yeah…" I shook my head, trying to clear it. "Long drive."

It was clear she had no idea who I was. I needed to get myself together and play things cool.

"You the guy Officer Rory sent up?"

I had to push through the fog to understand what she meant. She spoke like those I'd come in contact with around these parts, but it was so different from in the past. It meant I'd have to adapt quickly. "The officer I talked to, old enough to be my father?"

She smirked and approached. "Yeah, that's him. Glad you could make it."

I shut the truck door and met her halfway. "Astrid, right?"

"That's right. And you are?"

"Tyr," I said.

"Tyr," she murmured. I saw the internalization of my name through her eyes. My pulse skipped, hoping it might spark something. "Like the Norse god. That's not a common name."

So, she was familiar with my name, but I was sure she'd never prayed to me, meaning she couldn't be a practicing heathen. That was interesting. With my absence in Midgard, I'd faded from prominence except with those who actively worshiped me. My dwindling power was evidence of that. *It's fine, if I stick around, maybe it'll spark something in her.*

I held up my left hand to shake hers and glanced at my missing one. "I'd offer a proper handshake if I could."

Her eyes flicked down to my missing appendage. If she saw a

correlation between my injury and name, it didn't show in her expression as she looked back up at me and smiled. *Her mind might try to make sense of this as a coincidence, and tell her I'm just another wounded warrior, like most believe.*

Astrid slipped her soft, warm hand in mine and shook. A familiar jolt coursed through me with the contact, one I knew from the first time she and I had ever touched long ago. And like that first time, her motion paused for a moment, as if she felt it, too. "It's a pleasure to meet you, Tyr. If you decide to stay, I hope you enjoy it here."

I worked my jaw and looked around, taking in the house and the surrounding yard and forest. "What is here, exactly? The officer didn't quite explain that to me."

Astrid chuckled. "Sounds like him. Valkyrie's Reach is a therapy retreat. We specialize in helping those who are lost find themselves and soar higher than they ever did before."

"That's rather poetic," I said.

Her eyes squinted in the way I was familiar with as she smiled. "I wish I could take credit, but I have Aya to thank for that line."

A muscle in my neck twitched. *It couldn't be…* When mortals anglicized many of our names, Freya adopted the change with ease. She had to. A god who couldn't adapt disappeared from existence. But that wasn't all.

Freya embraced the change so well, last I'd heard, she'd begun going by an altered name—*that* name. "Aya?"

"A friend of mine and one of our employees. She makes sure our technical infrastructure is advanced and up to date, so no one has to go without comforts they're used to, like cell service and internet."

That didn't put my suspicions at ease. No, it made them worse. Like me, Freya held dominion over war. However, unlike me, where I still focused on the physical aspect of war, Freya had adapted to the change in technology, turning her attention to cyberwarfare, or whatever it was called. I hadn't adapted well to the technological advancements of this century. Hell, Davyn was the whole reason I had a cell phone. He was my only contact in it.

"So, this is a therapy retreat. That makes you a shrink?"

Astrid laughed. The songbird-like sound made my heart skip. It was achingly similar. "I prefer therapist. I would rather foster a more positive relationship with mental health and healing than perpetuate the outdated stigma of shame."

My lips pressed into a thin line. The job fit her, no doubt. It wasn't directly a physical healing job like she'd done in the past, but I'd seen the effects of poor mental health, particularly on warriors. The evolution of mental health healing, and as a result, physical healing, was an important change I agreed with. But for someone to get into my head… I wasn't thrilled by the idea, even if that person was Astrid.

She gazed at me sympathetically. "I can understand your hesitation. Taking the step to heal mentally isn't easy. And I want you to understand, therapy doesn't mean you're broken. We all can benefit from understanding ourselves and growing from that."

Astrid clasped her hands together. "Therapy sessions also aren't mandatory here. People come to heal here in many ways. And while Diego and I specialize in mental healing, we have resources for those who need to physically heal, or even just need a safe place to get away from the difficulties of their lives and reevaluate what they want."

That sounded like a better deal. I didn't need to heal. I wasn't lost. I was fine. Now that I'd found her, I was fine. A quieter place away from the noise of urban life to get to know her again sounded perfect.

"How much does this all cost?" Living as long as I had, money wasn't an issue. But it seemed like something mortals would be concerned about, so I had to ask.

"Valkyrie's Reach is a non-profit, and exists and runs solely funded by donations. We don't ask for up-front payments from our residents, as we understand many who come to us aren't in the position to shell out any monetary expenses. Of course, if you're in a financial position to donate during your stay, and you wish to, we won't discourage you, but overall, all we ask is that you consider donating once you've gotten back on your feet and are ready to go back out in the world."

A noble cause—something I'd expect from her. And that detail was good to know so I could plan how to support her here. "I'd like to give this place a try, then."

Her smile brightened. "Wonderful! Why don't I show you around, and then I can get you set up with your cabin?"

"Cabin?"

Astrid nodded. "All residents have their own cabins for privacy. You'll have a bed, bathroom, and kitchenette. Everything you need to fend for yourself if you're not up to group meals or activities."

She gasped. "Oh, are you okay with dogs and cats?"

I grinned. "I love dogs. Cats, I'm indifferent."

A relieved smile spread over her face. "Let me introduce you to Angel, then."

My gaze flicked to the dog, who still remained on the porch with the ball in its mouth. The dog hadn't moved a centimeter. Astrid called the dog's name and then made a hand motion to come to us. The dog's ears perked, and then it sprinted over.

"Good girl," Astrid praised when the dog sat at her feet. "This is Angel. She's our resident emotional support buddy, as well as our famous search-and-rescue hero."

I crouched to be at a better level with the dog. "A lady of many talents."

Angel stretched her neck and sniffed me, all the while refusing to relinquish her ball. I reached out and gave her a good scratch behind the ear, careful not to be too rough with her. Angel tilted her head into the touch and her tail thumped on the ground.

Astrid beamed at the positive interaction. It was clear she cared about this dog. We'd had a number of pets together in the past, but cats had been her favorite. It seemed things had changed in this life for her, and I didn't mind one bit.

She turned to lead me into the house, but stopped short. A teen girl with dark skin stood on the porch. She stared at me.

"Raeni," Astrid said.

"Who is this?" the girl asked.

"This is Tyr. He's a potential new resident."

The teen continued to watch me. She didn't seem fearful, but she had worried lines along her brow that pulled at the corners of her eyes. Was I scaring her? My appearance did that to some. "Does my mom know?"

"Not yet," Astrid said. Her tone was kind and calm. "He just arrived, and she's in a session with Diego. I'd planned to text him so he could break the news to her."

This all piqued my interest, and the girl seemed to notice. "My mom is afraid of men like you."

My brow lifted. "Like me?"

She shook her head. "That came out wrong. Sorry. I meant men who look a lot like you."

I nodded, understanding where this was going. Her mother had been a victim of something; my guess was some sort of violent crime. I'd unfortunately seen my fair share of such effects in my time.

"Astrid, can I be the one to tell her?" Raeni asked.

Astrid nodded. "If you think you can deliver the news in a way she'll handle well. If not, tell Diego, and he'll handle it from there."

The teen nodded and ran off the porch, on a path leading down the hill the house was built on.

Astrid gave me an apologetic look. "Sorry about that."

"Is my presence here going to be a problem?" I hoped not. After finding her, I didn't like the idea of having to leave.

She shook her head. "No. You're not the only person to arrive here who has fit the profile Carrie struggles with. And she knows we won't allow someone to stay if we don't deem them safe."

"I will do my best to give her space so she doesn't feel threatened," I said. I'd agree to just about anything if it meant I could stay.

Astrid smiled appreciatively and then led me into the foyer of the main house. Two staircases on opposite sides of the foyer wound up to the second floor with a loft. We stepped into the great room. Natural light streamed in from the enormous windows all over.

To our right was a full kitchen, with granite counters and modern appliances. A curved breakfast nook was to one side of the kitchen, while a formal dining space was to the other, along with what appeared to be a pantry.

Angel trotted into the kitchen to lap up some water.

"This is the main gathering area, where everyone is welcome. However, because this main building is home to my dad and me, plus staff, we ask you to respect the hours you pop in." Astrid pointed to our left. "My dad's room is over there. There is a set of stairs leading to the basement and upstairs. Beyond the kitchen is the laundry room and another bedroom, as well as the stairs leading to the basement and upstairs. That bedroom belongs to Xavier. He's Diego's dad and our groundskeeper, as well as resident chef. You won't meet my dad or Xavier for a while. They're on vacation."

I nodded.

"The deck can be accessed from the breakfast nook and the great room. My dad's room also has its own door for it, so just keep in mind which door you're using when you're out there."

I chuckled. That would be an embarrassing mistake I'd like to avoid.

"Upstairs is just the loft and bedrooms for me, Diego, and Aya. Downstairs is the full communal space for everyone. There's a gaming and recreation room with a bar for hanging out, along with the library and study, second laundry room, gym and sauna, and hot tub. You can access the pool out back from the basement, or by going around the house."

My eyebrows spiked. This was an impressive home. "You are a licensed therapist and you own this place? How old are you?"

Astrid chuckled. "I'm twenty-nine. But I always tell people not to compare others' accomplishments to their own. We all achieve our goals at different times. Mine are also rather deceptive. Yes, I worked hard to obtain my college degree and licensing, but when it comes to this place, my dad and I inherited it from my grandparents. They ran the retreat before we came here. So, they gave me a head start running this place."

I cocked my head. "What do you mean, before you came here?"

She smiled. "Pete and Randi weren't my bio grandparents. Dad and I came here as residents. We bonded and became a new family during that time."

I tried to smile back, but found it difficult. While I was happy she found herself with a good family in the end, and seemed to be safe now, what horrible event had she suffered to need to come here to begin with? What had I again almost lost her to?

I needed to not think about that. "So, you have this place, and then smaller cabins for residents. And this is all afforded through donations?"

She nodded. "For the most part, yes. We have a few particularly generous donors who make sure we're all comfortable. Plus, whatever townies donate, and what retreat residents give either during or after their stay here. Diego and I do sometimes take clients who aren't residents as paid sessions, and Dad does his own side work, so we funnel that income into the retreat as well."

Astrid showed me the communal downstairs. Just as the upstairs, all the rooms were well-furnished and comfortable. The view from the recreation room to the back of the house with the pool, landscaped lawn, and surrounding forest was idyllic. I could only assume the view from the deck above was even better.

"Where are the cabins?" I asked. I couldn't see them from here.

Astrid pointed to the path in the yard that angled for the forest. "They're spread out along the property. There are some that are in the forest, while we did some clearing around some others. You'll have your pick, as we've got plenty of space right now."

"How many residents are here?"

"Including you, four. You'll see Carrie and Raeni the most. Sean likes to keep to himself. The retreat gives him a place to live where it's quiet and close to nature. If you see him, he'll probably be doing some gardening, or spending time in the woods."

I nodded slowly. "I don't suppose you've got a cabin with a lakefront view?"

Astrid laughed. "If we did, I'd be living there instead of the main house."

It was good to hear she'd likely still love the lake house in Norway.

The sliding glass door slid open, and a tall, broad-shouldered man with a lean yet well-muscled frame around Astrid's age walked in. He brushed some wayward strands of his tousled hair out of his face.

Astrid's face lit up upon seeing him, and my gut twisted. I knew that look. It was the one she had upon seeing me before we admitted to any feelings we had for each other—the one she had for Baldur.

The man came up to us and draped his arm over her shoulder. The action, while innocuous to most, mixed with the way he looked at Astrid, came off as slightly possessive, as if he were staking a claim. When he spoke, I noted he had a voice that could easily charm a woman. "This our new resident?"

Astrid smiled up at him. "Diego, this is Tyr. Tyr, this is my best friend and our other resident therapist, Diego Santos Nilson."

"Just call me Diego," he said.

Best friend. Not lover, boyfriend, or any other romantic assumed title. I still had a chance, though it was clear I would have competition for her affection, and he already had a head start.

I pushed away all the feelings and offered my hand in an attempt to be cordial. I wouldn't mess this up by causing issues with someone she called a friend. Diego reciprocated the handshake.

"I was about to show him a few of the cabins to see if any interest him," Astrid said.

"That's actually what I wanted to talk to you about," Diego said. "Carrie made a request that he take a look at some cabins that would require him to walk past hers."

Astrid's brow rose high. "She said that?"

He nodded. "Raeni did a great job explaining the new situation to her, and Carrie decided all on her own that she thought it might help."

Diego looked to me. "That's if you're okay with this. I made sure Carrie understood we wouldn't force you to move once you're settled."

"Sure?" I really wasn't sure how to answer, since I didn't quite understand Carrie's situation. "I don't wish to cause anyone here any undue stress with my presence."

Astrid smiled reassuringly. "You'll be fine. Carrie is making this step on her own. It shows her healing progress and growth. All you have to do is be kind and give her plenty of space unless she says otherwise."

I could do that. "I'll grab my things."

"Would you like to see the cabins first?"

I shook my head. "I don't have much."

Traveling light was easiest, and I didn't need much beyond the necessities.

If Astrid thought my comment deserved pity, she didn't show it.

She merely nodded with a pleasant smile on her beautiful face. We headed upstairs while Diego left to speak with Carrie again. Angel followed us outside and down to my truck with her ball, hoping it was playtime. I had a feeling I was going to like this dog.

I folded back my truck bed cover and reached for my backpack. Curious, Astrid peered in. I didn't mind. I knew better than to carry anything compromising on me. Most people this day and age didn't react well to the idea of gods, immortals, and other creatures that fell under the supernatural walking amongst them, so we'd come to blend in and act as if old tales were just that.

"Is that armor?" Astrid asked.

Ah, forgot about that.

She reached in and lifted a maille hauberk and a tunic. Her eyes widened with wonder and her lips parted. *Does she recognize these?* Wars may have changed over the years, and I'd altered what weapons and armor I used if I participated, but I still held onto my old armor. I added to it for the sake of illusion, since gods required little in the way of armor, and carried it with me in hopes that the day I found her, she'd recognize some of it and see it was me.

But unfortunately, it didn't seem to have the effect I'd wanted.

"Are you a Middle Ages enthusiast?" she asked.

"Viking Age reenactor," I said without hesitation. I'd learned this was the easiest way to explain the armor and weapons if anyone found out by chance.

"Wow, really?" Her excitement was surprising. "In a couple weeks, we're holding our annual cultural festival. We pick a different culture each year to explore and teach. The whole town gets involved. And coincidentally, this year, we chose the Viking Age. It'd be fantastic to have someone else to act in character to help with the immersion. If you're up for participating, of course."

"Someone else?" I couldn't shake the oddness of this situation.

"Aya is the one who came up with the theme this year. She's a reenactor as well. She's from Norway, so she's got all kinds of great history knowledge from living there." Astrid cocked her head. "Actually, you two have similar accents. Where are you from, if you don't mind me asking?"

A muscle twitched in my neck. This was too coincidental. "I'm also from Norway."

She blinked. "Huh. That's a bit of a coincidence."

I wasn't so convinced. Finding Astrid as an adult, safe after some mysterious event that forced her to come to a place like this, and after she'd made friends with a woman with two traits too similar to the goddess I had a strained relationship with after the events that killed Astrid originally? Something was not right here.

"I look forward to meeting Aya. It'd be nice to speak to someone from the home country again." It was best to stay polite. I didn't need Astrid getting suspicious.

She watched me haul my backpack over my shoulder. "Have you not been there lately?"

I shook my head. "I haven't been home in a long time. Maybe sometime soon, after I've wandered enough to figure things out."

Astrid smiled. "Well, I hope we can help you with that while you're here."

If I played my cards right, she'd do more than just help. "I hope so, too."

THREE

DIEGO

EEP. BEEP. BEEP.

Heaviness weighed on my mind. Warmth cocooned me. And some annoying sound was ruining my perfect dream. *Cállate.*

BEEP. BEEP. BEEP.

The sound continued, dragging me closer to awareness. *My alarm.* I groaned and flailed my arm blindly, trying to find my phone. My hand slammed into the side of my dresser and I flinched, the pain jolting my brain awake more.

BEEP. BEEP. BEEP.

Shut up. My hand landed on the smooth face of my phone, but my half-awake brain didn't have coordination. The phone slipped from my fingers and clattered on the floor. *Fuck…*

Struggling awake, bright light filtering around my blinds assaulted my eyes. I groaned. That, mixed with the continued beeping of my alarm, forced me to wake up.

I flopped onto my back and sucked in a deep breath, yawning wide until my jaw popped. My eyes fluttered open, the vaulted ceilings of my room and gaming and movie posters and motocross trophies decorating the walls greeting me.

BEEP. BEEP. BEEP.

Grumbling, I rolled over and scooped my phone off the floor. I tapped my screen and turned my alarm off. The app paused and the most beautiful, smiling face greeted me on my lock screen.

Astrid's eyes squinted as they always did, and her smile filled her face. Angel, a ten-week-old puppy here, eagerly licked her face. Aya, a pale woman with long, blonde dreadlocks, hung off Astrid, making the funniest cooing face at the pup.

This was the day I'd surprised Astrid with Angel. I'd hoped after all the work she'd done to tackle her fear, Angel would be the tipping point Astrid needed to overcome it. Plus, she'd been talking about wanting a pet. The initial meeting hadn't gone smoothly, but it wasn't long before this photo was possible.

I tucked my arm under my head and unlocked my phone. A new wallpaper displayed. This one was of Astrid and me on a hiking trip just the other day. Angel posed at our feet, her tongue-lolling face just as happy as the two of us. I gazed at Astrid's face, a sense of longing pricking my chest.

A memory of the dream I hadn't wanted to end found its way to the surface. I held her close, stroking her cheek in an intimate way I longed to in real life. The way she looked up at me, it was clear she was used to that affection from me in the dream, and had been for some time. Years, decades even, maybe? I wasn't sure, but in my dream, I felt how long it was. And yet, we looked the same as we did right now.

I blew out a breath and sat up, hanging my feet off the bed and rubbing my face. *It was just a dream.* They happened—a lot. It was how I'd screwed any potential between us, because like the naïve child

I was, the night before I met her, I'd dreamed of a red-haired girl with a face scar I'd be best friends with. We were amigos forever. So, of course, when I saw her that day, I made my declaration.

Objectively hot. I ran my fingers through my disheveled hair. I deserved that. I'd tested boundaries so many times since I started seeing her differently in high school, and each time it was clear she took our friendship as it was.

I thought I'd had her yesterday. I knew I was attractive. I had my share of people to choose from in my attempt to find someone I didn't compare to Astrid, and I would become completely enamored with instead. And every one of those people, while not that special person for me, appreciated what I brought to those relationships. And there was no way Astrid wouldn't have come even a little undone after what I'd asked her to do if she did feel something toward me.

I sighed and turned my gaze to a photo sitting on my dresser. I lifted the frame and stared at the impressively tall woman with alabaster skin, pale eyes, and even paler hair I always swore was silver. She had her arms wrapped around six-year-old me, both of us smiling for *Papá*, who I remember taking this photo.

I was so happy that day. So unaware how much our lives would change the next day when they would tell me *Mamá* was sick, and we'd be moving from Spain to the States so she could receive specialized treatments.

My finger traced her delicate face. *I know that dream was only a dream, because you were there. And there's no bringing back the dead...*

My chest constricted until it felt like I was suffocating. I placed her photo frame back on my nightstand, turning away.

I was sure that if she were still here, she'd have some brilliant advice on how to approach my Astrid issue. I couldn't go to Papá. I loved him, but his advice would surely have me driving Astrid away with how forwardly romantic he'd suggest I be. That wasn't to say I wasn't a romantic. Hell, I learned from the best, watching Papá romance Mamá every day.

But Papá came off fairly strong. Even Mamá admitted to me one day, she was almost put off by his forwardness when they first met. *And like hell I'll talk to Darius about how to go about dating his daughter.*

I wasn't afraid of her father. No, he was a good man and didn't do the crazy overprotective thing. What I feared was him intentionally trying to make me look like a fool for the laughs. It would probably be effective, but I wasn't looking to embarrass myself into eternity to win Astrid's affections.

I shook my head of the thoughts and found my workout clothes. A strong routine would get my head on straight—or as straight as it could be for me.

Moving through the house, I noticed the stillness. No clicking of computer keys or anyone rummaging around in the kitchen. I knew Astrid would be outside doing archery practice. She mentioned it last night. But it was Aya's lack of presence that made part of this not feel right. She was always up before either of us and doing something on a computer.

Even Papá's and Darius' lacking presence felt wrong. It was like life was a little emptier with them missing.

I paused at the stairs leading to the basement. Music pulsed below. Not so loud it would wake someone sleeping on the first floor if they were around, but enough to have purpose. The beat had the perfect rhythm for sets. *Viking metal?*

That could only mean Astrid was using the gym. She had an eclectic taste in music, from nineties pop to heavy metal. I didn't understand her tastes one bit, and Aya hadn't helped. She was the one to introduce Astrid to Viking metal after finding out she enjoyed Nordic folk, and Astrid practically breathed the stuff now. It seemed to resonate with her in a way most other music didn't.

Though, it could be the new resident. Astrid told me he was also from Norway, so it was possible he liked similar music. He certainly looked like he would, though I knew better than to judge someone based on appearances.

So far, Tyr seemed like a decent guy. He was courteous to Carrie when they met, and he gave her the space she needed to feel safe. He also had no issues taking direction from Astrid. Hell, he seemed to hang on every word she said, as if enamored with her.

I couldn't blame him, nor would he be the first resident to become infatuated with her. But Astrid was always professional, and made sure they understood. Which was good, because otherwise, I might have some issues keeping her attention. Tyr certainly fit her type profile.

What got me about this guy, though, was his name. Tyr wasn't a common name. And his missing hand had my imagination going crazy with thoughts about Norse mythology. I shook my head. It was a coincidence. Of course it was. Myth was myth.

I reached the gym and paused in the doorway. As I originally suspected, Astrid would be my gym companion this morning. She worked the heavy bag, swinging hard punches in time with the music. I leaned against the doorframe, watching her. My gaze drifted down the curve of her body, over her shapely hips, and down her strong legs, then back up to her firm ass.

My pulse thrummed under my skin, desires from earlier resurfacing. What I wouldn't give to touch and taste her, even once. My cock hardened and strained against my shorts at the very thought.

"You know, it's rude to linger in doorways," Astrid puffed out. She didn't even glance back at me.

I shook my head clear. I'd come down here to do just that. She was going to be a distraction from that attempt, but I had to try. *Good fucking luck.* "I thought you were going to practice archery today?"

"I was, and then I woke up and felt like hitting something instead."

I ran my tongue over my teeth. "Do you want to talk about it?"

She shook her head and continued to beat on the heavy bag. I left her to it. If she wanted to talk, she would when she calmed down.

Most assumed Astrid was a pacifist. She always seemed to have control over her emotions even when she was enraged, to the point most only experienced her sassy mouth at her worst. And she tried to deescalate a situation before a fight could break out if she could.

But they didn't know her—didn't see her like I did. They didn't see the other side of her she tried to suppress.

Astrid was aggressive. She had a deadly eye when loosing an arrow or firing a gun, and didn't hold back when we sparred. Few saw how vicious she could be. They never learned how close she'd been to expulsion in high school for putting a kid in the hospital, defending me from his racist tirade.

They only saw the kind Astrid, the gentle Astrid, the always-smiling Astrid who hid her pain and aggression behind a wall, where she seemed to think it now belonged.

I wished she didn't. I wasn't a fan of violence, and liked it when something could be settled with conversation, but Astrid's approach wasn't healthy. She focused so much on her fear of dogs that she neglected the other side of her that needed healing. And as a result, she was imbalanced emotionally.

But I couldn't help her find that balance if she didn't want to let me in.

I started up the treadmill to do my warmup, however my focus continued to drift to Astrid. Not because she was distracting—okay, maybe a little of that—but mostly because of her form.

Exhaustion dragged at her, weighing down her arms and shoulders. She'd been at this for a while, and that usually meant she focused too much to give herself the necessary breaks to prevent injury.

Turning off the treadmill, I walked up behind Astrid and wrapped my hands around her forearms. She gasped and jerked, attempting to break free and throw me off balance as if I were some attacker. But she was too tired from her routine, and only managed to smack into my chest.

"*Oof.* Diego…"

I had to ignore the way her body molded into mine so perfectly. "Your form was poor. You need to take a break."

"I'm fine," she bit back.

I folded her arms to her chest, tucking her into me. My libido had cooled. This was too serious to have such thoughts. "Don't lie to me."

Astrid struggled against my hold, but I refused to let go. Any other day, I would have. I would see I'd overstepped and needed to back off. But something told me to hold on this time. Like it could hear her silent screams—see the anger still building up inside her with no realistic outlet to be released on.

"Diego, let go!"

My grip tightened. I pressed my lips against her ear. "It's okay to be angry, Astrid. It's okay."

She struggled more. Her eyes clamped shut and bared her teeth, as if she were fighting herself more than me.

"It's okay," I murmured again.

Astrid made a strangled sound and then screamed—something deep and agonizing as her fury burst through the dam she'd erected to keep it contained. I thought the ceiling lights flickered, but I was too focused on holding onto her to pay much attention.

Her legs buckled, and I supported her full weight as I slowly lowered us to the floor. She sobbed, though tears didn't fall.

I slid my fingers into her hair and pressed my lips against her forehead. "It's okay. It's okay to feel this."

She shook her head and struggled against my hold on her again. "No."

"Yes, it is. Don't bottle these emotions up. *Por favor.* Please, feel them. It's okay."

She slammed the flat ends of her fists into my chest. "No, I can't! Every time I do, someone gets hurt."

Her eyes burned into me. I knew that look. I knew the moment she meant, because after that day, she tried to suppress her rage—and that was the day the imbalance started. "Ben had what was coming to him."

"I tossed him *through* a brick wall, Diego. Even with adrenaline, that shouldn't have been possible. I hurt people." Her lip quivered. "I hurt myself..."

My chest ached. The anguish in her eyes was too much.

Her chin dipped, and she whispered out her next words. "I dreamt about her... my mom... what she did... what I did to cause it..."

"Do you want to tell me what happened that day?" She had never talked about it. Neither she nor Darius did. I vaguely knew her mom was a horrible person, and went to jail because of it, but Astrid never confided in me about the event or how it continued to affect her.

Astrid shook her head. "I'm not... I'm not ready."

"Okay." While disappointed, I understood. I couldn't push her to open up about it. I'd be there for her when she was finally ready.

A stray tear trickled down her cheek. I reached out and wiped it away with the back of my finger, feeling the texture difference in her skin when I touched her scar.

Astrid sucked in a tight breath and pulled away, rubbing furiously at her face. "I'm sorry."

I grabbed her hands to make her stop. "You have nothing to apologize for."

She wouldn't meet my gaze. "I made your morning more difficult than it needed to be."

I tucked a finger under her chin and lifted her face. Her stunning green eyes gazed up at me, almost through me, as if she could see into my soul. "No, you didn't. I'll always be there to help you, *mi cielo*."

She squinted. "Your… sky? Or is it heaven?"

Astrid may have learned Spanish from living with Papá and me, but there were many times the language still tripped her up.

"Both." I stroked her cheek. "You're a breath of fresh air—my reason to look forward to the next day, every day."

The flush on her cheeks from her workout and emotional break deepened, and it didn't go unnoticed by me. *No way…*

A wicked grin spread up the side of my face, and she blinked in response. "Besides, I've now learned from this. It would be better for me to pin you to a wall next time."

Astrid's eyes popped wide, and I caught the quiet hitch in her breath. "You wouldn't dare."

I snickered, enjoying this discovery a little too much, and leaned closer. "Watch me."

Her jaw set and she shoved her hand into my face, pushing me back on my ass. Astrid jumped to her feet and grabbed her water bottle. "I'm going to go shower."

I watched her go, chuckling triumphantly to myself. *Astrid, Astrid, Astrid. Objectively hot, your ass.*

Cold water splashed against my face. My shower had helped relax my tense body after my emotional dump, but it'd done nothing to ease the tumultuous feelings Diego had stirred up with his comments. Still, the image of him pinning me against the wall, ravishing me until I was breathless, lingered in my mind.

Unfortunately, it mixed with the shame still present within me, tainting the fantasy. As a therapist, I should be better at addressing my emotions and healing. Diego was right. it was unfair of me to chain my emotions. The therapists I'd seen growing up tried to get me to see and address the same thing.

I leaned on the counter, gazing at my reflection. The scar that marred my face mocked me. *I can't lose control again.* I learned what happened when I did—at seven years old. The reminder stayed with me. It caused people to flinch and avert their gaze. I used to cover the scar. I thought it'd help me. But it never did, so the ugly mark remained on display. It made it difficult to find someone to love me for me.

I tried from then on to be good. To be perfect.

But bottling up my emotions took its toll on me. I had to find outlets to ease the pressure. Target shooting. Martial arts. They were what I needed. I could focus all my pent-up energy into them, and it was freeing. I felt strong and powerful, but controlled.

And when those didn't work, I used my hands to create.

My fingers scraped on the granite counter. *I tricked myself into thinking I'd fixed myself.* Like many people, I fell into the trap of believing I was better, rather than just coping in ways I shouldn't. And I was reminded of that the day I almost killed someone.

I didn't mean to. I just… lost it.

I gazed at my hand and flexed it. *Adrenaline, they said.* Adrenaline mixed with my training caused me to throw a six foot, two-hundred-and-sixty-pound football player through a brick wall in a fit of absolute rage. I let them believe that. It made it easier to ignore the weird sensation I felt that day—to ignore the fact I'd never laid a finger on him, even though others insisted I had. I shoved it to the back of my mind, to never be revealed to anyone.

And yet, when my anger boiled over today, I felt it again. Some sort of tingling sensation that coiled and slithered like a snake deep inside my body, along my bones, and into my soul. Then it dissipated as Diego calmed me down—just like the time before. *His words… they…* I shook my head.

I didn't know if I was crazy, or what, but I couldn't tell myself it was just my emotions getting to me. I knew what I felt. But how could I tell someone about that? What would I say? That I needed intensive therapy? That I couldn't help others until I was fixed?

Turning away from the sink, I gazed out one of my windows, past the deck, and to the forest beyond. I couldn't lose everything I had.

The world out there… it was… tiring. Every time I had to go out, I felt a weight as if I'd lived a thousand lifetimes that only ended in pain. But here… it was peaceful. It was safe from all those feelings. It was home, and I never wanted to leave. *But it's lacking, too… something is… missing…*

I closed my eyes and took a controlled breath. I needed to get out of my head. All I would do is spiral out of control, and I couldn't do that. *I'll contact my therapist to pencil in for a session. I'm long overdue.*

But in the meantime, I went to my dresser and grabbed a necklace with a wooden pendant. An intricate rune was carved into the surface. The moment the pendant rested on my chest, a sensation of safety and comfort fell over me.

Aya had given this to me as a gift during college. She was a heathen—a Norse pagan—and she wanted me to wear it to keep me safe. I'd grown up understanding heathenism because of Dad. He never made me participate or believe, but some of the rituals were part of our celebrations and every day.

For the longest time I couldn't find myself fully believing like him. I never called out to gods or performed any specific rituals. But the more I was around Aya, and she and Dad conversed, I was finding my stance changing and questioning why I had been so reluctant to believe.

What if this necklace did have magical properties?

What if these rituals and beliefs were real and made a difference?

What if there was more to Midgard than was on the surface?

A sharp thudding sound echoed outside. I blinked and looked around, but didn't see what caused it. The sound happened again. *Is someone chopping wood?* We had a woodpile that we took care of throughout the summer, but it was something Dad and Xavier mainly took care of together.

I wouldn't know for sure what was up unless I went to check. When I made it halfway down the stairs from the loft, the warm, sugary smell of baking cookies greeted me. An enormous smile tugged at my face. This only meant one thing.

I practically ran down to the kitchen, where a curvy woman with dark umber skin and long, wavy dark hair danced in front of the stove while she pushed a tray of raw dough balls into the oven. A cooling rack with huge freshly baked cookies containing chocolate chips and M&Ms taunted me on the island.

The woman turned around and smiled brightly when she noticed me. She popped an earbud out of her ear. "There you are, Astrid."

"Good morning, Carrie."

"Feeling better?"

I winced. "How much do you know?"

She smiled sympathetically. "Only that you had a rough morning, like so many of us have during our journeys to recover. Have a cookie. They're fresh."

I wasn't going to say no, even if they were pity cookies. There was no need for me to feel embarrassed. Most came here to heal. But I knew I was harder on myself because I was the one they looked to for healing, and if I wasn't fixed, how could they trust me to help them fix themselves?

Nibbling on the cookie, I listened to the sound of the chopping wood again. "Is Diego taking a crack at the woodpile?"

Carrie shook her head. "No, actually he headed into town. Said he'd be back in an hour or less."

"Huh." I didn't know he'd planned to go into town today. "Then who?"

Couldn't be Sean. He'd never helped with the woodpile in the years he'd been here.

"It's that new man, Tyr. He's been splitting for a good thirty minutes."

I blinked. I didn't expect that for an answer. "Are you okay with that?"

Carrie gave a weak smile. "I'm working through it. The baking is helping, and so is listening to music. I think after a few days of adjusting, I'm going to get used to his presence here."

That was good. More than good for her. Carrie's particular fears had been quite a challenge over the years. We'd get to a point where she'd make enormous leaps, and then she'd backslide.

Carrie gazed toward the deck windows. "It's strange. I don't feel that same urge to run and hide from him, even though he looks so similar to my ex-husband. I'm nervous, yes, but he doesn't have that threatening aura my mind usually tells me exists."

My eyebrows raised. That was impressive progress. But she also wasn't wrong about Tyr's assessment. He had a stoic and hard look about him, and he'd clearly seen some shit in his life. But when he listened with his full attention, or he spoke, there was gentleness there.

Carrie took a deep breath and pointed to the cookies. "Why don't you bring some out for him and Raeni? I think she's still watching him."

I rolled my eyes. "Of course she is."

Carrie laughed. "As exhausting as it is for me already, I knew to expect it. I was just as boy-crazy as her at that age."

She then winked. "Of course, if you snag him, she'll leave him alone."

I shook my head. "Don't start. He's a resident. It wouldn't be appropriate."

Carrie snorted. "Like any of us would care. It's not right to pass up opportunities for happiness over silly things like 'professionalism.' You're not getting any younger, Astrid. And since you and Diego seem to insist you're only friends—"

"We are only friends." *I make sure I remind myself every day until one of these days it finally sticks.*

She popped her earbud back in and turned away to check on her baking cookies. "Uh huh, you keep telling yourself that."

Why does no one believe me? Shaking the thoughts from my head, I snagged a paper towel and a few cookies before heading outside. Angel greeted me on the porch and immediately tried to check out my precious cargo.

Following the path down to the woodshed, and dodging Angel, I found our new resident and Raeni. Raeni sat on a stump while Tyr stood with his back to her, his exposed, muscular back with a prominent and intricate tattoo on display.

Tyr lifted an axe above his head with one hand and slammed down on the vertical standing log set up on a chopping stump. It split with impressive ease and the two pieces flung to the side. He then moved to the next prepared log and readied to split it as well.

His muscles flexed with his movements. I swallowed and forced myself to breathe as a sudden, overwhelming need to feel the strength of his body pulsed through me down to my core.

I want to remember what he feels like.

I blinked, my mind stalling. *What the hell was that thought?*

Raeni noticed me and grinned. "Enjoying the view, Astrid?"

Tyr paused for a second, glancing over his shoulder before splitting another log.

I ignored her question. No matter how true it was, I would not embarrass myself by admitting to a resident's face that I found him hot. "I hope you're not bothering him, Raeni."

"Course not," she said. "I'm learning more about him." She noticed the goodies I carried and her eyes lit up. "Did Mom make cookies?"

I smirked and held them up. "Your favorite."

She squealed and launched off her seat. Tyr turned around in time to watch her snag one of the colossal cookies and shove it into her mouth. She moaned in delight and tried to talk with her mouth full, the words coming out in a muffled, indecipherable sound. Or, I thought it was indecipherable.

"She asked if there were more in the house," Tyr said when he noticed my spiked eyebrow. It rose higher when I looked his way and he shrugged. "Old friend did it all the time. Forced me to become proficient in food muffle."

Something in the back of my head twitched, like recognition or something, and then I laughed. "Well, at least one of us is. Yeah, there's more. She's still baking."

Raeni took off toward the house, muffling something else out. Tyr waved in response. Angel followed Raeni, happy to race her back to the house.

I focused on Tyr. "She didn't bother you, right?"

He shook her head. "No. She's a curious teenager, but she wasn't any trouble." He held up his arm with the missing hand. "Actually, she was quite *handy* with setting up the logs for me."

I pressed my lips together. *Don't laugh. Don't laugh.*

Tyr smirked, and I couldn't hold back my laughter. My hand flew up in front of my face, as if that'd help, but it didn't; not even to hide my heated cheeks, announcing my embarrassment.

"I'm sorry."

Tyr set his axe down and walked over. "Why? It was supposed to be stupid enough to make you laugh."

"I shouldn't."

He held up his arm again. "Why, because of this?" He shook his head. "I make these jokes all the time. I made a mistake that cost me my hand. I can either wallow in self-pity, or I can make the most of it. I choose the latter."

"And that includes dad jokes?"

His brow furrowed, as if he'd never heard the term before. Maybe it was a language barrier. I held up a cookie for him to change the subject. "Monster cookie?"

"Sure. Never had a monster cookie before."

"Peanut butter cookie with oats, M&Ms, and chocolate chips. Carrie is an amazing baker, and these are super soft and gooey."

He took the cookie and plunked down where Raeni had sat, biting into the treat. He chewed and nodded. "These are good. Strange, but good."

I took a seat next to him on another sitting log. "How was your first night?"

"Bed is comfortable. Sounds of the forest remind me of home, which was nice. Though, it's missing the soothing sounds of the lake."

I bit into my cookie. "Lakefront property? I don't think I could leave such a place."

Tyr stared at his cookie without responding. I spotted the unspoken sorrow in his eyes. He'd left for a reason, and possibly not because he wanted to.

I gasped and jerked back, almost toppling over, when Angel suddenly appeared in front of me. My heart raced in my ears and it took me several moments to calm down.

Tyr stared at me. "Are you okay?"

I sucked in a deep breath. "Yeah. I'm… afraid of black and mostly black dogs."

He leaned on his knees. "That's quite specific."

I nodded slowly. The muscles in my neck and back tightened. He, like many others, was curious about the origin of this fear, and my gut reaction was to avoid it. But I had to be open about my issues; I couldn't face them otherwise.

"When I was little, I started having nightmares where I was attacked by a black wolf or dog. I don't know what started them, but ever since, I've had an irrational fear." I turned my right arm, revealing the scars on my forearm. "Then, when I was seven, a black dog attacked me."

Tyr frowned and reached out to touch the healed-over skin, then flexed away. I took his hand and pressed it against the sensitive marks—partially damaged nerve ending firing in odd ways. A surprising jolt shot through me alongside the sensation. It was similar to when I shook his hand yesterday.

I didn't know why I did this. I'd only ever allowed Dad, Aya, and Diego to touch my scars.

His calloused fingers left my arm and grazed my cheek where a segment of my scar cut into it, sending an unusually pleasant shiver down my spine. His brazen behavior should have put me off, thinking it was okay to touch me like that. But a part of me didn't mind. The touch was so tender, like I'd felt something like it before, from him, as illogical as that feeling was.

"Did the dog do this to you?" he asked, his voice quiet.

I nodded. "My arm took most of the damage, but one of his canine teeth managed to get my face."

His attention shifted to Angel, who pawed at the ground, impatient for attention. "And yet, after all this, you have her."

"Diego got her for me. I wanted a dog, and I needed to overcome my fear, so he decided we'd have a hard go with exposure therapy." I scratched Angel behind the ear. She leaned into the touch, her tongue lolling out. "She's been the best thing for me. I'm still working through my fear, understanding that I may never fully overcome it, but she helps, day by day."

Tyr pat Angel, but his touch triggered her desire to play. He grinned and pushed against her muzzle when she got mouthy. Diego and Dad played with her like this, too. The muscles in my back tightened, and I worked on breathing to relax. This type of play always spiked a reaction.

Angel barked and then snatched her ball. Tyr chucked it a fair distance, impressing me. The extension of his arm drew my attention back to his tattoos.

"May I?" I half-reached for him to indicate my intent. Normally I admired from afar, but with him, I felt an unusual compulsion. I knew I should be more careful with myself so as not to cross too far over the line of professionalism, which was blurred in this place a lot, depending on how close to a resident I became, but I barely knew this man. And yet, here I was, acting as if I'd known him far longer.

Tyr offered his arm without hesitation. I traced my fingers up his arm, along the bands of runic lettering wrapped around his strong, muscular forearm. *Why do these feel so familiar?*

It had to be because of all the things Dad and Aya taught me. Certain symbols and runes were commonly seen in Norse culture and had returned with the revival of heathenism. It was how I could identify them at all. "These are protection runes. Are you a practicing heathen?"

"I am," he seemed surprised. "Are you?"

"Not exactly. My dad is. We joke I'm a part-time heathen since I participate in some parts of the practice, just not all."

Tyr chuckled. "Then, as a part-time practitioner, do you know what these mean?"

"They're for protection, strength, and mental fortitude." That was the simplest way to describe them. It was actually a little more complex, and I wasn't sure I could decipher the depth of these.

While my fingers didn't migrate higher than his bicep—I had some propriety—my eyes trailed the band of runes on his check and neck.

"Do you like them?" Tyr asked.

I nodded. "I like tattoos. My dad has two full sleeves. He would let me color them when I was a kid."

"Sounds like a great dad."

I smiled. "You'll like him. Everyone does." I squinted and pursed my lips. "Well, maybe not when he gets into his pranking moods. He can be a bit relentless."

Tyr grunted. "I'll keep it in mind to make sure I'm ready to retaliate."

"Do you mind showing me the one on your back?"

He turned, exposing his bare back to me. I took in the intricate tattoo of an enormous tree with branches that stretched from shoulder blade to shoulder blade. A wolf and dragon were designed on either side of the detailed trunk that ran the length of his spine, and tangled within the tree's roots was a helm of awe. An intricate knotwork weave with moon and sun accents hung from the tree branches around the wolf and dragon, and hooked into the roots.

I reached to touch his back and retracted my fingers, biting my lip. Heat pooled in my core, thoughts of running my fingers along his skin plagued my thoughts. *Not appropriate.* And yet, the desire to touch him didn't diminish.

Appropriateness be damned. My desires won out, and my fingers traced one of the tree branches. His muscles twitched reflexively under my touch. My fingers tingled from the contact with his warm skin. "This is a stunning rendition of Yggdrasil. Whoever you hired did a fantastic job."

"I'm happy with how it came out," he said. *Is his voice deeper?* I shook the thought from my head. I was imagining things. "But they didn't do the best one I have."

I blinked. *He has an even better tattoo?*

Tyr turned more, showing me his right side. On his bicep, in even more detailed ink, was a woman. Armor, a fantastical interpretation with skulls and feathers that didn't look practical for battle but was no less stunning, covered her lean, muscular body. She carried an intricately designed shield, and a sword and an axe hung at her sides. In her free hand, magic coalesced. Translucent black wings sprouted from her back, adding striking power to her already intense presence. But what stood out to me most was her face and hair.

Long red hair flowed behind her, in motion with her fighting stance. Her fierce look was enhanced by gleaming green eyes and—my pulse slowed—a face-crossing scar that looked eerily like mine.

She looks like me.

My heart thumped in my ears as I reached out to touch his ink. It was a coincidence. I was seeing things—trying to make sense of the similarities. My finger traced the woman's face, those intense eyes staring at me, looking into me, as if she were real and able to see directly into my soul.

And yet, something deep inside me screamed this was me. "A Valkyrie."

"That's right." Tyr's words cut through the fog of my mind. "And an important one where I'm from."

I lifted my gaze to meet his, his intense blue eyes snaring me. My heart thumped harder in my chest. "How so?"

"The story told says she was a powerful mortal völva who was so beloved by the gods, they turned her into a Valkyrie."

His words slowly sunk in and something deep inside me pulsed. I licked my lips to wet them. "Völva… a seer, right?"

Tyr nodded. "Seer, witch, sorceress. To the people back then, it was all the same."

I looked at the tattoo again, to find my fingers tracing the weapons at her side and taking in their runic inscriptions. I couldn't quite shake the feeling I'd seen them somewhere before.

"I'll admit, when I first saw you, I thought maybe the stories were true, and I'd driven right into Fólkvangr."

My head jerked up to find him smiling. "Fólkvangr? Not Valhalla?"

Most people knew of Valhalla. The hall belonging to Odin, where fallen warriors went, their souls ferried by the Valkyries. But Fólkvangr was lesser known by the average person. A place the goddess Freya ruled over.

He grinned. "I like to believe I might be blessed enough with a far more prestigious entry to the afterlife."

"What was this Valkyrie's name?"

"Astrid."

My heart seized and that deep pulse sensation happened again. *It was what?*

Tyr chuckled. "Now you can see why it took me a minute to process you were a real person with a fairly common name and not some folk legend come to life."

He's right. Astrid wasn't even close to a unique or obscure name. *But Dad always says, there's no such thing as a coincidence.* Yet, what else could this be? I wasn't a Valkyrie.

I blew out a breath. "Well, sorry to disappoint you, but I can't sprout wings from my back or cast mystical spells like some badass D&D spellcaster."

"If you could have one or the other, what would you pick?" he asked.

I pursed my lips and thought that over. "That's so hard. Both sound amazing. But if I must choose, cast spells. So much more potential to do cool shit. Plus, my dad knows fun and cool illusionist magic tricks. Ever since I was little, I wanted to be able to do it like him, to no avail. So having real magic would be like a dream come true. You?"

"Wings. I've always wanted to be able to fly anywhere I wanted." He grinned. "And magic sounds too complicated for me."

I laughed. I'd always wondered what type of rules life would have for magic if it were real.

Tyr stood. "Would you mind helping me set up more logs? Having one hand does slow that process down. Raeni was actually helpful in that respect."

I glanced around at the work he'd already done. "Are you sure you don't want to do something else? You've made quite the dent in this pile already, and we expected it would take us to the end of the month to get through."

He rolled his shoulders. "I prefer to do manual labor to pass my time."

"What about hobbies? We have a lot of resources here, and even if one in particular is missing for you, we can look into making it possible."

He thought for a moment. "That's a bit more difficult for me. I lost a lot of interest in hobbies I used to have because relearning with a missing hand was either too difficult and frustrating, or outright impossible. And don't try to suggest anything like painting, because I don't find it fun."

There went that idea. "How about baking?"

He chuckled. "Shove anything to eat in front of me, experimental or proven, and I'll eat it. But prowess in the kitchen was never a strong suit of mine, even before losing my hand."

Somehow, I believed that. "What about gardening? We have a greenhouse, and plenty of outside space."

His eyes squinted. "Last time I tried, I was banished from ever stepping foot around a garden again."

I couldn't stop the boisterous laugh. I didn't know why I found that so funny, but I did. He didn't seem to mind. In fact, Tyr appeared quite pleased by my response. "Alright, I'll have a think about it to see if we can get some extra excitement in your day."

"If you can't, just put me to work, boss."

"Don't tempt me."

Tyr grinned. The expression sent a pulse of heat between my legs. *No, don't, it's not appropriate.* I didn't care what Carrie said.

I snagged a log to distract myself.

Tyr looped his arm around another log. "Do you have any tattoos? I don't see any, but you seem too interested in them to not have at least one."

I nodded and set my log on a chopping block. "A sternum mandala. Not original, but I like it."

"That's what matters, right?" He smirked, his eyes trailing a heated gaze down my body. "And I'm sure it's the perfect choice for you."

I swallowed and told myself to move to the next topic. "Maybe you'll see it one day."

Fuck. Mouth, meet foot.

Tyr grinned. "Maybe."

My eyes darted away, looking for something to help turn this conversation to something else—anything else. My gaze landed on the axe. *That'll do it.*

I lifted the tool into my hands, noting its heft. This wasn't one of ours. The axe had a black head, like obsidian, and a well-crafted wooden haft. Silver inlays swirled and cut in an intricate design along the head. My pulse slowed, and I traced a finger along the design. Something about this axe felt... familiar.

My fingers trailed down to the engraving on the haft. A tingling sensation spread from my fingertips through my hand and up my arm into my chest—something... powerful and... comfortable—making me more whole.

"Do you like it?" Tyr asked.

"I do," I mumbled. "I've never seen an axe like this in person before."

"It's a family heirloom."

Family heirloom... Why did that meaning stick with me? Maybe because that meant this wasn't intended for chopping wood.

I glanced at him. "Why did you bring it out?"

"Tradition for me. Since I can't use it the way it had been in the past, I give it a good first swing when I do a log-splitting job."

I liked that tradition. Maybe it wasn't what his ancestors intended, but they would have never predicted how their children would have to adapt to an ever-changing world.

I set the axe down and grabbed the right one for Tyr to use. He thanked me and set up to split the logs. I sat down to watch. It would be wise for me to go and find something else to do, but I was enjoying getting to know this man.

"Oh, I forgot to tell you yesterday, but if you become a long-term resident, feel free to invite any friends or family you might have to visit. We want to make sure our residents still feel connected with their loved ones. We just ask that if they use any of our resources, they help replenish them before they leave."

Tyr paused for a moment and then slammed down on a log. "No need to worry about that. No family or friends to really contact."

"Do you want to share on that?"

He shrugged. "Not much to say. Family fell apart a long time ago, and in my nomadic ways, I ended up losing contact with most of my friends. I doubt if I contacted them now, they'd want to hear from me."

I kept my expression neutral. It wasn't an uncommon response from residents. But, by the time they were ready to leave, many of them found the strength to rekindle past relationships that would still be healthy for them. I hoped the same for Tyr.

"I noticed your tattoos don't have any typical imagery related to Odin or Thor, why is that?" Why had my brain gone back to the tattoos? We were done with that conversation.

Tyr split another log. "Because they're assholes."

My brow rose. *He said that like he knows them.* "What do you mean?"

He shrugged. "Everyone worships them like they're gods who were perfect. But they were far from it. They caused all kinds of problems for other gods and mortals, all because of various prophecies that had been told in days of old."

I squinted. "You say that like you were there."

Tyr rested the axe on his shoulder and glanced back at me, grinning. "My name is Tyr." He held up his arm. "And I am missing a hand. Who's to say I'm not the god heathens worship?"

I stared at him, unsure how to react to the claim.

Something pulsed deep within me, and for a moment, his form changed—to a tall, proud warrior in modified Norse armor, and long braided hair. I blinked, and the visage was gone. *I'm going crazy.*

"Most would say that's a coincidence, like that tattoo of yours."

Tyr watched me carefully. "Do you agree?"

"My father would say there's no such thing as a coincidence." I shook my head. "But he'd also say there's truth to all myths."

Tyr's head tilted. "You don't believe him?"

My brow scrunched. "Say gods exist, or they're based on real people who existed at one time, you want me to believe a god like Loki turned into a female horse and fucked a stallion, got pregnant, and gave birth to a seven-legged horse?"

"Eight-legged horse, and the stallion was a unicorn."

My eyebrows rose high on my forehead. "A unicorn."

"A shifted unicorn in human form, more specifically. And they're nothing like the sunshine-and-rainbow portrayals told in children's stories."

"Right, and why would Loki screw a… unicorn?"

Tyr shrugged. "A dare. Fuck a unicorn that wasn't caged or restrained for one's safety. And the asshole will do almost anything once, so he shapeshifted into a woman for the hell of it, survived the encounter, and ended up having to carry a unicorn to term."

I pursed my lips. There he went again, acting like he was there. *And why am I not calling this out as a grand, made-up story?* It was even more unbelievable than the myths and stories Dad told. Or it should be. And yet, a part of me seemed to believe him.

"And how about the story of Fenrir and Tyr? The Norse gods were so afraid of a prediction that the giant wolf-god would kill Odin that, instead of talking things out, they up and tricked him into imprisonment? And for the betrayal, he bit off the hand of the one god he trusted, who also betrayed him?"

"That's what the myth would say, yes, but what if that story is a twisted truth? The truth was, many of the gods mistrusted the wolf because of a prophecy that foretold he'd be the end of Odin. But the wolf and war god were friends regardless of such claims—not that the war god cared, because he had little love for the Allfather. But one day, in battle, the wolf turned on his friend and stole everything he ever cared about. Then people twisted the story to suit their needs."

My gut churned. There was something about the story of Tyr and Fenrir that never sat right by me. In the back of my mind, a thought always screamed, *"That's not right! They're friends. They'd never do that."* And now, with Tyr putting perspective to one possible origin of that story, those thoughts reared up again.

A sharp whistle cut into our conversation, stealing my attention.

Diego stood at the top of the hill by the house and waved. "Hey! I got something you're going to want to see."

He disappeared around the house before getting a response. I glanced to Tyr. "You up for finding out what surprise awaits, or are you gonna keep splitting wood?"

Tyr leaned the tool against a stump. "I could use a break."

He hadn't gotten much done since I'd come down here, but I wasn't going to point that out.

We walked up to the house. Diego had already disappeared inside. Angel paced by the door, whining.

"Aww, Angel, was Diego a jerk and shut the door on you?"

She looked at me and barked before spinning in excited circles. My brow lifted. This was odd. She got excited when Diego or Dad came home after a trip into town, but never this excited. This was usually reserved for me when I had to leave her home, even for just five minutes.

My back straightened. There was one person, however, who got the same reception as me. *It couldn't be.*

I grabbed the door handle and flung the door open, rushing in with Angel right beside me.

Diego stood by the island, speaking with a tall woman with fair skin. Her long, blonde dreadlocks cascaded over her shoulders and down her back. She wore ripped jeans and a graphic t-shirt on her well-toned body. A large fluffy cat in a harness perched on her shoulder.

"Aya!" I shrieked.

She turned, her bright blue eyes sparkling, and threw her arms out. "Surprise!"

I sprinted to her, Angel beating me. The cat on Aya's shoulders hopped onto the island where another huge cat lounged.

Aya managed to greet Angel for a moment before I threw my arms around my friend's neck. "I missed you."

She laughed and hugged me back. "I missed you, too. I'm so glad to be home."

Home. Her saying that felt so right. I called her my friend, but Aya was more like my sister. We had this special bond that just sparked the moment I met her.

I pulled away and punched her in the arm, making her wince. "That's for lying to me, you bitch."

Diego belted out a hearty laugh, which only worsened when I tagged him a few times, too. "And this is for being in on it."

Diego shot me one of his brilliant, heart-stopping smiles. "I have to keep you on your toes, Cielo."

"Ooh, we've moved into pet-name territory finally, have we?" Aya teased, a wide, shit-eating grin pulling at her cheeks.

I rolled my eyes, desperately fighting back the heat surging for my face. "Don't start."

Aya had a habit of "shipping" people. Anyone she thought needed to either get together or, in the very least, fuck, she paired them up in her head. The weird thing was, she had a high accuracy rate.

And unfortunately, she'd done it with Diego and me—day one of meeting us.

Aya winked, and I punched her in the arm again before turning to the cats on the island counter. "Buggy, Tuggy, how are you girls doing?"

The two Norwegian Forest cats, with coat patterns that looked a lot like armor, chirped. I happily scratched them under their chins, triggering the loudest purrs from cats I'd ever heard.

"Buggy and Tuggy, that's what you're calling them now, Aya?" Tyr's rumbling voice said.

I turned to see him leaning against the wall in the foyer, arms crossed, and fist clenched. His gentle demeanor with me from earlier had disappeared, and a stoic, hard one replaced it.

"Tyr." Aya smiled. "It's good to see you. It's been *forever.*"

Tyr's expression didn't change, and I noticed the tension in his shoulders. My eyes darted between the two. "You two know each other?"

"Sure do," Aya said. "Our families go way back. I told him about this place before, but it's taken him so long to come by, I thought he was ignoring me."

"You never mentioned this place."

She shrugged. "Or you weren't paying attention. You've done it to me before."

A prickling sensation trailed down my spine. Tyr was from Norway, just like Aya. It was supposed to be a coincidence. We occasionally had residents who came from other countries, and it just so happened he'd come from the same one as Aya. Dad's words bounced around in my head. *There is no such thing as coincidence.*

"I'm noticing some tension," Diego said.

Aya gave a tight smile. "We've had some family issues that we've been trying to work on for a *long* time."

"Very long," Tyr practically growled.

I sucked in a slow breath through my nose. "If this is going to be an issue…"

"It won't be," they both said.

Aya turned her attention to me, smiling kindly. "We'll work through it. That's why I wanted him to come here. This place has the *magic* touch on people and relationships."

I rolled my eyes. She always liked saying that.

Angel, now satisfied with the attention from Aya, wandered closer to the island with the two cats.

"Oh, this should be good," Tyr said.

Angel stuck her nose on the counter, sniffing Tuggy. The large cat bopped Angel on the nose in response. She wagged her tail and tried poking Tuggy with her nose. Tuggy playfully pawed her back, lowering herself onto the counter so she could use both paws. Buggy watched, eyes squinted and the tip of her tail curling and uncurling.

Tyr shook her head. "You've replaced them."

Aya laughed. "Nope, still the same two girls you know and love."

"They don't tolerate *any* canine."

Aya winked. "Angel is the exception."

Tyr shook his head and left without another word. Disappointment prickled in my chest. I suspected that was the extent he was willing to tolerate Aya for now. *Hopefully, they'll be able to work through it here.* The desire to ensure that was quite strong for me, in a rather startling way, too. Yes, Aya was my friend, but I'd never felt so strongly about helping a situation as I did right now.

"How was your trip, Aya?" I asked, trying to distract myself.

She smiled. "It was so good seeing my family. I missed them."

"How'd the grand re-opening go after the remodel of your brother's club?"

Aya's brother, Frey, ran an upscale burlesque club, and a few months ago was forced to close after the building sustained extensive damage because of a water main leak. Her brother had been thinking the club needed a remodel before the accident, so Aya joked the universe made sure he stopped dragging his feet about it.

I'd wanted to go and finally experience the place, with how often Aya hyped it up, but the timing didn't match up well against my schedule, so I had to promise a rain check.

"Oh, it went so spectacularly," Aya gushed. "Let me show you some photos I snagged."

She whipped out her phone and scrolled through all kinds of photos. My jaw dropped. The place was stunning, though there was a lot more purple in the décor than I expected—like, *a lot* of purple. Frey didn't seem the purple type from the way his sister spoke of him.

A few people appeared in photos, from guests to performers. Aya temporarily paused on a blonde woman with a well-toned athletic body passionately hugging a tall man with a lean but still muscular build. He had an unusual-looking prosthetic arm. There was something not quite right about it. Beyond its incredibly dark appearance, it seemed… twisted, like it wasn't made correctly. *It's probably the dim lighting in the place making it look off.*

A sensation of familiarity about these two people fell over me, but Aya continued her slideshow before I could think on it more.

A photo of her brother came up. He had long, dirty blond hair, a lithe body, and a similar complexion and stunning beauty Aya had. With him was a large, muscled man. *Fen.* He had short, blond hair and an intricate wolf tattoo along one of his arms, as well as some other Norse-inspired tattoos on his light skin. The two of them sat close and stared so lovingly into each other's eyes, it'd make any hopeless romantic weak.

As I gazed at the two men, a powerful sensation of familiarity rushed through me.

"Aya, are you sure I've never met your brother or Fen?" I asked. "Like, they never paid a visit to you in college and I saw them in passing? Because I swear, they look familiar."

She shook her head. "They haven't left Chicago much in the last ten years. If they have, it was to see our family. Frey is so busy with his club, it's hard for them to take time off."

I pursed my lips. *Then why can't I shake this feeling every time I see a picture of them? Especially Fen.*

Aya flipped to another photo of Fen. In this one, he passionately kissed a woman whom I could only describe as goth, with her long black hair, dark clothes, and black and purple make-up.

"Whoa, who is that?" I asked.

"Their girlfriend?"

I blinked. "Huh?"

Aya's brows pinched together. "What do you mean, 'huh'? I swear I've told you about Dahlia before."

"Nope." I emphasized, popping the p. "I would remember if you told me your brother was a lucky enough bastard to have *two* partners."

Was I jealous? Maybe a little. My dating life had all but dried up after college, and it hadn't been great during it, either. I wanted to form connections, and the people I seemed to attract either only wanted a 'wham-bam thank you ma'am' kind of night—many of whom didn't live up to their own hype—they had nothing going for them in life, or we just didn't have enough in common for it to work. And if they didn't fall into those categories, they were off-limits residents and my *just* best friend.

Aya tapped her lips. "Huh… I don't know how I managed to not tell you about her. You'd love her. She's a big nerd. She and her sister even love D&D."

My eyes popped wide. "What? How could you not tell me this? Why haven't you introduced us? I don't care if they have to video chat or something. We need more players at the table!"

Diego belted out a hearty laugh. "Look what you've done, amiga. You've gotten her all worked up."

Our friend winked. "I'm sure you could settle her down."

I was too excited to even care about the sexual hints she was suggesting. "No, you don't understand. Dad would be so happy to DM for a bigger table, and it'll add a new dynamic!"

Aya laughed. "I'll talk to them."

"You need to tell them to come visit, really," Diego said.

I pointed in his direction. "What he said. It's not fair they don't visit us."

Aya held up placating hands. "I've been trying. One of these days, I'll finally get them over for a visit." She winked. "I'm persistent like that."

I let out a breath. "Fine. In the meantime, let's get you settled back in."

"So you can pester me some more?"

I grinned. "Always."

FIVE

DIEGO·

The scent of musty paper filled my nose. I gingerly flipped a page of the cookbook in front of me on the counter, careful not to damage it. Mamá's perfect handwriting, along with other scrawls from generations of family members before her, filled the pages, sometimes accompanied by drawings or photographs.

It'd been some time since I'd seen this. I knew Papá wouldn't have tossed it. To this day, he still had almost everything that had belonged to her, just all stored away. I expected this book to be with those boxes. But I found it on his bookshelf while cleaning.

I wondered, as I flipped another page, how often he took it out and looked through it like this. I knew I couldn't ask him. To this day, he still struggled with the reality that Mamá was gone. It was like a part of him still expected she'd waltz through the door and act like she'd just been on some extended health trip.

I rubbed my forehead and shook my head. My dreams were bleeding into my reality. I'd seen her again, doing just that. However, I'd also seen Astrid sprout silver and gold wings from her back and take to the skies. *They're just weird dreams. Stop lingering on them like they were real.*

A page flipped on me, and the revealed recipe gave me pause. My fingers ran along the neatly written ink detailing a paella dish—my favorite dish that she would make. Not because it was some complicated, ultra-special meal, even though it was a special family recipe, but because Papá and she would always make it together. And he hadn't made it since her passing.

Sure, we'd had similar dishes, but not this one.

The sound of something snapping, and then someone chewing, drew my attention away. Astrid walked into the kitchen, munching on a carrot stick with her nose in a book. A burly, half-naked man posed on the cover.

"Are you reading Scarlett Summers' book again?" I asked, fake-exasperated.

Her eyes flicked up from her reading, and my pulse skipped. Her soul-piercing look sliced through me. "Don't you be making fun of me. It's damned good."

Aya poked her head over the loft and called down, "Is that the new bestseller everyone is raving about?"

Astrid nodded. "The Berserker Who Loved Me. It's as good as everyone says."

"Since you're reading it again, it has to be." She smirked. "What are your thoughts on it, Diego?"

I shrugged. "She won't give me the damned thing to read and find out."

Astrid stuck her tongue out. "Get your own copy. This is my special signed copy. No one gets to touch it."

Snaking my arm around her waist, I pulled her against my chest. Even with our height discrepancy, her body molded into mine perfectly. I bent close to her ear, her scent, lavender and vanilla, teasing and stirring. "We could read it together."

She paused, raising an eyebrow at me. "Read together? With your slow-ass pace? I don't think so."

I grinned. "Or maybe you should slow down. Savor and indulge in every moment instead of racing to the climax."

My fingers slid along her side, finding a portion of exposed skin where her shirt rose above the shorts she wore over her shapely hips, and glided along her enticing softness. One thing I was, was an attentive lover. And I'd be more than happy to show her exactly what that meant.

With my other hand, I spread her book open more, slow and deliberate, and peered at the passages on the pages.

My lips brushed Astrid's ear, and I dipped my voice to a huskier tone I knew she'd enjoy. "His large, calloused hands pinned my wrists above my head, and he raked his gaze over my naked flesh, drinking me in. Heat pooling in my core spread through me like wildfire, setting me ablaze with desire. I craved his touch—his worship—like the goddess he claimed me to be."

Astrid snapped the book shut, cutting me off, and Aya snickered. "Getting too X-rated for you, Astrid?"

Astrid placed the book down on the island and walked to the fridge without replying. I glanced up at Aya, who winked and disappeared to go back to her work.

I grinned. I didn't know what changed, but whatever was allowing me to get to Astrid so easily now, I was thankful for. Soon I'd get her to see how perfect we could be, and how serious I was about her.

Astrid poured herself a glass of orange juice, and then noticed the abandoned cookbook. "What's that?"

"Family cookbook I found while cleaning."

She leaned on the counter to take a closer look. "I've never seen you or your dad use this one before."

I drew up next to her. "It belonged to my mom."

Astrid turned her gaze up at me. I felt the weight of her full attention. She slid her hand in mine, lacing her fingers. It sent a pang of longing through me—the desire for such a gesture to mean more between us.

Any time she was close, that need to pull her into me until we were so tightly wound up in each other we might fuse overwhelmed my logic and control. Whenever she was gone, even for a short while, I felt lost—like a piece of me was missing. And with her like this with me, I could get lost in her quiet comfort, and be the happiest man alive.

"Talk to me," she said.

My lips twisted. "I'm not sure what to say. They're bittersweet feelings. I remember the good times and wish there'd been more. I wish Dad would cook these recipes again, but at the same time, I'm glad he doesn't. I want to make one, but I'm afraid reality won't be as good as my memories."

Astrid squeezed my hand. "It probably won't be the same."

My gut twisted. I knew she was right, but I really didn't want to hear the truth, either.

"It won't be the same—not because your memory is better than reality, but because she isn't the one making it." Astrid offered a kind smile. "No dish is one-hundred percent the same between chefs. They all have their own technique and flair to it. So what you make won't be the same as what she made. That doesn't make it worse or better, and it definitely doesn't alter the memories you cherish."

I gazed down at this perfect, beautiful woman. She always knew what to say to me.

Without breaking eye contact, I lifted her hand and pressed my lips to her skin. "*Gracias, mi amor.*"

She smiled and nodded, pink tinting her cheeks. Another one of my mess-ups, though not intentionally. I told her calling her that was something close friends said. And I wasn't wrong. But I also didn't expect that meaning to become more to me. And now I needed her to see that change, too.

After allowing my gaze to linger on her a moment longer, I turned back to the book. "I don't want to make this one. I know it's a more traditional recipe, so it'd be great to try and make, but I know we don't have any more rabbit left. And we definitely don't have duck."

My mouth twitched. "And this one was their dish together. I don't want to touch that memory with my own just yet."

I flipped the page to a variant of the dish. "This one is a more commonly made one, and besides the chicken, which we can leave out of Sean's portion, it's a safe dish to make for everyone, I think."

Sean was a pescatarian, making it sometimes tedious offering a wide range of meals for everyone without having to make multiple dishes. Papá didn't mind since he enjoyed cooking for everyone, no matter their varied needs. And it helped that Sean was a generous man, and donated more than he needed to allow us to cater to his needs, as well as others here.

"Aya, does Tyr have a seafood allergy?" Astrid called up.

"No, you're good."

It would be better to ask him directly to be sure, especially since the two had made it clear they hadn't seen each other in a long time, so food tolerances could have changed, but Tyr had been a bit more reclusive today than yesterday.

We suspected he needed time to process. I wanted to know what this family issue was between Aya and him, but neither seemed ready to talk about it yet, so my curiosity would have to wait a little longer.

If he couldn't have this, we'd work something out.

"I want to cook this with you," I said to Astrid.

She blinked. "Are you sure you want me to cook with you? I know I make a mean salted buttered pasta, but I think this might be a bit too advanced for me."

She pointed to one of the steps. "I mean, making our own fish stock sounds cool and all, but…"

I laughed. Astrid could do a lot of things, but cooking wasn't a skill she'd put a lot of points into for her character build. "I'm sure I want no one else making memories with me."

"Gag!" Aya shouted. "You can use a better line than that. Amp up the charm. Use that sexy voice to melt her panties! C'mon, I want to hear you trying."

I rolled my eyes, and Astrid laughed, the pink on her cheeks deepening.

We went about collecting the ingredients for both the fish stock and main dish. I popped on some traditional music, like my parents had when they cooked.

"Should I break out the candles?" Aya called down.

It was my turn to laugh while Astrid rolled her eyes. "Will you stop?"

"Can't, ship has already set sail."

"Well, I'm telling the navigator she's plotting the wrong course."

"Or you could trust me, and you'd be having the time of your life," Aya said in a sing-song voice.

"Bitch," Astrid muttered.

"Love you too!"

We peeled the shrimp and chopped the vegetables. Astrid did fine quartering one onion, but dicing the other proved more difficult for her.

I slipped in behind her and reached around to grasp her hands with mine. "Like this."

With careful precision, I sliced the onion with the knife. Her teasing warmth threatened to distract me—to fall into the beat of the music with her.

"That is easier," she murmured.

Onion diced, I grabbed the bell pepper and worked on that with her, too, falling into a comfortable rhythm.

Astrid giggled. "What are your hips doing?"

"Whoa, should I go to my room?" Aya called out.

"Shut up, Aya," Astrid and I both yelled.

"Killjoys."

We chuckled, and I didn't stop the motions the music swept me up into.

"Seriously, what are you doing?" Astrid asked.

"Dancing, of course."

She shook her head. "You've got a knife. That's dangerous."

"Live on the edge a little, take a risk."

Astrid grunted. "Says the motocross racer who likes to do crazy tricks he sees on TV."

I set the knife down and pulled her back by the hips. "Yes, says me."

She fell into step, knowing the dances. She grew up alongside me, sharing in my family's food, music, and culture. I may have grown up here, but Papá made sure I'd never forget where we came from. And occasional visits to family didn't hurt, either.

I'd bring her there someday, and show her the sights and culture firsthand. And hopefully, introduce her to the family as mine.

I took Astrid's hand and spun her slowly. She giggled, and I caught the kitchen lights flickering. *This again?*

Pulling her close, I dipped her low. She gasped and threw her arms around my neck. That only pulled her closer to me. I grinned, noticing the flush on her pretty face. "What, do you not trust me?"

She opened her mouth, and then shrieked when something crashed to the floor. I instinctively pulled her flush against me and jumped back.

We stared at the two knives that'd somehow fallen off the counter.

Aya's feet thundered down the stairs, and she appeared in the kitchen. "You two okay?"

"Yeah," I slowly released my hold on Astrid. "Just dodging flying knives. Pretty sure the house ghosts are dance critics."

She grunted. "Then maybe you should turn the dial down on the magnetism between the two of you."

Astrid smacked her forehead, and I shook my head. "That was a terrible one, even by your standards."

Aya only grinned, as if pleased with herself, then decided to move her work down to where we were. Astrid and I cleaned up the strange mess and fell back into cooking.

Though a part of me couldn't stop thinking about the flickering lights and the knives. *Call me superstitious, but something strange is going on.*

SIX

TYR

I slid the comb through my beard one last time and made a thorough check in the mirror. *Clean, trimmed, and styled…* My eyes narrowed at an unsightly single hair sticking defiantly out of place. I snatched my trimming scissors off the sink counter next to my beard oil, and snipped off the affronting hair.

Satisfied, I ran my fingers through my hair before cleaning my mess. Irritation still simmered under my skin; I'd tossed and turned all night. And when sleep didn't work, I had hoped going for a long walk and replaying my conversation with Astrid yesterday, and my attempts to get her to remember, would allow me to forget seeing Aya act so casually in that house, as if she belonged there.

When that hadn't worked, I'd done my damnedest to work off my frustration by making a dent in the woodpile. However, I had to stop after a while, or I risked someone noticing my lack of exhaustion, so I chose to take a long shower and tidy myself up. I had to look my best, after all.

Nothing ended up dissipating the chaos raging inside me. I'd had my suspicions that the Aya Astrid had talked about was the one I knew. Everything added up too well, but I hadn't been prepared to be proven right. *How long has Aya known Astrid in this life and not told me?*

I shut my eyes and sucked in a slow, deep breath, trying to clear my head. Allowing these thoughts wouldn't help me.

Didn't work. I couldn't stop replaying how Aya had spoken to me as if she had something to do with me showing up here... like she expected me. She didn't contact me. Her magic didn't call to me like it had in the past. I knew that call.

My hand clenched into a fist. *The call that told me we'd failed Astrid.*

Leaving the bathroom, I stalked through my cabin for the door. She had some explaining to do, and I wouldn't wait any longer.

I swung the door open and stopped short. Amber eyes peered up at me.

"Trjegul."

The cat's eyes squinted and her tail swished back and forth lazily. I crouched and scratched her behind the ear. She purred and rolled her head until I was scratching her under the chin.

"I can't believe Freya is calling you Tuggy now." I grunted. "Actually, it's her; of course she would."

The cat pulled away and gazed at me with eerily intelligent eyes. Back then, I had always assumed Freya had normal cats who would die when their time came, and she'd replace them. But no, these two lived on, and they showed signs to be more than just felines. But Freya never divulged what her cats truly were.

"You couldn't possibly tell me what the hel is going on so I don't have to deal with Freya, could you?"

Someone chuckled. "How long do you think you can run from your problems, Norse god?"

I snapped my attention to my right, where a tall, lean man with angular features and a freckled, pale complexion sat on a rock. The light breeze teased his tousled black hair. Vibrant green eyes gazed back at me. "Who are you?"

"A resident, like you." He had a strong, lilted accent.

There weren't many residents here. Astrid had told me the names of them all. "You must be Sean."

The man grinned. "That's what they call me here, aye."

A muscle in the back of my neck tensed. This man made me uneasy. *He knows what I am.* However, I didn't know what he was, and that didn't sit well with me at all.

Sean's grin widened. "Still haven't figured it out yet? Maybe this will help?"

Before my eyes, his ears morphed to a more pointed shape, and his eyes became more vibrant and inhuman in color. Had I not been a god, I may have also been overcome by the alluring beauty he now exuded, regardless of my preferences.

I tilted my head, eyes narrowing. "What business does an elf have here?"

He blinked too innocently and gazed around. "Why wouldn't I? This place is beautiful and quiet. It heals me to be so far from the advancements of this age."

"You could always go to the fae realm."

The fae had done decently well adapting to the developments of societies over the millennia, but this most recent century, with the ever-advancing technologies, had proven to be the most difficult.

More and more, the fae shifted to their own realm, sometimes choosing to never leave. Those who remained did their best to incorporate both technology and nature into their lives. They'd even gone as far as to make mortals reliant on their more modern deal schemes of credit cards and insurance, like Good Neighbor.

Sean's eyes shifted away. "You know as well as I, elves are not welcome in the fae realm."

I tilted my head. I did not know that.

One of his single, perfect eyebrows lifted. "Ùna didn't tell you?"

Hearing the fae female's name sent a sharp pang through my chest. "You know Ùna?"

He nodded. "That's how I was able to recognize your presence so quickly. She misses you."

I turned my gaze away, guilt clawing up from deep inside. "I'm sure she does."

"Don't worry, she understands why you don't return and waits patiently. Why, that is beyond me." Sean shrugged. "But it isn't my business who she swears eternal fealty to."

"You said you can't go to the fae realm. Why is that?"

His lip curled. "Just as Ùna is no longer perfect enough, *earning* her elf title, we born elves are not pure enough."

I frowned. *There are two types of elves?* I knew elves were the product of fae and mortals mingling, but I didn't know there was a way to earn that name. Nor did I know the fae cast out their own kind for such petty reasons.

Ùna never told me she couldn't go back. She was the sole survivor of a brutal massacre by mortals who feared the fae. Though, because of the cold iron they'd used, she'd never fully recovered.

I never once questioned why she insisted she was indebted to me. I'd never wondered why she wouldn't ask for a different debt repayment. I now regretted not caring sooner.

"I wondered how long it would take for you to show up," the elf said. "Aya has been here so long, I thought you'd make yourself known much sooner. How curious she didn't tell you."

My eyes narrowed. I didn't like what he was insinuating. "How long has she been here?"

He shrugged. "You'll have to talk to her about that."

"Does Astrid know? About you, that is." This would give me an idea of what she'd been exposed to.

She had talked about her exposure to heathenism, but I couldn't be sure which type. Theoretically, since she didn't seem to recognize anything I'd said to her about the past, I would guess her father was a mortal practitioner with no connection to the magical and supernatural community.

I also couldn't quite confirm because I was unsure if he prayed to me. I'd gotten his name through a passing conversation with Carrie, but Darius wasn't a name that stood out in the chorus of voices.

If Astrid was also ignorant about Aya's true nature, which I highly suspected based on the way the goddess had worded herself in our conversation, that meant Aya had been careful, too, with how much she revealed, which didn't make any sense to me. But if that was the case, I already suspected Sean's answer.

The elf shook his head. "No, the wingless Valkyrie is not yet aware of my true nature."

My eyes narrowed. "You know? How?"

"I've known since I first laid eyes on her. It is no accident she looks the way she does—that her scar resembles the one she was most known for."

My jaw set. I didn't like the way this fae said that. Only Freya, Baldur, and I knew about the spell and ritual we used. We'd agreed to keep it secret for her protection. Lot of good that did her, but we tried. So, if Sean knew… "What do you mean?"

"Magic is not a toy, wandering god of war and judgment. It is powerful, and should be respected." His eyes squinted. "You and Freya took a great risk with ancient and powerful magic, and this is what magic brought you."

My axe materialized in my hand, the wooden haft biting into my skin. "Is that a threat?"

The elf jumped off his rock away from me, but gazed up with defiance. "No. I wish no harm on Astrid. She was kind to us fae back then. She is kind now, even if she does yet understand the true ways of this world. Truthfully, I'm glad she was brought back, even if I'm not clear on the magic you obtained to do so. But, no matter what I want, magic's price comes due. You must be ready when it comes to collect."

My grip on my axe tightened. *What does that mean? Is Astrid still in danger? Does Freya know about this?*

Tuggy chittered and then trotted down the path toward the main house.

"Seems the war goddess' familiar has deemed it time for you to speak with the woman."

I blinked. *He understands the cat?*

Sean grinned and tipped an imaginary hat at me before waltzing into the woods.

Tuggy stopped and turned her head to chitter at me again. She really did want me to follow.

I took a deep breath to calm myself and dismissed my weapon. Whether I liked it or not, I was going to have to have this conversation with Aya. Hopefully not with Astrid around to witness, because I wasn't sure if I could keep my cool around the goddess.

The walk down to the house was peaceful. I could see why a fae would be drawn here. In some ways, it reminded me of home, and I understood how Astrid loved this place. Even if she had no memories of the past, a part of her had to remember, right?

I shook the thoughts from my head. Aya told me a long time ago, when she'd done the first ritual, despite promises Astrid and I made to each other in life, there were no guarantees. I had to treat this as a brand-new start, as hard as that was proving to be.

My pulse slowed. *But if she did remember, how would I tell her about Fenrir… and Baldur?*

Tuggy yowled, snapping me out of my head. She stood in front of the door, crying. Lively music played within.

"Don't be impatient," I mumbled.

I opened the door, and the fluffy feline scurried inside. I followed her, watching as she ran past the kitchen into the great room where Angel snoozed. The cat groomed the shepherd's head before curling up with her. I shook my head and scanned the room.

Aya sat in front of a laptop in the breakfast nook. She split her focus between the technology and the activity in the kitchen. My attention was drawn to the latter. Astrid dancing around was too distracting to not focus on.

Her body flowed with sensual movements in step with the Latin music playing. My eyes followed each jerk of her body and sway of her wide hips. It stirred desire in me. I almost stepped closer, ready to reach out and pull her firm against me and feel what she was like in this life, when a hand reached out and grabbed hers.

Diego pulled her to him, spinning her as she went. Her body molded into his and he murmured something in her ear. Her cheeks tinted a light shade of pink before she pushed away to dance some more. Diego snagged her back, their bodies syncing. My jaw clenched.

I'd hung onto the friend label she'd given him, but it was already looking like I needed to be careful or I'd lose my chance. *If I haven't already.*

I tore my gaze away and settled it on Aya. This was happening right under her nose, and from the goofy look on her face, she not only knew, but had no intention of stopping it. I stalked over to her.

Aya stroked Buggy, who sprawled on the table as if she owned it. "Poetry has changed quite a lot since the old days."

She spoke in an archaic language only us gods knew these days. While I appreciated our conversation would be a bit more private, her comment was another story.

I dropped into the spot next to her. "How long have you been keeping her from me?"

Aya continued to pet her cat. "I haven't been keeping anyone from you."

My hand balled into a fist, my muscles coiling. I used to have control over my fury. But without my Valkyrie to help curb my reactions when I struggled to maintain control, that control crumbled over the centuries. "Don't treat me like I'm an idiot. How long?"

Aya frowned and turned her focus on me. "Since she was seven years old."

My gut clenched, as if a raging Berserker slammed into me. Seven? *Aya had found her some twenty years ago…* "And you never told me?"

"You're here, aren't you?"

My eyes narrowed. "Don't play games with me, Aya."

"I'm not. If you really believe you showed up here of all places by chance, then you're a fool." She tapped on her keyboard, pretending to work for a moment. "I lured you here when I thought it was safe enough for you to know."

"Bullshit. I'm here because of Davyn. I haven't felt your magic."

Her perfect eyebrow spiked. "Davyn? Interesting. Then I suppose that's how my magic has decided to work, then. Because I sent out a call to you two years ago and then a few weeks ago."

Two years. That coincided with when Davyn first found me. And then again when he gave me my lead. But still, even if those were as a result of her magic, that didn't explain why she waited so long. "I had a right to know the moment you found her. You swore under oath—"

"I didn't break my oath!" She sucked in a slow breath, calming herself. "And what would you have done had I told you about her? Groomed her?"

I reeled back at the accusation. "The hel I would have."

"Are you sure? Because I know you, Tyr. I know you wouldn't have been able to stay away until she was an adult."

"I would have been there for her." I gestured in the vague direction Astrid and Diego danced, now apparently to some pop song I was sure I heard on the radio in the nineties. "I sure as hel would have made sure this wasn't a thing."

Aya smirked. "Jealous? You didn't have any qualms when she was getting close to Baldur."

"That was different."

She shook her head. I didn't expect a goddess of sex to see it the way I did.

"Beyond this fucking annoyance that I now have to deal with, since you're so content to let it happen, given you apparently were with her this whole time somehow—"

"I have magic, moron." Her eyes narrowed. "She has no idea I posed as the woman she calls grandmother. She doesn't know the lengths I went to to change my identity in her life to stay with her when she went off to college. All for the sake of protecting her."

She turned her attention back to her computer, a frown pulling down her lips and her shoulders drooping. "You don't know how bad it got, Tyr. I didn't tell you all the times she died."

My pulse slowed. *What does she mean by that?*

"There were three times as many deaths. I only periodically told you about them, because I knew it'd break you if you were exposed to too many of them." Her hands curled into tight fists. "I couldn't handle it after the last time I found her mauled and mutilated body. She was only a little girl, Tyr, just like every other time—six years old—the oldest she'd ever gotten."

Aya turned back to me, her eyes hard. "I made a promise that day I'd do things differently. I'd find her sooner and protect her myself this time. And still, in this life, I was almost too late."

"I could have helped you. I had a right to help you."

She shook her head. "No. I needed to take drastic action to save her, so I did. I used all my magic to conceal her. I pretended to be neutral when all manner of events transpired over these last two decades in order to keep her safe, no matter what others thought of me."

She held an unwavering gaze. "You weren't the only one who loved her. She was my family, too, and I'd do anything to keep her safe this time—even if it means you and others hate me."

My pulse beat slow and steady under the surface of my skin. I could appreciate her conviction. I could try to hate her for keeping Astrid from me, but I knew I couldn't. She was right, even if I didn't like that reality. But there was also a flaw in her claims.

"And yet, you still protect Fen, even after what he did."

Aya's eyes darkened, and she bared her teeth. "He didn't kill her, Tyr."

"I know what I saw," I snapped back. "You weren't there."

"And I know Fen, as do you. He'd never do that to her."

I opened my mouth to rip into her and how she always protected the wolf-god, when a gentle voice made a fake throat-clearing noise. I snapped my attention to Astrid, who now sat on the other side of the table.

She folded her hands in front of her, ignoring Buggy's pawing attempts to get affection. The corners of her eyes were tight, and her lips pulled into a neutral, serious position. "I think, given the tension, it would be best if we discussed this issue between the two of you."

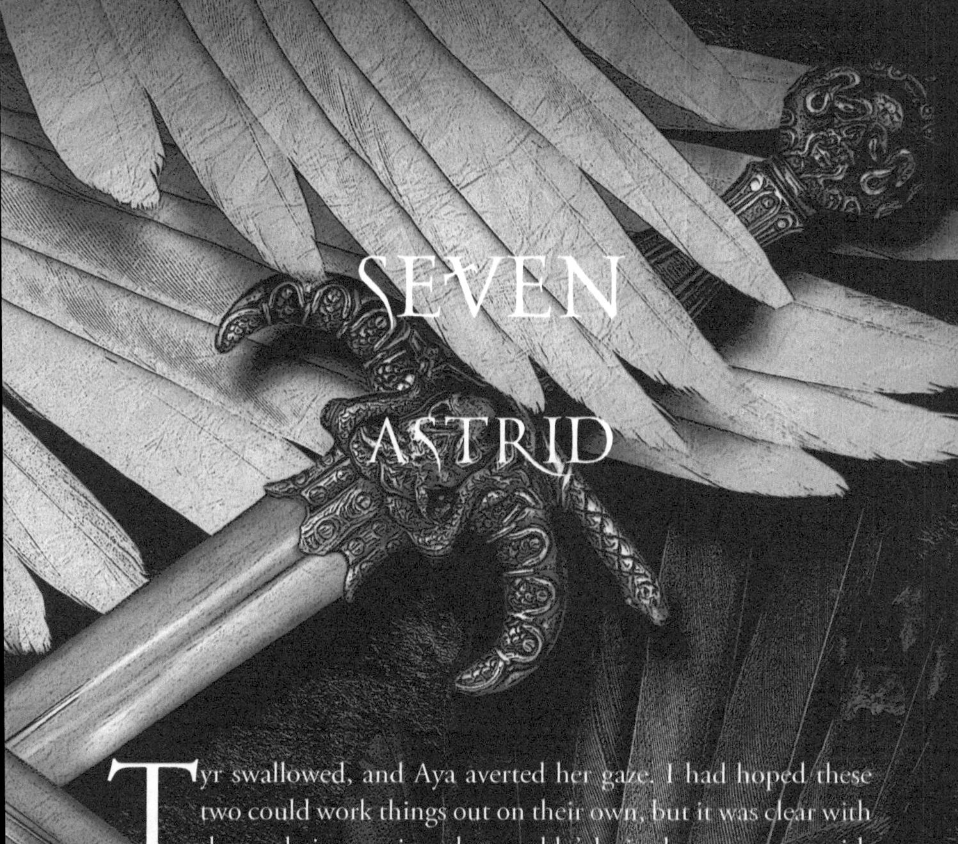

SEVEN

ASTRID

Tyr swallowed, and Aya averted her gaze. I had hoped these two could work things out on their own, but it was clear with the escalating tension, they couldn't be in the same room with each other without help.

"I understand this situation is a difficult one," I said. "However, I know you two can work through this together. I want to assist where I can, to help you both heal and move forward. Can we do this?"

Aya still didn't meet my gaze, and Tyr appeared unsure. I could understand his hesitation, but Aya's perplexed me.

Tyr finally broke the tense silence. "This isn't something that can be fixed by talking. I understand you want to help, but talking about feelings won't right this wrong."

"And without knowing the details, I don't believe it will," I admitted. "However, the goal right now doesn't have to be that grand. I'd rather tackle what we can, which starts with helping you two not only communicate with each other, but process all emotions that come with this conflict."

Aya finally looked at me. "He's right, Astrid. This isn't something a therapy session can fix."

This was the time I knew I should back off and just remind them the offer stood when they were ready. However, something nagged at me in the back of my mind; it urged me to keep pushing. And I did. "Why do you say that?"

Tyr's jaw clenched, and his hand curled into a fist. "Because it's about Fen murdering my wife."

My body chilled. *Murdered?* My mind blanked—I didn't know how to react. Aya had spoken so fondly of her brother-in-law and made him out to be this amazing man who was the perfect partner for her brother. I couldn't see her doing that for someone who would murder another person.

A part of me deep down twisted and turned, as if rejecting the very thought of Fen doing something so abhorrent, like I knew he would never. But that didn't make sense. I'd never met the man, so the reaction had to be based on what I knew solely from Aya.

Aya's hand slammed down on the table, and she practically snarled out her next words. "He didn't kill her!"

"I was there!" Tyr's eyes bore into her. "I know what I saw."

Aya didn't back down, the tension in the air spiraling out of control. "You saw wrong! She was like his sister. He would have never harmed her."

Tyr held up his arm with his missing hand. "I know what I felt. By the time Fen was done with her, she looked like she'd been mauled by a beast and I'd lost my hand trying to stop him."

My chest twisted. Something about this conversation hit somewhere deep within me, making me feel like I knew more about this situation than I really did. It had to be the stress. This was quickly growing far out of my experience level. *Still, I have to try to help.*

"Everyone, please stop." I did my best to keep my voice calm. "I'd like everyone in this room to take a deep breath."

Diego did just that immediately, as did I. However, Tyr and Aya didn't listen. They looked poised to attack each other.

"Tyr, Aya, please," I said.

Aya closed her eyes, her hands curling into fists, and she sucked in a deep inhale. She exhaled slowly and then repeated the action two more times before her shoulders relaxed and her hands fell to her lap.

Tyr was more resistant to my request, but when we made eye contact, his determination to fight softened. His shoulders relaxed a little and he let out a breath. He didn't release all the tension, showing he wasn't ready to let go of the pain raging in him, but I could work around that.

"Thank you," I said. "I understand I am limited here on how I can help, but I can see where I can. And if you're both willing, I'd like for us to talk about this."

The two passed unsure looks. It was a long shot, I knew this, but something just wouldn't allow me to let this go, so I had to try.

"Everyone will speak in turns. I won't allow anyone to talk over another person, and I ask you both, when speaking about each other, to refrain from using accusatory tones or laying blame. Is this agreeable?"

Aya nodded, and Tyr did as well after a moment of thought.

My eyes flicked to Diego, who gave a curt nod himself before going to lock all the doors. "Diego will remain here to observe. What we discuss here stays between the four of us. We are serious about confidentiality."

Uncertainty returned to their faces when I mentioned Diego. I suspected in the heat of their emotions, they forgot he was still here.

"I also have a few questions, so I can try to be more informed about the situation as a whole. Is that okay?"

Aya nodded. "I'm willing to answer questions you have the best I can."

"How long ago did this situation take place?"

Aya licked her lips. "Before you and I met for college."

I nodded slowly. Almost a decade ago, at least, which did track. Aya was a little older than Diego and me, by maybe two or three years. She'd told me once, family matters had kept her from going to school at the same age most did. I was beginning to think this was the situation. And given I'd suspected Tyr was also a few years older than me as well, it wouldn't be hard to believe him being widowed young. *Why does that conclusion not feel quite accurate?*

I shook the thought from my mind. "Were there any legal proceedings around the murder?"

Tyr tensed, and Aya chewed her lip. "That's where our fighting comes from. There was an investigation, but with Tyr as the only witness, and little other evidence, the investigation came up inconclusive, so Fen was never charged with anything, and the case went cold."

My brow furrowed. That was strange. If Tyr was there, as he claimed, that made him a witness. Even if he was the only witness, I would think that'd be enough for a trial. Of course, I didn't have any extensive legal knowledge around such cases, especially not when it came to another country.

"I see that look," Aya said. "I can explain why."

Tyr shot her an ugly glare, and I prepared to have to step in. "Please explain to me, Aya, what I'm missing."

"Tyr was the only witness, and there was a conflict of timing between the crime and when Fen was last seen, by me and a friend."

"It was him," Tyr nearly snarled.

I held up a placating hand. "Tyr, please allow her to finish speaking."

He sucked in a tight breath through his nose and sat back hard in his seat. I knew this was difficult for him—we were discussing the death of the woman he loved.

I turned back to Aya. "Would you be willing to elaborate on what you mean by the timing conflict?"

"Fen was with me and a friend," she said. "He'd gone missing for a brief period of time. However, the time it would have taken to commit the crime didn't add up to the distance and the time the murder took place."

I nodded slowly, understanding a bit more. Tyr was certain of what he witnessed, but not even the law could give him the justice he sought. That couldn't make this situation any easier on him.

"I'm now going to ask you both some personal questions. Some may be difficult to answer, but I ask you to do your best. I believe these questions will help with communicating." I turned to Aya first, as I had a feeling she'd be the easiest. "Conflicting evidence aside, you've been adamant Fen couldn't have done what he is accused of. Can you tell us why you feel this strongly?"

"Like I'd said earlier, the two were like siblings. He'd pick on her like any older brother would, and hel would freeze over before he'd allow anyone to hurt her." Aya shook her head. "Fen has a temper, I won't deny that. But he never once hurt her. She was the first person we looked to to calm him down if he got too bad."

Her eyes flicked to Tyr for a moment. "He loved the two of them together. He'd pick on them, and sometimes pretend to attempt to steal her from Tyr, but it was never serious. They were a perfect match that Fen would have died for to keep together."

Aya settled a determined gaze on me. The intensity made my pulse slow. "Nothing could make me believe he'd seek her out and kill her in cold blood."

Deep inside, I twisted, like some inner part of me was thrashing against a cage and screaming. She agreed with Aya, insisted something was wrong about this whole situation, and that Fen was innocent. *Stop, Astrid. You need to stay neutral and not allow your friendship with Aya make you biased.*

"And there was never a point where he had ever threatened her?"

Aya shook her head. "Not that I'm aware of."

I nodded, that inner feeling again saying she was right. "Thank you for sharing all of this."

I turned to Tyr. His hand clenched and unclenched. His jaw tensed so hard, I was certain it was pressing the blood vessels in his temple. "Tyr, would you like to say anything in regards to her claims of how Fen was around your wife?"

His jaw flexed. "No."

I did my best not to react. This was a common reaction. And if he hated Fen as much as he claimed, Tyr wouldn't want to think about any positive points associated with Fen.

Aya snorted. "Because he knows I'm right."

Tyr sat up quickly, his muscles bunched, and eyes filling with hatred. I reacted, my hand shooting out and landing on his. "Tyr, wait, please."

I snapped my attention to Aya. "Aya, don't antagonize. Please."

She frowned, and her eyes lowered. "You're right. Sorry, Tyr."

He didn't react. I shifted my focus back onto him, to find Tyr staring at my hand on his.

"Tyr?" I nudged.

He blinked and then locked gazes with me. My heart pulsed, and something within me warmed, spreading through my limbs. His eyes flicked back down to my hand and I realized how inappropriate my behavior was. I retracted my hand immediately, that warmth dissipating just as quickly.

"Do you accept Aya's apology?" I asked him.

"Yes." He still looked at his hand, even though I'd removed mine.

"Are you still open to talk?" I really wasn't sure why he was acting so strangely all of a sudden.

He sucked in a deep breath and then nodded.

"I'd like to ask you about what you saw that day." This is where it got risky for me. If I didn't handle this correctly, he'd shove me away.

This question grabbed his attention. "Why? I saw him kill her. That's all that needs to be known."

I nodded slowly, trying to make sure I worded this correctly. He was already on the defensive, and I didn't need to drive him off. "What I'd like to ask you isn't about the act itself, but what was going on around you at that moment."

His brow furrowed. "Why?"

"It's a memory exercise. It helps with re-solidifying memories, especially in high-stress situations, like this one. Recalling your surroundings, or what you were doing before Fen showed up, or remembering as many details as you can of what he was wearing, can all help figure out what we're missing."

Tyr's hand curled into a fist. "You don't believe me."

"That's not what I'm saying at all." Though the words came out, inside I was at war. I logically didn't know enough to form an opinion, not that I really should. But there was a strong part of me that believed Aya. Like an abnormally strong part of me, that went beyond the reasoning that she was my friend and I always wanted to believe what she said. "I'm asking these questions for your benefit, and mine. Maybe if you can paint the scene for me, we can find—"

"You believe Aya." He shook his head and stood. "No matter what I say, you won't believe me."

I frowned. "Tyr, please don't…"

He looked at me with pained eyes, as if I'd betrayed him in some way. I wasn't sure why, and that inner part of me that was siding with Aya withered under that agonizing gaze. It whimpered and felt like it was begging for him to listen instead of falling into the pain he had become so comfortable with.

Without another word, he walked out. Angel, who had been locked outside by Diego to ensure she didn't feed off any of the high emotions, watched him leave with keen interest. But, for whatever reason, she didn't follow him like she would another resident who was upset. Instead, she watched him leave like the rest of us and then trotted into the house, going to Aya and laying her head on my friend's lap.

My stomach knotted. I couldn't explain why, but something about his retreat bothered me. Maybe it was because, with the way this all started, I expected a more explosive denial. *Not something that sounded so defeated and broken.*

Aya turned her attention to me. "Don't let him upset you."

I shook my head. "I'm not. I knew this would be difficult. It's not something that can be tackled in one session."

Aya chewed her lip. "I think you're going to have more difficulties than you think."

My eyebrow ticked up. "Why's that?"

"You… share a lot of similarities with her," she admitted. "It's not like these qualities are unique in a person or anything, but…"

I nodded slowly, understanding what she was implying. "I wish I'd known. I would have considered having Diego handle this instead."

Diego rubbed the back of his neck. "I don't know. I don't think I would have been able to de-escalate his anger as effectively as you did."

"I have to agree with him," Aya said. "Tyr wouldn't have stayed for even five minutes if it'd been Diego reaching out. Your similarities with her is a double-edged sword."

My lips twisted. It was a 'damned if I did, damned if I didn't' situation. And it explained the feeling of betrayal I sensed from him.

I rose. "I'm going to go for a walk."

Aya frowned. "Are you okay?"

Deep down, I was reeling. There was all manner of chaos thrashing about. But I didn't know how to explain that, so I nodded. "Yeah, it's just a lot to process. Some time alone will help me sort things out."

"Alright. I do hope this conversation hasn't gotten you to see Fen in a lesser light."

I shook my head. "I wasn't lying to Tyr when I said I hadn't picked any side."

She gave a small smile. "I'll take neutral over you condemning him."

I headed for the basement. Angel followed; her usual bouncing steps calmed. I was sure she could sense the hidden turmoil within me. She'd stick to me like glue until I felt better. And I needed her presence.

Because I didn't know how to process this strange feeling inside me.

EIGHT

TYR

Water lapped at the shore of the lake. A raven called somewhere in the forest. I ran my fingers through my hair, breathing hard through my nose. *She didn't believe me.* That moment swarmed my mind and played over and over. Astrid didn't have any accusatory tone when asking questions. She genuinely listened to the whole situation with fresh eyes. But the fact she'd question me at all…

I sighed again. Even if Astrid didn't have her memories, some part of her did. She had to. *And that means, deep down, Astrid doesn't believe what I saw.*

I didn't understand. She saw Fenrir. She watched him kill her. And yet… even she doubted the events. *She has to be in denial… she has to be…* Because if she wasn't, and Fenrir wasn't the one who killed her—*No!*

I shook my head. I wouldn't doubt myself now. I wouldn't break after all this time. *Can you really say you haven't?*

Aya didn't tell me about all the deaths because she thought it'd break me—that thinking the reincarnation process just took a long time was better for my mental state. I only knew of three. Three.

Before seeing Astrid, I would have denied I was broken. I was just exhausted. *But the moment I saw her…*

A snapping twig drew me out of my thoughts. My senses went on alert, centuries of existing through war honing them into instinct. Someone approached. No, two bodies approached. Their pace wasn't consistent, as if they stopped and started several times.

Then I heard the familiar giggling and voice of the one person I craved to hear, even in my current state.

I turned just as Astrid waltzed out of the forest, Angel trotting excitedly next to her. The dog gazed up at her owner, watching the ball Astrid carried. Astrid laughed when her companion jumped to try and steal it.

She came to a sudden halt when she noticed me. Her lips pressed together, and she averted her gaze. "Sorry, I didn't mean to disturb you."

Disturb me? What, did she think her presence bothered me? I frowned. Maybe she did after how I had up and left.

Astrid took a step to continue on in some direction other than mine, when Angel decided to trot over. She came up right behind me and sat, resting her head on my shoulder. The dog gazed at me with unusually expressive eyes that reminded me of Aya's cats in a way.

I reached up and scratched her behind the ear. Angel's tail thumped on the ground and she tipped her head into my hand. I glanced Astrid's way, finding her smiling.

"Seems she thinks you need her company more," she said.

I frowned. I didn't like how she said that. "What do you mean?"

Her attention shifted away. "I'm not here to bother you. I'll just keep going."

Pain struck my chest. *I fucked up.* I'd gone and run her off. How had one moment made her not want to be around me? *Fuck.* "You're not bothering me by being here."

She shook her head. "You came here for solitude."

My heart rate slowed. That was why she didn't want to be around me? *Creation, why did I panic so quickly?* I should have known I wouldn't run her off that easily. "I would like it if you stayed."

"Are you sure?"

I didn't understand her hesitation. "I wouldn't have asked if I wasn't."

She still seemed unsure, but instead of leaving, she joined me at the shore. Astrid pulled her legs up to her chest and gazed out at the lake. I could take in this idyllic moment with her; enjoy the peacefulness that felt so familiar to what we had in the past, yet vastly new, all at the same time.

I watched her instead, taking in every beautiful detail of her I could—the way her eyes sparkled in the light; her fierce scar cutting a path over her skin; the freckles banding her nose; the angling of her heart-shaped face; how her orange locks cascaded over her shoulders—

She noticed my attention and blinked. "Um, do I have something on my face?"

I chuckled as she dragged her hand along her cheek. "No. Just enjoying the view."

Pink tinged her cheeks, and she tore her gaze away, half-laughing awkwardly. "You're looking in the wrong direction, then."

I made a thoughtful sound. My eyes swept over the view and came back to her. "The lake is beautiful, but I think I'm appreciating in the proper direction."

Astrid chewed her lower lip, drawing my gaze, and played with her fingers. "I like to come here when I need to think. It's so peaceful. I wish it were part of our property. I'd build a house right on that far side. It has the best view."

I turned my attention out to the tranquil water. It was clear I needed to be careful how much I pushed right away. If I had to guess, she ran into some self-esteem issues like in the past with that scar. Back then, we lived in a time where it was more acceptable, but she still had her share of experiences because of it. So, I could only assume the reactions she received now. "I hadn't realized I'd walked off the property."

"We don't mark it. Most don't feel like wandering this far out on the paths. Had I realized you might, I would have given you warning. Though, as long as you didn't wander too much farther, you wouldn't have gotten lost."

"I'm glad I could discover it myself. I think the experience was much better. And the view from this side of the lake is wonderful."

She smiled and nodded. "I don't know anyone who hates being here. It can calm the mind or bring out something beautiful in us. It might even make you want to paint or write a song."

"Or recite poetry."

She turned to gaze at me. "Do you recite poetry?"

I shook my head. "No. No, you don't want to hear me do that. It's more than just embarrassing for me." And like hel would I ever do that to her again. "What about you?"

"Hmm… not great, but not terrible, either." She smiled in a way that borderlined a sultry smirk. Or maybe I was imagining the sultry part of that. "Maybe we can make poetry together to change that."

She paused, pink rising to her face. My attention on her sharpened, and a grin pulled at the corners of my lips. I sure as hel wouldn't mind that, but was she serious? That wasn't a phrase most understood anymore. A part of me hoped it was the past her reaching out for me. But I could be hoping for too much.

Astrid flailed her arm and shook her head, her face turning redder. "Oh my gods, that did not come off the way I meant it. I am so sorry. Forget I said that."

I threw my head back, belting out a hearty laugh. Whether that was the Astrid I knew or not, it was clear this woman had not planned to invite anything—yet.

When I calmed, I smirked. "I'll have to think about your offer."

I swore to Creation her face was about to combust. She hid in her arms, as if that would save her.

"How have you felt while being here?" she asked, trying to steer the conversation elsewhere.

I thought about it for a moment. "Calm. It's allowed me to come down from the emotions."

She smiled and rubbed her arm. "I'm glad. I do apologize if I'm the cause of any of that. Aya… told me that I share some similarities with your wife, and I was worried that might have caused some issues in our session. If it did—"

I held up my hand. While I didn't like that Aya had made the comparison to Astrid, I didn't feel angry. More relieved than anything, if

I was honest with myself. "Please don't. Yes, you do remind me a lot of my wife, and that made the conversation difficult. It felt like it was her questioning the situation, when I knew it was you. But I think that's what I needed."

Astrid wrapped her arms around her legs. "Do you want to talk about it?"

Do I?

"I know it can be hard for a lot of men to talk to someone about their emotions. There's a lot of societal pressure to lock those up. That somehow your strength comes from how well you hide all that. Those pressures are wrong." She smiled. "That strength comes from acknowledging them as part of who we are and being open about them. It's something I have to tell myself a lot. Not because I have some pressure to hide my emotions, but because I don't want to burden people. So, I make the repeated mistake of trying to deal with them privately. I acknowledge this fault, and try to do better, even if I'm not perfect."

I worked my jaw. It would be nice to talk to someone finally, even if in a coded manner. And Astrid could be the best person to talk to. Old her and current her, she wouldn't judge. I could always be vulnerable with her. "I would be willing to talk through this, under one condition."

She cocked her head. "And what's that?"

"I don't want to feel like I'm talking to a shr—therapist." Astrid's eyes narrowed slightly right before I corrected myself. "I don't have much in the way of friends anymore. Makes it hard to… express myself. And I'd rather talk to a friend than anyone else."

Astrid's posture relaxed, and she turned toward me more. "I can do that."

Whether this was some act, or she really meant it, I didn't care. This new posture and her full attention already made me feel better. Angel settled in between us, rolling on her back for belly rubs.

While I spoke, I rubbed my arm along Angel's fur. "I should have been able to protect her. I was right there. She always trusted me to keep her safe."

I closed my eyes. The image of her bleeding and dying in my arms was so clear, as if a hundred mortal lifetimes hadn't passed since then.

Astrid's warm touch drew me out of my mind. Her hand rested on my arm, and the achingly familiar sensation of her healing pulsed through me. Yet, her hands didn't glow with magic. It was the same as when we'd been in the house, when she grabbed my hand to calm me. That power she had over me, it remained even now.

"What you're feeling is normal," she said. "And these feelings are okay to have. Surviving something so traumatic isn't easy."

My shoulders drooped. "I should have done more…"

"Did you do your best in the moment?"

Her words caught me off guard. Her expression was soft and kind, so I knew it wasn't accusatory. "I…"

"When you think about that moment, did you do everything you could have within such a stressful situation?"

Could I have done anything else? "I… don't think I would have done anything differently."

She nodded slowly. "It's easy for us to be hard on ourselves for the things we should have done. It's easy, once outside that situation, to criticize and question and see where we could have done something differently. But upon doing that, we forget that we're human. There's only so much we can do."

Her attention shifted out to the lake. "I've helped a lot of people. So many have gone off to be better versions of themselves and are living amazing lives. But that number isn't one-hundred percent. There are people I feel like I've failed. They've either gone back to their old ways, or worse. I find myself in the trappings of what-ifs and self-doubt. What could I have done differently? Do they blame me for not being able to do more? Am I not cut out for this job?"

Something pulsed deep in my chest. This was far from the sterile professional approach I suspected she was trained to take. She took my request to heart, because it felt like I was really connecting with a person who knew what I was going through, without me being able to put all the words out there myself.

"And for most, I know they don't," she said. "They would know I did my best, even if that best wasn't enough for what they needed."

My hand curled into a fist. My best hadn't been good enough. If I'd been better, I could have saved her. None of this would have happened.

Astrid offered a kind smile. "I don't know the woman you loved, but I've glimpsed just enough to confidently say, she wouldn't be the type to blame you. I know I wouldn't."

Those piercing green eyes of her peered through me, to the deepest parts I hid from Midgard. *She doesn't… blame me…* Something inside me cracked.

"You… forgive me?"

Astrid didn't stop smiling. "There's nothing to forgive, Týr."

She said my name… like she had back then. I didn't care if I imagined that or not. *The woman I loved, and the one tempting me now, doesn't blame me for what I couldn't save her from.*

The crack split even more and then opened up. I pulled Astrid into me and buried my face into her neck. The scent of vanilla and lavender enveloped me. So different from back then, and so fitting for her now.

Astrid let out a startled squeak and then placed a comforting hand on my head. Angel licked my arm, adding her own support. We remained like this until the emotional flood inside me subsided.

"I apologize if I put you in an uncomfortable situation," I said. As much as I needed that, and wanted her that close, I still was getting to know her in this life. I couldn't assume I hadn't put her in an uncomfortable situation.

Astrid smiled and cupped my cheek with a soft hand. "You wanted a friend. You got a friend."

The light weight in my chest was a new feeling. If she wanted to be my friend, I'd take it. I wanted more, but I could be patient. I'd woo and romance her like I had before, with even more modern tools at my disposal.

"Thank you… for being willing to open up," she said. "I appreciate that trust."

I smirked. "Do I get a reward for such good behavior?"

She pursed her lips and her brow scrunched as she thought. She then reached into a back pocket and pulled out a flat, brown dog-bone-looking item. "I've got a dog treat."

Angel perked up and licked her chops.

"It's all natural and organic, made with peanut butter," Astrid continued.

I did my best to keep a straight face, which was a harder feat than it should be. "Are you calling me a hound?"

To her credit, she didn't crack, either. "Would that make you a lost puppy?"

I worked my jaw. I wouldn't be the first to crack. Her lip twitched and then she and I both sputtered out laughter. I took the treat when I calmed, and a melancholy feeling came over me. "Fen would have appreciated these jokes…"

Astrid observed me. She didn't push any conversation, and I was thankful. I wasn't ready to tackle the topic of him right now. I didn't even know why I said anything about him just now. *Because I miss what we had…*

"How did you and your father come to find this place?" I wanted to change the subject to getting to know her. "Where did you come from before here?"

Astrid sucked in a deep breath and relaxed in the grass. "We're originally from the D.C. area. I don't know how my dad knew of this place, though. He said a friend sent us here after my mom's trial, but he's never gone into detail about it."

That had to be the work of Aya's magic. It wouldn't be beneath her to manipulate someone with magic in order to protect Astrid. "How long have you and Diego been friends?"

"Since day one." She adjusted the way she sat. "Dad and I had only been here maybe five minutes before he and Xavier showed up. And that was the day he publicly declared we'd be best friends forever."

"And that's all you two are?"

Astrid rolled her eyes so hard I laughed. "Don't listen to Aya. She's obsessed with shipping us."

My brow rose. "Shipping?"

"Uh, hmm." She thought for a moment. "It's when you desire two or more people, real or fictional, to be in a romantic or sexual relationship. It's fairly common in fictional fandoms."

I grunted. "That sounds like Aya. It's weird how good she is at it, though."

Astrid's eyes widened. "Right? It's a little freaky."

Little did she know it was Aya's domain that allowed it. And that made things difficult for me. "But you insist she's wrong about you two?"

Astrid shook her head. "Look, Diego's a flirt, but it's obvious when he's set his sights on someone. He's relentless."

I wondered how much she was in denial and how much was her being oblivious, because it seemed even obvious to me. But I wasn't going to push that. If she was going to deny Diego, it gave me a better chance.

Aya's taunting words about sharing Astrid flitted into the back of my mind, but I shook them out. "Speaking of Aya, how exactly did you two meet? You mentioned college, but I don't see how your and her professions overlap for you to meet."

I assumed Aya had gotten herself some sort of college degree if she was going to sell her undercover story. I wouldn't put it past her. Sure, she probably knew more about that computer stuff than any mortal alive, but she was a known masochist, so no doubt she got some enjoyment from it in some way. *Probably by fucking all the professors.*

"Oh, we became roommates first," Astrid said. "My dad's friend, Nyx, owns a bunch of apartments across the globe, and happened to have a suite available for us in one of her New York City complexes if we were willing to have a roommate. That's how we met. And it just so happened we were attending the same school."

Nyx? There was no way that name didn't belong to the Fate, especially if Aya was involved. What business did she have helping? Why did Aya trust her to know of Astrid's existence?

"Do you know Nyx?" Astrid asked. "I noticed some recognition in your face when I said her name."

Shit. Well, no going back from that. "Yeah, she's an old family friend. How did your dad meet her?"

Astrid shrugged. "He just said he'd met her in Greece once. Never explained further."

"Huh, small world." Was that the truth from her father? Had he actually met Nyx? Or had Aya implanted that memory to ensure Astrid went to Nyx's apartment?

She'd be safe there, given all the protective magic Nyx would have had on the place. Little did mortals know, their separate living accommodations were all part of her singular realm that she shaped to appear like an apartment or hotel, with multiple connection points around Midgard. She typically kept mortals separate from supernaturals and immortals to keep up the façade. Astrid would have been one of the rare cases the Fate would make an exception for, with Aya involved. *Still, why would she involve herself?*

The Fates typically kept neutral stances, refusing to get involved with anything that would tip the balance one way or the other. Though, there was a rumor that Nyx wasn't as neutral as she led on.

Angel pawed my arm and whined. I realized I was still holding the dog treat. "Wow, you've been patient."

"I'm actually surprised she waited this long," Astrid said. "She hasn't taken her eyes off that."

I offered it to the dog. After that impressive display of obedience, how could I not?

Angel happily crunched down on her treat and then jumped to her feet.

"Looks like she approves of our improved mental states," Astrid said.

The statement intrigued me. Astrid said Angel was a therapy dog, but I didn't know the first thing about such a profession for dogs. And there was the strange sense I got from her that she was more intelligent than your average canine.

However, Angel did not seem interested in me finding out. She grabbed the ball Astrid had set down on the ground and dropped it in my lap.

Astrid chuckled. "Tag, you're it."

I laughed. "Does she swim?"

Astrid snorted. "Normally, she's charging into that water whenever we get here. Just know, you get her wet first, you're towel-drying her before she goes back into the house."

I could live with that. Securing the ball in a good grip, I chucked it into the lake. Angel tore off after it, launching herself into the water. Astrid laughed and shielded herself from the splash.

Angel returned a moment later, her drenched fur clinging to her honed body. Astrid gave a warning, but her dog didn't care, and the inevitable shake happened, water flying everywhere. Astrid shrieked, and I laughed.

The canine dropped the ball at my feet and impatiently barked once. I didn't hesitate to throw it for her again.

"I should have worn my bathing suit," Astrid complained, wiping at her wet shirt.

I smirked. "You did promise I'd get to see that tattoo of yours one day."

She laughed, her cheeks tinting. "I didn't promise. Just said you might see it."

"Well, it is summer, so I think there's a high likelihood I will." My eyes traveled down the tempting curves of her body. Preferably while she was topless, but a cropped shirt or bikini would suffice for now.

Astrid rolled her eyes, as if she could read my thoughts. "Don't even suggest I remove my shirt."

My brow lifted. "Why not? I'd remove mine to make it fair."

She snorted. "Not even close to similar."

I couldn't stop the grin spreading up my face. "The way you stared at me yesterday says otherwise."

Her cheeks turned a shade of pink. "I was admiring your tattoo. That's all."

Angel returned with her toy. I slowly turned my attention toward the dog. "Sure. You keep telling yourself that."

If she wanted to appreciate me, I'd give her whatever view she wanted. She only had to ask.

We settled in for more conversation and ball throwing. I was going to relish the time we had to spend here today. The more I learned about her, the better chance I had at making her mine again.

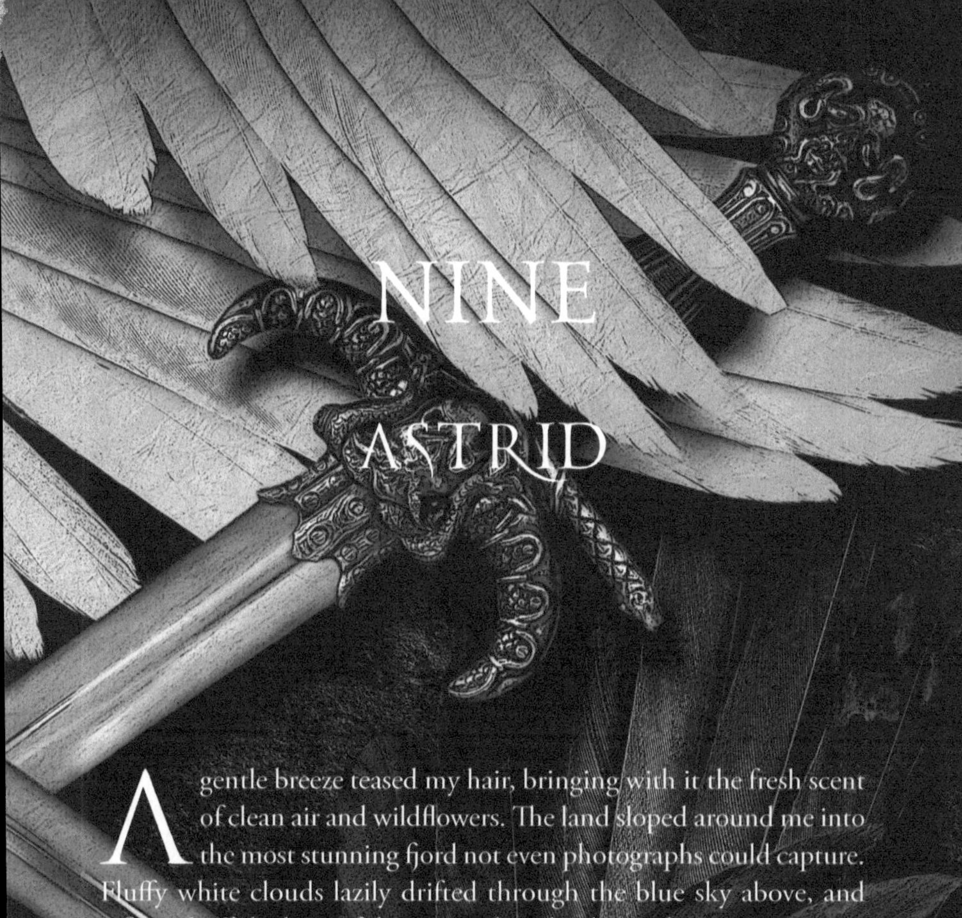

NINE

ASTRID

A gentle breeze teased my hair, bringing with it the fresh scent of clean air and wildflowers. The land sloped around me into the most stunning fjord not even photographs could capture. Fluffy white clouds lazily drifted through the blue sky above, and reflected off the beautiful water within the deep inlet.

Familiarity washed over me, as if I'd been here before, and yet, while I'd traveled before, I'd never gone farther than Canada. No place had been this spectacular.

I cocked my head when I caught the sound of flapping wings. *That's an unusual sound.* I'd heard various birds flying, but this wasn't one I was familiar with. *Is that sound getting closer?*

Turning, I looked around for the source of the steady wings. A large shadow cast on the ground approaching got me to jerk my head up. My eyes went wide.

Above me, a woman of pale complexion swooped down toward me. Long golden hair freely flowed in the wind behind her, and the black wings spreading from her back beat strong, propelling her through the air.

She landed with grace and elegance and gazed down at me with stunning blue eyes. Armor that looked more fantastical than real with its form-fitting, semi-revealing appearance with skulls and other detailed decoration, covered her slim, athletic form.

She smiled. "It's so good to see you again, Astrid. It's been so long."

"Kirby?" I blinked. *Where did that name come from?*

"I'm so glad you remember. I can't wait to see you in person."

I tilted my head, one eyebrow raising. "Huh?"

She grabbed me by the shoulders. Not roughly, more friendly, but it still startled me. "I've missed you."

Missed me? How could she miss me when I didn't know who she was? *And yet, I do?*

"It's time you finally grow into your wings."

Kirby stepped back and her wings flapped, black feathers flying out. I threw my arms over my face and shut my eyes to protect myself.

When I opened my eyes, I was faced with the view of the fabric of my canopy, and surrounded by the comfort of my bed. Morning sunlight slipped in through my windows.

I let out a slow breath and draped my arm over my forehead. "The fuck was that dream?"

Kirby. How did I know her name? Hell, why did she look so familiar? Did I meet someone like her at some point in my life? *Maybe a photo?*

I knew the mind transposed faces and identities onto people in dreams, even if it was someone we only saw in passing. *But the fact that I was so sure I knew her…*

A large body shifted in my bed, and I let out an *oof* when Angel dropped her head onto my chest. I smiled and scratched her along her chest. "I had the strangest dream, girl."

Angel's ears perked, and she cocked her head to the side. I loved it when she did her head tilt. She was so cute.

"I met a Valkyrie." As the words left my lips, my thoughts paused. *Was that a Valkyrie? How would I know that? Am I making assumptions because of Tyr's tattoo?* None of this made any sense.

I shook my head and sat up, gaining a displeased groan from Angel. I chuckled. For such an energetic dog, she sure was lazy in the morning.

"I have to get ready for the day and forget that weird dream. You can stay in bed a moment longer."

Angel gladly sprawled out when I climbed out of bed and I slowly readied myself. Today wasn't a workout day, though as I went through my routine, and the dream refused to fade from my mind, I wondered if I should change up my schedule. I just couldn't shake it. Her words clung to me, as if they were the key to a question I'd yet to ask.

I leaned against the canopy posts of my bed when I'd finished my morning routine. My fingers slid along the elegant knotwork and Norse imagery, engravings of Dad's handiwork, as well as some of my marks where we'd made the posts together.

"Ready for the day, girl?" I asked Angel.

She groaned in response.

I shrugged and turned away. "Okay, suit yourself."

I'd taken only two steps when Angel bolted from her spot and tore out of the room. I barked out a hard laugh. Her morning antics never ceased to amuse me. And I wasn't the only one, from the laughter downstairs.

By the time I made it to the first floor, Diego had stepped out with Angel. Carrie was cleaning the kitchen, and Tyr sat at the breakfast nook staring out the window while sipping on what smelled like coffee. Aya typed away on her laptop as always, nibbling on some toast. The two of them didn't appear tense, so it seemed this morning they were getting along again.

The last few days had been okay between them. Tyr usually kept his distance, but I'd caught the two conversing a few times, and thankfully, no more incidents had transpired.

Raeni wasn't around, though I suspected she'd gone to hang out with some friends. I remembered her asking her mom about it last night.

I greeted everyone before grabbing myself a hot mug of coffee. Aya smiled as she looked up from her computer, but it didn't remain. Her brow furrowed. "What's wrong, Astrid?"

I paused mid-sip. "Huh?"

"You look like something is bothering you."

Carrie and Tyr turned to look at me. I shrugged and took a seat next to her. "Had a weird dream. Haven't been able to shake it. Hoping the coffee helps."

She turned to face me. "What was it about?"

I pursed my lips. Aya was always asking people about their dreams. "I was standing at the top of a beautiful fjord. Then, out of nowhere, a blonde woman with black wings swooped out of the air and started talking to me like she knew me and then said something about me flying… or something like that."

I squinted. I'd known her name too, but now it escaped me. *Must not have been important.*

"That does sound odd," Carrie agreed. "Especially since Diego said he had a flying dream last night."

My brow arched, and she shrugged. "Coincidence, I guess."

I sipped my coffee. "Maybe…"

Why couldn't I shake the feeling it wasn't? *There's no such things as coincidences.*

Aya and Tyr didn't make any comments about my dream, though I swore they passed each other a strange look. *I have to be imagining that part.*

"What are everyone's plans today?" I asked. I figured it was best to steer the topic away from dreams.

Aya typed away on her keys again. "I have a freelance project due soon."

"Don't know yet," Tyr said. "Might work on that woodpile some more."

I nodded. While I didn't think he needed to work on it much more for a while with how much he achieved yesterday, I wouldn't tell him how to spend his time.

I turned to Carrie, who had a shit-eating grin. "You're up to something."

"I am," she said. "I have a working interview in a few hours."

My back straightened. "What? Really? When did this happen?"

Last I knew, she'd still been too nervous to take up work, in fear of running into people who triggered her trauma responses.

Carrie rocked her head back and forth. "Jessie has been trying to convince me to come work for her for some time. I saw her while shopping in town last week, and we got to talking. She offered to let me try out a few hours to see how I do, and after some thinking, and talking with Diego in my last session, I decided to give it a try."

I smiled widely. "That's fantastic, Carrie! I know you'll do great."

"I'll be doing everything I can to do well. I owe it to my daughter to get back on my feet and provide for her again."

I sobered. "Don't push yourself too hard. This is a huge step. Take things slowly and step away if you get too overwhelmed. You can't race up the mountain."

Carrie placed her hands on her hips. "I sure as hell can try."

I shook my head, smirking. She'd come a long way from the battered and frightened woman who showed up on our doorstep. I loved the tenacious woman she was reclaiming.

"What is the job?" Tyr asked her.

"In a past life, I was a hairstylist."

His brow furrowed, and Aya snickered. She spoke in another language to him, what I assumed was Norsk. I couldn't be sure, since I'd rarely heard Aya speak it, but it made the most sense.

Tyr nodded as she spoke. It seemed she was explaining the phrase to him.

"What are your plans, Astrid?" Carrie asked. She tilted her head to give me a pointed look. "It's your day off, so I expect you to not do anything work-related unless it's a legitimate emergency."

I shot her a sheepish smile. "Well, I had some paperwork I planned to get done——"

She pointed at me. "Absolutely not."

"It's just a little paperwork," I tried to defend. "It's important, and I'm behind."

I felt Aya's stern gaze on me as much as Carrie's. When a third set of eyes bored into me, I frowned and turned to Tyr. "Not you, too."

"Don't overwork yourself. Balance between work and the rest of your life is important."

I blew a strand of hair away from my face. "Not like any of you can stop me once you start going about your days."

Carrie lifted an eyebrow, and Aya snickered. "Tyr, you up for keeping an eye on our workaholic?"

My mouth fell open. "You can't volunteer someone to babysit me."

Tyr chuckled. "I'd be happy to."

"What are you happy to do?" Diego walked into the house wearing his motocross jersey, pants, and boots. Angel happily trotted after him, her tongue lolling.

Aya smirked. "We're making sure someone is watching Astrid, so she doesn't work today."

Diego shot me a pointed look. "You'd better not. I'll cancel my plans today if you're too difficult."

I huffed. This was ridiculous. If I wanted to get some quiet paperwork done, I should be allowed to do so. "Fine, I'll stay away from anything work-related."

Diego smiled and snagged a set of keys off the key rack. "Good. I'm going to head out, then."

"Got your brain bucket?" I asked.

He nodded. "All my gear is in the truck."

"Don't do any crazy stunts, and be safe," I said.

He chuckled. "I'll do my best."

I knew he would do one or two. He and his motocross buddies liked to show off, regardless of whether they were at the track or on the trails. They wanted to either one-up each other, or impress someone, usually a guest who tagged along. But I hoped he'd be at least a little careful.

"Have fun."

Diego smiled and left. I ignored the twinging sensation in my chest when he disappeared from sight. He was allowed to go hang out with friends all day and not with me. The motocross scene didn't interest me, and it was good for us to have separate hobbies. It was stupid to feel left out or hate the time apart from him, especially since we were *just* friends. *I need more friends.*

That was the understatement of the century. Most of the ones I had were from college, and not only were those few in numbers, none of them lived close enough to work out times to hang out. And while I had gaming nights with some of them, they were becoming fewer and fewer as my friend's lives changed, and they had less time to sit down and play.

Aya and Diego were my closest friends, with Zeke trailing a little behind them, and the last thing I wanted was to be that clingy friend who stole all their free time.

I noticed that stupid grin on Aya's face. "Don't you say a word."

Her shit-eating grin widened. "Don't forget to tell your *not*-boyfriend you love him and you'll be here when he gets back."

I rolled my eyes and hopped off my chair. I needed to get away from this topic she liked far too much. Tyr rose from his seat and took my empty coffee cup to throw into the dishwasher with his. "So, what's the plan for today?"

I pursed my lips. Seemed he was serious about babysitting me. "I still haven't figured that out, since the first four hours of my day are now canceled. I didn't plan to play any games until later tonight… I guess I'll walk the property until I figure it out."

Angel perked her ears at the word "walk" and snatched a ball, eager to go back outside. At least one of my companions was guaranteed to enjoy herself.

I didn't lead an exciting life like Diego. I liked my homebody lifestyle with a dash of hiking, hunting, or travel-excitement. But plenty would find it quite boring overall. I wouldn't blame Tyr if he wandered off after a while in search of something more stimulating.

"That sounds nice," Tyr said, surprising me a little. While I suspected he might be a fellow outdoorsy type, walks didn't come off as his thing. Then again, I still didn't know him all that well to make such assumptions.

"Have fun, you two," Aya said in her sing-song voice as we headed for the door.

"Not another word," I threatened, pointing back at her without looking.

"Don't do anything I wouldn't do!" she said anyway.

I grumbled a few insults, and Tyr laughed. "At least you're no stranger to her antics."

Tyr opened the door for me. "Oh, you have no idea."

The warm, mid-morning air greeted us. I sucked in a slow breath, relishing the freshness. Angel whined, and I shook my head before taking her ball and chucking it. She took off, and I picked a direction to walk.

Silence fell between Tyr and me until the house disappeared and Tyr took Angel's ball from me. He chucked it hard into the thick of trees.

"Hmm, maybe I threw that a bit too far," he mumbled while we watched Angel tear through the leaf litter in search of her toy.

I shrugged. "If she loses it, she'll come back with a stick. Or another ball she previously lost."

He barked out a laugh. "I suppose this place is littered with lost toys."

"You've no idea." I'd lost count by this point.

I glanced behind us to be sure the house was nowhere in sight. "You don't have to keep following me. I don't need a babysitter, and Aya and Carrie won't see you break off to do your own thing as long as you don't double back to the house."

His brow furrowed. "You actually think I agreed to Aya's request just to make her happy?"

I opened my mouth, and then promptly shut it. That was a fair point. I may have helped him through some of his issues the other day, but that didn't mean he and Aya were magically best friends again. "I suppose I didn't think you actually wanted to follow me around."

"What lost hound wouldn't follow a beautiful woman home when she promises to play with him?"

Heat flooded my cheeks. "You're never going to let me live that down."

Tyr grinned. "Never."

I averted my gaze. I still didn't know what came over me in that moment. Yes, he was attractive. And yes, seeing a man like him open up and be a little vulnerable was sexy to me, but it was so wildly inappropriate, even if he didn't mind. I also couldn't forget he was still struggling with his late wife's loss.

I had to remember he was a client right now, and I had to maintain a professional relationship with him. *Life's a bitch...*

"In all seriousness," Tyr said. "I'd like to spend time with you to better know you. My request to speak with a friend wasn't intended to only be for that moment."

I glanced up at him to find him smiling. There was something about that smile that sent a flutter through my chest. "I would like that."

Careful, Astrid. You're walking a thin line.

Even though he said he wanted to get to know me, a comfortable silence fell over us. It felt right, though, like we knew each other so well already and could just enjoy each other's company without the need for anything more.

A raven landed in a tree on a thick bough. It croaked as it look down at us. I blinked slowly up at it, an unusual sensation of familiarity falling over me. The raven clicked and then flew off.

"A good omen," Tyr said.

I smiled up at him. I was glad someone else thought of ravens that way. So many saw them as only bad omens, which couldn't be further from the truth.

We came to a split in the path and I directed us left.

"Do you go on these walks often?" he asked.

I nodded. "I may be a gamer, but I enjoy being outside, too. Diego and I try to get out and hike at least twice a month, and I walk the property all the time, sometimes even going beyond it to the lake, or further if I feel the need. It's nice just getting lost in nature. You can either clear your head or gain inspiration."

"How does it inspire you?"

I smiled. "My dad is a carpenter, and he passed his passion on to me."

This piqued Tyr's interest. "A carpenter? Is it a hobby, or job for him?"

"Both." I nodded, mostly to myself as I thought about our family line. I'd never met any family from either of my parent's sides. Dad's family had all passed away or were estranged, and I knew nothing of my mother's side. "Carpentry has been a family business on my dad's side for generations."

We came to a wooden bridge that arched over a stream. I ran my hand along the planed timber. "My dad never intended to take over the business. He enjoyed working with wood as a hobby. It just so happens a few people wanted to buy some pieces off him, and then he continued. He said it was good for him after he left the service. Kept him busy."

"Military man?"

I nodded. "Though now, you wouldn't be able to tell. His CO would have a heart attack if he saw what he looked like now."

Tyr belted out a hearty laugh. "I can relate."

"Did you serve in your home country?" I asked.

He nodded. "It's mandatory for men to serve at least a year, but I chose to serve longer."

I tipped my head skyward. "That's right. Aya mentioned once about how your country did that."

"So, when did your dad introduce you to the craft?" Tyr asked.

I guess he doesn't want to stay on that subject. I wouldn't push. "My earliest memories of him are in the workshop. He was always so proud of the things he did, even if they didn't turn out right. And when he deemed me old enough, he turned those moments into something for us to share."

A smile curled up my face. Thinking about those memories always did that. I'd cherish them forever.

"I'd like to see some of your work," Tyr said.

I nodded. "Sure. I was thinking of going to the workshop after this walk. You won't see any masterpieces, but I have fun, so that's what matters to me."

He grinned. "I'll save judgment until I see for myself."

A fallen tree on the side of the path begged for me to climb it, so I did. Tyr's strong and warm hand grasped mine, and he helped me balance as I ran along the tree trunk and then jumped off. Not that I needed it, but I didn't mind.

The touch brought an unusual feeling of safety with it. Like a promise that if I were to ever fall, he'd always been there to catch me—as illogical as that feeling was.

He chuckled when I jumped on a rock. "You're like a little woodland fae."

I couldn't hold back the grin. "Maybe I am."

Tyr snickered. "Even at your height, you're too tall."

I winked. "Magic."

His intense gaze didn't falter. "You're magical, all right."

Heat bloomed in my chest. Why did words like this from him do this to me? I'd never had such reactions so quickly with another man. It usually took time getting to know them first.

"May I ask you something?"

I blinked up at him.

"You talk about your dad a lot, but the only time you've mentioned your mom, it was about a sentencing. Why is that?"

My gaze lowered, and I bit my bottom lip. It was inevitable this would come up. I could choose to not discuss it. I never did with anyone, not even Diego. But I knew I needed to stop avoiding the topic. "She… she's the reason we came here. And the reason… I was attacked by a dog."

Tyr's pace slowed. "What do you mean?"

I shoved my hands into my pockets and chewed my lip. How to explain was on the tip of my tongue, but the words lodged. "It… she…"

Dammit, Astrid, just say it. Admit reality so you can heal.

"She was abusive, to the point she was locked up for trying to kill me."

Tyr came to a halt. Horror contorted his face. "She… how could someone do that?"

I shrugged. "I don't know. To this day, I still don't know why she hated me so much. Dad told me she was the perfect mom for the first few years of my life. And then something happened. She started acting weird, and…"

The memories swarmed in my mind. Dark and terrifying. "She laughed—laughed the whole time she had our family dog attack me. Like my screams brought her some twisted joy…"

I sighed and squeezed my eyes shut, blocking out the memories. "So, yeah. We don't talk about her."

A warm, calloused hand wrapped around mine. I stared at Tyr's massive hand engulfing mine. His grip was tight, but didn't hurt. It felt protective. "I'm sorry you went through that. And I'm thankful you were willing to share it with me."

I forced a smile, though I did notice I felt a little lighter.

We continued on until the forest opened up with the house coming into view. I swerved us down the back, past the pool and woodpile to a large building tucked in at the edge of the clearing. I opened the door, the musky, sweet woodsy scent of wood shavings and lacquer greeting me, and let Tyr in, though I had to stop Angel from following. She whined and pawed at the closed door, but she wasn't allowed in here for safety reasons.

"This is the workshop," I said, stating the obvious for no other reason than to break the silence.

Tyr gazed around at the various tools and projects, both in process and finished. "There's a lot to admire. Anything I'm not allowed to touch?"

I shook my head. "Not that I'm aware of. Pretty sure all stained and lacquered projects are dried by now."

He nodded and wandered over to several tables. I watched him take in every little detail, more than the usual person did.

"Do you have experience with carpentry?" I asked.

"I've done a few home-fixer projects, but nothing like this." His hand traced a bone inlay adhered to a tabletop's edge. "Reminds me of the work by my late father-in-law."

I cocked my head. *Interesting.* "Profession or hobby for him?"

"Profession. It was a family trade. His son took over the business when he died."

I pursed my lips. *Even more interesting.* Made sense why Tyr was so interested in what my father did, at least. Though, something felt like it was more than that, and I didn't know why. *How strange her family and mine had the same profession.*

He turned to look at me. "Do you have any active projects?"

I gestured to two large, natural boards. "I don't have any personal projects started, but my dad and I are working a resin table project."

Tyr walked over to the pieces. "How much will you cut these down?"

I drew up next to him and felt the rough bark. "These came from an old log, so we'll probably have to refine them to be rid of any unstable parts. Hopefully not too much, as I like the shape these create as it is."

I walked over to a pile of oak planks. "I do have a personal project planned, though. I want to replace a lot of the older outdoor seating we have at the cabins."

His lips twisted. "I want to scold you for thinking about working, but I think this is skirting the line enough that I'll let it pass."

I grinned. I didn't care if others considered it work. I didn't, so that was all that mattered to me.

He looked over the pattern. "Why type of chair is this?"

"They're Adirondack chairs. We make them a lot, but usually sell them or auction them off. I've always meant to make them for use here."

Tyr lifted one of the planks. "I don't know what kind of chair that is, but would you like assistance?"

I smiled. That sounded nice, actually. "I'd be happy for some help holding these down while I trace the patterns."

Tyr grabbed the boards to line up while I pulled out the templates and a pencil. Each plank was enough for me to mark out a few pieces, and with Tyr's help the task was much easier—when he wasn't messing with my pencil.

I laughed and smacked his arm away when he nudged the top of my pencil again. "If this trace ends up wonky, it's going to your cabin."

He smirked. "Fine by me."

I rolled my eyes and shook my head, trying my best to fend him off while finishing these last few stencils.

"There," I announced. "Finished."

I'd traced out enough for four chairs to start me off with this project. That'd cover two cabins if I did two per building, which was ambitious for me to do alone, given we had twenty-four buildings.

Tyr peered over my shoulder. "Hmm."

"I believe that means this is Witcher approved."

"I don't know what that means."

I stared up at him, eyes wide. "What? You've never watched the show?"

Tyr shook his head.

"Played the games?"

"I don't know what you mean by a game."

How is that possible? "You've surely at least read one of the books?"

He shook his head again.

"This is a crime."

He chuckled and plucked my pencil from my hand. "A worse crime is this wiggly line here."

I gasped and looked down at the line he was reaching for. "It's not wiggly!"

Tyr traced my line. And not well.

"Now it's wiggly."

"Now it's perfect."

I rolled my eyes and tried to snag my pencil back. Unfortunately, he had good reflexes and kept it out of my reach. I even jumped for it while he dangled it above my head. "Tyr, give it back."

He snickered. "I don't think you've tried hard enough to reclaim this."

I pursed my lips. If he thought this would work, he was wrong. I had no issues playing dirty.

Tyr teasingly wiggled the pencil. *Yup, he's sealed his fate.*

My shoulders drooped, and I puckered my lower lip as I glanced up at him. Tyr froze. My inner evil-self did a little dance while I kept up the pleading puppy face. "Please, Tyr?"

"Oh, she got you good with that one, Tyr," Aya's voice rang out through the workshop.

I whirled around to find her leaning against the doorframe, holding onto Angel's collar so she wouldn't come in. "Hey, Aya."

She smirked. "Hey. I just came down to let you two know, Carrie is starting dinner."

I blinked and jerked my attention to one of the windows, where the orange light of the early evening filtered in. "Wow, I didn't realize we spent all day in here."

"I'm glad he could keep you occupied all day. You'll have about thirty more minutes before the casserole is done. She's got great news to share over dinner." Aya turned away. "Oh, and careful playing keep-away with her, Tyr. She's nimble enough to climb you like a tree."

My mouth gaped. *She did not just say that.* "Aya!"

Tyr roared with raucous laughter and Aya winked before slipping out.

When he calmed, he tipped the pencil in my direction, and I thought he might give it back finally. But instead, he tucked it behind his ear.

I huffed, and he chuckled. "You don't need it. You said you were done."

He might be right, but that didn't mean I had to like it. And I just didn't want to risk losing it. "Just don't walk off with it. It's my favorite right now."

"If I do, it just means we can do this again."

I rolled my eyes, heat rising in my cheeks. "You can work in here whenever you want."

"With you?"

The warmth on my face increased. "If you'd like."

He smiled, his eyes lingering on me a moment longer before turning to the project. "So, are we done for the night, or do you want to get more finished?"

I thought for a moment. "I'd love to toss some of these on the table saw to cut them into individual sizes. Then I can see if I'll be able to shape any on the bandsaw before dinner or not."

"Just tell me what to do and I'll do it."

I had him grab the safety glasses and cut-resistant gloves from the drawer while I pulled out the respirators and earmuffs. I also donned an apron.

Dragging over a few pieces to the saw, with Tyr offering to hold the extras, I adjusted the saw and then flipped the power switch. The saw whirled to life. Using a push stick for safety, I cut into each board, sawdust flying.

With Tyr's assistance, I flew through the trimming process faster than I expected, so I decided to cut at least one chair's pieces into shape. Taking my time with the band saw, I shaped the arms first, as they were the most complicated.

I managed to get through both arms and half the back slats before my phone pinged with a reminder text. I almost rolled my eyes. She could have done that the first time, but no, she had to come embarrass me. *Most likely, she was hoping to find us in a compromising position.* She was always making that attempt whenever I was alone with Diego.

I chose to call it quits there, so I'd have time to clean up. Tyr helped me stack all the pieces in a way I'd know which went to what chair assembly, and then we stored away all the safety gear.

"Okay, I'll take care of the sweeping," I said. "That's really all I have left to do."

"I can help you with that."

I shook my head. "No, I've got it."

The barest of a downward turn touched the corners of his lips. "Okay. I'll go freshen up before dinner."

He gazed at me for a moment and then reached out, plucking a splinter of wood from my hair. "You have a lot of sawdust in your hair, just so you know."

I chuckled. "I'll definitely keep that in mind. Thank you for helping me, by the way."

Tyr took the pencil he still had and tucked it behind my ear. "Thank you for including me. It was nice spending this kind of time with you."

The barest of touch of his hand caressed my cheek; something so gentle from such a large and imposing man, it sent my heart fluttering.

I opened my mouth to speak, but as my eyes met his snaring blue irises, my words died on my lips. Tyr dipped down, and his lips brushed mine, his beard tickling my skin. I sucked in a startled breath, his intoxicating aroma of spice and musk enveloping me, but didn't pull away. *I should. I know I should stop this.*

But as his firm lips pressed against mine, deepening the kiss, the only desire I had was to peel off his clothes and fall together in passionate bliss while exploring each other's bodies with greedy hands.

My hands slid up his chest, tremors of raw desire coursing through my entire being. My heart beat louder until it echoed in my ears, drowning out every thought beyond my growing need. Familiarity raced through me, as if I knew this touch—this feeling with him.

Dirty images of us together invaded my mind—of how easily he could bend me over the table, or of me slipping my fingers under his shirt, exploring the hard lines of his body and tracing his scars while I kissed him, lower and lower.

I clamped my thighs together, trying to quell these sensations.

Tyr pulled away, drawing my breath with him. "I'll see you at dinner, Valkyrie."

I said nothing, my mind hazed. My heart beat hard in my chest, and I placed my hand over it. His words—*that* word—wrapped around me like a comforting, protective blanket I didn't know I needed. *What is going on with me?*

I shook myself and grabbed a broom. I needed to get a hold of myself. That wasn't appropriate for me to allow. But even though the chastising thoughts floated through my mind, my heart beat louder. He was interested in me, and for some reason, my heart was already yearning for a man I didn't know, but also felt like I did.

Someone knocked on a door frame. I whirled around to find Diego leaning against it. Dirt coated him from head to toe.

"Finally got your attention," he said while smirking.

Heat prickled my cheeks. "Sorry. Lost in thought. Welcome back. Did you have fun?"

Diego nodded and showed himself in. "It was a good day. Andrew ate shit and then had to chase his bike down a hill after he failed miserably, trying to show off for his *novia*."

My head flew back with my laughter. That didn't surprise me one bit. Diego always had a good story about Andrew every time they went out. He was always doing something stupid on these excursions.

"Would have been better, though, had you gone."

I shook my head and held up a hand. "Oh no. You know I don't even have a fraction of the skill you all have to remotely keep up."

"Doesn't mean I wouldn't want you there." He wrapped his hand around the handle of my broom. "Why don't I help you? You can tell me what kind of trouble you got into."

I chuckled. "I behaved."

"Uh huh, sure."

I rolled my eyes and fetched a second broom while showing him what I'd gotten done.

TEN

DIEGO

Oil popped and then sizzled upon contact with the folded and filled dough I gently slid into the pan. My body swayed along with the soft music played from the Bluetooth speaker. I scooped out the turnovers when they were golden brown and deposited them on a waiting paper towel to soak up the excess oil before coating them in cinnamon sugar. While I got my next batch ready for frying, someone walked into the room. I spun around, hope blooming it was Astrid. I should have heard her returning home, but I could have missed the signs.

That hope plummeted at the sight of Tyr. He chuckled. "Am I that much of a disappointment?"

I shook my head. "I thought you might have been Astrid trying to sneak past me and Angel."

Angel huffed from her spot on the couch. She always got mopey when Astrid left her home. I understood her sentiments. Astrid had only been gone a few hours, but it felt like an eternity today.

He touched his chestnut hair. "Sorry, no red in these locks."

I laughed and went back to cooking.

"Where is everyone?" He grabbed a glass from a cupboard and filled it with water before helping himself to the fridge.

"Raeni is out with friends, Carrie is doing laundry, I think."

"I sure am," she called out.

My lip twitched in amusement. "And the power twins went out shopping."

Tyr's brow lifted. "Power twins?"

I scooped the recently fried turnovers out of the pan. "You'll learn those two are an unstoppable and dangerous duo. If they want it, they're getting it, one way or another."

He chuckled and shut the fridge door. "I believe it."

Angel lifted her head suddenly, ear perked. A moment later, she was rushing for the front door, barking.

"Ah, there they are." I could see Astrid's Jeep rolling up the front drive through the window.

Tyr sipped his glass of water before making himself a sandwich and sitting down at the island.

Not long after, the front door flew open and Aya breezed in, her arms full of shopping bags. "We have returned with spoils of war."

I snorted, and Tyr laughed. "What war did you two fight in this time?"

Aya's expression grew serious. "The foretold battle… of Christmas in July craft sale."

A beat of silence and then laughter filled the house. It only increased when Astrid's voice carried into the house. "Angel, stop. Angel, move out of the way. Aya! They sent reinforcements."

Astrid staggered into the house, Angel trying to trip her up. Her sundress fluttered around and clung to her curves in all the right ways at a teasingly high length at her thighs. Her red hair, pulled back in a partially braided ponytail, draped over her shoulder on one side, offering the perfect profile view of her stunning face. "I swear, she acts like it's a crime for me to leave the house."

"Well, clearly you abandoned her," I teased.

Astrid rolled her eyes, making me laugh. "Carrie, are you inside?"

The woman in question poked her head around the corner. "I'm right here."

"We chauffeured Raeni home, and she brought two friends. They wanted to go swimming."

"Thanks for letting me know. I'll keep an eye on them." She flicked her gaze to me and then to Tyr. "You two best keep your shirts on, unless you want a gaggle of giggling girls following you around."

I shook my head. "Astrid, I don't remember you being this bad."

She set some bags on the island. "That's because I wasn't. I was too busy drooling over muscled action stars and boy-band members."

Tyr paused mid-bite of his lunch. "That is a strange array."

Astrid shrugged. "What can I say? I've got an eclectic taste in men and music."

That was the understatement of the century. "Aya, were you this bad?"

Tyr snorted. "She was worse."

Aya gestured to him, an unapologetic look on her face.

Carrie laughed. "At least I wasn't the only one."

She wandered off after that. I reached blindly behind me and grabbed a sneaky little redhead trying to snag her treat before I gave permission. "I don't think so."

"Aw…" She pouted, those temptingly kissable lips drawing my gaze. "But those look like the surprise you promised. And you know I love your empanadas."

That was definitely why I picked this treat over mozzarella sticks. She could live off the two of them for the rest of her life.

I held Astrid close against my side, enjoying the feel of her body molding against mine. "So you did get my texts?"

She tsked. "Of course I did. I was just being entertained by the battle of the century." She put on her best announcer voice. "Aya versus Knitting Nancy in aisle five, battle of the fifty-percent-off wool yarn skeins."

My eyebrow spiked as I glanced at Aya. "And who won?"

Our friend plopped down at the island with a dejected sigh. "Knitting Nancy used her knitting-needle finisher on me."

My head tipped back as I barked out a laugh. Tyr watched with a bemused expression.

"This Nancy individual sounds like quite the opponent," he said.

Astrid snickered. "She's the undefeated champion of the annual Christmas in July craft sale. We had high hopes for Aya this year, with all the training she put in."

"I was so close, too," Aya grumped. "If I didn't care about this tapestry so much, I'd use cheaper materials. Now I'm going to have to hope my online shipment arrives in time."

For the cultural festival, Aya was going all out. She knew traditional sewing and weaving techniques that she'd been sharing with Astrid and me over the years. This allowed her to accumulate a range of crafted items to use for the event, but she apparently still wanted more.

"Well, if it doesn't, can we somehow use it to show as a work in progress?" Astrid asked. "I don't expect us to be able to move that loom, but maybe use pictures?"

"Oh, we're using that loom as a prop," Aya said. "I don't care what kind of muscle I have to wrangle up to help, but we're using it."

"Your family loom?" Tyr inquired.

Aya nodded. "The very same."

"I'll move it," he said. "I'm intimately familiar with that thing, with how many times you've made me and your brother move it for you."

She clapped, a beaming smile accompanying it. "You're the best!"

I grabbed a cooled empanada and offered it to Astrid. "Now you can have one of these."

Astrid eagerly took the treat.

"Just be careful. It might be a bit messy to eat." I'd never made this recipe before, so I wasn't sure how it'd go. Theoretically, the time I let it cool would make it less messy.

Astrid turned the treat in her hands. "What's in it? This has a sugar coating, so it's not your chicken empanadas."

I smirked. "Abuela's *cajeta* recipe."

Astrid's eyes lit up. "Caramel? You made caramel?"

She bit into the snack without waiting for me to respond. The most adorable, delighted squeal came from her as she danced around.

Tyr laughed. "I believe that's a stamp of approval."

I smiled. It didn't taste like Abuela's, even though I followed the recipe. It had disappointed me since I wanted Astrid to have a taste of what I always bragged about after returning from a trip to see the family. But if Astrid loved it regardless, then I'd happily accept that.

"Did you find this in that cookbook?" Astrid asked, her mouth still full.

I shook my head. "No, I spoke to her today. Of course, she had trouble figuring out how to send it to me, and she wrangled in *Tía* Camilla."

Astrid made a face. "Did she behave this time?"

My lips twisted. "Unfortunately, no."

My eldest tía wouldn't let it go that Papá and I never returned to Spain after Mamá died. Even now, she hounded me about when I would finally return to be with *la familia*. She just didn't get it.

Mamá knew the doctors wouldn't be able to fix her. Even though she tried to be brave when I was a kid, I now understood why she wanted to come back here. This was where she grew up. She'd worked at this very retreat when Pete and Randi ran it, and they'd repaid that in full by allowing us to stay while Mamá went through her treatments. They let us stay even after we lost her.

We buried Mamá in the cemetery in town, with some of her ashes spread at the base of her favorite tree deep in the forest of this property. Papá wouldn't leave with her here. This place was the last thing we had of her. We made a new life and formed a family here. Pete, Randi, Darius, Astrid, and now even Aya and Zeke, when he came around for visits. Everything I loved now was here.

My tía could try to tell me I needed to come back home to be with the familia, but I couldn't abandon this family to do so.

My eyes flicked to Astrid, where she munched away on her treat and sifted through her bags. I especially wouldn't give her up for anything. Gandalf himself could show up and call her the chosen one, and I'd go to the depths of Mordor as her personal Samwise.

I grabbed the waiting plate of empanadas and set it in front of Aya. She grumbled out an "about time" and snatched one to eat. Astrid greedily tried to steal the whole plate, but we fended her off until she decided to find something to supplement.

Astrid pulled out a jar of pickles from the fridge. Just the pickles.

She ate them on their own like they were the perfect snack, and to this day I still found it weird.

She twisted the cap, only for it to not budge. Her brow creased and she twisted harder. I laughed when frustrated sounds came from her pretty mouth.

"Do you need help?"

She grunted. "Tch, no. Do I look like I want to be an embarrassment to my ancestors? I'll just smash this stupid jar if I have to."

Tyr and Aya laughed. I shook my head and reached for the pickle jar. Astrid ducked away, insisting she had it. I grinned and lunched for her, wrapping one arm around her waist, and snagging the jar with the other.

"Diego," she whined.

"Let me help." With ease, I popped the stubborn lid off and offered her the jar.

She grumbled out, "I loosened it for you," and pulled out a pickle spear.

I chuckled. "What did you manage to buy, Cielo?"

She shrugged, her fake sour mood vanishing. "While Aya was battling it out with Nancy, I swiftly snagged up various other items on her list, and got some more picture frames."

My brow lifted. "I thought we had some in storage."

"Just big ones. I needed small ones." She pulled out a thick envelope stuffed with photographs. "Dad sent me a batch of photos he wanted printed. He didn't specify which, so I did them all. I thought I'd hang a few of the best ones up, and leave the rest for him to choose for his albums."

I helped her clear up the counter of all the shopping bags so she could spread the photos around. The subjects ranged from a small town to people to the woods. Some even should have been vetted out, with how blurry they were, or had a finger in the way of the camera lens. But Astrid and her dad were weird when it came to those. They liked to keep the bad photos and put them in an album or scrapbook. Darius always said the imperfect photos told their own story, and made the perfect ones even more special.

Tyr reached across the island to look at one of the photos. "Where were these taken?"

"A small town called Bifrost in Manitoba. My dad's friends, Hurrit and Arran, run a hunting and fishing charter camp up there. Dad likes to get up there every few years if he can."

Astrid sifted through the stack and pulled out a photo with two men. The taller of the two had a lean, muscular build, medium brown skin, and long, braided black hair. The other man was of a larger build, with lighter tan skin, and short, dark brown hair. "Here we are. Hurrit and Arran. I've met them a few times. They're both awesome."

She smiled. "Hurrit actually contributed to me choosing to overcome my fear of dogs."

"How so?" Tyr asked.

"He told me once that it wasn't the wolves you could see that you should fear, but the ones you couldn't." Astrid gazed at the photo in her hand. "I know he was probably referring to people, but that got me thinking about my fear."

She was quiet for a moment, and we all watched her. Something in my neck prickled, like a warning.

Then Astrid said the strangest thing.

But be wary of the snarling wolf
Cloaked in shadow he'll prowl close
Snapping teeth and drawing blood, he'll follow the fallen Valkyrie
to her other life

She didn't blink—she hardly moved. Astrid just stared at the photograph. It was almost as if she didn't even realize she'd just said something odd. Then she sifted through the pile of photos as if nothing strange happened.

My lips pressed together, and my brow furrowed. A quick glance at the others told me they, too, were confused or concerned about her sudden weird behavior.

I wanted to say something, but I wasn't sure what, or how. It was just so strange.

I spotted a photo of Darius, a tall, broad-shouldered man with heavily tattooed tan skin, green eyes, slicked back salt-and-pepper hair, and well-groomed beard, and Papá, a slightly shorter late-forties version of me, distracting me. It was a closely cropped selfie-style image of them by a river, with Papá holding up a decently sized fish he'd caught.

Aya let out a dreamy sigh. "They really know how to create the perfect romantic getaway for two outdoorsy men."

I rolled my eyes, and Astrid groaned. "When are you going to give that up?"

She shook her head. "I don't have to. I'm right most of the time."

"Most, not all," I said.

"Yeah, it's more of a bromance than anything," Astrid added. "And that's all it'll be."

Aya shook her head again. "Well, you two had a fit when I flirted with them, so this is the next best thing."

I winced, and Astrid made a gagging sound. She'd tried twice with Darius and once with Papá since we'd met her. It'd been uncomfortable each time.

"I swear, one of these days we're going to find where you store all your shipfics," I said.

Tyr's eyebrow lifted. "Shipfic?"

"Fictional writing for her shipping habits," Astrid explained.

He shook his head. "You'd be looking forever for nothing, then. That'd be all done as commissioned art."

Aya unapologetically pointed his way in confirmation. Astrid laughed, and I groaned. "I don't want any of those awful visuals in my head."

"Any juicy thoughts are all your own, and you should share them with the class." Aya winked. "Especially any that include our favorite redhead."

I choked on a laugh. She would be so brazen to say that in this setting. Astrid's face turned as red as her hair and she growled Aya's name in warning.

In her irritation, she hit a small stack of photos, and one fluttered off the counter onto the floor. I scooped to retrieve it, finding myself looking at a pale, smiling woman with wavy copper hair. *I wonder who this is.*

I jumped when a cacophony of sounds assaulted my ears. Phones went off like crazy, sending Angel into a fit. Tossing the photograph onto the island, I rushed over to my phone. My screen glowed with a warning message:

Emergency Alert
SAR ALERT – Endangered Missing Child

My attention snapped up when Astrid answered a phone call. She spoke urgently with Officer Rory on the other end. My pulse spiked as she confirmed information and then hung up.

"Ten-year-old boy," she said, already getting into motion. "His family was camping up on the mountain where he went missing, about three hours ago. The rangers requested our immediate help."

I angled for the door. "I'll get the vehicles ready."

Aya volunteered to collect the gear, and Astrid needed to change and gear up Angel.

Tyr rose from his seat. "What can I do?"

"Have you done search and rescue before?" I asked.

He nodded. "A few times."

That was good. More trained eyes to help, the better. "Come with me to get the vehicles ready. We may not use them, depending on where the hikers went into the mountain, but we like to make sure we have them, just in case."

Carrie came around the corner. "I'll clean up the kitchen. Go find that child."

ELEVEN

DIEGO

I wandered through the dark house, sleep far from my mind. The search earlier was still too fresh of a memory. We'd found the boy, not unscathed from a nasty fall he'd taken into a ravine, but alive.

Angel's impeccable find record remained near perfect. To this day, I still didn't understand how she was this good at finding people. But it was thanks to that record we'd been called in so early compared to other SAR teams.

I paused at the base of the stairs in the foyer when I noticed a light on the back deck. Had we left a light on? Then Angel appeared in one of the windows. I cocked my head. *The hell?*

Walking through the house, Angel greeted me when I opened the door. "What are you doing out here, *chica*?"

"Diego?" a quiet voice said.

I snapped my attention to my right, finding Astrid curled up on the swing she and her dad built together. I then glanced down at myself and winced. "Sorry, I didn't expect anyone to be up."

She chuckled. "Like you didn't walk around half naked in your boxer briefs in college."

I grunted. She had a good point. I'd gotten rather comfortable living in that apartment.

"Besides…" She stuck her leg out. "I'd be a damned hypocrite if I got on your case this time."

My gaze flicked to her bare leg and slowly traveled up to her shapely hips, barely covered by eight-bit heart panties. My eyes continued up along the milky, freckled skin of her bare stomach to the tantalizing cropped shirt with retro controller buttons printed over her barely covered breasts.

I sucked in a quiet, hard breath, and tore my attention away, using Angel as a convenient excuse. The last thing I needed was an awkward boner in my underwear. "I didn't realize you still wore that."

Aya had given the outfit to Astrid as a Christmas gift our first year sharing the apartment, and after a lost bet that same night, Astrid had to wear it as her lounging outfit until we graduated. It'd been painful to resist the thoughts of coming up behind her and gliding my hands along her bare skin until I lifted the front up and—

My cock twitched, and I gave myself a mental slap. *Not the time.*

Astrid chuckled, as if it was clear what this tempting outfit did to me, and she got great amusement from my struggle. "I got so used to wearing it, it's become part of my normal comforts."

I chuckled. "And here I thought you were going to say you were lying in wait to use it to seduce someone."

She snorted. "And who would I seduce? It's just you and Aya here at the house."

Not being considered an option to seduce was one way to cool my libido.

I finished scratching Angel behind the ear and approached. "If not to lay a seductive trap, why are you out here?"

She repositioned so I could sit down next to her. "Couldn't sleep, so I thought sitting out here might help. What about you?"

"Also couldn't sleep. I keep thinking about the rescue today."

She nodded slowly and gazed out into the darkness beyond the house. "That's been on my mind, too. That boy… is really lucky."

I made a thoughtful sound. "Yeah. I'm glad they didn't wait to call us in. I don't want to think about what could have happened if we hadn't been."

She made a sound of agreement, and my brow lifted. She still gazed out. "That's not what you were thinking about?"

Astrid worked her jaw, as if she were hesitant to tell me what was on her mind. I did my best not to react outwardly, though inwardly I couldn't stop the concern mixed with disappointment she was still hiding something from me. I didn't know what I had to do for her to trust me. We were friends. The closest of friends. There was hardly anything we didn't share with each other. I didn't understand why she didn't think she could confide in me about everything.

"I had thought about that, don't get me wrong," she finally said. "It's just not what I've been mulling over."

Astrid pulled her legs up to her chest. "The way his parents fussed over him after they were reunited… he's lucky to have two parents who love him."

I turned toward her, my senses sharpening. *What does she mean by that?*

Astrid chewed her lower lip. "My mom… tried to kill me."

Everything fell from under me. *She what?*

Neither Astrid nor Darius ever spoke of her mother. It was obvious the subject of her was a sensitive one by the way they reacted whenever someone asked questions, no matter how innocent their intent was. *But that…*

Never in a million years would I have guessed those words would ever come from Astrid's mouth.

She turned her gaze to me—something so painfully sad, my chest ached. "I've wanted to tell you about it before, it's just always been too difficult to admit out loud. Knowing one of your parents never loved you… it's not easy to come to terms with. Knowing they found enjoyment in your pain and wanted to see you dead, it…"

She sighed, her shoulders drooping. "It takes so much time to heal from something like that. Especially when you try not to let other happy relationships get to you."

My stomach knotted. She was referring to the affectionate way Papá and I spoke about Mamá.

Her gaze fell away, and I didn't like that. I reached out and pulled her into me, tangling my fingers in her hair and holding her against my chest.

Astrid sucked in an unsteady breath and snuggled into me. "I never wanted you to see that jealousy I felt. I never wanted you to know the anger I had at the universe for taking her away from you, when she loved you so much—in the way I had always craved for a mom to love me."

Her fingers curled against my bare chest. "I wanted so much to be content with having a dad who loved me like I was the best thing in Midgard, and that it didn't bother me she was never there for all the big milestones I had. I wanted to forget the awful things she said and did and pretend my life was the best without her. But I could never forget the feelings she left behind. The ones that made me feel like I'd never be good enough."

Her voice cracked. "Because, if she couldn't love me, then why would anyone else?"

My grip tightened, emotions of rage, anguish, regret, love, and so much more swirling chaotically inside me. "You *are* the most amazing thing in this world. You *are* worthy of so much love, Cielo. Don't you ever think otherwise."

We remained like this, in silence, for several long moments before she pulled away. My fingers remained tangled in her gorgeous hair, and I stared into her eyes—bloodshot from previous tears shed before I arrived and didn't notice until now.

She always cried alone when she thought no one was around to hear her. Astrid never wanted to be a burden to anyone, and now I understood why.

The pad of my thumb ran along her jaw. Her eyes widened a bit. They flicked to my mouth for the briefest of moments, but just long enough for me to feel that magnetic pull between us. This was the worst possible time. I could pick any other—I should choose another.

My thumb brushed her bottom lip, making just enough contact to pull it in the most tempting of ways. I leaned in.

"I have my own confession to make," I said before my lips brushed hers.

The contact was feather-light and tentative at first—just enough to tease and tempt with my intent, as well as allow her to push away before I continued. Astrid's breath hitched.

My fingers curled around her neck, tangling in her hair and pulling hard against me until my mouth claimed hers in a desperate hunger sizzling under my skin and down my spine. She moaned quietly, the sound stoking the heat of desire building in me, and her body melded against mine, falling into the connection threading us together.

Years of denial and yearning broke through the barrier that'd kept us apart all this time, fuzzing my mind as I took in her taste and smell, searing its delicious existence into my mind where it'd never be forgotten.

I was the first to break the kiss, my breath heavy. Astrid's eyes fluttered open, her lips still parted with a hitch to her breathing, and cheeks pink. "I don't want this to come off as me capitalizing on your vulnerability and willingness to open up to me. That wasn't my intent. I just couldn't keep this to myself anymore."

Her mouth moved, but nothing came out.

My lips twitched with amusement. "I won't pressure you to decide now. I want you to think on it first. Whatever decision you make, I'll respect it."

Astrid's mouth closed, and she wordlessly nodded.

I stood, as difficult as it was to release her and give her space, I wasn't going to push this. I'd done this all in a way that I'd rather not have. There were so many better ways I could have made my intentions and desires known. But what was done was done. And if she was willing to give me a chance after some time with her own thoughts, then I would work my ass off to make sure she understood just how amazing she was to me, and how much she deserved to be loved.

And with whatever god out there listening as my witness, I'll love her until my last breath.

TWELVE

ASTRID

My fingers drummed on the table, echoing through the quiet house. Everyone was off doing their own things or working, giving me the quiet needed to get some early study time in for my online anatomy class starting up next week. Unfortunately, my brain couldn't focus on such an important task.

No, instead, it wanted to replay the past few days, with all my interactions with Tyr and Diego. Especially when they'd each kissed me.

Heat inflamed my cheeks and pooled between my legs. I groaned and hid my face in folded arms. *Stop! Stop! Stop!* If I thought about that, I'd start fantasizing… again. And those two really liked to star in my dirtiest dreams.

What am I going to do? Logically, the answer should be clear. Tyr was a resident, and therefore off-limits. And I'd been crushing on Diego for years. I should be rejoicing he was interested. But no, I was foolishly conflicted instead.

How long had I not been seeing the signs? He was always so flirty. Was I mistakenly not seeing that as his attempts to get me to see things had changed? But how would I have known that, when he was always so forward with those he ended up dating? *How could I not have seen his flirtatious nature as just being one of his quirks?*

I ran my fingers through my hair. Did these questions matter? He'd made his intentions clear now, and he left the rest in my hands to choose.

But my heart was tempted by someone else now, and I didn't understand why. There was something fascinating about Tyr, but it wasn't like I knew him all that well—even if a part of me felt like I had known him for longer than a week and a half. And hell if I wasn't aware of how odd this last week and a half had been since he showed up.

From Carrie's sudden progress, to my dreams, it was like life was throwing me signals I didn't understand how to interpret. *Or I'm just trying to make sense of things that aren't even connected.*

I rested my forehead in the palm of my hand. *What I wouldn't give to ask Leif. He is always good at helping me sort out my thoughts.*

I blinked. *Who the hell is Leif?*

A chair slid across the floor. "You look like you're about to make a decision that will either cure world hunger or make Midgard explode."

I jerked my head up. Aya sat next to me, hands clasped neatly in front of her. "Oh, hey."

Her eyebrow spiked. "What's eating you?"

I sighed, and my shoulders drooped. "I don't know how to put it into words."

If I knew how to explain this problem, I would with her. I trusted Aya. She was as much a best friend as Diego, even though I hadn't known her as long as him. *No, she's more like the sister I never had.*

Aya poked fun and teased me relentlessly, but only because we were that close, and I did the same back to her. If I had a serious issue, she was there. And she'd helped me through my share of guy problems before.

"It's a guy issue again. Or, in this case, two guys."

Aya lifted her hands and rested her chin on them. "Go on."

I chewed my lip. "I found out recently two guys are interested in me, and I don't know what to do. I've never been in a position like this before. And while there's a logical, quick answer to who I should pick, that doesn't seem to be making this situation any easier."

Her expression didn't change, and she said nothing, giving me the floor to go at the pace I needed. I let out a slow breath and told her what happened between Tyr and me in the workshop, and then with Diego. I told her how subsequent interactions with them over the last few days had only intensified these confusing emotions, and I told her the thoughts I'd been mulling over just before she showed up.

"I don't know if it's a good idea to see where things go with Tyr, because I'm not clear on whether he's moved on from his wife, and I sure as hell don't want to feel like a replacement for her. And Diego… How did I miss all the signs? And why now? I've dated before, and not once did he ever say anything. Why did he have to pick now of all times, when I was starting to wrestle with these feelings around Tyr?"

Aya gazed at me sympathetically and waited a moment to speak, to make sure I was done brain dumping. "One, don't worry about Tyr and his past wife. We may have a strained relationship right now, but I know him. He'd never treat you like a replacement. Yes, a part of him will always love her, but that doesn't mean he can't have room in his heart for someone new. You know that."

She was right, I did know. I'd helped my share of people come to terms with the death of a partner, and learn it was okay to love again after.

"And two, I think you're missing an option here. You're worried about choosing, when right now, you don't have to."

My eyes widened. "What? Of course I have to choose!"

She tipped her head. "Why?"

"Why? Because no one in their right might would go up to two people they like and go, 'Hey, I can't choose between you two right now, so I want to date you both to help me decide.' No one with an ounce of dignity would agree to something that idiotic."

Aya laughed. "It's quite the take on what I said. I didn't expect that direction."

I blinked. "Then how else did you mean it?"

"You tell them you want to date them both without having to make a choice in the end, of course."

I stared at my friend as she smiled as if she'd just hacked the internet's most-impossible-to-crack password in less than a second. When my brain finally finished processing her proposal, heat inflamed my cheeks. "Aya, are you crazy?"

She held up a hand. "Perhaps, but I am serious. Why choose when you can have it all?"

I hid my face in my hands and groaned. "I can't believe you even thought that was a viable option."

"It is for plenty of people."

"But *I* am not them. I can barely handle one guy, let alone two. Plus, I don't think I could handle them giving someone else attention, too, because let's face it, if I'm asking them to allow me to split my affection between them, I need to allow the same."

Aya smirked. "I really don't think they're going to be interested in looking elsewhere."

"Whether they do or not isn't the issue. I have to allow it as a possibility because it's only fair."

She rose and kissed me on the head. "You're still overcomplicating this. Don't think too hard. Feel. Trust your heart. And if your heart says both, then it's both."

She walked away. "And, if you'd rather step away from them both, then that's fine, too. There are plenty of abs and breasts to caress out there."

I gawked at her retreating form. *Did she really just swap fish in the sea out for caressing abs and breasts?*

I shook my head and shut my laptop. That talk hadn't helped me at all. Unfortunately, I think it made things worse, which wasn't like our typical conversations.

I chewed my lip as I headed up the stairs to put my computer away. The last part of her comment stuck with me. *Maybe the answer is neither.* I really didn't want that to be the case. I was tired of being alone. *But really, if I can't pick, am I deserving of either of them?*

My shoulders slumped. Tightness wound in my chest, constricting my heart. There was the truth of it all. I'd never felt worthy enough of Diego to ever fess up. I held my feelings close to my chest and urged him to find happiness elsewhere because I didn't deserve it. And Tyr, what I had learned so far about him, was enough of a glimpse to know it was the same. Someone else would be more worthy of him.

And with them both suddenly showing interest in me, at the same time, it was like the universe was slapping me across the face.

Of course, the defiant side of me wanted to agree with Aya and give the universe the middle finger. But that side of me was foolish and impulsive, and shouldn't be listened to.

When I walked into my room, Angel lifted her head from where she lounged in my bed.

"Huh, that's where you went." Normally she wanted to sleep wherever I was.

My dog repositioned herself, hamming it up. After laughing and setting my laptop down, I jumped on the bed and curled into her. I rubbed her belly. "I don't know what to do, girl. My head is so messed up."

Angel rolled into me and licked my cheek. I pulled her into my arms and buried my face in her coat, inhaling deeply. Calm flooded through my mind, and all chaotic thoughts dissipated until my mind emptied.

I inhaled again, my eyes growing heavy. A nap to forget all about this problem sounded wonderful right now.

My eyes snapped open when a hard breeze whipped my hair. With it came the stench of blood, bile, and vacated bowels. Weariness clung to me, so deep that I felt it not only in my bones, but in my soul. *What the hell? Where am I?*

"We need to get to the others."

I turned my attention to a tall man with long chestnut hair. *Tyr?* He looked different, mostly because of the clothes and hair, and the fact he had two hands, but it was most definitely him.

My head nodded, as if agreeing with him, even though I had no idea what was going on. I opened my mouth to speak, when a wolf snarling interrupted whatever I was about to say.

I whirled around and my heart lurched. A horse-sized wolf prowled toward us. *The hell? How the fuck is a wolf this large?*

Blood caked its black fur, plastering it to a frame that didn't seem all that healthy, and the beast walked with an awkward gait, as if injured. Its golden eyes pinned their full attention on me. My pulse raced. *It's him…*

But instead of shrieking and running away like I wanted to, my body reacted in a completely different way. A gasp came from my mouth. "Fen, are you all right? Do you need healing?"

Fen? As in Aya's brother-in-law? No, that couldn't be right. This was a monstrous wolf. But why did it feel like I was correct? *Fenrir?* And what did I mean by healing?

The wolf only responded by prowling closer, his lips pulling back into a chilling snarl. My brain screamed to run. This wolf was dangerous. That *I* was in danger. And yet, this odd dream-version of me didn't agree.

I stepped forward, hands reaching out. "Fen, what's wrong? Are you in pain? I can help."

"Astrid," Tyr warned.

I stopped and looked back at him, confused by his caution.

"Don't get any closer to him. He's not in control of his wolf." Tyr advanced, weapon at the ready. "Fen, you need to come out of that form. I need to talk to you, but not man to beast."

Things happened in a flash. Fen snarled and then lunged. Tyr readied to fight this wolf, when he pivoted unexpectedly. My heart raced at the sight of the approaching teeth. I flung my hands up, as if that would do something. Nothing happened. I backpedaled and screamed.

Teeth sunk into my neck. Agony exploded through my entire body. My lungs seized and the stench of fresh blood filled my senses. My eyes met his crazed, hungry golden ones, then he disappeared.

"Astrid!" Tyr shouted.

My vision blurred and my senses dulled. He was there, but I didn't know where.

"Hold on, Astrid. Hold on."

I couldn't breathe. My vision darkened. *"Freyja, please… take care of him for me. He'll need… you…"*

Cold seeped in along with the emptiness that surrounded me, and then I heard his voice one last time. "I vow to find you, Valkyrie. No matter how long it takes. I will not rest until I do."

My eyes snapped open. I lurched upright in my bed, gasping for air and scrabbling at my neck. My pulse pounded in my ears. *The fuck was that?*

THIRTEEN

TYR

Shink. Shink.

My sword blade slid smoothly against the whetstone. I lifted the blade and tested the sharpness before dripping more water on the stone and repeating the motions. I may not use my sword often these days, but I made it a point to keep it ready in case. Plus, it helped settle my mind.

The last few days had been difficult. I'd made my intentions known with Astrid sooner than I planned. I wanted to take time to get to know this new her. I wanted to be sure I wasn't comparing her two lives, and that I wasn't only in love with a woman who didn't exist anymore. She didn't deserve to be treated that way.

Especially after she told me the horrifying truth of her mother. How could someone be so cruel to someone they should love? Randi had been the true mother Astrid deserved. After everything she'd gone through, she deserved another mother like that. *And to know that bitch is the reason I almost lost her again...*

Shink.

I let the sound of metal grinding draw out the negative feelings raging inside me. Astrid didn't need me treating her like someone else. She may share the same name and similar appearance, but she was her own person. She had different likes, and likely had different dislikes. Sure, some might overlap, but she would never be a one-for-one, and I accepted that. *Though, I can't stop calling her Valkyrie like in the past. I don't know if I can call her anything else…*

Spending that day with her, it felt so right. I got to see the unguarded side of her, and I had no complaints. She was an amazing woman in this life. One I wanted to be with more and more.

I couldn't lie to myself, however. I struggled against the hope that she'd remember who I was and what we had. Though, I didn't know what remembering would do to her. I couldn't be sure it wouldn't harm her in some way. And I didn't want that. Even if it meant her never knowing.

My mind wandered to that moment in the workshop. When the chance came, I couldn't stop myself from kissing her. I knew I shouldn't—that it was too soon. But that need to taste her for even a moment was so damned strong.

I sucked in a deep breath, and my cock twitched. It was better than I'd imagined—better than I remembered. *And the fact that she didn't push me away…*

These last few days after, though, had been up and down. Sometimes she acted as normal before the workshop moment, like when we had open conversation before the search and rescue, and others it felt like she was avoiding me, if she wasn't tossing me odd, indecipherable looks.

It wasn't just me she was doing that with, either. I'd noticed the same behavior with her around Diego. Something happened, and I was at a loss what it was and how I could fix it.

I paused my task when hurried footsteps crunched on the dirt path leading to my cabin. They were heavy, but not as heavy as I'd expect from a male individual. *Female… emotional… Astrid.*

I jerked my head up, and my pulse elevated. She stormed my way, fiery hair flowing behind her, adding to the fierce expression on her face. It was similar to the one back then, but also different. Admittedly, this one may be slightly more of a turn on. My cock was already straining against my trousers.

Astrid came to a halt in front of me. Her face said she was furious, while her eyes gave way to confusion. "I want the truth."

My brow rose. "The truth?"

"Yes." Her hands clenched and unclenched. "Who are you, really?"

"I told you, my name is Tyr." I wasn't sure where this questioning would go, but something was off. Something had her distressed.

She sucked in a tight breath through her nose. "That's not what I mean!"

I set my sword down and turned to give her my full attention. This was the first time since arriving here that I'd seen her so distraught. I had heard the worst of the breakdown she'd had the second day I was here, but even that had been short-lived and hadn't happened again. If Astrid didn't lose her cool often, this meant that whatever was causing her distress was not to be taken lightly.

"Valkyrie." The name I loved calling her tingled my tongue as it rolled from it. "I'm afraid I don't understand what you mean. I'm not sure what has you upset, but I'll help you as I can."

She ran her hands roughly through her hair, tangling her fingers in the red tresses. Her eyes clamped shut, and it appeared as though something was harming her mind. "The dreams came back. That vicious dog I banished from my mind came back—all snapping teeth and menacing golden eyes. I haven't had them for years. Then other weird shit happens. And it all started when you got here!"

My fingers curled. Her distress pained me, but I knew I had to let her get this all out to understand fully—even though I was getting a good picture of what was going on.

"And then I have even more dreams that don't make sense, but do. A blonde-haired woman with wings who knows my name, and I swear I know her, too. Then just now, some chaotic battle. You were there, but you were different. I was there. A wolf with Aya's brother's name was there."

My pulse picked up. Aya and I suspected Astrid had dreamt about Kirby when she'd mentioned the dream. We'd talked about it later.

Aya admitted to her attempts to slowly get Astrid to tap into those previous memories, with no seeming success. She'd think there were moments, but then Astrid acted like nothing had happened later.

But now, between dreaming of Kirby, and what I believed was a past moment of our history from what Astrid was ranting about, Aya may have been more successful than she realized. Astrid had just convinced herself she'd made those moments up.

Her hand clutched her neck. "I felt it—his teeth on my throat. I saw the rage in his gleaming eyes."

All the muscles in my body locked and my lungs squeezed. *She saw her death?*

"Who are you really, and what the hell is going on?" Astrid demanded, her voice raising and quaking at the same time.

I stared at her for a good, long moment. Astrid was remembering, and in the most distressing way possible. I didn't know how to tell her the truth without making this worse. This wasn't how I wanted her to learn everything. But I had to tell her. I had to be honest.

"My name is Tyr. I did not lie about that." I reached for my sword, and when I grasped the hilt, I willed it to vanish.

Astrid gasped and took a startled step back. She stared with wide eyes. "That wasn't a fancy illusionist hand motion. What the hell did you just do?"

"I'm not just any Tyr. I am *the* Tyr heathens name their sons after— the one your father claims to pray to. The one you prayed to in order to save your family, hundreds of years ago."

Astrid audibly sucked in air. I continued, figuring there was no going back now.

"I know you from another time, when you were a völva who healed as much as you conjured offensive magic." I gestured to my arm, where I'd had a tattoo made of her. "Back when you were my wingless Valkyrie."

Astrid shook her head slowly, back and forth, taking a step back. "That's not… this can't be…"

I rose to my feet. Maybe it wasn't the smartest option, since I towered over her, but I had to make sure she understood I was serious about this, no matter how much some of her wanted to fight this.

"The wife I spoke about before… was you. We were in love and happy once, until you were taken from me. I failed to protect you, and you paid the price. I couldn't live with that loss. I couldn't live without you, so I had you brought back to life. But you couldn't come back to the same body."

My eyes flicked down to my missing hand before refocusing back on her. "I vowed to find you again, no matter how long it took. When I first arrived here, you said I was lost, and you were right. Until I laid eyes on you, I had been."

Astrid ran her hands through her hair. "I want to say you're lying. I want to call you out for making up a farfetched story. But why can't I? Why does what you're saying make more sense than anything I understand in my life right now?"

My feet stepped forward without my say-so. I reached for her, pulling her against me, and surprisingly, she didn't fight me. "Astrid… Valkyrie…"

I spoke those names with as much love and affection as I'd always done in the past. The words tumbled off my tongue with the same accent her past-self knew.

Astrid jerked her head up, those green, soul-stealing eyes wide. I read the fear in her from those eyes—the conflict that raged inside her, bubbling to the surface to the point even my battle senses began to pick up.

Her entire reality had been shattered, and now she was struggling to understand it all. I wasn't sure how to help her. I wasn't even sure if I'd handled this well in any sense of the word.

Astrid stepped back, and I let her, as much as I didn't want her to put distance between us. "I need… space. I need to process this…"

I nodded. "I won't stop you. I'm here to help you through this, should you want it. It wasn't my intention to cause you any more distress. I just… didn't know how else to tell you the truth you sought."

She nodded slowly and turned.

Watching her walk away wasn't easy. Each footstep she took sparked pain in my chest I didn't wish to feel. *Creation, please don't allow this to have been the biggest mistake of my life.*

FOURTEEN

ASTRID

A warm breeze blew around me, bringing with it the potent scent of the forest. My mind raced, unable to focus on a single thought.

Tyr was a god. No, he can't be.

I'm someone from his past. *That's not possible.*

He made a sword disappear like magic. *Like magic…*

My thoughts halted, and I slowly straightened. Magic. I had loved what I thought was magic ever since I was a kid. Dad did all kinds of magic tricks I still didn't know the secrets to. But those weren't real magic.

The necklace Aya gave me, the protection in the pendant. I felt it. *No, I didn't.* Yes, I did. It was why I began questioning if her and Dad's faith was real.

What Tyr did wasn't real magic. *Yes, it was.*

No matter what plagued my mind right now, I couldn't shake what I'd seen—what I felt. Real magic. Magic was real.

I looked down at my hands. I hadn't touched Ben when I threw him through that wall. Sometimes when I got overly emotional, the lights went weird in a room. And, thinking back to that darkest moment of my life, our dog should have killed me before Dad had the chance to come to my rescue.

Am I magic?

I continued to stare, waiting for… something. Anything. If it made sense of this whole situation, I didn't care how the answers manifested. I just wanted them.

A tingling sensation prickled my fingers, and then a warm and chaotic sensation filled my chest. *What is this?*

My temple pulsed, and I flinched. *Ow! The hell was that?*

The pulse happened again and then searing pain split through my skull. I grabbed my head and gritted my teeth.

My vision flickered and my surroundings changed. I was in a timber home. Then I was in the forest. Then I was in front of a lake. Back in the forest.

Back and forth my vision went, experiencing some other places for split moments of time—like I was there—but I was here.

People came and went. But some came more often. A woman with gorgeous red hair and a soft smile, but a dangerous air about her. A rugged man with a bushy beard who radiated warmth. A young man with braided hair shaved on either side of his head, who made me feel annoyed and happy at the same time.

Mom? Dad? Leif?

I shook my head. No, those weren't my parents. That wasn't my… *Brother?*

A hand touched my shoulder. I gasped and launched off the log I sat on, whirling around and backing up as I did. Aya stood there, her arm still outstretched. Worry lines creased her brow.

My vision slipped again, but this time, it was only her who changed. A blur, almost like an overlay, of Aya, but with a much different outfit, something from an older time period, and braided hair instead of dreadlocks.

My sight solidified to the woman I knew. Or the one I thought I knew until this very moment. *She and Tyr know each other. And they have for a long time.*

"How long have you known?" I demanded.

The worry in Aya's gaze didn't go away. "Astrid, you look like you're in pain still. Let me help."

I took a step back. "Tell me the truth."

She let out a long sigh, her shoulders drooping, and then she plunked down on the log. She patted the spot next to her. "I would like it if you sat with me while I did so."

I hesitated, struggling to want to trust the friend I thought I knew, and mistrusting the woman she might end up truly being. She waited patiently, watching but not asking, allowing me to decide my comfort level. I'd get the truth either way, but I had to decide how much I trusted her.

And as messed up as this whole situation was, I still trusted her the most right now.

Aya smiled when I tentatively perched on the log. "Thank you. I don't want this to be difficult for you. Hel, I wanted this to go far differently. Had I known it would happen like this…" She pinched her nose and sighed. "I would have intercepted before Tyr could make things worse."

"He always did have trouble with words," I said before I could stop the words from tumbling out. *Where had that come from?*

Aya chuckled. "Yes, especially with you."

She frowned and then sighed. "I'm sorry. I owe you an explanation. And I will explain everything. All I ask is you hear me out all the way through."

I swallowed, my pulse thrumming under my skin, and nodded. I asked these things of my patients all the time when doing group therapy. To hear a person out entirely before forming opinions and comments.

"As I know you are suspecting, I am the war goddess Freya. We knew each other a long time ago. We were close then. When you died, Tyr was distraught and forced me into a blood oath to bring you back."

She shook her head. "I would have made the attempt regardless, but given the situation, I understood his demands. The magic I used couldn't give you a body, so it reincarnated your soul. That's when the search began."

Aya's shoulders slumped. "We found you… but we were too late.

You were dead. You were only a child."

I swallowed, and my heart lurched.

"I performed the ritual again, hoping the next time we'd get you back." Her fingers dug into her skirt, her shoulders tensing. "I performed that ritual seven more times."

My blood ran cold. *Seven more?* That put me on my ninth reincarnated life.

"Tyr only knew of three. I couldn't bear to tell him about the other ones. I knew it'd break him. It nearly broke me. And that's why, the last time, I did something different. I added more magic into your revival so I could find the unique signature that is my magic. I vowed to find you sooner, and keep you safe from whatever was hunting you this time, no matter the cost."

Aya shook her head. "I almost failed again."

I swallowed, my pulse pounding in my ears. *She knew about me back when my mom tried to kill me?*

"You were so young when I found you, but older than any other time." She worked her jaw. "I don't know why that was. I don't know if my magic protected you longer this time, or if it was something else, but whatever it was, that luck ran out almost immediately. I was speaking with your dad, pretending to be a new neighbor to start integrating into your life, when we heard the scream."

My brow furrowed. "I don't remember someone else coming to my rescue."

She nodded. "I don't expect you to. There was so much going on, I doubt you processed much after that beast had his teeth in you."

Aya tipped her head up to gaze at the canopy. "That was when I knew I'd have to do more. You needed all the protection you could get. So, I found this place. It was quiet, and Pete was a good man. It was the perfect place to hide you. I used my magic to make sure you and your dad came here, where I could keep you safe personally. I made Pete think I'd been his wife for decades, as well as all the townsfolk, that way it wouldn't be strange for me to be near you."

I stared at her a good long moment before it clicked. "You... You were Randi?"

I then pulled a face. "Wait, don't tell me you acted as his actual wife."

She winked. "I'm a war goddess, but also a goddess of sex and fertility. Girl has her needs."

I shuddered and shook my head. Pete became my grandfather. I already struggled with witnessing her trying to flirt with Dad on two occasions, I didn't want the image of her getting it on with my grandpa in my head.

"Why did you pick the persona Randi?" That name had felt familiar when I was a kid and first met her. It had to have significance.

She smiled. "I didn't know how the revival magic would work for you and any ancestral memories you might have. I thought maybe, if you were meant to remember, that name might trigger something."

Randi... her—my mother back then. I ran my fingers through my hair, struggling to really process this. Were these memories mine? Or just one that belonged to a woman who was a lot like me?

I jumped to my feet and paced. Back and forth, back and forth. My mind went a mile a minute, trying to absorb and process.

"So, what, this was just some elaborate plan to fill an oath?"

"No." Aya shot to her feet and grabbed my hands. "No, Astrid. My oath was fulfilled the first time. We found you. You may not have been alive, but the reunification clause of the oath didn't require you to be living. I did this because we were friends."

She slid her soft hand along my cheek, cupping it. "Because you're my family—my sister. And I didn't care if you remembered me or not. I'd cherish what we had and embrace the new you, forging a new bond that was just as strong, if not stronger."

My eye twitched when pain sparked through me again.

"We're friends, right, Freyja?"

"No." She pulled me closer. "We're family. And we always will be."

I pressed my palm to my forehead. "I'm so confused. What you say makes so much sense, but it doesn't at the same time."

She held me by the shoulders. "I understand. I don't expect you to be able to take this all in at once. Just know, everything I've said is true."

"Why now?"

Aya frowned. "I'm... not sure. I tested the waters with you every now and then, including going as far as to pretend I was a heathen in hopes my talks about us gods and magic would trigger something. I assumed I hadn't after a while. Now, I'm wondering those memories were being triggered in some way, and we just missed the signs. Especially since it's not uncommon for mortals to rationalize something strange related to magic into something they better grasp, or forget completely."

She chewed her lip. "Like earlier in the week, you remembered the prophecy your past mother spoke before she died, but it was clear you weren't aware of what you were saying, nor did you seem to remember saying it after the rescue was over, so Tyr and I weren't sure what to make of the situation. I should have seen that as a sign something had changed."

I squinted. *I'd recited a prophecy?* My mind flashed, and the day at the island counter, before the search and rescue, I'd been talking about Hurrit. I'd recited something without thinking about it.

Aya shook her head. "But, even so, I never would have guessed you to be hit so hard by the memories now. I've been trying to get Tyr here for some time, using my magic to lure him, since he never answers me any other way. But he claims he never felt the magic, even when he did finally show up, which is peculiar. He claimed it was a lead that brought him here."

She shook her head. "It's like Creation didn't think any of us were ready until now, but for what reason, I'm still not sure."

I sucked in a deep breath and plopped down on the log again. "How do I deal with this? How am I supposed to process these memories that aren't mine, but are?"

Aya sat next to me and held my hand. "I don't think I can give you those answers. I can talk to Kirby to see if she can help. She'd gone through something like it when her memories came back. Otherwise, all I can say is that you have to decide if these memories are yours or not."

My eyes popped. I knew that name. "Kirby? Why—"

Pain pulsed in my head again, and images flashed—various kinds, of a woman with blonde hair and black wings. All moments where I, or this past version of me, interacted with her. Some happy, some sad.

I gasped, my vision returning to normal. "I know her. I dreamed of her…"

I cocked my head. "She was in one of the photos on your phone from your brother's party." Which now I wasn't so sure was actually a grand re-opening party like she'd claimed. "You intentionally stopped on that photo on your phone in hopes it would trigger a memory, didn't you?"

"Yes, that was my hope." Aya smiled. "Kirby will be happy to know you're alive and remember her now."

I squinted, memories solidifying in my mind. "She died… Odin… killed her?"

Aya nodded. "Yes, he cursed her to live and die until she remembered what it meant to be a Valkyrie. At some point during this current life, she finally broke it."

I pursed my lips. "To know what it meant to be a Valkyrie… wouldn't a Valkyrie know that best?"

She chuckled. "We all said that back then, too. Odin's ego knew no bounds."

I scowled. "I hate him."

Her brow arched. "You, or your memories?"

A moment passed while I thought about it. These memories, while I didn't presently experience them, were mine. These feelings, they were mine at one time. "Both."

Aya smirked. "Well, then you'll be happy to know we did kill him."

My chest pulsed. The feelings that came with it were warm and relieving, like my soul had been waiting for that news. "I died… before I knew that."

"Yes." Aya nodded. "I heard you pray to me shortly after, and rushed back to find out what was wrong."

I ran my fingers through my hair. "How did I die? Tyr… didn't exactly say, but… I had a dream that started all this."

She worked her jaw. "That's… a complicated situation. What I'm telling you is Tyr's account, because there were no other witnesses. At the end of your battle, where you and Tyr stayed behind to keep Odin's armies off us, the two of you came face-to-face with a wolf shifter. You both thought it was Fenrir. He'd acted strangely before the battle, and when he showed up, something seemed wrong, so you tried to reason with him. Instead of listening, he attacked and killed you."

I swallowed. Fenrir, the wolf-god of war. I knew that much about him, without needing my surfacing memories to tell me this. But my chest twisted. Something didn't feel right about the story. Brief flashes to my visions said he was a friend—family.

"At least, Tyr claims it was Fen." Aya shook her head. "Like we tried to hint during that coded conversation we had last week, I know it wasn't him. No matter how wild his wolf got, he never harmed you—ever. Hel, you figured out ways to calm him when no one else could, like you could with Tyr on the occasions his anger got the better of him. I know it was another wolf shifter who looked similar enough to Fen that, in the heat of the moment, both of you misidentified the shifter."

Her hands clutched her skirt. "The problem is, Fen doesn't even remember that day. He knows he killed Odin, but that's it. And we lost contact with him for so long after then. It wasn't until my brother found him and brought him back, did I even get the chance to try and talk to him about that day."

She shook her head. "That's why Tyr and I are at odds. I understand his feelings, but I don't agree with what he saw, and he won't listen to anyone when they suggest he might be wrong. This has gone on for so long that even Fen was starting to wonder if he might have."

This was all too strange. Deep in me, the past part of me, felt like it was screaming that Aya was right, just like before when I tried my intervention. It told me Fen would never do that, even at his most uncontrollable moment. But there was something else that stuck in my mind.

"You're convinced Fen is innocent, beyond him being like family to that past me. Does it have to do with how I died again after that first time?"

Aya gazed at me, as if surprised I was actually thinking about this. "Yes, that's exactly it. Each time you died, it was an animal attack. And not just any animal—it was always canine in nature."

I swallowed, my stomach knotting.

"Even if by some chance it was Fen who killed you the first time in a moment of lack of control over his wolf, he would have no reason to kill you a second time, or any more times after that. Plus, I know for a fact, after confirming with my brother, and from a conversation I had with Fen almost a year ago now, not only did Fen not know anything about the resurrection ritual, he was with my brother when we found you some of those times. So, it couldn't have been him. Which leads me to question: why did you keep dying?"

My brow furrowed. That was a great question. I was still too confused about how this world really worked, now that someone had ripped the blindfold off to really offer any plausible explanations.

"It's possible the magic I used cursed you," Aya said. "And made it so you were bound to die in a similar manner as before. Hel, even in this life, the dog your mother tried to kill you with looked more wolf than domestic dog. But you were a child all of those times. If the curse was to take effect, you should have been an adult."

I chewed my lip. "You think someone is targeting me?"

She nodded slowly. "Your dad doesn't believe in coincidences, and neither do I. It's the main reason I wanted you to remember your past. I thought, maybe if you remembered, we could figure this out. Because I know they're out there. No matter where I erect my magic barriers to keep you safe, I'm feeling this presence just outside my reach of understanding, lurking. It's why I gave you the warding necklace for whenever I had to leave your side. I refused to take any risks, fearing somehow this entity had figured out what we'd done and was just waiting for a moment you were left unprotected."

My hand tremored. *Someone wants me dead? But why?* What could I have possibly done to make them try so hard to track me down, just to kill me that many times? "Is that why you wanted to do the theme for the cultural festival?"

Aya nodded. "I thought this might be my last big chance to try. If I immersed you in that world you used to be part of, you might remember. But if you didn't, it would tell me you weren't meant to, and I would have stopped trying… and accepted I'd be protecting you from some unknown enemy for the rest of your mortal life."

Mortal... "I was immortal once... right?"

"Yes. At some point after you and Tyr married, you unlocked the ability to become immortal. But you aren't anymore."

I chewed my lip. So much still swirled in my mind, and it wasn't easy to process it all. "Am I... magic?"

Wow, Astrid, great full sentence there.

Aya chuckled. "You're pretty damned magical, yes."

I rolled my eyes, and she laughed.

"But seriously, I believe you do have magic in this life. You may not cast spells and heal like you had back then, but the way you interact with people and make them feel better, it's far faster and better than any therapist I've seen. I think, perhaps, because you didn't have the same exposure to magic like in the past, it's been leaking out differently."

I chewed my lip. A memory surfaced of me screaming, and a man with a weapon going flying. "I think... I think I did use magic like in the past."

Aya's brow rose, and she waited.

"Remember when I put Ben in the hospital?"

She grunted. "Sure do. The shit deserved that one."

I tried not to laugh. When she posed as Randi, she'd had some choice words about Ben and rewarded me with ice cream every night for a week, and several gaming and movie marathons. "I didn't touch him. Yet he flew through that wall, regardless."

Her eyes squinted. "That does make sense. The doctors claiming you had an adrenaline rush was a decent way to explain it, but it never quite sat right with me. And the first time you used magic in your first life, it was in a similar way, but to protect your father."

"And if I'm honest, I think I used it for the first time when I was attacked by our dog," I said. "I shouldn't have come out of that with just a scar on my face and arm."

She nodded slowly. "I can't deny that, either. I think that settles it, then. If you had training, you'd be capable of casting magic like before."

"Is that you offering?" The prospect sounded promising. Seeing this magic may solidify what the hell I was experiencing right now.

"Of course. I trained you alongside your mother back then; I'll do it now. And maybe the more you remember, the easier it will be for you to pick it up."

I liked the sound of that. *I like the idea of actually being someone special. Even if only a small number of people know.*

I frowned. Diego wouldn't be one of them. He was my best friend, and sure, I kept some things from him, but I'd never had to keep something so big a secret. It made my gust twist.

Aya cocked her head. "Something the matter?"

"Just thinking." *Actually…* "I have another question. It's about when I told you the dilemma with my feelings for both Diego and Tyr. You had the perfect opportunity to steer me toward Tyr, but you didn't. And over the years of knowing you as my *college* friend, you constantly teased me about my relationship with Diego, as if you were pushing me to pick him. Why? Why would you do that when you knew Tyr was looking for a second chance?"

She gave a nonchalant shrug. "Because I want you to be happy. That's my first priority. If you would be happy with Diego, then I want that for you. If you wanted Tyr more, then I'd push you two together with reckless abandon."

I let out a laughing snort. Sounded like her.

"My point is, both are great options for you. Which is also why I said you can have them both. We gods don't often settle down with one person. Tyr is one of the rare exceptions. Even you, after some time with your immortality, were on the path of taking another partner."

My brow furrowed. No memories came up to solidify or contradict her claim. "I was?"

She made a thoughtful noise. "Maybe it's best you don't remember that. At least, not right now."

The creases in my forehead deepened. *What is she not telling me?*

"Anyway"—she waved her hand—"you'd have more fun with both of them, so I still say pick them both."

I rolled my eyes. "With everything going on, dating is the last thing from my mind now."

Aya winked. "Never said dating. Sex is a great distraction. And mood booster."

I shook my head, rolling my eyes once again, making her laugh. "Either way, I think it's clear, even though I don't know how to feel about this situation with Tyr, Diego can't be a choice. I can't live with keeping secrets from Diego if I did get into a relationship with him. It wouldn't be healthy. Even as friends, it's not healthy."

Aya shrugged. "Then tell him. The magical community melted into the shadows because Midgard stopped being safe for us. But that doesn't mean select mortals can't know. Hel, plenty do. I trust Diego. He can know if it makes things easier on us all. And really, with the way the world is going, it's not like hiding is sustainable. We're going to have to find some way to live alongside each other in the open, like before."

I chewed my lip. *Maybe...*

Aya stood. "I'll leave you to think and sort things out. It's been a lot. Don't hesitate to come to me with questions. I'm here for you." She took my hand in hers. "You're my family, always remember that."

I stared at our hands and then squeezed when she went to pull away. "I do have something."

The thought had swum in the back of my head for a while, mixing with the memories of Fenrir. How I'd tease and laugh with him. How I'd helped him through some tough choices. Healing him and bickering like he was another brother to me.

"I... want to see Fen."

Her hand tensed.

I looked up at her to find surprise written all over her face. "Deep down, a part of me agrees with you. Fen, no matter how feral and out of control he might have gotten, would have never turned on me like that wolf in my dream—my memory. But... given the situation... I also can't say that Tyr is wrong, either. So, I want to see him. I want to look him in the eye and make my decision that way."

Aya's lower lip trembled, and for a moment, I thought she might cry. She smiled instead. "You have no idea how long I've wanted to hear someone tell me I wasn't crazy for not siding with Tyr."

She squeezed my hand. "You know Tyr is going to be pissed if he finds out."

I held up a finger. "When. Because we know it would only be a matter of when. And honestly, I don't give a shit. It's not his choice."

Aya grinned. "I love your sass, you know that?"

I haughtily tossed my hair over my shoulder, making her laugh. She then left, promising to take care of everything, leaving me to process the insanity that was my life now.

FIFTEEN

ASTRID

My fingernail tapped on my dark phone screen, competing with a mourning warbler imitating a squeaky wheel nearby in the brush. Okay, it wasn't actually making that noise, but it sure as hell sounded like it in my pent-up state, and it wasn't helping my nerves.

Aya was going to text me when she was about to come back with Fen. She'd given me a day and a half to process everything; it hadn't been easy. I had struggled with all the memories I'd received. No new ones had come about since, and I was grateful for that.

The memories I did have bled into ones I knew I'd personally experienced, making it difficult to remember what were mine and what were hers. And that brought me to the crux of my problems—how I was going to see all of this.

A part of me tried to reject the reality of everything I'd experienced and tried to rationalize what I'd seen. But another part told me that was running away, and I couldn't do that. I had to embrace what really was, and that included accepting these memories weren't from someone else, but mine, and mine alone.

It took me some time, but I had sided with that choice, and when I did, accepting this new reality of mine became so much easier. Of course, that hadn't helped my relationships.

I'd distanced myself from Diego in all the obvious ways. I knew it was hurting him, and me, too, if I was being honest with myself. Being this removed felt incredibly wrong, like I was cutting off a piece of me. Logically I knew I should stop acting like this, but I was dealing with too much to also figure out how to navigate around him. I still didn't know what I was going to do about his confession and all my harbored feelings.

And then there was Tyr. Whatever had been building before the truth came out had up and died—I didn't know how to deal with the emotions. I wasn't sure if they were present-mine, or past-mine. And for him, I couldn't be so sure he was desiring me now, or the woman I used to be. So, until I was ready to tackle that, I kept my distance from him, too. *But it's also uncomfortable being distant with him…*

My phone chimed and the screen lit up. My pulse jumped, only for it to skitter and plummet to my stomach.

> Diego
> *Where are you?*

I chewed my cheek, then typed.

> *Out on a walk with Aya. We'll be back later.*

This was the cover we'd worked up before she'd literally disappeared in front of me. That had been one hell of a heart attack. And the bitch had the audacity to send me an *"Oops, sorry"* text a moment later, explaining that she had the ability to teleport anywhere she wished, and it was something I'd relearn, too, once we figured out my magic.

It also explained why I was sitting in the middle of the woods, alone. It might be good for me to help get my thoughts in order, but it was also ideal to keep this meeting more secretive. This way, neither Diego nor Tyr would be aware what was going to happen, but I didn't have to go anywhere. Aya was quite concerned about that last part, and wanted me to stay within the protective magic she'd apparently erected around the property.

I hadn't realized to what lengths she'd gone, protecting me with her magic. Even when she faked her death as Randi, and followed me to college, she'd made sure that if I wasn't going to be in a building she could use her magic around, she'd be with me. And if she had to leave, she had me wear that warding necklace, which she admitted had a compulsion spell component to ensure I wore it. If I didn't know now how many times I'd died, I might have found her paranoia concerning. But I was touched, and also concerned she had to worry so much for my sake.

Leaves crunched. I jerked my head up from my phone to spot Tyr approaching. He had a relaxed posture, though I spotted hesitation in his steps.

"Hey," I greeted.

"Hey." He looked around. "Why are you alone in the woods?"

"Thinking, and waiting for Aya to get back."

His brow rose. "Did she walk off?"

"No, she went to another city real quick." He gazed at me, and I blinked. "What?"

"It's just…" He shook his head. "You said that so easily. I thought you might still be struggling, with how distant you've been."

I pursed my lips. "I've needed the space to think and process. That made it easy to accept when she disappeared right in front of me."

He chuckled. "Sounds like her. Do you mind if I join you?"

I glanced at my phone, which showed I still hadn't received a text. "Sure."

He sat next to me. "You expecting a call?"

"Aya said she'd text me when she was about to come back. I think she wants to make sure I don't scream when she shows up right in front of me out of nowhere."

Tyr chuckled. "Would you do that?"

"I'd probably punch her, too."

He belted out a hearty laugh.

My phone chimed and lit up with a received text.

> Aya
> *Kirby agreed to come.*

I chewed my lower lip and responded with a quick acknowledgement. I knew she was going to talk to Kirby. Aya thought it would be a good idea to have her as support for Fen, as the two had a good relationship in this life. And, in the event Tyr did find out about this meeting, which was appearing to be much more likely, and sooner than I wanted, she would do what was needed to keep the peace. At least, Aya thought she would.

However, she didn't give me any indication regarding how much Kirby wanted to be here. I didn't know if she was doing this out of a sense of duty, or because she wanted to see me, too.

I wasn't sure why this bothered me. My memories of her were still hazy. But I knew we were friends once, and Aya had been so insistent, I felt like she wanted to see if we could rebuild that bond. That, of course, was if we wanted to, once we found out if the two of us had compatible personalities in this life. I still wasn't sure how to feel about these gods' desires to bring back something from the past.

"Kirby?" Tyr said.

I jerked my head up, finding him looking at my phone screen. I turned off the screen. "It's rude to read someone else's texts."

He held up a placating hand. "Sorry, I didn't mean to offend. I just noticed her name. Is that what Aya is doing, grabbing Kirby?"

I contemplated telling him and decided it couldn't hurt. "Yeah. She thought it would be a good idea for us to meet."

"You remember her?"

I rocked my head back and forth. "Kinda. Very few memories. But that's not why she wants us to meet. Well, it is, but also, she's experienced with this memory thing, so she might be able to help me."

It wasn't a lie. Sure, I was dodging the main reason, but Aya had said Kirby had experience with how this memory-regaining bullshit worked.

"Would you be okay with me staying so I can see her as well?" Tyr asked. "I haven't seen her since she originally died. It'd be nice to catch up with her. And with the four of us in one place, it'd be almost like old times."

My gut clenched. *Why does him mentioning only four bother me?* I knew he'd exclude Fenrir, but something nagged at the back of my mind that I was missing someone else. And yet no one else had ever been mentioned around me so far.

Though there was more to his wording that didn't settle well with me, either. "Tyr, we need to talk about that."

His brow pinched together. "What's wrong?"

I took a deep breath. "I need you to understand—no matter what you might have hoped when finding me, I'm not the Astrid you knew. We may share a name, and some similarities, but I'm a wholly independent person, with different likes and dislikes."

Tyr frowned. "I'm aware of that. I'm sorry if anything I've said made you feel otherwise. That's not my intention."

I rubbed my temples. "All of this is a lot to take in. And I know you specifically sought me out because of a past we shared. But I also know how dangerous that can be, based on expectations. There is nothing that will guarantee I'll see you the way I did back then."

Even as the words left my mouth, a big part of me didn't agree. Even before I'd been told the truth, I'd found myself drawn to him. But I also didn't know whether that was because of the past and the magic that affected me, or whether those feelings were really mine.

"Astrid, if you want me to leave, I will. I won't cause you any pain or trouble. That will never be my intention." I caught the pain in his words.

"I… don't know what I want right now." I chewed my lower lip. "Telling you to get lost doesn't sound right, but I don't know how to feel about you being here with expectations about me."

Tyr reached out and lifted my chin. It was a strange feeling, expecting a hand and feeling the hard bone of what remained of his wrist. "Valkyrie, I have no expectations, only desires. The moment I met you, I knew I had to let go of everything I'd wanted to embrace who you are now. I willingly have done this. If you want to be my friend, I will accept this. If you want to be my lover again, I will gladly accept as well. But I will never lay out the pressure of expectation for either."

Gazing into his intense blue eyes, a lump formed in my throat, and heat sizzled my veins. I believed him. "You call me, Valkyrie, why? What is the true reason, not the one you gave me last time?"

He smiled. "Because that is what you are to me. I did not lie. You hold the power to soothe or enhance the rage of battle in my soul, then and now. You were never a true Valkyrie, but others saw what you could do."

"The wingless Valkyrie…" I murmured, something pinging in the back of my mind.

"You remember?"

"Just that. Everything else is a blank."

The corner of his lip tipped down, but he otherwise didn't voice any disappointment I suspected he had. I still had no memories of us. I believed what he and Aya told me about my past together with him. But I still had nothing to compare it against yet. And that was what made me so confused about what I felt with him.

It was too fast for it to be my normal pace. But clearly, no memories influenced me. So why did I feel a draw to a man I didn't quite know, but felt like I knew everything about?

My eyes flicked down to my phone, and my pulse skipped. The screen darkened just before I noticed the text from Aya. I scrambled to turn it back on and read the text.

Aya
We're on our way.

My heart lurched. I typed a response faster than I swore I'd ever texted before.

Wait! I'm not ready. I'm talking with Tyr.

My heart dropped into my stomach, where it twisted in a tight knot when I sent it and heard the telling *ping* of a phone a little ways away from me in the woods. *Shit.*

"Too late, Astrid," Aya said, appearing a moment later.

My lower lip caught in my teeth and I struggled against the urge to hunch my shoulders and wring my hands together. This whole meeting was going to be tough enough as it was. I didn't want to deal with Tyr, too, once he found out what was actually happening.

Tyr flicked his attention between us, his brow knitted. "What's too late? Valkyrie, why do you look like you've eaten something rancid?"

I took a quiet, calming breath and relaxed. "It's nothing. Aya and I have something to do. We'll see you later."

"But what about Kirby?" he asked. "I thought she was going to—"

Tyr stopped dead when someone else approached from the woods. The newcomer was big and muscular, with dark golden blond hair cropped tight above his ears. He wore torn jeans and a tight tank top, which showed off an intricate wolf tattoo that wrapped around his shoulder and arm. Runic tattoos littered the rest of his skin on other parts of his body. A few of them were broken up by the scars that marked his skin. *Why am I surprised he's fully clothed?*

With him was a woman with a slim, athletically honed body. Her long golden hair trailed behind her, and her ice-blue eyes watched us with keen interest. *Kirby...*

"Fenrir," Tyr snarled, his body tensing. "You've got a lot of fucking balls coming here."

"Tyr, stop," I said. I didn't know where the strength came from, because I was fucking terrified out of my mind right now, but my voice did it.

Unfortunately, Tyr either didn't hear or didn't care, because he summoned an axe.

"I said, stop!" I threw my hand out, and tingling power suddenly exploded from my chest, bursting out.

Dirt and leaf litter kicked up. The trees and underbrush shook. Aya jumped back and shielded her face with her arms. Black wings sprouted from Kirby and she launched herself in front of Fenrir, using a sword to slice through the concussive magic.

Tyr was the only one unprepared, and found himself flung back several feet. He crashed to the ground—hard—and almost lost his grip on his weapon. He recovered quickly and propped himself up, staring at me in disbelief.

My breath came out ragged and hard, as if I'd just run up fifty flights of stairs. My fingers trembled and weakness flickered in the back of my mind. *That magic… did a number on me. Great.*

Of course, I refused to let that stop me.

"Astrid, why?" Tyr demanded. "Why would you—"

"Quiet." My tone was as strong as before when I first told him to stop, even with the difficulty breathing. "I asked Aya to bring him here. I'm the one who wanted to talk to him."

I took a calming breath. "I get you're angry, but you're not the one who stared down the wolf as he clamped down on your throat and ripped the life out of you."

Tyr climbed to his feet, conflict raging in his expression.

"This is my choice, and I expect you to respect it." I turned to face my past.

Kirby still stood in front of Fenrir, but she had a bit more of a relaxed posture. She shook her head when our eyes met. "We've certainly got a lot to talk about, don't we?"

I gave a small nod. "I think so. But after."

She nodded, her wings folding back against her back and then disappearing alongside her weapon before she stepped aside, leaving Fenrir exposed to my full scrutiny.

His pale blue eyes focused on me, his pupils slightly dilated and the corners of his eyes tight. His hands clenched and unclenched, as did the muscles in his jaws.

"Astrid." His deep and rough, almost growly voice rolled over me. That one word sent a flood of memories through me. Some, I'd already seen, but now were more solidified. Others were new but not unpleasant.

My head tipped for a moment while I processed the remaining memories. "Hey, Fluffy."

Fen's nervous tics stopped, and the corner of his mouth quirked. "You remember."

"It's complicated."

"Like the rest of this situation." He rubbed the back of his neck. "Look, Astrid—"

"I don't want you to say anything." I took a deep, calming breath. I couldn't believe I was about to ask this. "I want… you to shift."

He stiffened. "Are you—"

"I'm sure." The muscles in my back tightened all the way up to my neck. "I need to confirm for myself what I saw."

Aya rested her hands on my shoulders. She knew how difficult it would be for me to face this. To stare a black wolf down was to face this fear in the most literal sense possible.

Fenrir took a deep breath. "Okay. I'm sorry if I frighten you."

His body grew and twisted. Dark hair spread all along his body until a massive wolf the size of a truck towered over us. I swallowed hard, my body locking up. My lungs seized.

"Breathe," Aya murmured.

I sucked in a hard breath through my nose. And then another. I knew this form. It was the same as my memories of him. And those memories told me he was always gentle with me, even after I became immortal.

I took one step forward. And then another, lifting a hand to reach out to him.

Fenrir's ears pinned back, and his front legs bent, lowering his torso and head. His lips pulled back, showing his gleaming teeth. The sight of them made me pause for a moment, but only a moment. *He's not being aggressive. He's scared, like me.*

My eyes didn't leave him, taking in everything he was. I got within an arm's reach, feeling his hot breath wash over my skin.

My vision flashed back to that day I died, and then blinked back. It continued to do so until it felt like the past and present were overlapping.

Strong, powerful body. Lean, damaged body.

Large. Medium.

Pale blue eyes. Golden eyes.

I paused.

Golden eyes.

Golden.

I threw my arms around his massive neck, digging my fingers into his coarse fur and burying my face until all I could smell was his musky, woodsy scent. "It wasn't you."

The moment the words left my lips, a dam broke inside of me. All the tension left, and warmth spread. Hot tears leaked down my cheeks. "It wasn't you, Fen."

His body trembled, and in a blink, his furry wolf shape was gone. Strong arms pulled me in for a tight hug and he collapsed to the ground. "Fuck… Astrid, you have no fucking idea what those words mean. Aya said… that I didn't do it. And I wanted to believe her. I didn't want to believe anymore that I'd gone feral and killed you, of all people. That guilt ate me alive for so long."

I tightened my grip around his neck. "Why do I always have to be the tiebreaker so you'll have faith in yourself?"

His grip tightened—almost too tight. "Because you always saw the best in us."

I did. That was a truth I knew, and it was part of the person I was now. It was part of the reason I became a therapist. I wanted everyone to see the best in themselves.

My pulse slowed. How much of my past life influenced my current life without me knowing? Was I really that different from that person then? Were she and I really different people?

Aya shifted behind us. "Tyr."

I pulled away from Fenrir to watch him approach. Fen and I both rose, with me blocking him with my body as much as my short self could. Tyr still held his axe, and while I could see the conflict raging in his eyes, I wouldn't allow him to attack Fen, should he try. I was also aware of the tense stances Aya and Kirby took.

Tyr didn't stop until he was practically on my toes. My gaze flicked between the two as they stared each other down. Then Tyr shifted his attention to me. "What were the differences?"

I blinked. *He wants to know… Oh!* Of course. He'd gone centuries hating Fenrir. Just claiming he's been wrong the whole time wouldn't change anything. Hell, I should have expected him to ignore my claim and still try to kill Fenrir.

But he respected me enough to hear me out. *He's always respected what I had to say.* I took a calming breath.

"The wolf that killed me was smaller. It also was leaner… no…" I squinted, trying to parse out the memory. "Emaciated? It wasn't healthy. But the telling sign we should have noticed right away were the eyes." I held Tyr's gaze. "That wolf had golden eyes."

Tyr's jaw set. The conflict in his eyes still raged.

"The blame falls partially on me," I said. Both men opened their mouths to protest, but I silenced them with my hand. "Tyr and I both incorrectly identified the wolf. Regardless of how exhausted I'd been, I still made that mistake of reacting before taking in the situation. I let my guard down, and I will own that."

I softened my gaze as I looked at Tyr. "And I understand where you stand. I won't invalidate everything you've felt over these centuries. Even if they were based around incorrect information, no correct information had come forward until now to change things sooner. But, knowing what I do, I'm not going to stand down."

Tyr stared with intense, almost intimidating intensity. Almost. "Please step aside, Valkyrie."

I wouldn't. Not when I couldn't be sure he wouldn't attack Fenrir.

"Astrid."

He grunted when I refused to waiver. "How is it that you've become even more stubborn in this life?"

"You say that like it's a bad thing," Kirby said.

I chuckled. *Dad and Diego would think so, but that's another matter.*

Tyr sighed. "Please, Astrid. Trust me this once."

My lip twisted. His pleading did not help this resolve of mine. *Not fair.*

Fenrir tapped my shoulder. I looked up at him and he gestured with his chin to move.

My brow furrowed. "You sure?"

"If he hasn't barreled through you by now to sever my head from my shoulders, regardless of his insanely strong loyalty to you, then I think we're okay."

That's a fair point. I took a deep breath and stepped away, standing next to Aya. She held my hand, and I knew neither of us could relax just yet.

"I fucked up," Fenrir said first. "I'll admit that without hesitation. If I hadn't lost control, maybe none of this would have happened. I'll own my part in all of this, even if I'm not the one who killed her."

My eyebrows rose. I hadn't expected that out of Fen. In the past memories I had, he struggled to admit when he was wrong or at fault for something. If he did, he'd brush it off like it wasn't a big deal. It was one of my biggest gripes I had about him.

"Yeah, you fucked up, Fen," Tyr agreed.

The hard edge to his voice made me tense. Aya squeezed my hand, keeping me rooted in place.

Tyr lifted his axe and pressed the blade to Fenrir's chest. "You fucked up so bad, I swore an oath to spill your damned blood because you couldn't muzzle your wolf."

My blood ran cold. *No… No, Tyr, you didn't…*

Fen grasped the head of the axe and pressed it harder against his skin. "If you have to carve out my heart, then so be it. Do what you have to, Brother. I won't stop you. But know, Dahlia won't be happy, and you don't want a pissed-off dragon hunting you down."

Dragons? Dragons were actually real?

"Well, we can't have that now that I've finally found my Valkyrie," Tyr murmured.

The axe dug into Fen's skin, and then Tyr slashed the blade. Blood splattered on the ground. I gasped, and Aya had to grab me to prevent me from lunging for Tyr.

Fenrir looked down at the large gash in his chest. It was deep, but not life-threatening like I had feared. "Ow."

Tyr grunted and dismissed his bloody axe into nothing. "Don't complain, mongrel."

Fen placed a hand on his wound. "I won't. You have my thanks for using that loophole. And I'll wear this scar as a reminder."

"I'm going to need some time to fully get over this," Tyr admitted. "But we'll get back to the way things were."

He placed his hand on Fenrir's shoulder and held up his arm with the missing hand. "Now I have to find the real wolf who ate my hand and gut him for daring to take my Valkyrie."

Kirby leaned around Fenrir, her brow furrowed, and gazed beyond the two men. "Uh, who is that?"

We all turned, and my gut clenched seeing the one very stunned person I hadn't wanted to be here. "Diego, how long have you been there?"

He ran his hand through his hair. "What the actual fuck did I witness?"

I exchanged glances with everyone else. Well, shit.

SIXTEEN

DIEGO

I ran my hands through my hair again, my mind racing with all the information just fed to me. Gods, fae and other supernatural beings, magic… it was all real. They weren't just stories people told for fun, or as ways to scare children into behaving. Well, some were, but there was truth within the lies.

Aya, our best friend from college, was actually the Norse goddess of war and sex, Freya, who had been protecting Astrid since she was a kid. She'd pretended to be Pete's wife to do it.

Tyr, the new resident who I thought I didn't need to worry about around Astrid, was actually *the* Norse god, Tyr, who was her lover in the distant past. *No, her husband.* She was the wife he and Aya had talked about dying.

Then there was Fen, *the* Fenrir from Norse myth, and a damned Valkyrie also in the living room, standing around watching me as I took this all in.

This can't be real… can it? I'd seen with my own eyes a monstrous wolf the size of a truck become a man. I saw Tyr banish an axe into nothing.

My eyes flicked to Astrid, where she sat on the opposite side of the couch, her forehead pressed into her palm as if it were bothering her, while Angel sat at her feet, resting her head on Astrid's knee. *This all happened in front of Astrid, and she acted like it was normal...*

"So, three of you are Norse gods, one of you is a Valkyrie." I had to repeat my thoughts out loud a bit, hoping it'd solidify what they'd told me. "And Astrid is—"

"Just me," she mumbled. "I'm just me."

My brow furrowed. "Are you okay?"

She shook her head. "I'm dealing with a memory thing."

"What are you remembering?" Aya asked.

"Stupid shit," Astrid grumbled. "Like stupid things I don't need to remember, ever."

Kirby snorted. "I remember those. Hopefully, they're few and far between, like mine were."

"And fucking Leif." Astrid jerked her head up to look at Aya. "Gods, he got annoying, didn't he? All four of Frida's pregnancies, he was a damned worrier to the millionth degree. How did I not kill him?"

Aya laughed. "Because you loved him. You have no idea how much he prayed to me during all those. Though, believe it or not, it wasn't as much as your father when your mother went through all three of hers. She had no idea of how much of a worrier he remained."

Astrid massaged her temples. "That explains it."

My brow lifted. "Who is Leif?"

"Her brother in her first life," Aya said, her tone so matter-of-fact it was a little off-putting.

I ran my fingers through my hair. "Okay, so Astrid lived during the Viking age at some point. And she came from a family of sorcerers..."

"Just the women up to that point," Astrid corrected. She then squinted. "But I think... there was one time a son inherited the magic. My memories are still patchy around that."

Aya nodded. "That's correct, actually. One of Leif's descendants was born a twin. Both he and his sister, Randi, inherited the magic."

"Randi..." I murmured. "You used that name when posing as Pete's *esposa.*"

"Yes. That was Astrid's mother's name. It became a namesake after her death. Even in recent generations, there are a few surviving from that family line who have carried on the tradition. I thought it'd help her remember her past if I used it."

"And Astrid lived… how long?"

Astrid shrugged. "That's still blank for me, unfortunately."

"A few centuries," Tyr supplied. "She became immortal around twenty-five."

"A Valkyrie," Fen said.

Tyr shook his head. "She was never a true Valkyrie. The rumors claiming I made her into one were just that."

"The wingless Valkyrie…" Astrid murmured.

"What triggers someone to become immortal?" I asked.

I couldn't believe I was entertaining all this. But as crazy as this all was, I believed every word so far. And I'd be lying if some of this wasn't fascinating as well.

"It's different for each individual," Fen said. "Some are born immortal, others have the potential to become immortal, and it comes down to whether they unlock that potential."

Astrid shook her head and sat up straighter. It seemed this memory stuff was finally subsiding. "I think I know how I did."

All eyes fell on her.

"It's a vague memory, one that's not fully there, but is. It was after I'd recovered from… something, and…" She squinted as she processed the partial memory. "I drew Tyr's blood on accident when making a promise."

Tyr ran his hand through his hair. "Shit, you're right. We'd made an eternity vow at that moment. I hadn't thought we'd turned it into a blood oath. That would explain everything."

My brows pulled together. "Blood oath?"

"Blood is powerful," Aya explained. "It has an unusual property to bind with magic and enhance it. That's why there are so many stories about blood sacrifices. Those were real, and powerful. We gods used to gain much of our power from them."

Interesting… There was so much about this world I didn't know, and

I would have gone through my entire life blissfully unaware of what was right under my nose, had things not changed for Astrid. *Or that she hadn't died in the first place.*

My gut clenched. I didn't want to think about what my life would have been like not knowing her.

Astrid scratched Angel behind the ears, who excitedly snatched a squeak toy off the floor and squeaked it against Astrid's leg.

Astrid razzed the dog before shifting her focus to Fen with a mischievous grin. "What's wrong, Fen? Feeling left out? There are plenty of squeak toys you can play with. Or we could play a round of fetch with all the tennis balls we've got."

Fen rolled his eyes while the others laughed. I didn't join in, too preoccupied with taking in Astrid's behavior. They said she'd only started remembering two days ago, but she was already so comfortable with these people from a distant past.

Astrid released Angel, who wandered over to Fen and ate up the attention the wolf-god eagerly gave her, and turned her focus to me. "What's wrong, Diego?"

I shook my head. "I'm just trying to process all this. I don't know how you're doing so well."

She gave a weak smile. "Honestly, I can't say that I am. It's pretty overwhelming for me. There's a lot of chaos in my head right now. Some of these conversations and memories are coming to me naturally, but at the same time, my mind is at war trying to understand why."

I frowned. That made me feel worse about all this. I didn't want her struggling. I'd rather hear her finding this far easier to accept than I was.

"So, what now?" As the words came from my mouth, tension hummed through the air.

Tyr scowled. "We find and kill the bastard who killed Astrid and framed Fen."

Kill? These may be gods and immortals who had different codes they lived by, but the idea of someone speaking so openly about killing someone didn't sit well with me.

"And train Astrid in her magic," Aya added. "She actively used it earlier today instead of the subconscious level she has been her whole life. It'd be dangerous for her not to train now."

"And once she has control over magic, then what? She just has it and can use it?" I wasn't even quite sure what magic was. Would it be like in D&D, or more like myth, with rituals, reagents, and chants?

"I use it for whatever I want." Astrid's expression grew serious—no, dangerous. "And to kill a shifter."

My blood ran cold. I'd never seen this expression from her, even when she wanted to hurt Ben for what he said to me. This was the expression from a woman who'd seen battle and death—the past her.

"You can't… really mean that…"

Astrid set her jaw. "I do."

"That isn't you talking." I couldn't believe I was hearing this from her mouth. "Astrid, you aren't a killer."

"What do you expect me to do?" Her voice rose. "Sit back and let this shifter kill me again?"

"No." I shook my head. "Just… something other than this madness you're talking."

Call me a pacifist, I didn't care. I couldn't stand violence. I could accept people had aggressive tendencies, even Astrid, but to embrace violence and death…

"Do you really think she can sit by and do nothing?" Aya asked. "She's on her ninth incarnation since her first life because of this bastard."

Nine? This shifter they keep talking about killed her nine times?

"You don't get it, Diego…" Astrid didn't look at me. She stared at her hands in her lap. "My memories coming back to me aren't just of that first life I had. It's also of all the others… where I was just a little girl. That's all I ever was. So few memories, but all ending with a frightening, painful death."

I gazed at her like I'd never done before. I saw the weariness and age that didn't match her physical body. I could see the weight of several lifetimes in a way others only alluded to.

An old soul, they called her. A homebody who enjoyed a quiet life.

An old soul… who was tired of the world. *An old, tired soul who wants more to life than mere moments…*

"I can't hide anymore." Astrid lifted her gaze to hold mine. "And I won't wait around for the wolf to come at me again. I will be prepared this time, and I will get him first. I don't want to kill someone. The idea of killing someone doesn't sit well with me, even if my first life thinks it's okay. But if the choice is my life or theirs, I'm choosing mine."

I worked my jaw, my desires to be supportive and protective of her at war. This confidence and determination was something I always admired from her. But it now put her in danger, too. "You're mortal, Astrid. If he gets you again…"

"Yeah, about that."

Everyone turned to Kirby. She'd been fairly quiet this whole time, watching Astrid with only a few comments here and there.

"This is going to sound crazy, so much I'm having a hard time believing it myself, but destiny is a fucking annoying bitch and I really shouldn't be surprised. Astrid, do you remember telling us about a vision your mother Randi had about Valkyries?"

Astrid thought for a moment. "Yes. It was a strange vision about women in unusual clothes becoming Valkyries."

Her back straightened. "Strange clothes, as in our modern clothing?"

Kirby nodded. "Yeah, apparently that vision was true, and it was about me. And, ironically, you're one of the Valkyrie souls I've been searching for."

Silence.

Dead silence.

Until I broke it. "What do you mean by Valkyrie soul?"

Kirby crossed her arms. "It's exactly as it sounds. Her soul resonates with what it means to be a Valkyrie."

"What it means to be Valkyrie," Astrid mumbled.

"Ironic wording, I know," Kirby said, making Astrid laugh. I was clearly missing something. "Until these last recent years, I was the last one. I—"

Astrid gasped, her eyes going wide. "The last one? But there were so many back then. What happened?"

Kirby shrugged. "They died somehow."

"A majority of them volunteered to be sacrificed in a ritual Odin was conducting before we killed him," Aya said. "The rest… well, they followed the tides of battle. And unfortunately, after mortals began to fear supernatural creatures, they became targets as much as everyone else."

Witch hunt suddenly had an all-too-real meaning, and I didn't like it.

"So, you said you were the last until recently," I said. "What changed?"

"I found out I'm destined to bring them back, though not in the form of revival." Kirby rested her hands on her hips. "Like some gods and immortals can sense the dormant power of a potential soul, I can specifically feel a soul's Valkyrie potential. It calls out to me, though some calls are stronger than others."

She leveled her gaze on Astrid. "Your soul's call was the weakest; I suspect because of how much Aya was protecting you this whole time."

She shot the goddess a displeased glare, and Aya responded with a shrug. "You understand I had my reasons for keeping her a secret and staying out of events because of it. Don't get on me now about it."

"You could have at least used better excuses than the half-assed ones you gave."

"Can we stay focused ¿por favor?" I said. I didn't know the situation between them, but I didn't think it was relevant right now.

Kirby nodded. "What little pull I did feel, was so recognizably you, Astrid, I thought I was going crazy. I died before you and Tyr ever got together, let alone you becoming immortal. The idea that you were alive… just didn't make sense."

"What effect does this soul have on me?" Astrid asked.

"Your soul is a bit more active than the others I've found. I suspect this may be due to your reincarnation. As a result, you already feel its pull." Kirby ran her fingers through her hair. "A battle is a battle to a Valkyrie, regardless of how it comes to form. As a therapist, you guide souls through their own personal battles."

"What about the souls I fail?"

Kirby shook her head. "You can't see it that way with our power. It's not that you failed or succeeded. It's that your inner Valkyrie chose who was ready and who wasn't. It may not sound fair, but our power doesn't consider fairness. It doesn't pick sides."

Astrid frowned, but nodded. "And what makes it so important for me to know I have one?"

Kirby shrugged. "I'm supposed to find all potential Valkyries. I suspect it's to stop Ragnarök, but not even I have a clear idea of why I have this ability, or need to bring Valkyries back on the immortal chess board."

My back straightened, and Astrid sucked in a tight breath. *Ragnarök is a real event?*

"I'm not a total bitch, where I'd force you to promise to help me in order for me to manifest this power. I'll do it regardless of whether you join whatever cause this is, and you can use whatever abilities the Valkyrie power bestows on you, in whatever way you deem." Kirby gave a weak smile. "We were friends once, and I know you'd make an invaluable addition, so I would like you by my side in this, but I still will leave that decision in your hands."

My eyes flicked between Kirby and Astrid, who now mulled over the offer. *She could really make it so Astrid could live forever?* My gut twisted as realization set in.

This left me as the only mortal here, should she take the offer. Astrid would outlive me. *She may not want to watch me grow old and die...*

"I'll do it," Astrid said. "I'll help you stop Ragnarök."

Kirby smirked. Aya and Fenrir whooped and slapped hands while Tyr nodded with approval. I couldn't celebrate, however.

"Astrid, wait, don't be so hasty," I said. Everyone turned to look at me. I wouldn't back down. "Take more time to think about it. I don't know what will entail stopping a world-ending event, but it can't be easy. You don't know yet what that'll require of you. Saying yes to something you don't understand... isn't smart."

I didn't care if she activated this Valkyrie soul and became immortal. If that was something she wanted, then I'd support her there, even if that guaranteed she'd not find it worth her time to choose me when she could have an immortal god instead. But I wouldn't let her just jump into danger without thinking.

"I don't need to think about it," Astrid said. She got up to sit next to me, pulling her legs up onto the couch as she faced me. She reached out and cupped my face. "I feel it, deep in me, this is something I have to do. I haven't felt so sure about anything the way I do about this decision."

"Why do you feel this way?" I asked. "What makes you so sure?"

"Because of the number nine."

My brow knitted. "What?"

"Nine was an important number for me and my people in my first life. It was associated with magic and completion. I died nine times. The ritual was used on me nine times. I am on my ninth life since the first reincarnation."

Her green eyes peered into me—through me, as they always did. These eyes of hers always had this soul-piercing feeling, and now I was seeing why.

"Kirby broke her curse during this specific life of mine. I have a Valkyrie soul, possibly since the beginning. I always felt drawn to the Valkyries, wishing I could be one."

"You also had developed Valkyrie-like habits the longer you were immortal in the past," Tyr added. "It's why so many thought I made you into one."

Astrid nodded, though didn't look at him when she did. Her focus on me remained strong. "The odds of me having one now, with all these other boxes checked… remember, there's no such thing—"

"As a coincidence." I closed my eyes and sighed. When I opened my eyes again, I cupped her cheeks, like she did mine. "If you go through with this, mi amor, don't expect me to walk away. I'm staying right here. I don't care if I'm some basic, mortal human. I'm not going anywhere."

Astrid smirked in a way that made my pulse jump. "That's what I want."

I pulled her into me, wrapping her up in my arms. I pressed my face into her gorgeous hair and inhaled her intoxicating scent. My heart beat strong in my chest. Calmness fell over me in a way I'd never experienced before. This felt right.

It was like the dream I had of us, only she would live forever without me. *That's fine. I'll be with her until I draw my last breath.*

When I was ready, I let her go. I didn't care that we had an audience. Their opinions of my and Astrid's relationship didn't matter to me.

Astrid grabbed my hand and squeezed before standing and facing Kirby. "Okay, I'm ready."

Kirby approached and had Astrid reposition while Fen moved the coffee table out of the way. When Astrid's back was to the windows, Kirby and she clasped their hands and pressed them against Astrid's chest.

"Any strange feelings you experience, don't fight them," Kirby said.

Astrid nodded and took a deep breath in anticipation. Kirby's brow furrowed while she concentrated. Nothing seemed to happen for a long moment, and then suddenly, tendrils of golden light sprang out from Astrid's hands.

Aya gasped, and I sat up straight. *Holy shit, that's real magic.*

To Astrid's credit, she hardly reacted. Her eyes widened, but otherwise, she didn't move a muscle.

The golden light slowly floated through the house. Angel lifted her nose to it, sniffing the air. Her calmness around the magic intrigued me about as much as the tendril loosely wrapping around me.

Warm and inviting. That was the best way I could describe the feeling it wrapped me in. It was the same feeling as when Astrid and I embraced.

I noticed a black thread mixed in with the gold, and when it touched my skin, a powerful sensation rushed through me, sapping my lungs of all its air. *This sensation…* I couldn't describe it. Whatever it was, it seeded deep in my bones.

A flash distracted me. I watched as dark, form-fitting armor with skull and feather accents manifested on Astrid's body, and brilliant silver wings sprouted from her back. Golden feathers mixed with the silver—like gilded accents. *It's like my dream…*

I rose to my feet as Kirby released Astrid's hands and stepped away. *She's stunning.*

"How do you feel?" Kirby asked.

Astrid gazed at her hands, watching as the golden magic dissipated, and then down at her armor, before looking back up at the rest of us gawkers. "More whole."

She turned in place, trying to check out the wings on her back. "They're not as heavy as I expected."

"They're an interesting color, too," Tyr commented.

"Is there something wrong with them?" I asked.

Kirby shook her head. "No. Valkyrie wings come in many colors. It all depends on what their soul feels they specialize best in. However, it's not often they're two-toned."

"I don't care," Astrid said. "I love them. Baldur will love them, too, when he finally gets to see them."

She paused, her gaze going out the window and glazing as if she were remembering something, though not in the painful way from earlier. "Baldur…"

She missed the *zing* of tension immediately filling the room. I watched the gods and Kirby exchange glances, all clearly worried. My knowledge of Norse history and myth wasn't the best, despite Darius being open about his pagan beliefs, but I did know that name, and if what I knew about that myth was right, I had a feeling I knew why they were concerned. *All myths are steeped in truth.*

Astrid turned, her eyes wide and painfully hopeful. "Where is he? Aya, why didn't you grab him, too, when you fetched Kirby and Fen?"

No one spoke, the tension increasing.

Astrid's hope faded, replaced with concern. "What?"

When she still didn't receive a response, her expression darkened. "Where is Baldur? Why won't anyone answer me?"

Aya chewed her lip. "Astrid… there's no easy way to put this…"

Astrid's eyes widened, as if she realized what was about to be said. "No…"

"Baldur… is dead."

SEVENTEEN

ASTRID

ead? Baldur was dead?

My mind flashed with memories of a man with blond hair and blue eyes with a kind smile who made me laugh and my heart flutter when I knew it shouldn't.

My skin itched, and my lungs struggled to take in air. My stomach twisted until I was nauseous.

He couldn't be dead.

I threaded my hands into my hair, gripping tight as pressure built up in my head. *He can't be dead.*

I dropped to my knees, and a scream tore through me.

Energy exploded out of my body in every direction. Something smashed. In an instant, pressure wrapped around me, but the agony raking over me overpowered all my senses.

He can't be dead. He's not dead. He's not.

"Astrid," a deep, gravelly voice murmured. "Astrid, please calm."

Diego… It was that special voice of his. One he didn't use often, only when he really wanted to tease me or make sure he had my full attention. The way it wreaked havoc on my brain and made me weak in the knees, it was like he knew.

But instead of making me weak, it wrapped around me like strong arms lifting me up from a fall into a dark abyss.

My scream died. My ears rang in the sudden silence, and my sore throat struggled with the hard, gasping breaths I sucked in and out.

Diego murmured my name again in my ear, sometimes saying something in Spanish, drawing me further and further out of the darkness. My senses returned, and I realized there was more than him to the comforting pressure surrounding me.

Angel pressed against my chest, her head squeezed between my arm and neck. Diego wrapped his arms protectively around me, one of his hands on my head while his body shielded me from something. My wings had spread, like a curtain.

Tyr, Kirby, and Aya hovered over me, their arms extended with shields as a wall. And even Fen had transformed and loomed over us.

A warm breeze blew through the room, and my gaze fell to the shattered glass all over the floor, glittering in the sun.

My hands slid from my hair, and as the sensation of pain splintered through my chest, I wrapped my arms around Angel. I sobbed into her fur, tears trailing down my cheeks.

He's gone...

I cried for a man my past knew. I cried for a man my present would never reconnect with again. I cried for all the unspoken words, now never to be said.

I cried as a piece of my heart withered and died.

Here, in this room, filled with those who would do anything to protect me, I made no attempts to hide my vulnerability. I didn't try to stop the tears just so they wouldn't fuss.

I embraced this breaking pain until I couldn't cry anymore.

Diego rubbed my back when I'd been reduced to sniffles. No one said anything, allowing me time to express my grief—and my building rage.

"How?" I croaked out. I cleared my throat. "How did he die?"

Gods were immortal, and while not invincible, they were tougher than the average immortal. It took a major act to kill one.

Aya brushed off glass shards from her shoulders. "We should get you out of this mess first."

"Tell me how!" I snapped.

She flinched. Any other moment, I would have regretted my harsh command. But the anger that had replaced the despair overpowered such typical responses in me.

"Loki," Tyr said.

"Loki," I murmured. "Just like in the myth."

"For the most part," Tyr said. "It wasn't at some banquet, though. He took notice of my and Baldur's activities when we were searching for you, and laid a trap. We thought we'd found two possible strong cases of you being alive, and split up to check."

He bowed his head. "When I realized my lead was a clear ruse, I rushed to Baldur, but I was too late. I'm sorry, Valkyrie."

It wasn't his fault. If anyone was to blame, it was me. They wouldn't have been caught that way had I not died.

"Why did he do it?"

"We're not entirely clear on that," Kirby said. "He's proud of what he did, going as far as naming his organization after the deed."

"What is this organization called?"

"The Order of Mistletoe, or TOM for short. They claim they try to prevent prophecies from coming true, their ultimate goal being the prevention of Ragnarök. But they're only in it for themselves, and actively impede our efforts to prevent the end of the world."

"He'll pay for what he did." My hands curled into fists. "I'll see to it that Baldur is avenged. I swear it."

A powerful sensation rolled through me. Determination, most likely. I felt it as strongly as my conviction to become a Valkyrie.

"Astrid, be careful what you say," Diego said. "Don't go down a path you can't come back from."

I turned my attention to him, trying to keep my anger in check. It wasn't like he was telling me to forgive Loki. "He killed Baldur. I can't let him get away with that."

"She's also just sworn a blood oath," Tyr said.

We both looked at him, and he pointed at my hand. Blood oozed where it appeared some glass had managed to stick to me, and in my anger, I squeezed down on it.

"She'll now have to avenge Baldur, one way or another."

Diego frowned, and Aya gave him a sympathetic glance. "We know you're not a fan of violence, Diego, but this is our life. We're at war, and Astrid chose this path. It's what you've agreed to by sticking with us."

Diego sat back against the couch. He didn't like it, but Aya had a fair point.

I picked at the glass shards while fighting off Angel's attempts to lick my hand, watching as the small cuts healed up quickly on their own. The sensation was strange. My brain was having a slight issue processing a multi-day process happening in seconds. "I can't say killing sits right with me in this life, but I've killed a lot before in my past. And that past part of me demands justice."

"Good to hear," Kirby said. "Azzie, one of the other Valkyries, is currently hunting Loki. He's got it out for her because they're connected by a prophecy. At least one of her two protectors, Davyn, while sometimes difficult to work with, would probably be grateful for the help getting rid of the Loki problem."

"Davyn…" I murmured. "I know that name."

"He's an old friend of ours," Tyr said. "An immortal bear Berserker."

Berserkers were… warriors who took on the shape of werebeasts, like wolves and bears. That's what Dad claimed with his beliefs, and my memories confirmed that. *How much does Dad truly know?*

"Starkad was a Berserker…" Memories solidified in my mind. I jerked my head up to find Kirby smiling. "You found him again, right? Aya showed me a photo of you, that I think also had him in it."

She chuckled. "Oh yeah. Long, complicated story, but yes. He's gone through some changes, but he's still the same pain in the ass."

"And here I thought you enjoyed the pain in the ass he offered."

She and Aya laughed while I smirked. That may have come a little too easily off my lips, but I was getting used to my situation, little by little. I was sure this would all be normal for me soon enough. I just needed some time. "I would like to see him and Davyn."

"I'll let them know." Kirby glanced around the room. "After we clean this up."

Aya flicked her hand, and the glass began piling up on its own. "I'll work on fixing the windows and electrical wiring today. Last thing we need is for Carrie or Raeni to see this."

"Or Sean," I said. We could claim a wind burst, but that would only explain the windows, not anything else that I apparently damaged in my distraught state.

"You don't have to worry about anything with me, lass."

A muscle in my neck stiffened, and I turned to see Sean standing by the island with Buggy. But he looked different. More stunning? *Are his ears pointed?*

Sean smiled. "Your wings suit you, Astrid. It'll be nice seeing you grow into them."

I opened my mouth, but nothing came out.

He chuckled. "I'm not human, but an elf. Your family has made a great place here for me to live. I hope you can forgive me for the obvious deception."

I nodded. "I think we can work through that with a friendly conversation."

Sean smiled. "When you're less overwhelmed. I had come to check on the commotion. There was a lot of magic and I was concerned. But it appears all is well, so I'll take my leave again."

He grabbed an apple from a nearby bowl and waltzed out. *Okay, that was weird. Are all fae that way?* Were elves fae? I wasn't getting any memories to confirm or deny, so I'd have to make it a point to learn more actively. Maybe that'd help me remember.

Fen shifted out of his wolf shape. "Now that we've settled everything, can we talk about the giant dog thing in the room?"

"We're not talking about your large tail."

He smirked. "Frey and Dahlia are quite pleased with my tail size, thank you."

I rolled my eyes.

"I mean your dog, however."

I blinked and glanced at Angel, who sat calmly in front of me. "What about her?"

Before Fen could respond, Tuggy jumped up on the couch and padded over to Diego, rubbing her head affectionately against his. Fen took a step closer to her, his eyes hopeful, but the feline turned and hissed at him.

His shoulders drooped. Pity flitted through me. He always tried so hard to get those cats to like him.

Then Angel went up to Tuggy, who began grooming the canine's head.

Fen threw his arms out. "What the hel?"

The room erupted with laughter.

"No, seriously, what the hel is that dog of yours?" he demanded. "She shows no fear of magic, and rushed to you when you had your meltdown instead of running away from the damage your magic caused. On top of that, I can't get in eyesight of those miniature beasts because they get all moody. But they want to be friendly with your dog? I don't think so."

Aya calmed herself. "I can assure you, Fen, Angel is one-hundred percent dog."

He gestured to the animals, who were now playing.

Aya turned her attention to me. "You know how we talked about the possibility of you using your magic passively?"

I nodded, not sure where she was going with this.

"I believe you weren't only channeling that into others to heal. You've been slowly making Angel into a familiar, which means the girls don't see her as a canine anymore."

A… familiar? I didn't quite know what that meant. I knew fictional stories, but I wasn't sure which ones were accurate or not. And my past-self memories had heard of them, but never learned about them, it seemed.

"What does that mean?" Diego asked for me.

"Familiars are beings that magic has converted to assist a magic-wielder. The most common stories are of witches and their animal familiars. Those combos were the most common, though not the only ones. A familiar can be non-animals, like people or fae, though it's rare."

I tapped my chin. "What does it mean for me and Angel, though?"

"Animal familiars become more intelligent the longer they're exposed to the magic within them. And they live as long as their magical masters."

My eyes widened. "Angel will… live as long as I do?"

"If you complete the familiar conversion, yes."

I was a Valkyrie now. That made me immortal. Angel could live as long as I did. *I won't ever have to say goodbye to her.*

"Wait, is that what Buggy and Tuggy are?"

Aya smirked. "You're the first to finally guess it correctly. They were ordinary cats until I made them my familiars."

Tyr gave her a long look. "Really? You made it seem like they were something more than just familiars."

Aya wagged a finger. "No, everyone assumed they were. I just never corrected you because it was more fun."

She cocked her head when she glanced my way. "What's wrong, Astrid?"

A thought had come to me. My memories knew Buggy and Tuggy's real names, and something about Tuggy sparked the wheels in my head. I made a face suddenly. "Aw, Aya, I just realized the innuendo that is Tuggy's name. How could you do that to her?"

The room filled with laughter. Aya winked. "Because it wouldn't be me if I didn't."

I gave Tuggy a good scratch under the chin before she went back to grooming Angel again, which earned another disdained glare from Fen. He really wasn't going to let up on this.

"So, how do I finish making Angel a familiar?" I asked Aya.

"When we get a better hold on your magic, I'll show you. Then we can go over what that bond will entail."

I liked that idea. "So, the first goal is to get me caught up on my magic skills."

"And train you in the ways of a Valkyrie," Kirby said. "You're going to need to understand how that works, now that you are one."

I nodded. "We also have the festival next weekend that we need to prep for."

Aya waved a hand. "I've got that all covered. All the supposed prep-work I've been having us do was just to keep the façade up. Now that you two know the truth, don't worry."

"Wait, so was your insistence for this year's theme all an elaborate plan because of Astrid's memories?" Diego asked.

She nodded. "My hope is if we immerse her into something that is similar to her past, she'll remember quicker. Originally, I thought it'd help her remember at all, but that happened on its own. If Astrid can remember all of her past, we might figure out who insists she needs to stay dead."

He nodded, his jaw setting with determination. I was grateful for his support. I knew this whole situation was fucked up and difficult to wrap one's head around. If it weren't for the memories and all the magic flying around, I'd probably think this was some weird, fevered dream I'd wake up from any moment now. I could only imagine what Diego was going through as an ordinary person.

And it made me that much happier he wanted to stay by my side. *I'll need to figure out my guy issue eventually. But for now, saving Midgard takes precedence over my love life.*

EIGHTEEN

TYR

A fly buzzed by my ear. My training helped me ignore the annoying pest, but between it and this unusually hot summer heat for the area, even my patience was put to the test. I didn't know how Astrid could act like the heat didn't bother her as I watched her face Aya, both sitting on some patio furniture on the deck. Sure, she was sweating, even in the distractingly short shorts and low-cut tank top she wore, but the way she focused on her hands, trying to create a ball of light per Aya's instructions, it was as if she wasn't aware of anything around her.

"Breathe, Astrid," Aya said. "Don't hold your breath."

Astrid sucked in a tight breath without looking up from her hands.

I had paid little attention in the past when she trained Astrid. I'd always used that time to spar with Fen and Baldur. And back then, Astrid had prior experience with magic before Aya had started training her, making her lessons far easier than what Astrid experienced now.

I paid attention now. Not only because the instructions were fascinating, but I suspected that understanding how magic worked would help me synergize with Astrid in a fight. *We'd done well in the past, but there's always room for improvement.*

Fen swatted at the flies buzzing around him, unable to handle their annoyance. *Some things never change.* I still felt some animosity with him, but I was working on that. He came over daily, and Astrid even insisted on us having therapy sessions with Diego. I wasn't sure why she didn't want to, but to my surprise, Diego handled our conversations incredibly well for someone who'd been thrust into the truth of the world so recently.

Astrid let out a frustrated breath. She dropped her hands into her lap. "It's not working."

Aya tapped her lips with a finger. "This is so strange. You shouldn't be having this much trouble learning magic of any kind."

Astrid hadn't been doing well on the healing training, either, which surprised us all, given she'd been so adept at it before. It was like there was something holding her back. But what could it be?

"We all saw her use it against Tyr the other day," Fen said. "Sure, she was pissed, but if she could use it then, what's so different now?"

Astrid frowned. "I wish I knew. I hadn't even thought about using magic against him. It just happened. Just like when you all told me about Baldur. And it was the same with Ben. I was angry and then power exploded out of me, sending both flying with the power of the force."

The force? I ignored the comment while Aya and Fen snickered, as if they understood the reference, and instead focused on something specific she mentioned. *She was angry…*

I'd hardly ever seen her angry since showing up here. The last few days were the highest in frustration levels, and only around her training. Once that ended, and she did something else, it was like no negative bone existed in her. And maybe that was the problem.

I'd heard her rage the day after I'd come here. It was a powerful response to something, but I'd stayed away, as advised by Raeni. She had said it was something that happened every once in a while with Astrid, and we were to never discuss the situation with her. Only Diego and her father helped her through those.

How often did she suppress something like rage? How natural was it for her to be so happy all the time?

And then there was her distress after the news of Baldur. It was like her powerful emotions had opened up whatever blocked her.

My eyes flicked around to assess the area we had to work with. *The deck should be large enough.* I pushed off the wall and gestured for Astrid to rise. "Let's try something. Stand up."

Astrid's brow furrowed, but she did as I asked. "What's this idea you have?"

"I don't think this way of teaching you simple tricks, like a cute light, is working for you. I think you need something practical to start with."

Aya shook her head. "I don't like that idea, Tyr. Magic is dangerous if not used properly. She'd be better off learning something small and simple until she understands how her magic works this time. I can tell her all I like to just think of the thing she wants and the magic will do it, but until she understands her power at all, that won't happen. That's the purpose of this light-creation exercise."

"And what if her magic doesn't work that way?" I asked. "This clearly isn't working for Astrid. It's only frustrating her."

"This way worked for her before."

Astrid shook her head. "But we can't treat it like before. I'm not that person. How I learned then was even different from how my mother during that life had learned. I want to hear Tyr out on his idea. It's better than beating my head against a brick wall."

I smiled at her, grateful for her support. I may not understand magic like Aya, but as a war god, I knew a poor plan of action when I saw one. And I was sure, if Aya wasn't so close to this magic conundrum, she'd see it, too.

"You were angry two of the times you used your magic, and distressed the other."

"And scared the first time, when I was a kid," Astrid added.

I nodded. "All are potent emotions. I'm not about to put you in a situation that will frighten or distress you, and I don't like it when you're mad at me, but it's rather easy to simulate the feelings of anger."

Astrid's brows pulled together. "You want me to get angry?"

I summoned my shield. The sun gleamed off the silver and gemstone accents. It had been a gift from Astrid on our one hundredth wedding anniversary. I held it in front of me. "I want you to simulate that anger and attack me with magic."

She took a step back, her eyes going wide. "Were you hit on the head or something?"

Aya, Fen, and I chuckled. I tapped my head with a finger. "A number of times, before and after you were around to accelerate the healing process."

Astrid narrowed her eyes. "I'm not going to attack you."

I repositioned myself into a defensive stance, using the shield. "I want you to."

"No. This is stupid." She turned to Aya. "Tell him this is stupid."

"Oh, it's stupid," she agreed. "You should do it."

Astrid stared at our friend, her mouth agape, while Fen roared with laughter.

I smirked at Astrid when she turned her attention back to me. "Come now, Valkyrie, you know you want to. I know you've got some sort of irritation toward me over something that you can use to fuel the anger."

To my curiosity, that didn't bait her. She crossed her arms and held a serious expression about her. "No."

Before I could question her stubbornness, a phone rang. Astrid snatched hers from a nearby table and shook her head. It wasn't her phone. Fen and Aya checked their own. It was Aya receiving a call.

She answered and listened to the person on the other side. "Okay, I'll be right there to check it out."

Aya hung up and grabbed Fen's arm. "I might need you. Tyr, stay here with Astrid."

And then they were gone.

Astrid pursed her lips. "I wonder what that was about."

I made a thoughtful noise in agreement, feeling as though something big was happening.

"Now what?" she asked.

I shook my thoughts free and focused on Astrid. "Now, we try my theory."

She rolled her eyes. "No. I'm not going to attack you. Or your shield while you hold it and possibly hit you on accident."

I couldn't help but chuckle at her specifics. "And why not?"

"Because I don't want to hurt you."

"I'm a god, Astrid. It takes a lot to cause me issues."

Her gaze faltered. "And I know that magic can have some nasty effects on gods. That's why… Baldur isn't here."

I studied her, watching the smallest changes in her. She flickered in and out of a mask so subtly that most would miss it. And that mask covered pain and rage.

I dismissed my shield and approached her. She didn't move. She didn't even look up at me. "Talk to me, Valkyrie."

Her focus slid to my missing hand. She reached out and took my wrist in her hands, her warmth seeping deep into my bones. "Your hand never grew back…"

"I made a rash decision," I said. "In my grief, I decided I wouldn't allow it to grow back until I found you. I didn't think about the possibility that I wouldn't be able to after a certain amount of time passed."

Astrid frowned. "You were hurt… because of me. You made strong vows because of me. You searched endlessly because of me."

Her grip on my wrist tightened. "Baldur is dead… because of me."

"No." My voice came out harder than I wanted, but it was needed. "Baldur is dead because of Loki."

"Loki was able to set a trap because you both were looking for me."

I tucked a finger under her chin and lifted so she'd look at me. "Loki is a cunning bastard. He would have found another way to go after Baldur had you still been around. You are not to blame. For any of this."

She shook her head. "If I hadn't made my mistake—"

"It doesn't matter, Astrid. I made my own choices. You are not responsible for those, even if they were in response to yours."

Astrid tipped her gaze down to the ground again. "People get hurt when I'm angry. I have to stay controlled, so that doesn't happen. I can't allow myself—"

"Valkyrie, stop." I lifted her chin again. "Stop suppressing a piece of you. It only hurts you. Stop hurting yourself."

The corners of her eyes pinched together, and tears brimmed her eyes. "I want to be good. I want to be a good, kind person, Tyr."

"You can be. But you can also be fierce. Good and fierce don't have to be at odds." My thumb grazed her cheek, wiping away a tear that had broken free. "You know that balance. You had that balance before. You were good and kind and gentle. But you were also fierce and lethal. You knew when each side was needed, and never apologized for being who you were. You have to find that balance in this life now."

Astrid stared, the emotions raging in her eyes subsiding. "You're the first to tell me that side of me isn't a problem. Why?"

"I'm a war god, Valkyrie." I grinned. "And when you're fierce, you get that look that's sexy as hel."

She rolled her eyes so hard I couldn't help but laugh. "That's one thing I can say I do remember. And seriously, what the hell was with your and Baldur's reaction to whatever look I gave when casting magic?"

I smirked. "It was only when you cast offensive magic, intended to harm or scare. It was an incredibly deadly look, and damn, was it a turn-on."

Astrid rolled her eyes again. "You are something else."

I chuckled. I wouldn't apologize for something I wasn't ashamed of. "Are you ready to try using magic without suppressing another side of you?"

She nodded slowly. "Yes, but I want to try something else first. Before we try your idea, where you might find yourself with a hard-on from some look I give—"

I belted out a hearty laugh. "Being around you already does that."

Her cheeks turned a perfect shade of pink. Astrid's eyes flicked down for the briefest of moments, and my cock twitched in response. "Be as that may, I want to see if I can do something. Give me your wrist."

I held up my arm. "I'm afraid I can't detach that like I did my hand, so this offer will have to do."

To my delight, that got her laughing. "Let's see if I can do this."

Astrid took my wrist in her hands again and concentrated. For the longest moment, nothing happened, and I thought she might give up on whatever it was she was attempting to do. Then, golden light sprang out of her hands.

Astrid gasped, and the magic wavered.

"Concentrate," I said. We could marvel and rejoice after.

She nodded and focused. The magic spread out, as if it had a life of its own, but then pulled back in as she figured out how to control it. The magic solidified on my wrist, and took a form vaguely shaped like a hand.

Astrid's mouth thinned as she concentrated, but the magic didn't change any further. She let out a strained breath, and the magic disappeared.

We both gazed at my wrist before she lifted her head, eyes sparkling. "I almost did it!"

I laughed when she burst into a happy jig. She took me by surprise when she launched herself at me and wrapped her arms around my neck. Instinctively, I wrapped my arms around her waist, pulling her off the ground and flush against me; the soft curves of her breasts and hips molded against my hard muscles. Her soft lips pressed against mine, igniting the embers of desire for her that simmered under the surface. That one touch snapped all the control I had used to rein myself in around her in order to keep the promise I'd made.

I tangled my fingers in her hair and used my other arm to lift her higher. She wrapped her legs around me and slid her fingers up along the back of my neck, threading them into my hair.

I slammed her back against the wall, and she let out a deep moan, surging the desire in me into a fiery inferno. I kissed her harder, my tongue pressing against her lips, demanding her permission—permission she granted.

My pulse roared in my ears. Her taste and smell seared into my senses, revitalizing my memories and creating new ones with her differences in this life.

My chest rumbled with a groan and my cock strained against my trousers, pressing against her, desperate for Astrid to feel what she did to me—to know how much I needed her.

Astrid suddenly pulled away, pressing a hand against my chest. The air filled with our gasps for breath.

"I'm sorry." Her eyes struggled to meet mine. "I shouldn't have done that."

I wanted to argue with her—wanted to show her just how good we could be together in this life. But I bit all my arguments back and eased her to her feet. "I should also apologize. I promised I wouldn't push anything unless you wanted to. I got a little... excited."

Her gaze flicked down, and she worked her jaw as she tore it away from my all-too-obvious erection no clothes could hide, her slightly flushed cheeks turning pinker. "I, uh, can see that. Sorry for causing that. I'm not intentionally leading you on or anything. I haven't really had much time to think about things, with everything else going on."

She didn't have to think. She just had to go with what her gut told her. I'd take whatever she wanted, even if it was casual sex or something right now. It wasn't what I wanted in the long run, but hel, I'd take something.

However, I didn't voice any of that. She clearly was struggling with something around us, but if she didn't want to talk about it yet, then I would respect her wishes and wait until she did.

Backing away, I shoved my hand in my pocket. "I gave you my word that I'd respect your wishes, and I'll do just that. I can be patient." I grinned. "Though, after a kiss like that, I can't promise I won't try to sway you to give me a second chance."

She chewed her lower lip and twirled a lock of her gorgeous hair, refusing to look up at me, as if what she was doing wasn't enough of a tease. "It wouldn't be you if you didn't try."

I cocked my head, gauging her. Was that from an assessment she'd made from interacting with me these past two weeks, or did she remember more of her past that included me? She'd been quiet when it came to memories about us. She seemed to remember others and her relationships with them just fine. And sometimes she let on she knew things about me from memories, but they always seemed to be from memories that involved someone else.

"Oh, I've been meaning to give these to you."

Astrid blinked up at me, curious about what I suddenly had to offer.

I summoned an axe, the same one I'd purposely had out the day I was working on the woodpile, hoping it'd trigger a memory. "You've done well with your training. I thought it was time you had your weapons back."

She accepted the axe, taking it in. "You kept this, all this time on you?"

I summoned her onyx blade sword with rune engravings next. "Neither of these have gone far from me. I wouldn't risk anything happening to them."

She held them close, her eyes going distant. "Thank you. These were… important to me. The axe was made from my mother's staff, and… this sword once belonged to you." She frowned. "I don't know why you gave it to me, though."

"It was part of our marriage vow exchange."

Astrid cocked her head, thinking about this. Then she shook her head. Seemed she wasn't going to remember that just yet. "Well, now Kirby can get off my back about why I'm incapable of summoning these. She thought that after I became a Valkyrie, they should come back to me instantly, or fate would give me some, I guess."

I rubbed the back of my neck. "They probably would have, had they not been bound to my storage dimension."

"Thank you for returning them. Now I can practice with these instead of relying solely on my magic or borrowing from her or Aya."

I showed her how to store them, something she picked up on oddly quickly, given her previous issues with magic. *Maybe our talk helped more than that single attempt she made.*

Astrid gasped and jumped back. It triggered my need to protect, and I summoned my axe, turning to face the intruder. I relaxed when I came face-to-face with a tall man with long, dirty blond hair and a dark-haired woman wearing all black. *How the hel is she not boiling in that outfit?*

"Frey?" Astrid said tentatively.

He gave an awkward smile and gestured to the black, shadowy weapon-shaped objects hovering in the air around him that I hadn't noticed until now. *That color…* "I'm glad to see you too after all this time, Astrid, but would you mind not pointing those in my face?

While I'm not opposed to a little knife play, I'm sorry to say, I'm not interested with you."

Astrid let out a slow breath and the magic faded, allowing me to relax and dismiss my weapon. This place should be safe from unwanted intrusion, thanks to Aya's magic wards, but my instinct to protect her was even stronger. "Try not to appear suddenly in front of me, and I won't accidentally proposition you."

He smirked and opened his arms. Astrid smiled and embraced him, like the old friends they were. She hadn't been close with Frey back then, but they certainly weren't strangers.

"It's so good to see you again," she said.

He pulled away and touched the tips of her hair and her shoulders while giving her a once-over. "You as well. I dare say reincarnation is quite becoming on you."

She wagged a finger at him. "Careful. I'm not easily impressed and swayed by pretty words in this life."

Frey's eyes flicked to me. "That must be extra difficult for you, given how often you're known to be tongue-tied around her."

I grunted, and Astrid laughed. While he was right, he didn't need to call it out like that.

Astrid turned to the woman who'd come with Frey. "You must be Dahlia."

I jumped back when she exploded in what sounded like a happy shriek, and bounced like one of those excitable small barking dogs. She threw her arms around Astrid. "I'm so excited to finally meet you! Are you a hugger? I hope you're a hugger, because I am."

Astrid and Frey laughed while I blinked and listened to this woman ramble at the speed of sound.

"Fen and Frey have told me so much about you since you two reconciled, and I really wanted to meet you and get to know you. It sounds like you two are close, like brother and sister, which is a lot like my friend Magnus, who I see as my sister. And that would make you family, and I really like having a bigger family now."

Astrid squeezed her. "I'm glad you're a hugger, because so is this family. And if you're part of this family, you have to get used to hugs."

I shook my head. "You understood her?"

Astrid cocked her head. "What, like it's hard?"

Frey laughed. "I knew the two of you would get along."

Astrid then went to rambling, just like Dahlia, as if she were emulating the woman's bubbly nature. "I'm excited to get to know you. Fen hasn't shut up about you, in the most adorable ways. He's like a lovesick puppy. I don't have any siblings in this life—Aya is the closest I've got to a sister, and Kirby and I haven't connected the same way as we had in the past, so I don't know how that's going to play out, but I'm more than happy to have another sister. Same with Magnus, if she wants that. Kirby said Magnus is another Valkyrie, so I need to meet her anyway, meaning we can see if we click. My dad won't say no to another daughter or two… or five."

She squinted. "That's if you want a dad… or another dad. I don't know what your family life is like. Fen doesn't talk about it much. I gathered it was a bit of a touchy subject, but if you want to talk, I'm willing to listen, and offer advice if you want it. But only if you want it."

She suddenly stopped her emulated ramble and jerked her attention to the forest. "Oh hey, they're back."

Everyone turned as Aya and Diego strolled into the open.

Astrid raised her voice to call out to them. "Where the fuck you been? Burying Fen's body?"

Aya cackled, and Diego shook his head. A moment later, Angel barreled out of the trees at top speed, an enormous wolf charging after her.

Fen chased the happy shepherd, digging up the ground every time she forced him to pivot quickly.

"You're fixing the lawn when you're done, Fluffy!" Astrid called out.

Fen ignored her, enjoying playing with the dog instead. Angel barked and growled in her play, even nipping at the large shifter god without fear. Even though Astrid had trained her to be a therapy and SAR dog, Astrid didn't seem too concerned by this behavior. *Dog has to be a dog sometimes, I guess.* Even after learning Astrid was passively turning her into a familiar, which would make her more intelligent over time than other dogs, Angel would always be a dog at her base nature.

"Oh, and you have visitors," Astrid added as an afterthought.

Fen skidded to a halt and gazed up at us, his tongue lolling. *"You two showed up finally."*

His words sounded from outside and inside my head. While they were words I understood, they were distinctly wolf in origin, distorting them a bit. I did my best not to twitch. I used to be accustomed to this way of speech, but the centuries apart would require me to get back to that.

Frey leaned against the deck railing. "I need to know your secret to domesticating him so quickly."

Astrid laughed, and Fen gave an indignant snort.

I turned my attention to the kitchen door when it opened, Aya and Diego walking out to join us. "So, care to share what's going on?"

We'd known Diego had gone off on a walk with Angel while we worked with Astrid, to ensure the dog didn't get in the way, and it could be guessed that Aya had gotten the call from him, so why Aya and Fen met up with him in such a hurry needed to be understood.

"Wait, don't be rude," Astrid chastised. "Frey, Dahlia, this is Diego. Diego, Frey and Dahlia."

"Hey, nice to meet you." Diego smiled in a way that made Dahlia's eyes flutter for a moment.

"Hey, yourself," she responded.

Frey slid his arm around Dahlia's waist while offering a polite greeting back. *A little possessive, Frey, are you?* I could see now what Astrid meant when she said Diego was a charmer by nature, and how she might misinterpret his interest in her because of it. Unfortunately, I was also aware he'd made that interest clear to her recently at some point, thanks to Aya letting it slip, so I really did have competition for her affection.

Now that she was immortal, I theoretically shouldn't have any issues coming out on top. But even I was swayed by her when she was mortal, so Diego's shorter life expectancy wasn't a guaranteed deal breaker.

"Anyway," Diego said, "I was making sure I understood where Aya's magic shield ended when Angel started acting weird. If I got too close, she tried to force me away, which proved to us she is very much aware of Aya's magic, even though she's not yet a full familiar. I thought the behavior was strange, when I spotted some weird scratch marks on a tree just outside the border, so I wanted Aya to take a look."

He pulled out his phone and showed us a picture of crudely carved runes in a tree trunk. A muscle in my neck twitched. Could it really be that this shifter had found Astrid like Aya worried?

Aya nodded, as if she could see my thoughts. "It was the shifter. Fen confirmed there was a distinct wolf shifter scent in the markings left, but he was struggling to identify them as an individual, so he's not sure if he just doesn't know this one, or something else is at play, as, strangely, that was the only area with a scent of this shifter."

"We crossed paths with Sean while out there, and he and the forest also couldn't provide more answers for us," Diego added.

Astrid set her full attention on Aya. "What does this mean? What was the purpose of leaving such a mark? It's clear it was deliberate."

My hand curled. "It's a calling card."

Everyone shifted their attention to me. Fen even left his wolf shape and climbed up to join us like the uncivilized mongrel he still was, leaving Angel to run into the house on her own.

"It was fairly common back in the day," Fen said. "Shifters and Berserkers would leave them to declare something, usually to settle a score. Given we're sure this wolf is the same one who killed Astrid before, no doubt that's his intent."

"There has been a lot of immortal activity here lately," Astrid murmured. "If this shifter has been watching and waiting for an opportunity to strike again, the changes wouldn't go unnoticed."

"How would they know?" Diego asked. "Besides Tyr, who drove here, everyone else has teleported in." His eyes flicked to Frey and Dahlia. "I assume you two teleported in, at least."

Dahlia nodded. "Aya said it was okay to do."

"It is," Aya said. "And that magical activity is possibly the telling sign. The ability to sense magic isn't just relegated to those who can use it. There are plenty out there sensitive to it, especially if they've been touched by it themselves."

"We know nothing about this shifter," I said. "So it'd be best to assume they can sense it, especially if they're cocky enough to leave a calling card."

"It would also be best if Astrid doesn't leave the retreat without someone there to protect her," Aya said. "Until she's trained enough to hold her own, we can't allow this mongrel to get too close to her."

"What about the festival this weekend?" Diego asked. "Will she be safe? Do we need to protect the whole town from this shifter?"

Aya shook her head. "I can't make a shield that large, and I won't risk taking this one down to move it just for the festival. If they somehow get into the house while we're out, and then I erect the barrier again, it won't evict them. We'll just have to make sure Astrid isn't alone."

Astrid frowned, and I could understand why. She was strong-willed enough to not want a babysitter, but smart enough not to argue. *Don't worry, Valkyrie, we'll get this shifter, and then you can be free.*

Astrid took a deep breath and latched onto Dahlia's arm. "This is getting too serious for me. I'm told you're a dragon. I seriously need to see that."

Dahlia's eyebrow lifted. "You want to see the cute humanoid version, or the big winged lizard?"

"Yes," Astrid said, making Dahlia laugh. "Oh! And I'm told you and your sister play D&D, and we need more players at our Saturday table."

Dahlia beamed. "That sounds like a lot of fun!" She then paused to think. "Though, I'm not sure about Magnus. She's got twin newborns to take care of right now."

Astrid's eyes lit up, and it made my pulse skip, reminding me of the family we tried and failed to have back then. *Maybe this time, we'll get another chance.* "Even better! My dad is seriously baby-crazy right now."

Diego barked out a laugh. "Baby-crazy is an understatement."

After rolling her eyes, Astrid deepened her voice as she mimicked her father. "Astrid, when are you going to give me grandbabies? Astrid, you're not getting any younger. Astrid, you know the little pitter-patter of tiny feet would make this old man so happy to hear. I know you're not dating anyone right now, but I won't judge you if you became a single parent. I think I did a fine job on my own, and we've got more family now to help raise kids."

She then gave such a deep eye-roll I wondered for a moment if it was possible for them to pop out of her skull. "Seriously, a baby, especially two babies, would distract him from pestering me. He'll scoop them both right up and give Magnus a moment to herself. Hell, he'd babysit any time if she needed. Course, we'd have to figure out the logistics, since he doesn't know about real magic and stuff, but I'm sure we'll figure it out."

Dahlia regarded her for a moment. "Really? For someone he doesn't know?"

Astrid nodded. "Yeah, it's that bad. Though, like I said before, he'd take anyone in as one of his kids, so it's not that strange. And you can trust him. He'd treat those babies like his own grandchildren, and I swear, mortal human attributes be damned, he'll become one hell of a papa bear to protect them if needed."

Something flashed in Dahlia's eyes when Astrid mentioned "papa bear" before she made a thoughtful noise. "I'll have to think about it and bring it up to Magnus."

Astrid tugged on Dahlia's arm. "Now, show me the dragon! I wanna see."

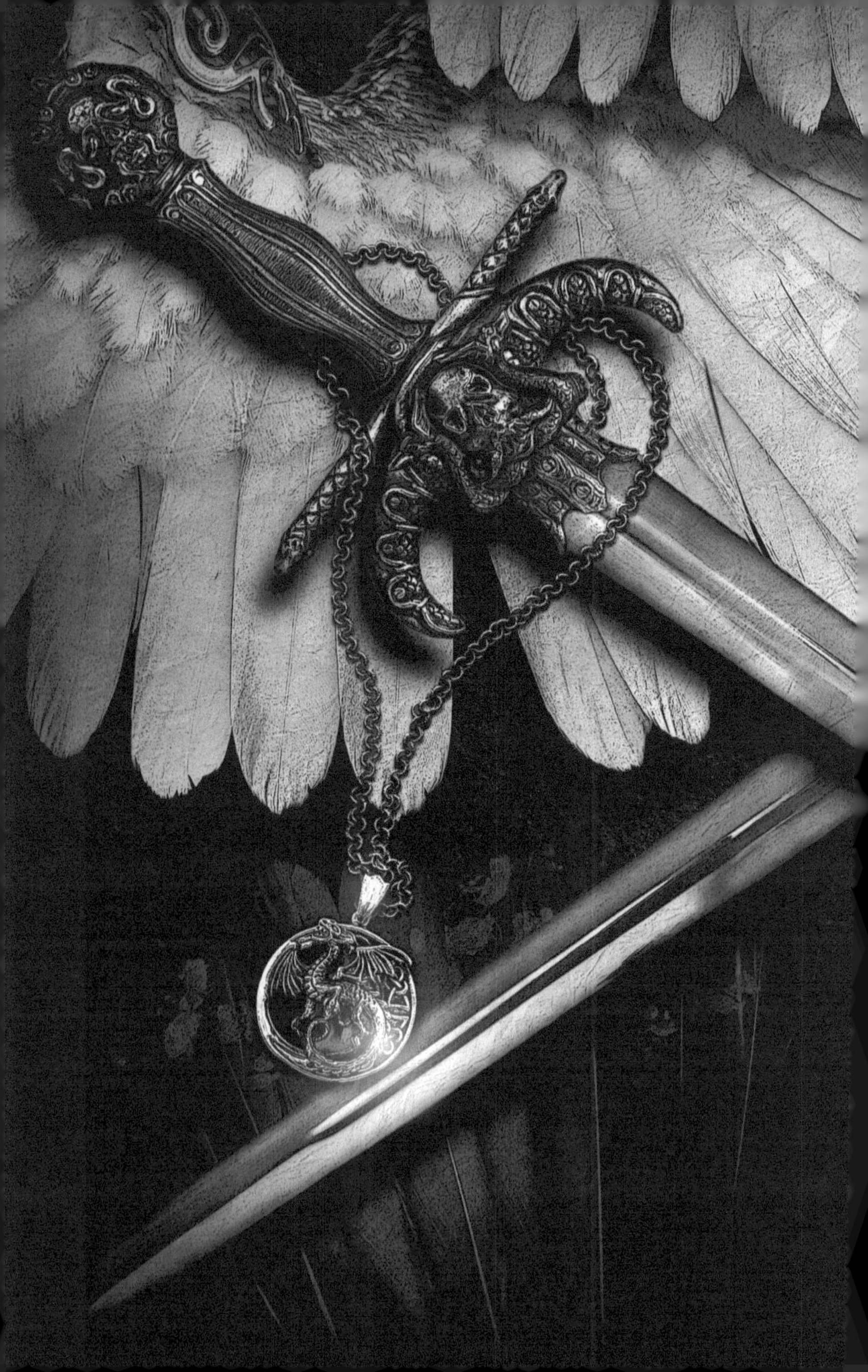

NINETEEN

DIEGO

Cool metal shifted in my hand as I absently rolled it. I watched Astrid spar with Kirby, my muscles bunching any time Astrid was thrown down or showed more aggression than I was used to seeing from her. The last few days had been a whirlwind of things to grow accustomed to, and I wasn't doing so well with it.

It was one thing to learn there was more to our world than you thought, and another to actually experience it firsthand. Magic, gods, the world of the supernatural as a whole, learning which myths and aspects of religion were real and what were fabricated, even learning that some influential figures in history were actually immortals in disguise… it was a lot.

Through it all, Astrid and I had to find our way through the world with our eyes wide open now, and we weren't going to be the same in the end.

Astrid had already begun to change. Being around these gods and immortals, it impacted her in ways I never expected to see. This aggressive side of her came out more often, but it stayed controlled. She hadn't had one of her episodes since this change.

I hated violence. I'd rather work things out peacefully than resort to such measures. However, I could see how that didn't work for everyone. And that included Astrid, it seemed.

I was so worried this new path for her would change the woman I loved into someone I couldn't recognize. But that hadn't happened. She was still the same caring and thoughtful woman, to the unfortunate point of self-neglect, whom I knew her to be. She just seemed more... whole now.

When will I feel whole? I looked down at the circular pendant in my hand. Carved into the silver metal was the tree of life and other Celtic symbols. Three lines that looked like ribbons wrapped loosely around the tree and tangled in the roots. A small gemstone surrounded by tiny elements of magic was set into the trunk.

My thumb traced the engraving. *Where do I, a mortal with no supernatural abilities to speak of, fit into all this?*

I'd promised to stick by Astrid's side, no matter what, no matter how much this so-called war would wear on my understanding of morals and make me question what was good and evil. But what did that promise mean? What use was I, if I was only in the way?

My attention shifted to the sparring when someone yelled. My heart leapt into my throat at the sight of Kirby slashing a sword Astrid's way. Astrid lifted a hand and golden light sprang out. It formed into the shape of a shield, blocking the strike and dissipating on impact. She didn't hesitate to go on the offensive. Her hands moved as if summoning something, only nothing appeared.

Astrid paused and cocked her head, confused. "Weird... my magic is active..."

My eyes flicked to the dozen or so swords and daggers—more solidified than her previous shield—now surrounding me, their pointed tips angled in not-so-friendly ways. "Uh, Astrid."

She gasped, and the weapons disappeared. In an instant, she was landing on the deck railing, her beautiful wings spread wide. I couldn't stop myself from gawking.

Aya said angels didn't exist—that they were a myth borne of various other winged supernaturals, including Valkyries. And gazing at Astrid, I could see why they would. *My Valkyrie. Claim.*

Astrid crouched. "You okay?"

I shook myself and nodded. "Yeah, just a little startled."

She frowned. "I'm sorry. I didn't mean to."

I poked the corner of her mouth and pushed up. "I know, and it's okay. Not a bad trick if you learn to do it on purpose."

She rocked her head back and forth and made a thoughtful sound. But instead of responding to my comment, her eyes flicked to my other hand. "What's that?"

Shit. I hadn't wanted her to see this yet.

I acted cool and shrugged, trying to slide it into my pocket. "Just something I found in my junk box."

She snickered. "Anything you find in your *treasure hoard*, I want to see. You've got a lot of fun things in there."

I grinned. I loved that was how she saw it. Ever since I was little, I'd collect things and put them into a box. Most thought it was random junk, but it wasn't. I didn't have lint or random trash wrappers in the box.

A small acorn? From a hiking trip Astrid and I took a few years back.

A torn, beer-stained ticket? From the first concert Aya treated the three of us to in college.

A shiny pebble? I found it when Mom and I first walked the retreat after arriving.

Every item had meaning to me, and I treasured them all.

But this wasn't from that box. This necklace was even more special than any item in that box.

Astrid made grabby-hands. "Well, let me see it."

I stepped away, keeping it out of reach. "Go back to training."

She hopped down, reaching for it. "Please?"

The shifting of her wings caught the sunlight, and the gold and silver feathers seemed to sparkle, dazzling me. Kirby explained that the silver feathers meant Astrid's soul resonated with healing the most. Not just magic healing, as apparently all Valkyries were capable of that, but restoring the mind, body, and soul.

Kirby said they were drawn to those who were out of balance and were the Valkyries most commonly seen on the battlefields, comforting the dying and collecting the most souls to carry—the heaviest burden of a Valkyrie's purpose. It fit Astrid's character to a T.

But the gold meant it also resonated with protection, and at any cost, which made sense with how self-sacrificing Astrid could be sometimes.

"Ha!" Astrid shouted in triumph.

I blinked and found her with the pendant cradled in her hands. "Cielo…"

"Wow, this is so pretty." Her loving gaze on the necklace made my chest swell. It was the exact reaction I'd hoped for. She turned it in her hands. "It looks really old."

It was. I had stored it away until the right moment to give it away—and that moment was soon, but not right now, no matter how lovingly she gazed at it.

Astrid was too engrossed to care about my desire to have the necklace back, even after I said her name. I huffed, and then smirked when a devious idea came to me.

Walking up behind her, I reached around and grasped her hands—no easy task with her wings, but I managed. I bent closer, my lips brushing her ear, and spoke in my special low tone. "Mi amor, give it back."

She stiffened, and I grinned. Plucking the necklace from her hands, I spoke again before stepping back. "*Gracias, hermosa.*"

Her breath hitched and then a moment later, after I'd gotten several steps away, she shook herself and whirled around.

"Not fair!" she complained, her cheeks pink.

I smirked. "All's fair in love and war, Cielo."

I'd always known that voice did something to her. At the very least it'd always gotten her attention, but now, with that barrier between us gone, even if we hadn't had the chance to sit down and talk about where we stood, I could see just what it did to her.

I could ask endlessly how long this unspoken attraction had been between us, but I knew, deep down I knew, it'd been a similar length of time. But because of my damned childhood declaration, we both tried to pretend it wasn't there. *Maybe if we'd come to realize how foolish we were sooner, we wouldn't be in this awkward predicament we found ourselves now.*

I slipped back into the house to allow her to get back to training, and clear my head. This limbo between us wasn't easy, but I also didn't want to pressure her. She had a lot going on, and I couldn't imagine the difficulties navigating around my and Tyr's declarations to her.

I wished I could point to all the reasons why the answer should be easy—that answer being me—but I knew I couldn't. I wasn't in her position.

Pausing in the kitchen, my fingers drummed on the island counter and I looked down at the pendant in my hand. *Am I making this more difficult for all of us than needed?* I wasn't going to give her up unless she told me to, that much I was sure. But I feared she might avoid this forever if the pressure was too much. *And I know the exact answer she'll have to give both of us if it comes to that…*

Closing my hand around the pendant, I slipped it into my pocket and looked around. I wouldn't let it come to that.

Time passed as I got things together. I pulled out ingredients, pillows and blankets, queued up a movie, and searched for Astrid's favorite selection of bath relaxers.

I felt her, in my mind. This little niggling presence where I was vaguely aware of where she was. I always had a strong connection with her, but this feeling was something… more.

Astrid entered the house around the time I finished drawing hot water. I rushed downstairs to meet her. She was alone, and she was a mess, with her disheveled hair and dirt smeared… everywhere. Her body also drooped with exhaustion.

"They pushed me hard today," she murmured before I could say anything.

"I can see that." I looked around, but we were the only ones in the house. "Where is everyone else?"

She gave a half-hearted shrug. "Said something about participating in a magical fight pit or something."

Her lack of caring showed how exhausted she was. She and Darius had a family tradition of watching UFC fights and wrestling together. No one would know someone as kind as her loved seeing people beat the shit out of each other for entertainment, fame, and money. And if she didn't care about a magic fight pit, she definitely needed this surprise I'd cooked up.

"Well, let's get you relaxing."

I reached for her, but she pathetically tried to push me away. "I'm going to go lay down."

"No, you're going to enjoy this surprise I have."

Her shoulders drooped more. "Diego…"

I slipped my arms around her and guided her to the loft. I'd carry her, but I knew she'd freak out at me for trying that on stairs.

Astrid's feet dragged in her exhaustion and I worried she might actually fall asleep while walking. She'd never been this tired after training. *Why did they push so hard this time?*

Even though she was tired, she still noticed the setup I'd created in our personal lounge up in the loft. "What's that?"

I veered her away and toward her room. "Part of your surprise. But first, a bath."

"Bath?"

Guiding her into her room, I nudged open her bathroom door, where a hot bath with salts and bubbles waited for her.

She gasped. "Diego…"

She looked up at me with watery eyes and wrapped her arms around me, burying her face in my chest. I hugged her back, smiling. I knew she'd appreciate this treatment. *Spoil her. Pamper her. Claim her.*

I shook the strange thoughts from my mind. I didn't understand why they were popping up all of a sudden. I'd never thought to claim someone before. *But I would claim her if she let me.*

When she was ready to pull away, I motioned with my finger. "Turn around."

She eyed me, suddenly suspicious. "I don't know if I should trust you."

I chuckled. "I said turn around, not bend over."

Astrid sucked in a breath through her lips, her cheeks turning a shade of pink. She turned around, and I allowed my gaze to trail down her figure.

I slid my hand along her hip and pulled her against my chest, bending close to her ear. "I'd be sure to warm you up first before I ask you that."

She pressed her lips together, and I felt her weight shift. "As if it'd be easy, like turning the keys of a car."

I hummed thoughtfully, allowing my hands to teasingly trace up her arms and along her collarbone. "I'd take my time. Slow and steady, until you're purring."

She visibly swallowed.

I grinned and finished clasping the necklace around her neck before stepping back. "I hope you like your gift."

Astrid blinked and tipped her head down, now noticing the piece of jewelry. I didn't wait to see her reaction. We could talk about it after she bathed, and at this rate I didn't trust myself not to ask her if she needed help getting into the bath, with nothing on but that necklace. *Turn back. Take her. Claim.*

I paused in the threshold of her room just before leaving, and sucked in a deep breath when an image of her slowly stripping down flitted through my mind's eyes. Her milky, freckled skin, a little bruised but quickly healing with her immortal Valkyrie power, all exquisitely tempting me to touch and feel… to kiss and lick.

I groaned and shook the thoughts from my head, desperately trying to ignore the painful hard-on that image gave me. This was supposed to be a romantic gesture, not a way to seduce her into my bed—yet.

I breezed my way down to the kitchen and distracted myself by making Astrid something to eat. I finished before she completed her bath, but I didn't mind. It gave me time to take a breath and play the guitar.

With Carrie only needing a session once a week, Tyr and Fen being my only frequent sessions, and no outside clients, I'd found myself with more personal time. Any other time, I'd go out for hikes or call up my buddies to go out riding, but that didn't appeal to me these days.

I needed something calm that didn't take me too far away from Astrid. And something that grabbed her attention. Papá made sure I knew one instrument. *"Serenade your señorita, mijo. You'll never lose."*

I sure as hell hoped he was right. Astrid listened to me play all the time. Even if she had something to do, she took time to sit down and enjoy what I played.

My fingers plucked the strings and my hand slid along the guitar neck. I fell into the sound, everything around me slipping away. My mind traveled, following the music where it went through flashes of images and events—memories, I assumed, even of some I didn't recognize. I didn't pause to think on any of them, allowing the music to travel until my hands finally stilled.

A moment after sitting in silence, I looked up where I sensed Astrid's presence. She leaned against the doorframe of her doorway, her hair pulled up in a messy bun with a few strands hanging free to frame her face, and her hand fingering the chain of the necklace I gave her.

"How long have you been there?" I asked.

She shrugged. "Long enough."

My gaze traveled down her body. She wore that teasing gamer crop top and the matching short shorts, instead of just panties. Hunger simmered under my skin.

My eyes flicked back up to meet hers. She didn't flinch.

"Like what you see?" she asked.

"Absolutely."

She pushed off the doorframe and sauntered over. The hypnotic sway of her hips and bounce of her breasts, barely held in by her shirt and tempting a wardrobe malfunction, captured my attention.

She halted at the couch and glanced around at the setup I'd created. "What is all this?"

Resting my guitar on its stand, I gestured to the plate of mozzarella sticks and mug of hot cocoa waiting on the coffee table. "I made you food. Come sit down."

Her eyes lit up, and she squealed. I laughed as she did a little happy dance and rushed over to the plate. Astrid plopped down next to me and bit into the breaded cheese stick. It wasn't warm like I'd wanted, but she clearly didn't care.

I watched her, noting how much better she looked already, if still tired. "How are you feeling?"

She smiled. "That bath really hit the spot. Between it and my accelerated healing, which is still weird to me, I'm only just feeling fatigued."

Astrid lifted her mug and sipped the hot cocoa. "You avoided my question."

I ran my fingers through my hair. "I didn't. Just prioritized."

She gave me a long look that had me chuckling. "This is my way of contributing—of holding up my promise."

Astrid cocked her head. "What do you mean?"

I shrugged. "I can't help you with this training. I can't use the force or shoot laser beams out of my eyes."

She giggled and sipped a little more of her drink.

"I won't be able to fight the big evils in the world with you. I'm just an ordinary mortal man." I gestured to the comfortable lounging setup I'd created with soft lights, pillows, and blankets. "So, I'll help in a way I can. I can give you what you need to relax and heal. I'll make your favorite treats, queue up your favorite movies or games, and make sure you take care of yourself. I'll do whatever normal, mundane thing you need."

Astrid set her mug down and framed my face with her hands. Her soul-piercing eyes stared into mine and then she pressed her forehead against mine. "Thank you. This is exactly what I needed."

I closed my eyes and breathed in, enjoying this simple closeness. "I have *Lord of the Rings* queued up for us to watch. As much as playing some games would be fun, I figured it was best to do something calming."

She pulled away. "Extended edition?"

I smirked. "Of course."

Astrid smiled and then touched the necklace. "Before we do, I have to ask, how does this fit in with all this?"

"It doesn't." I couldn't stop myself from sliding the back of my finger along her hand before pinching the pendant between my fingers. "This is an unrelated gift. I was waiting for the best time to give it, when you caught me with it."

"When did you get it?"

"I've always had it." My thumb traced the tree trunk. "It once belonged to my mom."

Astrid's breath caught, her eyes going wide. She then suddenly started scrabbling for the clasp.

I stared at her, unable to understand what had gotten into her. "Astrid, what are you doing?"

"I can't take this."

My pulse spiked, and I grabbed her hands to make her stop. "Why not?"

She gazed at me. "Because it belonged to your mom. I can't take something that special from you."

I sucked in a deep breath. *It's not a rejection, Diego. It's fine.* "Hear me out, por favor. It belonged to her, but when she gave it to me, she had me make a promise. I was to give it to someone who was special to me. They had to be capable of cherishing it like she did—like I do."

I curved her hands around the pendant. "That person is you, Cielo. I know, no matter what, you'll cherish this."

I hoped she understood what I meant. This wasn't me trying to force an answer out of her. I wanted her to have this, regardless of what happened between us.

Astrid closed her eyes and then nodded before leaning into me, her face pressing against the crook of my neck. "Thank you."

I wrapped her in my arms and rested my cheek on her head. Warmth bloomed in my chest and that near-magnetic pull I felt with her tugged harder, as if telling me we were still not close enough. This was what I wanted—every day, her in my arms. *Claim her.*

"I like it on you," I said. "*Muy bonita.*"

She hummed. "You should speak Spanish more often. I like it when you do."

So, I did. I said so many things to her. Whatever I could think of that told her how I felt about her, as both my friend and the woman I wanted—how smart she was—how talented and tenacious she was—that I loved and hated her stubbornness and how it was such a driving force that encouraged me to never give up—how I didn't have enough words to describe how beautiful and special she was to me.

As my rambling came to an end, I didn't know how much she understood, especially with how quickly I realized I was talking, but it didn't matter. I said what I wanted to say, and I did what she asked. Anything to make her happy.

My fingers slid through her loose strands of hair, grazing her cheek. Astrid gazed up at me with soft, kind eyes that could pierce any defense if I had any against her. My fingers stroked her cheek and her eyes fluttered.

I dipped my head and brushed my lips against hers. She sucked in a quiet breath before tangling her fingers in my hair and embracing me back with her own tender kiss. Our lips moved in sync as the moment stretched on forever, my heart immersing itself in her feel and taste, and all that she was, committing this moment to memory, never wanting it to end.

Astrid pulled away suddenly, her lips pressing tight together. Disappointment swooped in my stomach. I'd done something wrong. Something deep within me writhed, refusing to accept the rejection.

"I'm sorry," she whispered. "I… shouldn't have done that."

My brow furrowed. I didn't understand what she meant.

She didn't meet my gaze. "I've been too busy to think about anything but my training. It's not right for me to—"

"You're not leading me on," I cut in, realizing where this was going. "I don't mean to feel like I'm pressuring you. It wasn't my intention. I just fell into my feelings without thinking." She lay her head on my chest as I tucked her into me. "I'll try to keep myself in check."

She snuggled into me. "It was nice."

I kissed her forehead before reaching for the console controller to start up the movie. I'd take that as a consolation prize.

While I should have paid attention to the movie, with her reciting various lines, I found myself more interested in watching her. Astrid had been quick to blame herself. She always did that. It was a response that had been one of her most difficult to break. Knowing her mother had caused most of her trauma, I better understood where these responses came from.

Her admittance to putting thoughts regarding my confessions to the side didn't surprise me. It wasn't a slight against me, or her way of not wanting to change things between us, even though I'd opened that bag of pixies. It showed the side of her she leaned into too much—the one where she put herself last.

Tyr and I were both vying for her affection. We'd both made that quite clear. But she wasn't thinking about it. She was putting the prospects of love to the side, when it was something she heavily sought just a week ago, because she deemed saving the world more important. *Why can't you put yourself first for once, Astrid?*

My fingers slid along her arm. She didn't react—her slow breathing, and now lack of line-quoting a clear sign that the exhaustion she'd been fighting had won. I took in her peaceful expression, loving the way she found comfort in me, even when there was so much up in the air between us.

I cocked my head and paused my touch when my fingers reached her hip. A still-healing, yellowish bruise peeked out of her waistband. My eyes scanned her body, finding another one around her ribs, and one more on her forearm. My gut clenched—not because of the forearm bruise, but because of the other two.

Astrid had been wearing a t-shirt that covered her stomach when she had come in after her training. I couldn't see these bruises, and yet, they matched the exact placement when I'd pictured her stripping down. How was that possible? Maybe I'd finally cracked after everything I'd been exposed to. I wouldn't be surprised.

"I see her training has caught up to her."

Aya's hushed voice made me jump. We both flinched when Astrid grumbled in her sleep, but luckily she didn't wake up, and instead snuggled into me more in sleepy protest.

I let out a quiet breath. "Don't do that, amiga."

She shot me an apologetic look. "Didn't mean to startle you. How long has she been out?"

"Maybe ten minutes. I made sure she took a relaxing bath and got some food in her before popping the movie on."

Aya smiled. "I can always count on you to make sure she's taken care of, even when she insists on pushing herself too far."

"So, her extra-hard practice was her idea?"

She nodded. "She just wanted to keep going, so I figured we might as well see what would happen. When she uncharacteristically opted not to watch Fen and Tyr beat the snot out of other immortals at the fight pit, I knew she'd pushed herself past her limit."

I ran my fingers through Astrid's hair. "We'll just have to find another time for her to experience that."

Aya smirked. "I'll let everyone else know to be mindful, so she gets her rest. I presume you're fine staying right there?"

"I've got my movie and the perfect woman sleeping in my arms. As long as Angel doesn't require me, I've got no plans to move."

The dog in question lifted her head up from where I'd made her a comfortable bed of blankets and pillows and yawned before snuggling back in.

I chuckled. "And I don't think she's interested in going anywhere right now."

"Well, that's good. Hopefully she'll bother me first, so you don't have to disturb Astrid. She needs the rest. I'll be in my room doing some work if you need me."

"Wait, Aya," I said as she turned her back. "I have a question for you."

She didn't turn around. "Which side I've picked?"

I gauged her posture before speaking. "More of, what's your angle? You've not been subtle at all about your attempts to get the two of us together since college." *Maybe even before that, when she was posing as Abuela Randi.* "But I also know you haven't dissuaded Tyr, either. And you even knew he was looking for her with the intent of trying to get her back. So, what game are you playing?"

"It's not a game. I am a goddess of war and sex and fertility. They are my domains. It's my business to see over many wars, and encourage all relationship possibilities, and have fun while doing it."

She turned, her eyes a startling seriousness I'd never seen in her before. "But Astrid is different. She is not a fun game where I have no stake in the end outcome, regardless of the result. My angle is seeing her happy. I want her to make choices that ensure that outcome happens. I will offer her whatever advice she asks, without forcing an opinion or trying to sway her in one direction over another, because I can't decide what will make her happy. I can only advise her on the two excellent choices in front of her."

I watched the goddess closely. "What advice did you give her?"

"That she had four options to choose from."

My brow furrowed. *Four?* "What are they?"

Aya grinned and turned away. "You already know them."

She walked off without another word. *I know the options?* Sure, I knew of three. Pick me, pick Tyr, or neither of us. But what was the fourth? Both?

Everything in me paused. I looked down at Astrid's peaceful form. *Is that an option?*

TWENTY

ASTRID

The brush snagged on a tangle in my hair. I grumbled and worked it out gently before continuing. I was trying not to rush, but I also didn't want to be late.

Aya was out getting last-minute touches set up in the event field with her magic, and she told me all I had to do was get ready at this ungodly hour of the morning. Except, beyond my clothes, which were fairly straightforward to put on, I wasn't sure what I was supposed to do about hair and makeup. I knew this was a test for me and my memories, but damn, was it frustrating.

Unsure what to do with my hair once I finished brushing it, I let it be for now and worked on dressing. *Maybe putting on the clothes will jump-start something.*

Around the time I was sure my dress was on right, someone knocked on my door, and then Tyr's voice drifted in. "Astrid?"

He poked his head in before I got the chance to answer. I gasped and brushed one of my legs behind the other. "Wait, my ankles are showing!"

He laughed. "How indecent."

I stuck my tongue out. "Maybe that'll teach you to wait to be called into a lady's room instead of walking in immediately."

Tyr paused and made an apologetic face while rubbing the back of his neck. "Ah, yeah, sorry about that. Old habit. I'll be sure not to do that again."

I nodded. He'd done this a few times this week. Nothing compromising, and he was always sincere in his apology. I could understand where he came from now that I had so many memories. Hardly any were of the two of us and the life we had, but a part of me accepted I'd been his wife once, and being around me would trick him into leaning on past behaviors if he wasn't diligent.

I cocked my head when I realized there was something different about him, beyond him wearing time-period-appropriate attire that matched my memories. "Your hair is long."

He ran his hand through the long chestnut strands. "Aya's idea. She thought it might help. We're pretending it's a wig."

"You seem uncomfortable."

He shrugged. "It's been a long time since I first chopped most of my hair off. And feeling her magic buzz around my head is strange."

I gazed at him, an urge hitting me. "Mind if I do something?"

He grinned. "You can do whatever you want to me, Valkyrie."

I rolled my eyes, fighting back a wave of heat that smile created in me, and then motioned for him to sit on my bed. When he did, I let my body run on instinct, taking strands of his hair between my fingers and braiding them.

This felt so normal. My past said it was. Memories flickered in, filling in that gap of why. Simple and sweet moments, where he let me play with his hair all the time, for whatever reason I wanted.

Tyr held up a wooden box made of red wood while I worked. "I brought these for you. I thought you might want to use some with your outfit again."

Pausing my work, I took the box. A carving of Yggdrasill covered the lid, with gemstones embedded into the wood around her roots. Runes and smaller images complimented the tree and gems, adorning the box on all sides. The silver hinges on the box were sturdy, and the craftsman had even taken the time to detail those as well. *He gave this to me for a special occasion…*

I flicked open the lid. Inside was a stunning selection of jewelry. Familiarity rushed over me as I fingered through the contents, as did another sensation. It reminded me of my magic, but also… different.

I stopped when I found some metal beads. More memories flitted through my mind. "I had you break some of these. After… after Odin killed Kirby."

"That's right."

"It was raining that day… no, it was a storm. I'd been out in it because Leif and I had a disagreement." I squinted, thinking hard, then frowned. "That's all I have of that day."

Tyr hummed thoughtfully and leaned closer. His gaze on me was intense, and my heart thumped hard against my ribcage. "I'd be willing to incur Aya's wrath, making you late if you'd like a reminder."

His powerful scent wrapped around me, along with his large presence. My pulse picked up, and I swallowed and my body reacted to an idea of a reminder it wanted. *Sex. Sex happened in this missing memory.*

Flashes of a timber home warmed by a fire, fighting over a tunic, me straddling his lap, the feeling of a dress ripping—I tore my gaze away and focused on my box's contents. I… wasn't ready for such intense reminders.

Tyr chuckled, as if he could see the memories that came back to me. The heat flooding my face was most definitely an obvious blush.

I found more beads and rings I had liked, my favorite pair of earrings, and—I pulled out a simple but beautiful necklace with beads and a center pendant carved with a swirling pattern dedicated to Freya. "You bought this for me. In the market."

I made a face. "After the king tried to make me marry him."

Tyr laughed. "And you tried to fight me the whole way with every purchase I made."

My lips twisted. "I'm not much better now, either. Just ask my dad and Diego."

Tyr snorted. "That doesn't surprise me."

Something is missing in here. There was plenty of jewelry to choose from, but a dark spot in my memories niggled my mind. Something important. I didn't go anywhere without them. Bracelets? The memory burst to life. Many of them.

"Tyr, what happened to the bracelets you and Baldur gave me? It was on the same day…" I paused to process. "You were annoyed he didn't wait for some reason. And I almost always wore them after that."

He frowned. "The battle with Odin. Mine broke and his was missing from your wrist. We never found the lost one."

"Oh…" My gut twisted. One less thing I had from Baldur. *He did give me other gifts. Maybe they'd survived the test of time.*

I gazed at the jewelry. "I'm surprised all of this is in such good condition. The fact so much lasted during my time as an immortal, let alone to this point."

Tyr tapped on the box. "You got good at enchanting items. The box protects them from the typical breakdown of time."

I pursed my lips. That explained the sensation I felt. "Hopefully, I'll figure out this magic shit better and be able to enchant items again."

Tyr rested his hand on my leg. "You will. I have faith in you, like I always have."

Warmth seeped through my leg and throughout my body. I swallowed hard as he held eye contact with me, my heart's pace picking up erratically. An invisible pull tugged at me, urging me to be closer, but I wasn't sure I wanted to heed it. I knew what that pull wanted, but I didn't know what I wanted.

Sometimes I thought I did, and then the next moment I was unsure again. This was all so confusing.

I tore my gaze away to pick through my jewelry.

It was better this way right now. I hadn't really told anyone, but I couldn't say I understood who I was anymore. I understood what everyone expected me to be, on different levels, but that made things worse.

How could I make important decisions for myself if I didn't know who I was?

Tyr touched my elbow. "Valkyrie, what's wrong?"

I paused, conflicting emotions flickering through me like always lately when he called me that. "I'm just… processing."

"You tend to get quiet when you remember things," he said.

"I just need time to figure things out."

His grip tightened just a bit. "You never come to us to help you, though."

I shrugged. "What can you do to help me?"

"I don't know," he admitted. "But I want to, however you need me to."

I looked up at him. "Have you ever gone through life knowing who you were, only to have that security ripped away one day, and you're left trying to figure things out under a deadline?"

Tyr frowned. "No, I suppose I can't say I have."

"Don't get me wrong, Tyr, I'm glad to know more about the world I live in, and I get to experience some cool shit with people who are awesome. I am enjoying learning new things and experiencing the memories of the people I knew, and seeing how I can incorporate those bonds into my life now. I accept this past I'm remembering was mine. It's just not as easy as fitting a round peg into a round hole. I have to process each memory and feeling, and figure out how that affects who I am and my understanding of that person. And right now... I can't say I know who I am."

And there was the truth, out in the open.

He worked his jaw. "Do you want us to stop? Would you rather... we walked away?"

"No. I just want people to be patient with me." I pulled his large hand between my smaller ones. "I need *you* to be patient with me. I know this isn't easy on you in different ways. I can't imagine being in your shoes and having to measure your expectations after you spent so much time and energy to get me back. And I'm sorry I can't live up to those exact—"

"No." He curled his hand around mine. "I don't want you to apologize. I was warned not to have these expectations when we started this path I forced us all down, and I didn't listen. That is for me to handle, not you. I have made it clear, I'm not here to cause you problems. I've been open about what I would like, and I'm not ashamed of that, but that doesn't mean you have to give what I've asked for."

Tyr squeezed my hand. "I want you to figure out who you are first, and then decide what you want. And I will respect whatever you choose."

Warmth bloomed in my chest. I appreciated his honesty, and I did find his boldness quite appealing.

But there was something I wanted to know that I hadn't known how to bring up. And now seemed the best chance I'd get. "How often do you compare the present me to the past?"

Tyr didn't respond right away. His eyes grew contemplative and his tongue absently dragged along his lower lip. My gaze followed and an urge to lean in and kiss him—to taste him—like I did on the deck earlier this week, flashed through me.

He opened his mouth to speak finally when Diego appeared in my doorway. "Hey, Astrid, you decent?"

I peered around Tyr. "What is it with people barging into my room before me acknowledging them today?"

He rubbed the back of his neck. "Sorry. Aya's back, and she has some people she wants you to meet. Seemed important with how many of them there are."

My brow pulled together. She hadn't said anything to me about me meeting anyone important today. Hell, she made sure I understood that today I was supposed to have fun and relax so that if I did remember things, it wouldn't cause a scene around the townsfolk. "How many people?"

"Like, twenty."

My eyes bugged, and I looked up at Tyr, who shook his head. "I know nothing about this."

"Well, I guess we'll find out," I said. "Can you let her know I'll be down in a minute? I need to finish Tyr's hair, as well as my own."

I wasn't meeting anyone until I had my hair done. I could walk around without makeup just fine, but I refused to look half-put-together.

Diego agreed and left, though not before his gaze lingered on me for a moment. I watched him go, enjoying the view of him in his tan tunic with the way his belts hung around his hips. He pulled off this reenactment look quite nicely.

With people waiting, I focused on finishing Tyr's hair, adding a few beads into my work. We could finish our discussion later.

When I finished, that left me with my own hair, and I wasn't sure where to start. "How did I used to wear my hair?"

Tyr thought for a moment. "You had a few styles, but the style you went with the most was two large front braids, with the rest allowed to drape over your back."

I squinted as I tried to remember doing my hair this way, and after a moment, those memories flitted through my mind. I immediately went to work braiding locks of hair and then holding them tight at the end in a decorative bead cuff. Tyr helped me with a few other hair decorations, as well as a headband I remembered wearing frequently before being married, and I also put my necklace and earrings on.

"I have something else for you," Tyr said when I was finally satisfied. He untied a vambrace on his belt that I hadn't noticed before and handed it to me.

I took the piece of armor and turned it in my hands. Warmth and longing filled my chest. "This belonged to my mother."

I'd inherited them after she'd died, and rarely went out without them.

"But, where is the other?"

"It's still safely stored away. I thought it'd be difficult to wear with this." Tyr tugged on the vambrace he had around his wrist and removed it.

He handed it to me, and I stared at it in my hands, taking in its worn state. This had seen better days, but had yet to succumb to ruin thanks to an enchantment I felt on it.

"This is… Baldur's."

"It's a bit big for you, and it doesn't match your mother's, but I thought, with everything going on, you might want to wear it."

I held the vambrace against my chest, my heart aching. These memories I had with him… they hurt. Unlike the others, this was one person in the past I'd never be able to rekindle anything with, and there was nothing I could do but grieve in silence.

"This one also doesn't have a pair," I managed to say without choking up.

Tyr scowled. "Loki took the other as a trophy before I could kill him after finding him kneeling over Baldur's body."

The pain in my chest hardened, and my grip on the vambrace tightened. "The cocky bastard will pay for that."

Tyr nodded and then rested a gentle hand on mine. "But for now, let's work on getting through today."

He was right. It wasn't like we'd run into Loki at the festival.

Sliding both vambraces on, and doing a little extra finagling to make sure Baldur's stayed secure—I'd have super glued it to my arm if that was going to be needed—I found myself ready to face whatever guest Aya had in store for me.

Tyr followed me out of my room. My skirts swished around my feet, almost trying to trip me up on the stairs. Tyr took the stairs so close behind, I wasn't sure what would be my undoing first.

When I reached the landing in the foyer, I looked around for Aya and these supposed guests. No one was inside, and someone left the front door wide open to allow the bugs in.

Angel appeared in the doorway and barked, wagging her tail, her tongue lolling.

"We're outside," Aya called.

I think my familiar and best friend are conspiring against me. It was strange to call Angel a familiar, especially knowing she wasn't official still, until I worked out my magic a bit more, but Aya insisted I get used to it now, so it'd feel natural by the time that happened.

I shook the thoughts from my head and walked outside. Aya and Diego hung out on the porch, and just as Diego had warned me, a good twenty or so people mingled together outside in period attire.

Most were men, though a few women added to their numbers, and they clustered around a tall and burly man. He had blond hair shaved on both sides of his head and the rest pulled back into a ponytail, and tattoos littered his light skin.

Even though he stood with his back to me, and he had an imposing aura about him, there was something… familiar about him.

One person noticed me, turning their attention my way. Then another. And then another. As they did, their faces flickered to life memories deep within me.

The man in front of me turned around last. An intricate bear paw tattoo on his chest peeked out around the collar of his tunic. His green eyes went wide. "Astrid."

Silence filled the air. My pulse fluttered under my skin, memories licking the back of my mind, but not quite surfacing.

"It really is you," the man said. "Aya wasn't pulling a fast one on us."

"I told you I wasn't," Aya muttered. "No faith in me. The hel has happened to our followers? Seriously."

Laughter rumbled through the gathered people, though all of this barely registered with me. I stared at the man, and took a step closer.

He smiled. "Do you remember me, Astrid?"

All at once, memories flashed through my mind of a man who would have been my husband had it not been for a chance offer to a god my father made when he delivered our family from injustice. A man who became a close friend when I encouraged him to follow his heart, and who I practiced my magic on to ready for the time I'd finally join battles or raids.

The man before me became a confidant when I found my immortality, a shoulder to cry on, and to equally console when we both lost our fathers to the same battle, and then later when I lost my brother. The man I helped through his own ascension to immortality when his time came.

A smile pulled up my face so high, my cheeks hurt, and warmth nearly exploded out of my chest. "Bjarke!"

I launched off the porch, ignoring all the steps. Bjarke caught me in his arms and spun me around. I hugged him tight around the neck and laughed, my chest swelling.

When he finally put me down, I smiled up at him and found myself crowded. Each person—each face, I knew, and put a name to. "What are you all doing here, growly pants?"

Bjarke skimmed his hair. "Aya asked us to help with some cultural festival she was putting on. She wouldn't tell us why, but was insistent we needed to help. Since it's her, we agreed."

"Then she sprang it on us, right before teleporting us here, that it had to do with you," Aric, a tan, middle-aged man with graying golden-brown hair, said.

I nodded. "That makes sense. My safety hinged on no one knowing about my existence until now."

Bjarke shook his head. "This is so surreal. You're really here. And… you did die, right? You look different, but…"

I *booped* his nose. "It's a long story. But, yes, I died. A lot of magic was used to bring me back, but not as I was. I was born and lived a brand new life, and I'm still recovering memories from the past. We're hoping what's missing will recover during this festival and it'll help us find the shifter who killed me."

The air around us tensed, and Bjarke snarled a bear-like snarl. "They're still alive?"

I nodded. "We're fairly certain it's an immortal wolf shifter."

A chorus of wolf and bear-like snarls echoed around me. It sent a shiver down my spine, though not an unpleasant one. I knew this sound so intimately. I'd lived with these Berserkers. I'd fought with them. I'd experienced their protectiveness. It was nice that even after all this time, they'd provide that to me again.

Bjarke's head twitched, a sign he was fighting a shift. "Whatever you need, you've got it from us."

I smiled. "I know I can always count on all of you. Is this all of you who have managed to survive after all this time?"

Bjarke rocked his head. "A few stayed in Runavík, not hearing this was all being done for you. Others either died during the war with Odin, or unfortunately met their end during the various purges the mortals caused."

My fists clenched. The very idea that those I once cared for met such horrific, prejudiced ends infuriated me. "I'm surprised Runavík is still around."

He grunted. "What, do you think I'd give up my Jarl position? No. Randi, one of Leif's descendants, still lives back home. She erected a protective barrier there to keep us hidden. You won't find Runavík on any map."

My back straightened. *A descendant of Leif's?* I wondered how many were out there after Aya had mentioned some of the family line still existed.

"You're always welcome home," he said. "Those who stayed behind will be kicking themselves for missing this. Townsfolk who have only grown up hearing your stories will want to meet the legend herself. And I'm sure you'll want to meet Randi."

Home. Images of Runavík flashed through my mind. No doubt it was different now, but this was how I remembered it to be. And how strange that it invoked a longing in me similar to when I left this place. It seemed, with my soul filling in with more memories, it wanted more than it had in a long time.

A house on a lake island appeared in my memories, and an even more intense homesickness washed over me. *That place...* My and Tyr's home. We lived there with...

I glanced around, feeling as though I was missing something... or someone. My eyes fell to a small woman hiding just behind those gathered around me. Large gossamer wings hung limply on her back, draping on the ground behind her, drawing my gaze to her ethereal tail lazily swishing back and forth.

I took a step closer to her; the Berserkers surrounding me made a path. Instead of rounding at the tips, the woman's ears had a pointed edge, and she blinked up at me with large, multi-colored eyes. "Ùna?"

The woman's eyes lit up, and her wings shimmered and then tried to flutter. "Astrid!"

Energy welled up in me as vibrant memories came with the uttering of her name and the sound of her lilted accent. I rushed to the fae, scooping her up in my arms and holding her close.

She wrapped her dainty arms around me and cried. "You're back! You came back."

"Yes, I'm here." I did everything that I could to hold back the tears that threatened to leak from my face. I embraced the joy this brought me. I loved the memories I was recovering of her. This tiny, important fae was one of my most precious memories.

Ùna finally pulled away, and I flinched when she smacked me on the head. "Don't you ever do that again. You promised."

I chuckled, smiling at her. "And I didn't break my promise. I came back, just as I said."

"Yes, you're right." She hugged me around the neck again. "And you'd better not go anywhere again."

I laughed. "I'll do my best."

After a moment longer of embracing, we let each other go, though she didn't leave my side, grabbing my dress with a small hand.

I noticed how intently Diego watched the scene in front of him. I winced, smiling at him apologetically. "You probably want some introductions."

He chuckled. "I knew if I was patient, I'd be looped in, eventually."

I introduced everybody, one by one. "Ùna is an elf, and everyone else but Siobhán are Berserkers."

Diego looked at the stocky, dark-skinned woman with curly black hair and amber eyes, wearing a green dress different from the other women gathered. A gold torc and natural jewelry decorated her neck, wrists, and hair. "What are you, if you don't mind me asking?"

She smiled and spoke in soft tones wrapped in a lilted accent. "I am a druid."

He tilted his head. "You'll have to explain to me what that is. I'm still new to all this."

Siobhán continued to smile. "We are descendants of elf and human breeding. Diluted our blood may be, we retain our ability to touch nature, and our lives are extended over our pure human counterparts, should we not unlock immortality in our souls."

"How did a druid get mixed up with a bunch of temperamental werebeasts?"

His comment received a rumble of amused chuckles.

Siobhán's sharp gaze darted to Hilda, a burly woman who looked like she bench-pressed Siobhán on the regular. Hilda smirked. "One might say, their wildness was appealing for a free spirit like me."

She then refocused on Diego. "What are you?"

He shrugged. "Your everyday mortal man."

Siobhán cocked her head, her eyes contemplative. "Are you sure? The energies surrounding you are much different than that of a typical mortal."

I pursed my lips. That was quite strange. I didn't sense anything different about Diego, though to be fair to myself, my magic wasn't the same as Siobhán's, and I still wasn't nearly as skilled as I once was. "Have you seen this energy before?"

She nodded slowly. "Once, yes. But…" She shook her head. "It couldn't be possible. Never mind me."

I looked to Ùna. "Are you able to see this, too?"

The small fae nodded. "Yes, though I don't know this energy Siobhán means. I've never met anyone with it. Perhaps nature favors him similarly to the being Siobhán means."

"I do enjoy the outdoors," Diego said.

Ùna beamed. "That could explain it."

Perhaps it was, but I had to admit to myself, something about that conclusion didn't sit with me as fully correct. I couldn't say why, maybe it was Valkyrie instinct, maybe it was something else. Either way, it wasn't like we'd get answers anytime soon.

Diego's eyes swept over the gathered Berserkers. "There's a larger male-to-female ratio here. Is that the norm for Berserkers, or just this group?"

"It's rare for our souls to resonate with the Berserker spirit," Hilda said. "The shift is taxing on the body, and few female bodies can handle the stress."

"Odin also never intended for women to inherit the Berserker soul," Aya supplied. "It was a surprise to us all he even made the first Berserkers capable of producing children, though it ended up being a blessing, given he forgot how to make more, and Berserkers were so prone to dying in battle."

Diego's brow furrow. "Why was that a surprise?"

"Because when he made his Valkyries, who were created before the Berserkers, he made them infertile," Tyr said.

I blinked. I hadn't even known that.

"He was a paranoid and possessive old bastard," Aya nearly spat. "He frequently admitted he didn't want his precious Valkyries *tainted* by another man's seed. Any Valkyrie who took an outside lover also found themselves deemed *disloyal*."

My stomach twisted. What a disgusting man. It made me wonder how much of Kirby's extreme punishment had to do with his demented thoughts. Then another thought hit me. "Wait, Aya, then how did Magnus become pregnant?"

Aya placed a hand on her hip. "Because she's not one of Odin's Valkyries. That's confirmed to us that Kirby and the Valkyrie souls she is unlocking are different from his originals. It's why I told you to be careful."

Eyes turned to me. Bjarke tipped his head. "Uh, what?"

I smiled weakly and held up my hands. "Surprise, I'm a real Valkyrie now!"

A clamor of excitement built around me. Naturally, several thought I'd been a Valkyrie in my first life, and I had to explain to them I never was. Then came the requests to see the wings. Aya assured me she'd made subtle slits in my dress to accommodate as a "just in case" so there wouldn't be any issues showing them off.

If they'd been excited with the news before, it was nothing compared to the moment my wings popped out. It was as if seeing a Valkyrie invigorated their Berserker spirits. I didn't doubt it. Valkyries and Berserkers had a connection. I suspected it was a major contributing factor to why I had the bonds I did with my Berserkers.

Even if I hadn't been an official Valkyrie in the past, I strongly surmised my Valkyrie-like tendencies back then that earned me my title were a hint at what my soul was meant to be.

Bjarke eventually calmed everyone down and had Aya spirit them off. I'd caused a slight delay in the schedule—not that anyone minded, but we needed to be sure everyone was in place for all the visitors who would begin entering the festival grounds within the hour.

Bjarke stayed, wanting a rundown of what happened leading up to their involvement in the event. I needed to put my makeup on and invited him inside so we could do both.

Una grabbed my hand. "I will do your makeup. We will use fae compounds so you stop poisoning your body with these commercial human brands. It will be good for your magic, too."

She had insisted this before with me in the past. Something about the makeup the fae used did have a positive effect on me back then. I would have guessed it was because people didn't understand the toxic properties of the materials they were using, unlike now. But if Ùna still felt that way, I wouldn't argue.

"How do you know Astrid can use magic?" Diego asked while Ùna pulled out makeup from what looked like thin air.

"Like you, Nature Blessed, there is an aura around Astrid," Ùna said. "It's not the same as us fae or you, but common for the few humans who can touch magic and don't have fae or demon ancestry."

He leaned on the island counter. "What do you mean by 'few humans'? No one has seemed surprised Astrid has magic in this life, but it sounds like it should be questioned."

"We're not actually sure how Astrid has magic," Tyr said. "It's possible the ritual used on her soul has caused her magic to transfer to her new body, or it's something else."

"I suspect it's the ritual," Ùna said. "That was powerful magic Freya used. And, unless Astrid has a magic ancestor in this life, it is unlikely she is naturally the first of her new blood line. It's too rare."

My brow knitted together. *Could I have an ancestor who could use magic?* It was possible. We had Scandinavian blood, that was evident even by our family name, but also Dad was open about our family history. He even had documents about a few prominent members of the family, though none of them screamed "secret witch" or anything.

There was Dad's heathenism to consider. He followed a lot of old rituals that he claimed were passed down. I hadn't actually asked my gods about that, not even Aya, despite her knowing he was a practitioner.

"Why is it rare?" Diego asked. "If one human can do it, why can't more?"

Ùna shrugged and started applying a foundation to my face. "A long time ago, before my time, humans could touch magic in great abundance. But, something happened, and now only a rare handful are capable of harnessing that same power."

My memories told me magic was rare. It was why so many were surprised that my family had been a long line of witches, and continued to be so from what Bjarke mentioned. And yet, this information Ùna gave was a surprise to me. "So, no one knows what happened?"

She shook her head. "The oldest fae sometimes tell stories of a time where humans achieved a great many things with their magic, and lived peacefully with all other creatures of the world. But some dark event stole the magic and brought great ruin on the humans."

Diego's brow knitted. "That would imply there was civilization beyond what is in our recorded history."

The small fae gazed up at him, but before she said anything, Sean waltzed into the house. "In a world of gods and powerful immortal beings, is it so strange to you that someone might have changed history as most know it, in order to protect us from experiencing such a horror again?"

Diego made a thoughtful sound in his throat. "You've got a point."

Ùna rushed over to Sean and greeted him by clasping their hands together. "Aengus, it's so good to see you."

He smiled pleasantly. "It's good to see you again, too, Ùna. I go by Sean these days."

She nodded. "I will remember that."

"Astrid, Aya has informed me she recruited some others of Celtic origin for this festival of yours, and I've decided to join them."

I smiled. Sean didn't involve himself in much, so when he did, I never said no. "I'd love it if you added some of your flair to things."

Ùna looked to me and then Tyr. "I would like to join that as well, unless you need me for anything you have planned."

I didn't have any plans, but then again, I had only just barely remembered her.

"You know you don't need permission to do things, Ùna," Tyr said. "Even if we'd planned for something specific that included you, we could work around it."

The little fae's damaged wings tried to flutter in her excitement, and she hummed to herself as she went back to working on my face.

Bjarke tapped on the island counter. "So, about that explanation."

I shot him an apologetic look and gave him a quick rundown of the events leading up to today.

"So, this elaborate plan is to gain back the rest of your memories so we might possibly find the bastard hunting you?" Bjarke asked.

"Yeah, that's about the gist of it." I didn't open my eyes as Ùna applied some form of eyeshadow.

"And if the memories don't help?"

I shrugged. "Then we'll just magic the fuck out of the problem until we conjure a solution."

He barked out a laugh. "Just the response I expect. Excellent. Whatever you need, we'll do our best to help. Our loyalty to you won't end, even after our deaths."

I opened my eyes and smiled up at him, my chest swelling. "I know."

TWENTY-ONE

ASTRID

The festival grounds bustled with activity, the air alive with the sounds of laughter and music. People from all over came to experience the event Aya had coordinated, a feat only she could pull off, with the mix of mortal reenactors and immortals we shared a past with. In these last few hours, I had seen a variety of people, from those wearing street clothes to those donning their favorite costumes and cosplays.

Activities were set up everywhere, from craft-making to battle training, feats of strength, games, and drinking and feasting. Bjarke wandered around the fake town that'd been erected, acting as the Jarl. His mortal wife, Alecia, accompanied him.

Tyr and Fen were off a little ways from me, teaching children how to perform the perfect shield wall. Kirby and Starkad, whom I happily greeted the moment I saw him, were teaching the adults. Her partner Gwydion hung with Siobhán, Sean, and Úna, to create a small Celtic bubble of information. The two fae donned human disguises.

Kirby's other partner, Min, volunteered to play a household adja-cent from Aya and me, with Carrie and Raeni. Carrie, upon meeting him, managed to call him "handsome" and "a sexy beefcake" in one sentence and have it make complete sense. Though that may have had to do more with me knowing Min was a sex god than anything.

Her last partner, Brit, had disappeared somewhere. Much like Dahlia, who sat nearby splitting her attention between watching Fen and Frey, she wasn't doing so much participating, other than being moral support.

Frey and Diego engaged in a flyting, the Old Norse version of a rap-off, going back and forth with no clear winner yet. Aya had been the instigator of the match, but what impressed me most was Diego's ability to keep up with Frey. I had no idea he had this kind of skill.

As for me, I crushed some herbs in a mortar. I'd grown bored of sewing a shirt I was supposed to finish before the event, and decided this was a better choice to keep me busy.

Aya hadn't planned a lot of activities for me. She just wanted me to slip into the simulated time period and allow my memories to flow freely—and it worked.

Between the people I knew, Runavík's replication, and various activi-ties, my mind flooded with memories—nothing that actually helped us in the end with my death, but a piece of me felt a little more whole with each memory.

It was a strange feeling to accept, and it defied logic. *Why should experiencing a past life of mine make me feel whole? Why can't I feel whole without it? Does that make this current life fake?*

I shook the negative thoughts from my head. Losing all sense of who you were and trying to find the real you wasn't easy. I was trying to be gentle with myself, and accept whoever came out at the end, but I did have my concerns, too. I constantly questioned whether my thoughts and feelings belonged to me, or a past version of me, whereas before, I would have always assumed it was me. I didn't trust myself, and that was maybe the most unsettling part of not understanding who I was anymore.

The flyting ended, Frey coming out victorious. People cheered and clapped before Aya ushered them on to me with her special guided tour. I knew what to do, taking up my part as a völva. My past guided me through the motions and lectures, from herbs and healing to rituals.

I even leaned on Dad's teachings and performed several blood rituals that the onlookers believed were fake, but I'd secretly used real animal blood. And it was clear, to my eyes, that it had their desired effect on the gods here I'd performed these for. To an untrained eye, some might think they were joining in the revelry of the ritual, but it was clear to everyone else that gods didn't get the same power boost from sacrifices and prayer that they had in the past. *I'm going to have to add this to my list to do on the regular.* We needed the gods to be at their highest strength possible if we were going to win this fight.

After my demonstration, Aya guided the tour away for a bit, giving me a breather. Diego sat down with me and whittled on some wood. He wasn't very good, but it gave him something to do. And I also gave him a few pointers, even going as far as taking his hands in mine to show him when he insisted he didn't understand. I wasn't fooled, but he was a little too charming to resist.

Some of it reminded me of my time with my brother. He ended up taking over the family trade, as was customary at the time, but my father hadn't prevented me from learning or teaching Leif when he was old enough to start. It sent a pang of longing through me. *I miss them.*

My attention was drawn away by the sounds of Tyr and Fen roaring. The children with them also roared, imitating their brawny teachers. The way Tyr handled the children made my ovaries do an annoying happy dance. *If I could punch my own ovaries, I would.*

Unfortunately, that wasn't the end of my hormonal torment.

A little girl wandered away from the sewing activity Hilda oversaw and came up to Diego. He smiled at her and encouraged her curiosity, taking her into his arms and showing her the same techniques I'd just taught him, in a gentle and safe way so she wouldn't get hurt but still could give the whittling a try. *Yup, I'm doomed.*

I rose. A walk would do me some good. "Does anyone need anything? Going to stretch my legs."

Diego looked up at me. "Food would be great."

A few others agreed. I grabbed a basket so I could bring some back immediately, and planned to have more delivered.

"While you're wandering around, can you keep an eye out for Raeni?" Carrie asked. "She went to get something to drink a bit ago and hasn't returned. I'm sure she got distracted with everything going on, but I just want to make sure."

I smiled. "Of course I can."

Holding my basket against my hip, I wandered at a leisurely pace. I wouldn't take too long to get everyone's food, but I didn't need to rush. And it was good for me to do this. Much like I did in my current life, my memories told me I used to go out for aimless walks on the regular just to have some time alone and think.

There was no pressure, no one breathing down my neck with expectations—just me and my thoughts, something I needed. Remembering so much had taken its toll on me.

I gasped when I collided with something solid and stumbled back, my basket clattering on the ground. The decently sturdy object I'd collided with grunted. I snapped my attention up and my eyes went wide. I'd walked right into a pale man with gaunt features and black hair. He had a large scar cutting across his face.

A feeling of familiarity came about with this man, and not in a good way. I couldn't pull a memory with any clarity as to where I'd met him.

"I am so sorry," I blurted. "I was so lost in my thoughts I wasn't looking where I was going."

He chuckled and picked up my basket. When he offered it to me, he rasped, "No harm done."

An almost too-difficult-to-hear voice whispered along my senses. *"Be wary, Sister."*

A shiver ran down my spine when my eyes met his strange amber-gold ones. Something deep inside me screamed to run. *This man isn't safe.*

He continued down his path. "Take care where you step, young völva. You don't want to accidentally run into trouble."

My feet moved without my say-so, my pulse thrumming in my veins. I needed to get away from here ASAP and still I didn't know why. *He called me völva.* Of course he had. Aya had used me in her tour. He probably was part of that group, and since we were to be in character as much as possible, people would respond to that.

And yet, I couldn't shake the feeling plaguing me that danger was right around the corner.

Rounding the bend, I came face-to-face with a wall of people. Peering around them, I found them waiting in line for one of the food stalls. *Good thing those working the event get to skip the line.* I didn't want to think how long it'd take to get my food otherwise.

Weaving around the crowd, I looked for the employee line I'd been told about earlier. I smiled when I found Raeni standing in that line. She noticed my approach and waved.

"Come to find me?" she asked.

I shook my head. "Your mom was curious where you went, and asked me to keep an eye out for you, but I'm here to stretch my legs and get everyone food."

"Is Mom doing okay without me there?"

I nodded. "You're able to go off on your own without worry."

She toed a rock on the ground. "She's doing really great lately, and it's all thanks to you and Diego, so I try not to worry, but I can't help it. My father really messed her up, and it's taken her so long to get to this point. I'm seeing so much of the mom I knew when I was little, it's amazing. But I'm worried she'll disappear again, too."

Raeni rarely did therapy sessions now that she was a teen. We'd managed when she was younger, and it'd been good for her, given how deeply the situation with her father affected them both, but as she hit adolescence, she became more resistant to talk. We never pushed, knowing she'd come around when she was ready.

"Do you want to talk?" I asked her. She'd know what I was implying.

Raeni chewed her lip and then shook her head. "Not right now."

I respected that and didn't push. Instead, I made an order of food to be delivered to everyone, and a pitcher of mead and some fruit for me to carry back. Raeni was hungry now, so she got herself a bowl of stew.

"What do you think?" I asked her as we made our way back.

She pursed her lips. "It's interesting. It's like I'm tasting more than what veggies and meats are in here."

"That's because the broth is created from several days' worth of stewing. When the ingredients are done cooking, they're taken out with a little bit of broth, and the next batch of ingredients is added."

She made a thoughtful sound. "Interesting. I think I'll still stick with our modern meals, especially with Mister Xavier's cooking."

I chuckled. We were quite spoiled, with him being a former professional chef.

"Thank you," she said. "For picking Min to play family with us for this. He's so gentle with her, and I haven't seen Mom this happy in so long."

I watched as several emotions flickered across her face.

"I hope one day she'll be able to find someone new. Someone better, who will love her like she's their entire world." She flicked a braid over her shoulder. "And maybe they'll be willing to be my new dad."

I rested a gentle hand on her shoulder. "They will. You're the most precious thing to your mother. She wouldn't settle for less for either of you."

She gave me an appreciative smile.

A flash of orange-red caught the corner of my eye. I turned, and the world around me seemed to slow as I watched a red-haired woman walk down the road. I froze, everything in my body winding tight. My pulse pounded in my ears, and my throat dried. *It can't be...*

"Astrid?" Raeni tentatively asked.

"Flee, Sister!"

I broke out of my state and whipped around, grabbing Raeni by the arm and hastening our steps away.

"Astrid, what's wrong?" Raeni asked.

"Give me a moment." My mind raced, and I tried desperately to calm myself down. *It wasn't her. It wasn't her.* There was no way she was here. Red hair wasn't unique. The shade of red we had was common. I didn't see her face. Maybe subconsciously I had when she passed, but I didn't actively see it. So, I had no reason to think it was her. *So why can't I ignore my instinct to run?*

"Astrid, you're hurting my arm," Raeni whimpered.

I gasped and released her. "Sorry."

She rubbed her arm. "What happened?"

I chewed my lip and shook my head. "I saw someone who… looked a lot like my mother."

Raeni gazed down at me, her eyes sympathetic. "She's like my dad, isn't she?"

I nodded. She slid her hand into mine and squeezed.

Taking a deep, calming breath, I squeezed back and smiled. I wouldn't allow that woman to poison my day. She wasn't here. She had no idea where I was. *I should have worn my protection necklace.*

When we made it back to the others, they were all grouped up differently, and Aya had an eager look about her. No, it was more than that. She smirked in a way that made my insides crawl with apprehension. *What is she up to?* "Need more of my magic?"

The smirk didn't disappear. "No, I need you for something completely different."

"Why do I feel like it's going to make me want to punch you?"

"Because you love me."

I rolled my eyes. This only meant one thing: it was going to get real uncomfortable between me and someone else, and given I was supposed to be remembering my past, I had a very good idea who that person was.

"You brought the first tunic you finished, right?"

I pursed my lips and thought for a moment. I had finished that one weeks ago, but did I remember to grab it? "You snagged it off the counter this morning."

She snapped her fingers. "That's right. Then, did you finish that second tunic?"

I frowned. "No. I didn't have enough time before this all started, and can't concentrate well enough here to complete it."

"Good."

My eyebrow spiked. *Good? Why is that good?* I still didn't understand why she had wanted me to make the first tunic, let alone a second one. The second one was large enough to fit Tyr, but he had one, and the other was a good size for Diego, but again, he already wore one.

Wait… isn't there a ritual that has something to do with clothing?

Aya addressed the gathered crowd. "Now, we're going to discuss something I know many of you are curious about—romance."

She received a mix of responses, from excitement to eye rolls and groans. I was one to internally groan. *I knew it.*

Normally, this wouldn't bother me, and I knew I needed to remember *everything* of my past, but this was Aya. She was meddlesome, and definitely had something up her sleeve. *And still I love her. Apparently, I am a glutton for punishment.*

"Many look at this time period, and the Norse and Scandinavian people of the time, and think freedom—these freedoms also being extended to women. And as I've taught throughout the day, sometimes this was true, and sometimes it wasn't, especially between separated communities. The aspect of romance and family is one such occasion where it is both."

She walked around, staying animated to keep people's attention. "For the majority, marriage was still used as a means of alliances. They were business contracts, first and foremost. Arranged marriages were the norm, for both men and women, though some were lucky enough to have more of a say in their union. It wasn't uncommon, even if arrangement was chosen, for those being married to be consulted, as, unlike many other cultures, divorce was possible, so they considered it wise to try and make agreeable matches that also worked positively for the families."

Aya gestured to me. "Astrid here will be acting as our young fair maiden for this demonstration."

I placed a hand on my hip and tried not to glare at her. *There is no going back now.*

"While her father isn't here to stand in to show what negotiations looked like, there would have been a discussion of bride-price, dowry, and any other political advantages that would come with the union. Once an agreement was made, the betrothal would be set, and then it was highly encouraged for the betrothed couple to get to know each other while wedding preparations commenced, especially if they hadn't done so prior to the proposed marriage."

Aya continued to move about, graceful as always, bewitching her enthralled onlookers. "Men and women would show their tokens of affection and love differently. You couldn't show public displays of affection, such as kissing, sharing drinking horns, and lap-sitting, until courtship was official. However, you could show other forms of interest before the official betrothal."

I startled when a small bouquet appeared in front of my face. I glanced at the pretty flower arrangement and then up at Diego, who smirked.

This was a moment for me to remember my past, and I would have expected her to pick Tyr for something like this—but it seemed Aya was up to something else. I was vaguely aware of Tyr's intense gaze on me, and I could only imagine the jealousy he may be experiencing, as no doubt he also would have assumed Aya would use him in this demonstration.

"Men would commonly present women with flowers, much like we see today." Aya chuckled. "Though, unlike today, and for some reason that still baffles many of us to this day, men would slap women across the face with said bouquet."

The crowd laughed, and then roared when I pointed at Diego. "Don't you dare."

He snickered. "I wouldn't dream of it, Sunshine."

Something inside me pulsed. No one called me that in this life. However, my soul had experienced that name—long ago, in my first life. My mother would call me that. Baldur began calling me that at some point... in the same way someone else had before Tyr had come along.

I took the flowers and smiled while I inhaled their sweet scent. This may be a demonstration, but Diego would be the type to give flowers. And it was a romantic gesture I enjoyed.

"For women," Aya said, continuing. "To show their affection, they'd take the time to sew a tunic."

She briefly gestured with her eyes for me to grab the red bundle on a nearby seat before continuing. "Some may think this to be a strange way to show affection, but given one couldn't simply walk into a store to buy something premade, and only nobles and other wealthy individuals could afford to pay someone to make clothes for them, the ability to make clothing was crucial to women. And, given how long it took to make something even as simple as trousers or a tunic, one could appreciate the effort and time placed into such a gift, especially for exceptionally crafted clothing."

"Don't hold your breath about getting anything exceptional," I muttered, garnering several laughs, including from Diego.

He winked as he took the folded bundle from me. "I'm sure it's spectacular."

Warmth pulsed in my chest. It really wouldn't be amazing. Turns out, I wasn't very good at making clothes. Aya did most of the measurement work in the end; I just had to put the pieces together and add details.

Yet as Diego unfurled the red runic and rubbed the material with his fingers in appreciation, that stopped mattering. The warmth in my chest spread, and deep down I craved to hear praise from his lips.

That gentle warmth kindled into something hotter when Diego began pulling his tunic up.

"Diego, what are you doing?" I hissed.

He paused, his spectacular abs on display. "Putting the new tunic on. You spent all that time making it, I want to wear it."

A few in the crowd found that rather sweet, while I hid half my face in my hand and fought the heat rising in my cheeks. Just because that's what he said, didn't mean he told the truth. He had a wicked grin on his face. Diego knew exactly what he was doing. He wasn't playing fair.

Diego pulled his tan tunic over his head, and I swear I heard the drool drop from salivating onlookers. Someone even wolf-whistled. A bizarre sensation of possessiveness flashed through me and I squashed that quickly.

To my dismay, Diego took his time putting the new tunic on, insisting on feeling the fabric again while he was half-naked. *This man...* Immortality be damned, I was going to go to an early grave at this rate.

When he finally pulled the red fabric over his head, I should have found myself relieved. Instead, I watched the garment slide down his body and fit him perfectly. My heart did that stupid pitter-patter thing, and I mentally shushed it. Right now wasn't the time for me to swoon over a man—not in public, and not when I hadn't put in the time to figure out what I wanted.

But the heart rarely listened to the mind, and it refused to behave.

"It looks great on you," I managed to say with an even voice.

Diego adjusted his belt to hang around his hips just right again. "It's perfect. You did an amazing job."

Heat seared my cheeks, and my tongue caught when I tried to confess how little I'd actually contributed to the shirt. *Past me's doing, I know.* She wanted me to take the credit and bask in his praise. And I couldn't deny a part of present-me desperately wanted to as well.

Diego took my hands in his, and I prepared myself for him to say something, when Aya spoke up instead. "There was another form of affection that was displayed during this era—one thought so power-ful, it became outlawed later, to never be used on unwed maidens."

My fingers tingled, memories surfacing faster than Aya could speak. I knew what she was about to say. Would Diego actually do it? *Of course he would.* This man danced with me in front of everyone without hesitation.

"Poetry," Aya said.

A mixed rumble of mocking laughter and excited clamor responded to her reveal. No surprise. Poetry wasn't as well received as it once had been. And the idea of professing one's love in such a way was deemed too soft and ridiculous to many.

"Don't be so quick to laugh," Aya said. I pictured her wagging her finger in scolding. "To the Norse people of the time, poetry was a gift from the gods, and as such, had great power. Skalds were hailed over the lands for their way with verse. The best were in direct service of kings and jarls."

Aya breezed around, as if she were dancing or something—I wasn't sure. My eyes refused to leave Diego's face, the anticipation growing within me.

"And because poetry was seen as something so powerful, it was believed to be an ultimate form of confessing one's love, if used appropriately. There were times when it was believed to be an insult to women to recite them love poems, while other times, it would undoubtedly ensure you weren't spending the night alone."

I licked my lips, waiting for Aya to finish and for Diego to speak. My soul yearned to hear what he had to say, as if starved and hungry, and he had the only source of sustenance for it to survive.

His grip on my hand tightened, and then he animatedly recited his poetry.

> Let her kiss me over and over, for her love is better than wine.
> She draws me after her. Oh! My heart desires that she would be mine.
> Honey-sweet lips beckon me near, my fingers ache with hers to twine.
>
> If she would kiss me sweetly once, from happiness I would sing.
>
> Her locks fall free, like daisies red across the mountainside.
> They draw me after her, binding my soul to hers, tethered and tied.
> Silky crimson tresses washed in tears the gods on her behalf have cried.
>
> If she would let her hair fall over me, from peace I would sing.
>
> The velvet of a new lamb cannot compare to her milky-soft skin.
> Her scent draws me after her, forsaking my home and kin.
> Moonlight maiden, soft and sweet, how can a mortal your love win?
>
> If she would let me breathe her sweet skin, from love I would sing.
>
> Her twinkling eyes put the stars and new life of spring

to shame.

They draw me after her, consuming me in a passionate flame.

Emerald eyes beckon me near. Time ceases. On my soul they lay claim.

If she would let me stay in the depth of her eyes, through eternity I would sing.

Diego finished his poem by bringing my hands up to his lips and brushing a gentle kiss against my knuckles. He didn't break eye contact for a moment.

My mouth gaped, my heart soaring and soul roaring with overwhelming satisfaction. "That was... That..."

Were there words to describe this sensation? *What are words?*

"I believe he's bewitched her," Carrie declared.

Aya and the crowd laughed, but I hardly heard it. As I stared into Diego's eyes and processed the poem, memories stirred. A dark-haired man with just as deep, kind eyes. A warm smile and skin different from most in Runavík; darker, more exotic. *Ragnvald.*

My mind swam with memories of fifteen-year-old me, an adult by those past standards, falling for a merchant's son. Captivated by his different appearance and softer, gentler way of speaking, and Creation knew he had a way with words.

He was so different from the men I was used to, I didn't stand a chance resisting his charms. I'd found myself glad my previous betrothals had failed, and ecstatic when my father agreed to Ragnvald's marriage request.

Why am I remembering him? Why did this moment with Diego make me think of Ragnvald?

Diego tipped his head. "Is it true, Sunshine? Have I bewitched you?"

My soul pulsed. He couldn't... Diego couldn't be... *Could he?*

I licked my lips to wet them. "I'm just trying to find the appropriate words to praise your poetry skills."

"Is that so?" He kissed my knuckles again and leaned down, his lips brushing against my ear. He lowered his voice so only I could hear. "Or would you rather show your appreciation in a more… physical way?"

A tingle ran down my spine. Biting back the heating sensation building inside me, I pushed against his chest. "I think you've gotten a little ahead of yourself."

He chuckled, that low rumble that got my lady bits all excited, and pulled away. "No, I don't think I have."

Diego continued to pull away, taking one slow step at a time. I cocked my head. *What is he doing?*

"Marriages happened quickly, and at young ages," Aya told the crowd. "Living in such a volatile time of sickness and war, twelve became the age of adulthood, with most marrying by age fifteen, and no later than twenty. A wedding typically took a year to plan, but much could happen in that year."

My pulse slowed as Diego's fingers slipped from mine. *No…*

"And a carefully planned marriage could fall apart, especially if one of the soon-to-be-wed individuals met an unfortunate, untimely end."

My soul writhed, flooding aching pain throughout my body. *Aya… why?* I knew why, but… why? Why did I have to remember this pain? Why did I have to relive seeing Ragnvald's family be taken, one by one, by the same sickness that took my own younger sister, only for me to be by his bedside when he, too, succumbed to the illness?

What point was there, except to show me that as much as my past self had pushed away all that pain, I'd never truly gotten over his loss? How did that help me in any way?

I plopped down on my seat and rested my cheek on my palm. I heard the pity from the crowd, yet I didn't want it. Just like I didn't want to experience this sensation of anguish in my soul. *Why is it reacting so violently?* It was just Diego backing away.

But was it really?

My sight suddenly picked up a flash of purple. I jerked my head up and came face to face with a large bouquet of purple flowers. Stunned, I merely blinked at the offering.

"While disheartening at times, there was always a chance for a new opportunity at love," Aya said, amusement in her voice.

I lifted my eyes above the bouquet to find Tyr crouched in front of me. He smirked. I looked back down at the beautiful arrangement, memories stirring of a day in the village when he'd presented me with an arrangement very similar to this.

I then became a little suspicious, and didn't hide it. "You'd better not smack me with these, either."

Tyr chuckled and then *booped* my nose with one of the flowers sticking farther out than the rest. "Just for them, I had to."

I smiled despite myself, and took the offered bouquet. "I can accept that."

He watched me with an expectant gaze. When I didn't immediately understand what he was waiting for, his eyebrow cocked. "Well?"

"Well, what?" I asked. "I'm waiting for you to continue to impress me."

He adjusted his weight, and a wicked smirk slipped up his handsome face. "I do believe that for this demonstration, that's been assumed."

Aya talked in the background, heckling the two of us while still keeping to her presentation. I ignored it, refusing to back down with Tyr. He was trying to avoid something, and as we stared at each other, my past pieced itself together as to why.

He blew out a breath. "You're really going to make me do this, aren't you?"

I smirked. "Absolutely."

Tyr sucked in some air and ran his hand through his hair before reciting a poem.

> My love has fair skin, like fresh washed sheep.
> Her hair is red as if in her enemies blood it has seeped.
> Her breasts rise and fall like empires when she is asleep.
> She is my love, and I have loved her forever.
>
> Her green eyes bring men to their knees in conquests.
> Sweet aromas come from her skin, tempting the mightiest.
> Like she has a sachet of Freya's flowers between her breasts.
> She is my love, and I have loved her forever.

The crowd laughed while I pressed my lips together. I refused to laugh, no matter how bad that was. "I have to admit, that's actually better than the first one you recited me."

He hung his head while chuckling. "I'll take it."

"Luckily for Tyr here," Aya said through barely contained laughter, "good poetry isn't a requirement to secure an alliance or win a beautiful woman's heart. A strong, proven warrior like himself would have enough clout to secure a betrothal, and could be seen as impressive enough to give him leverage to woo her."

When Tyr looked at me again, those stunning blue eyes of his snagged me. "Now that I've embarrassed myself in front of an audience, I think it's only fair you stop withholding your side of this agreement."

I blinked. "I don't have anything."

Truly I didn't. It wasn't hard to guess that he was expecting a tunic, too, but I hadn't finished it. Unlike with Diego's, where Aya had given me help making it over a matter of weeks, she didn't with the second one. She only told me the measurements and to go from there. And I'd had less than a week to do it, on top of all my training. Even the time I took during the event wasn't enough to make it wearable.

Tyr gestured to a spot beside me. "Then what's that right there?"

I looked, and my heart stopped. The blue tunic I'd tucked away in a basket when I no longer felt like working on it was now neatly folded and on display for everyone to see. I caught a flash of movement and spotted Ùna slipping into the crowd.

"Ùna," I growled.

She winked and disappeared. *Meddlesome fae.*

Tyr reached for the tunic and I grabbed his hand. "No, you can't. It's not done."

He grinned wickedly and easily overpowered me, snagging the folded clothing. "I don't believe you."

I lunged for him, but he easily dodged my grabbing hands, and stood to his full height. Face burning, I desperately jumped for the tunic, but to no avail, as he easily kept it out of reach. I huffed and crossed my arms. The crowd laughed at our antics.

Tyr released the cloth just enough to allow it to unfold itself, revealing a finished blue tunic. Well, wearable at least. It was missing all kinds of details, but it definitely was in better shape than where I'd left it. *Una, what did you do?*

That meddling fae was clearly behind this. She'd always finished projects for me in the past. But how did she manage to do this in such little time?

"It's not nice to lie, Valkyrie," Tyr rumbled out while enjoying the feel of the shirt between his fingers. "If I didn't know any better, I'd think you were trying to keep it for someone else."

"It wouldn't fit anyone else, you lumbering bear," I muttered.

Tyr grinned again. "Good, because I wouldn't allow you to give something so nice to anyone else."

My mind and soul pulsed with a familiar memory, the missing pieces to what I'd begun remembering this morning.

Tyr proceeded to do exactly what Diego did, and removed the tunic he currently wore. My face burned hotter than it had all day, as my eyes refused to not watch as his corded muscles flexed and pulled taut as they were put on display. The dusting of hair across his chest trailed down in a line that disappeared beneath his pants, adding to the dangerous temptation in front of me.

Need pooled in my core, and the desire to reach out and feel every sexy inch of him was almost too powerful to ignore. *The fuck is wrong with me?*

I was a woman with needs that hadn't been sated by someone else in an agonizingly long time, battling past memories and histories that left me craving things I wasn't sure were my desires or hers, and I had two hot men each asking me to pick them, and doing everything in their power today to really push that button—*that* was what was wrong with me.

Tyr pulled the new shirt over his head, and this one, while the same color as this other one now piled on the ground, fit far better. *Has to be Una's doing.* No way had I made it this well.

Aya continued her presentation, and as I expected from her, she made a few more jabs at us. "Normally, this would be where we'd demonstrate a marriage, but Astrid would skin me alive if I put her through that. Lucky for her, we couldn't afford to put on two feasts today, so I wasn't in a position to risk her wrath."

The crowd laughed as I glared imaginary daggers at her. Though, at the same time, I wasn't sure why she'd used this excuse. Putting us through a fake marriage would be something she'd do to me, just for her own amusement, even if it wasn't necessary for my memories. *Unless, because gods are involved, it puts too much risk into making it real.*

That was not something I'd thought about. Gods didn't exactly marry all that often. And I wasn't sure if a fake marriage for a demonstration would count toward destiny or whatever the Universe counted as the real thing. As much as Aya liked to mess with me, she wouldn't put me into a marriage, even a spiritual one, unless I enthusiastically consented.

My soul pulsed at the idea, and I squashed that. *Jumping a little ahead of itself.* I needed to actually be dating someone before I started thinking such things. *Or dating multiple someones.* I banished that thought immediately as well.

Aya continued her presentation of homelife. Tyr sat down and pulled me onto his lap. His lip brushed my ear, and I suppressed a shiver that ran down my spine caused by his hot breath.

"Is this okay?" he asked.

I swallowed. "Yes."

It was more than okay. Sitting here with him, his large presence surrounding me, it felt right—just like when I was close with Diego. *But, are these sensations mine, or do they belong to past-me?*

The day passed quickly. I spent most of my time with Tyr, pretending to be his wife, without stepping over any boundaries. Memories surfaced in my mind throughout, cementing in my brain and forcing me to process them faster than normal, without anyone noticing. They brought with them emotions I struggled to handle.

Tyr whispered a few compliments as I painted a small clay cup, and when I helped him with his, he pressed his lips against my forehead. My heart fluttered and my knees weakened, even with me sitting. I was so pathetic when it came to forehead kisses.

A few times, a sense of foreboding washed over me. I casually scanned the area each time, but never found anything out of place. However,

I did spot that man from before, in the crowd talking with someone I couldn't see. He and I never made eye contact, and I brushed off his presence. He didn't seem dangerous enough to cause this feeling.

Unfortunately, Tyr noticed my behavior after a while and got me to tell him what was up. He wasn't willing to dismiss my nerves, which only made me more uneasy, and he discreetly sent Fen and a few others out to scour the area. There were, in fact, shifters here, but none were wolves from what they'd found. Unfortunately, Fen and the Berserkers found it difficult to sniff anyone suspicious out with so many bodies around. Despite their enhanced senses of smell, even they had limits.

I decided it was best just to ensure I was with someone at all times. That would keep me safe, and would make sure I didn't stop enjoying myself. And enjoy myself, I did.

TWENTY-TWO

TYR

Astrid giggled when Diego stumbled into her. He slurred… something, and she laughed again while trying to keep him upright long enough to get him up the porch stairs. I'd offered to help, but she insisted she could handle him, so I watched the entertainment.

Diego handled the stairs with far more coordination than I expected. Then again, with how much he drank at the feast, I expected a mortal like him to be catatonic. He drank like an immortal.

Una opened the front door, where Angel waited to greet us. I was surprised how quiet she was, but given she was becoming a familiar, I wondered if she had some sort of understanding of time now. It was late.

"Tyr," Carrie said. She held her very exhausted daughter against her. "Would you mind helping me get Raeni to our cabin? I'm worried she'll trip, and I certainly can't carry her."

My eyes lingered on Astrid, whose attention didn't leave Diego, before I turned to Carrie and nodded. "I can do that."

I wanted to speak with Astrid about today, see what she remembered.

But I could either do that after helping Raeni, or wait until tomorrow if I had to. I wasn't even sure if Astrid was up to talking.

"Raeni, I'm going to carry you. Is that okay?" I asked her.

She grinned up at me sleepily. "To be carried in your strong arms is a dream come true."

Carrie roared with laughter, and I shook my head. This girl was entertaining. Lifting her into my arms, I followed Carrie to their cabin.

I'd planned to only go as far as their front porch, so as not to cause Carrie any discomfort, but Raeni ended up falling asleep in my arms. With no other choice, I accepted Carrie's invitation to enter their home when we arrived, and gently deposited Raeni on her bed.

Carrie kept her distance, watching me carefully, and then she unexpectedly smiled when I turned around. "Thank you."

There was more meaning in those two words than on the surface. The way she watched me wasn't as guarded or fearful as the first week we'd met. She was grateful for more than just my help tonight.

Not sure what to say, I rested my hand on her shoulder for a brief moment before leaving.

I took my time heading back to the main house. I almost went to my cabin, but I felt a need to see if Astrid would be up for talking. I wouldn't rush back and make myself seem desperate, even though a part of me was. I desperately hoped today had helped her with memories of our past. She seemed to remember a part of one when we were talking this morning. It might have made me a little hopeful.

I came up short when Astrid came into view on the path. Small lights flickered in and out around her, like fireflies. *Like starlight.*

She noticed me and stopped. The lights, clearly her magic, flickered around her in the most mesmerizing way, tangling in her red tresses and catching in her skirts. I gazed at my Valkyrie, the ethereal and perfect creature she was. My heart lurched. How was it she was even more beautiful now? I thought she was the most magnificent creature then. I never thought it possible for her to be even more so.

Astrid smiled. "Care to join me for a walk?"

I nodded, finding myself unexpectedly tongue-tied. She was the only woman who had that kind of power over me. No one else had ever come close.

She slipped her arm around mine, pressing her full body against me. I relished the softness of her and noted the differences in how this body felt compared to her previous. Yes, she was the same height as before, but her fuller breasts pillowed my arm differently, and her swaying hips brushed against me more often.

Astrid's hand wrapped over my wrist, as if it were a hand to hold, and rested her head against my arm. She didn't flinch or hesitate when most would. She never averted her gaze from my scars, or showed me pity, even after knowing the truth of my missing hand. Warmth built in my chest. She was so perfect—almost too much so. A part of me worried this was all some fevered dream, and at any moment, I'd wake up alone, wandering endlessly until Creation took pity and finally put me out of my misery.

Astrid looked up at me. "What are you thinking about?"

"Wondering how someone so small can be so perfect." And there went my mouth. My awkward courting skills were legendary, according to Aya and Frey. It was honestly a miracle I hadn't blundered my chances with Astrid back then.

And by the way she was laughing, it seemed I was lucking out again, though by how much was yet to be seen.

"Dad says we only grow until we're perfect." She had a bit of a skip to her step. "And I agree. I am a respectable height, thank you."

I smirked. She barely came up to the middle of my chest. But I couldn't say she was wrong, either. I was a giant even among men, though not the tallest immortal out there, either. Davyn and Baldur both had about twelve to thirteen centimeters on me.

"How are you feeling?" There, that was a normal thing to say. *Hopefully, my mouth will function better the longer we talk.*

"Okay," she said, bobbing her head. "It's been a lot—more memories than I've had in a single day, and that's saying something, considering the memories that came back to me in the first three days of all this happening."

"Good memories, I hope."

A demure smile pulled at her lips. "Yes, they were very nice."

My pulse skipped. Did that mean Aya's plan worked? She'd pre-informed me of her plans to get Astrid to remember our relationship. It'd been a bit of a risk, since Astrid could have felt too uncomfortable to agree to it on the spot. Luckily, she hadn't, and my check-ins to make sure I wasn't pushing too much for her comfort seemed to reinforce her surety of the situation, much to my delight.

"Do you want to talk about anything you remembered?" I asked tentatively, so I wouldn't seem too pushy.

Her lips twisted. "In a moment. I'm still processing—it's why I wanted to go on this walk instead of immediately going to bed."

"Did you enjoy yourself today?" I wanted to be sure that out of everything, she at least enjoyed her time. She'd been doing so much training, Astrid deserved time to relax and have fun.

Astrid nodded. "I had a lot of fun. And, as strange as the feeling is to adapt to, quite glad becoming a Valkyrie means I can't get drunk."

"So scratch the plan where I go hunt down Olympian wine for you?"

"Huh?"

I chuckled. "It's rumored wine of the Olympian gods is the only stuff that can get an immortal drunk. But they guard it so closely, it's hard to say whether it's true, or if they're just stingy bastards."

She made a thoughtful noise and then shook her head. "Trying the wine to know what it tastes like would be nice, but that's it. As much as I enjoy recreational drinking, getting drunk, and the dreaded hangover after, are not my favorite parts."

"Not even if it means you can forget about something for a moment?" I distinctly remembered a night after a war celebration, learning Astrid had wanted to be drunk so she could avoid her troubles that I later realized were caused by me.

She shook her head. "I've only ever done that once, and I refuse to do it again."

I could respect that decision. It took a lot of courage to face your problems instead of burying your head in the sand.

The tingling sensation of Aya's magic around my head disappeared. I reached up and ran my hand through my normal-styled hair.

"Hey, your grays are back."

I snorted. "I don't have grays."

"Uh huh, you keep telling yourself that. If I got grays at twenty-one, then you definitely have some."

I glanced down at her. "You don't have grays."

She stuck her tongue out. "Sure do. Nearly had a heart attack when I found them. Diego thought my freakout was hilarious, until I found one he had. He then tried to blame me for all the stress in his life and Aya thought it was *so* hilarious."

I shook my head.

"Were you always a god?" she asked.

I nodded. "As far as I remember. Though, that's not saying much, because there is a point where my life is just… blank. I know I was born and grew up and then never aged past my mid-thirties, but I don't have any of those memories. My parents, childhood friends, anything, I don't remember them. I just remember being a war god that the Norse people took as their own."

"Strange…" she mumbled. "Maybe it's your old age at play."

I rolled my eyes, and she laughed.

Silence fell over us, something calm and comfortable. Her magic lights floated around us, and I couldn't help but try to catch one. She giggled.

"This is a rather creative way to use your magic."

"I wish I knew how I was doing it."

I cocked an eyebrow. "You're not actively using it?"

Astrid shook her head. "Just started doing it. I also don't recall any memories where I did something like this, making it extra odd."

She was right. I couldn't think of a time she used magic lights in this manner, either. But it was the passive use of the ability that was most interesting. This hadn't happened before, though her magic did sometimes seem to have a mind of its own when she was training.

"Well, I hope you figure out how to use it at will. It's a neat trick."

Astrid made a thoughtful sound and tried to catch one of her lights. I watched her. She had a thoughtful look about her. I wanted to ask her what was wrong, but also wanted to give her the space to share at her own pace.

"Can souls reincarnate on their own?" she asked.

That was a random question. "Yes, though I couldn't tell you how often or why. I'm not sure there's anyone out there who could answer that. There are some mysteries to Midgard not even us gods know the answers to."

She nodded, that contemplative look about her remaining in place. *What had prompted this line of thought?* Had she seen a soul that made her think this? I didn't know how Valkyries touched souls, let alone how they saw them. I could see the strength of a warrior's soul if I concentrated on them long enough, but I couldn't touch them like Aya had figured out how to, or the way Valkyries did.

And Kirby hadn't gone over the soul-collection part of Astrid's training, as far as I knew. We'd focused more on making sure she was capable in a fight, and in control of her magic. But there had to be some sort of innate instinct for her to lean on when it came to souls.

That led my thoughts down to wondering if Kirby collected souls now. It was part of a Valkyrie's purpose. At least, it had been for the Valkyries of the past. I remembered Valkyries becoming restless if too long of an interval had passed since their last collection.

But if Kirby and her Valkyries were collecting souls, where did they go? Valhalla? Odin didn't oversee it anymore, with him dead, so I could see them being okay with sending the souls there. Or maybe she worked with Aya to send them to Fólkvangr. *Who holds domain over Valhalla with Odin gone?*

A whisper of a voice flitted through my mind. *A prayer.* For the first time in a long time, I listened. I listened to each word, as a warrior somewhere asked me for strength. I granted it, and a moment later, a pulse of power rushed through me. Nothing as strong as in the past, but it was something.

Another prayer came. A woman asking any god who could hear her for justice for her son's death. The conviction of injustice in her words called to me. I answered her prayer.

More prayers flitted through my mind. Some I answered, others I didn't. I listened to each one, regardless—until something tapped my arm.

I looked down at Astrid's beautiful, soul-snaring eyes gazing up at me.

"Do you want to sit while you answer prayers?" she asked.

I realized we'd stopped walking and stood in front of a bench. How long had I been unaware of our surroundings? That'd never happened to me in the past. Though, with my Valkyrie here with me, I did feel more comfortable letting my guard down.

I took the invitation to sit. "How did you know I was answering prayers?"

"You always get this look." Her expression changed to the most serious and almost grumpy I'd ever seen on her. "You have a serious case of resting bitch face when you answer prayers."

I threw my head back and laughed. "I don't look like that."

"Oh yes, you do." She made another serious face. "You normally look like this."

I shook my head, still chuckling. I knew I had a rather serious look about my neutral expression, but I'd never had someone try to mimic it. Not even Astrid had in the past.

"You said I have this expression every time I answer prayers." I regarded her for a moment. "I've never answered any in your presence since arriving here."

She played with her fingers, her sudden shyness intriguing. "I remembered some things."

Sliding my arm along the back of the bench, I leaned closer, though not too close as it would risk shutting her down. "How much have you remembered, Valkyrie?"

Her lower lip caught in her teeth, sending a pang of need through me. "Everything."

That need heightened in intensity, though I did what I could to control it. Just because Astrid remembered didn't mean she'd beg for me to bury my cock into every perfect, fuckable hole of hers. "And how are you feeling with all these memories?"

She was quiet for a moment. "Conflicted."

I cocked my head and waited for her to continue in her own time.

"It's been easy to accept the events as I see them. That's been the only easy part of this memory stuff. It's the emotional side that's been difficult."

She chewed on her lip some more. "There are times I can firmly say thoughts or emotions belonged to the past part of me, and do not belong to me, like my past acceptance of slavery or ambivalence of those who were not Norsemen. Then there are times those past feelings and thoughts belonged to past me, but I also find it easy to accept into my current life, like old friendships."

Her lips pursed. "Then there are the ones I'm not so sure about—mostly emotions. They feel like mine at present, but also like mine of the past. But does that mean the past is influencing my present? And if so, are they really mine?"

It wasn't hard to guess what she meant by these unspecified emotions. It was me. She wasn't sure if what she was feeling were truly her feelings.

Astrid had always been an independent person, then and now. She wouldn't like feeling like her emotions were being manipulated, even by herself.

"Do you agree with these emotions?" I asked.

She pursed her lips. "That's why I'm confused. I—"

"No, don't think about it so deeply," I said. "Do you agree with those emotions?"

Astrid was quiet for a long moment. "Not to the same intensity."

Warmth flared in my chest. That was better than I could have asked for. "Then that part is yours. Your past will influence your present. That's unavoidable. There's nothing wrong with that, either."

I brushed a strand of hair away from her eyes, my finger grazing her cheek. "It all comes down to how comfortable you are with the fact."

She worked her jaw. "I don't like feeling as though something is influencing my thoughts and emotions. But I guess, given my situation, I have to get used to it."

I didn't like that take. I didn't like her being reluctant to experience what were really her feelings. "May I do something?"

Her brow spiked. "Sure."

Taking a quiet breath in, and sending a prayer to Creation I didn't fuck this up, I reached out and slid my fingers along her cheek. Astrid's breath caught, her eyes widening ever so slightly. Yet she didn't stop me as I tucked my finger under her chin and tipped her head up. I dipped closer and brushed my lips across hers.

I kissed her slowly, not quite deeply, but enough to get my point across. And to tease my senses with everything she was, tempting me to go beyond my point.

I pulled away when I felt the tension in her jaw relax. Her eyes fluttered and the pink in her cheeks didn't escape my notice. "Whatever you felt from that, did it feel like your reaction and only yours?"

She licked her lips slowly, and my eyes tracked the motion. "Yeah. Yeah it did."

"Then there is your answer."

Astrid gazed up at me with those stunning eyes in a way that made them seem more innocent than I knew she was. It sent a rather conflicting wave of sensation through me. "I heard the vow you made when Aya released my spirit with the ritual."

I blinked, my brain not quite fast enough to keep up with such a sudden topic change.

"Did you really not stop trying to find me?"

I nodded.

"You never tried to walk away?"

"No, never, Valkyrie."

Her brow drew together. "You never tried to move on?"

I regarded her. I wasn't sure if this was a baiting question where she'd be offended if I did, or upset that I didn't. "Did you want me to?"

Her eyes widened. "I would have never wanted you to never love again. When I was mortal, I accepted you'd have to move on with your life after my death. I wanted that for you. I didn't want you to be alone. Even when I became immortal, that thought never changed. I knew I wasn't invincible. Just more difficult to kill."

I clasped my hand over my wrist in front of me and bowed my head. "There was a moment in time I was overcome with loneliness. I hadn't successfully gotten you back, I didn't have Baldur, and I'd all but shut out everyone else I knew. I never planned to stop looking for you. I never break my vows. But I wanted companionship, and a part of me did want to move on."

I shook my head. "I never achieved that last part. And after a while of moving from one woman to the next, I realized I had a pattern… they were all attempts to replace you."

Astrid's lips pursed, but she said nothing, allowing me to tell the story of this pitiful part of my life.

"Either a feature, or a quirk, they all shared something close enough to you, I realized I was either trying to pretend you never died, or desperately hoping one of them would turn out to be you."

"How did you come to realize what you were doing?"

"The last woman was the most similar to you. And I… called her by your name once."

Astrid winced. "Yeah… that would do it."

Definitely wasn't my proudest moment. "That's when I decided to focus solely on finding you."

She was quiet for a moment. "So you never tried to make a full attempt to move on."

My mouth twisted. "You were my heart, Astrid. I loved you more than life itself. Losing you to death… I would have joined you had Aya not been able to use her magic on you. Life wasn't worth living without you there. And I can't say I ever fully recovered from that."

Her gaze softened, and I hoped this confession didn't guilt her. That was not my intention. She was the only one I could be this vulnerable with.

"You used 'loved' in the past tense."

I nodded. This had been something I'd thought about a lot lately. "I think it would be incorrect to say I love you now. Desire you, yes. I definitely feel that. But your past and present are different Astrids, even with your strong similarities. You haven't lived a thousand years alongside me. You've lived two separate full lives, with many shorter ones between."

I brushed her cheek with the back of my finger. "I want to get to know you in this life. And I hope, in time, I'll be able to change that tense to present."

"How often do you compare me to my past?"

I wasn't surprised she brought this up again. It was inevitable we'd talk about it. And I wouldn't do her or our building relationship a disservice by lying or avoiding the question. "Frequently."

She chewed her lower lip. "Do you… like me more now or prefer me how I was then?"

I curled a lock of her silky hair around my finger. "That's not a simple answer. There are times I think a quirk of yours in the past was more to my liking, and there are other times I'm enjoying a new or even enhanced quirk of yours now. I'm not good at articulating what those differences are, but I don't think it's necessary. I don't want you to be the Astrid of my past. I want you to be the Astrid you decide to be."

Her lips quirked into a sultry, teasing smile. "For a man who can't recite poetry, you certainly figure out the right thing to say."

A low growl rumbled in my throat. I leaned in. "You owe me for that. I swore I'd never embarrass you or myself like that again. And you had to make me do it in front of a bigger audience. In front of Aya, no less. She still hasn't let me live down the first one I ever recited, before you came into my life."

"You've still not told me what that poem was."

I chuckled low. "And you never told me how you got that fierce scar in your first life."

Creation only knew how hard I tried to earn that secret. There were a few times I thought I'd finally seduced her enough, but no, she stuck firm to her promise.

Astrid smirked and fanned her fingers across my chest. "And I won't. I honor that vow I made."

Her touch simmered my veins. I dipped my head until our breath mingled and her lavender and vanilla perfume enveloped me. "You made a vow to me, Valkyrie. A few, in fact. Do you plan to honor them as well?"

She made a thoughtful sound. "Perhaps. I do want to test some of these memories."

I trailed my finger up her arm, my veins fanning hotter and hotter, and cock straining against my trousers the longer this flirtatious banter continued. "I know a few memories I could help you recreate."

I wanted nothing more than to tear this dress off her and indulge in her sweet, tempting curves and hear her pleasured moans until she was screaming.

Astrid's lips brushed mine, and she practically purred before speaking, "I do hope you can. My past self seems quite adamant you're hung like a stallion."

I chuckled. "Do you not believe what your memories tell you? I am a god, after all."

The color of her eyes deepened as lust crawled through her. "God or not, I can't be so sure magic isn't involved in making sure a supposed horse cock fits so well in a human body. Especially someone of my size."

"The only magical one here is you, Valkyrie. But if you need more convincing"—I wrapped my hand around hers, and dragged it down my chest to my hard cock—"Why don't you feel for yourself."

I bit back a groan when her hand wrapped around me over my trousers and I heard her suck in a sharp breath through her nose. Astrid's eyes widened and the lust in them deepened even more. An alluring flush tinged her cheeks.

"Well…" She licked her lips. "I can't say I'm disappointed with this confirmation."

I was just about out of restraint with her slowly stroking me. "I can promise you, Valkyrie, riding me wouldn't be a disappointment."

The impish smirk on her temptress lips confirmed she was well aware of that fact. "You act as if you're once again a wild stallion needing to be broke."

Gliding my fingers along her cheek and into her silken locks, I gripped her just tightly enough to make her look up at me with parted mouth. "I am."

Our eyes met with a heated intensity before I fiercely crushed my lips against hers without hesitation. Her pleasured groan mingled with mine, and her grip around me tightened. I kissed her like I never remembered kissing her before, the desperation and need for her after losing her for so long taking over.

Her other hand grazed over my shoulder and up my neck, blazing a trail of fiery heat in its wake. Her fingers tangled in my hair and her tongue pressed against my lips, demanding entry. I didn't deny her, eager to devour her and sear everything that she was into every recess of my mind.

My pulse pounded in my ears, my veins blazing with desire. I needed more of her. I needed to feel her against me. My hand brushed over her neck and shoulder as I sought to tear away the fabric blocking us from one another.

Astrid laughed breathlessly against my mouth, pulling away all too soon for my liking. The absence of her left me cold and aching with need.

I swiped at her as she quickly retreated. "Astrid…"

She giggled, an alluring and mischievous grin on her lips, and slowly backed away down the path. "You're not the wild one needing to be tamed this time, Tyr."

"Valkyrie," I growled, low in my chest. "You're playing a dangerous game. If you make me give chase and I catch you, there's no going back. You are at my mercy."

Her grin said everything for her. That's what this tempting vixen wanted, and that was what she'd get.

I stalked after her—not setting a fast pace, but not a leisurely one, either. Astrid giggled and ran at varied intervals, glancing back or stopping when I didn't pick up my pace to keep up. Her lights danced around her, adding to my Valkyrie's luring dance. Yet, even with my pulse pounding in my ears and my body screaming to catch her and show her what it meant when she teased a war god, I held fast to my control, enjoying the build of this chase.

For a little while, at least.

When she'd lured me deep into the forest of the property, and she ceased slowing down, I picked up my pace. Still not a run, but all predator.

My longer strides allowed me to not only keep up, but advance on her. She tossed back glances to gauge the distance. Each time she did, I gained on her. Astrid squealed when I came in swiping distance and narrowly dodged when I grabbed for her.

She bolted. I chuckled. "Run as much as you want, Valkyrie. I will catch you."

Her teasing laughter drove me on, my pace increasing. I wanted to catch her now.

Astrid set a jogging pace for herself, but it wasn't quick enough to outpace me at my fast walk. I gained on her, my muscles straining against my control. Swiping at her again, I snagged the fabric of her skirts. Astrid gasped and then the sound of fabric tearing echoed through the forest.

I halted when Astrid's visage disappeared before my eyes and I looked down at the scrap of fabric in my hand. Her lights hovered for a moment without her and then zipped down the path. A moment later, she squeaked as she reappeared several meters up the path, tripping over her own feet. She managed to stay upright, but it was a rather comical sight.

She gazed back at me, wide-eyed. "Did I just…"

I chuckled. "Well, at least you didn't end up in a tree this time."

Astrid rolled her eyes, knowing the moment of time I was referring to.

I cocked my head when I noticed where her skirt ripped, and grinned at the view of her shapely legs and the profile of her ass on display. Astrid noticed and gasped, sweeping the tattered clothing up to cover herself.

I advanced on her again. "Don't be like that, Valkyrie. I'm enjoying the view."

Astrid took several steps back before fleeing at full speed. Carnal desire surged through me, breaking my restraint. My feet dug into the earth as I raced after her. She did decently keeping the distance between us, especially after she stopped trying to clutch her torn skirts, granting me the occasional peek at her bare ass, but it wasn't enough.

Just as we burst through the trees and came to the lake, I reached out and grabbed a fistful of her dress. The clothing tore some more, but held enough for me to yank her back into me. Astrid gasped when she slammed into my chest and then struggled to break away.

I wound my arm tightly around her waist before yanking us both down to the lush, carpeted moss beneath our feet. "You're mine, Valkyrie. You're not going anywhere."

My teeth grazed the tender skin of her shoulder, and I didn't hesitate to rip her dress again. Astrid sucked in a breath and bit her lip. The clothing gave easily under my strength, splitting open along her back and falling loose without the tension keeping it around her tantalizing figure.

Astrid struggled and managed to break away just long enough to shed the dress before I snagged her back. Her tantalizing soft curves pressed against me. She squirmed, but it was clear she wasn't actually trying to escape.

I glided my fingers down her smooth skin, and she arched her back.

"Is this how you like it, Valkyrie?" I growled in her ear. "A chase that ends with you on your knees and at my mercy?"

She grinned. "Some days I crave slow, sensual worship. Other days, I want my hair pulled while being called a dirty whore and fucked senseless."

I tangled my fingers in her hair and yanked. She gasped, the sound crawling along my senses. "I can do that. Though, before I do…"

Releasing her, I slid my hand along her bare back, down to her firm ass. After a nice appreciative squeeze, and ensuring my other arm supported her, I drew back and slapped her pale skin. Astrid responded with a gasping moan.

"Punishment for leaving me," I growled. "One for every century."

Astrid gasped again when I spanked her a second time. "Punishment, or reward? Feels more like a reward to me."

My cock twitched, and my pulse increased at her bratty challenge. I slapped her ass a third time. "And then one for each day since I arrived here, unless I hear you begging for my forgiveness."

She glanced over her shoulder at me, her eyes gleaming in challenge. "And if I don't?"

"You will."

She wiggled her ass in defiance. I spanked her again and then again. Her last one for the centuries I'd been without her, the sixth, was harder than the rest, and it showed in her response that was more of a grunt than pleasure. Her grip on my arm also tightened, nails digging in.

I massaged the globes of her ass, easing the sting. Her Valkyrie healing would take care of most of it, but that didn't mean I wouldn't take care of her, too.

Astrid looked at me with apologetic eyes, understanding the anguished length of time I'd wandered alone, desperate to find her again, yet she didn't voice her apology.

"Apologize, Astrid."

She refused me again. I slapped her tender backside, not hard, as the first day I found her was a reward. She moaned, her eyes hooding. I spanked her several more times, each one at a different strength that corresponded with the difficulty I felt being so close to her, but not with her. I ordered her to repent, but still, she held out.

Her body trembled beneath my touch and soon, her desire dripped over my wrist. Watching her enjoy her punishment drove me wild and tempted me to end this early and show just how much I missed her—wanted this new her.

Then, when I'd gotten over halfway through the days' count, she whimpered out, "I'm sorry."

I paused mid-pullback. "What was that, Valkyrie?"

She opened her eyes and gazed back at me. "I'm sorry. Please forgive me, Tyr."

A glimmer of rebellion still lingered in Astrid's gaze, but I knew I wouldn't bend her will to total submission. She was too willful for that. And I could tell she had outgrown this playful game.

I slid my hand along the curve of her hip, along her side, and cupped one of her full breasts, pulling her against my chest. Astrid's eyes hooded, and she snaked her arm around my neck.

"I forgive you," I murmured before dipping my head and kissing her.

Astrid arched into my hand as I squeezed and played with her, her nipple pebbling under my touch. I circled the erect bud with a finger, teasing her just long enough to make her groan out desperately for more. The groan deepened to something temptingly primal when I rolled her nipple between my fingers.

Her hips rocked, and she rubbed her pussy eagerly against my wrist. Her bare, slick folds slid back and forth, grinding into me. She moaned when she hit the perfect spot for her.

I chuckled, breaking our kiss. "Greedy little Valkyrie, you are."

"I am," she moaned. "I want so much from you."

"And I'll give it *all* to you."

I devoured her with my eyes as she panted and grinded against me, relishing the sensation of fondling her soft breast in my hand, and her slick, needy heat against my wrist. Our eyes met and a current of intense desire locked us together.

This was a part of Astrid that differed from the past. She wasn't as timid about what she wanted. She'd never been shy, but she had a more reserved nature when we'd enjoyed each other. That reservation didn't seem to exist with this present version of her. *And I like that a lot more.*

Her breath came out fast and heavy, and a smile split my face. "Come, Valkyrie."

She closed her eyes and rocked her hips more. I pinched and tweaked her sensitive nipple and Astrid threw her head back into me. She screamed and her hips bucked as her orgasm tore through her.

I didn't cease my attention until she lay boneless beneath me, gasping for air and trembling from the aftershocks of pleasure. Pleased, I tucked a strand of hair behind her ear before trailing my tongue down the sensitive shell of her ear. "I hope you don't think I'm done with you."

She grinned seductively as her hands dropped from my neck and she turned to face me. "I've got enough practice in me to not be a one-hit wonder. And I believe becoming a Valkyrie gave me an added stamina boost."

Not wanting to think about the other men she'd fucked, I distracted myself by allowing my hungry gaze to roam appreciatively as she reclined back. Her legs casually spread, putting her spectacular body on display for me, the glow of the moon lighting her flushed skin in an ethereal glow, mixed with her magic lights still floating around us—each supple curve begged to be caressed; splatter of freckles needing to be kissed; her sternum tattoo deserving to be traced and appreciated for adorning her so perfectly; glistening folds unobscured by a curtain of curls requiring to be—

"You're overdressed," she said. "It's making it difficult to appreciate you like I'm allowing you to for me."

I reached behind me and grabbed the collar of my tunic. "Well, then let me fix that."

Before I even had my shirt halfway pulled over my head, her hands were roaming my body. I sucked in a sharp breath when her soft lips pressed against my skin. "You don't waste any time, Valkyrie."

She chuckled and fiddled with the ties of my trousers. "I apologized, and you didn't seem to believe me with how you just treated me, making me do all the work. So, I think I need to show you that sincerity."

My trousers dropped, and my throbbing cock sprang into her waiting hands. I groaned deep in my chest, feeling her wrap around me and stroke without hesitation. Her strong, sure strokes teased and pleased me all at once.

She kissed my torso, licking swathes of hard skin hungrily whenever she pleased. Her mouth pressed against a particularly sensitive scar on my ribs. I didn't remember where I got that one, but it had always been sensitive. And usually, if I touched it, it came with a sensation of shame. But when she touched me there, I only felt forgiveness.

Astrid trailed a leisurely pace down, sending a wave of anticipation through me. I grabbed a handful of her hair to steady myself as she sent jolts of pleasure through me with every teasing bite and lick. When she nipped the sensitive area of skin under my navel, I twitched in her hand, eliciting a throaty chuckle from her.

I blew out a breath. "I'm starting to think this isn't an apology at all, Valkyrie."

"Oh, really?" Her words vibrated against my skin, and I twitched again. "Well, we can't be having that now, can we?"

I closed my eyes and sucked in another slow breath when she slid her tongue along my shaft. I opened them again to gaze down at her when she hesitated. "What is it, Valkyrie?"

She swallowed, her eyes fixated on the head of my cock, the foreskin partially retracted. "I'm… I will admit, you're the first intact guy I've been with. I don't know… do you need me to, uh, do anything specific?"

My brow rose with interest. I wasn't aware that circumcision was so widely practiced she hadn't experienced anything different. And if her memories weren't clear enough on how I liked it in the past, then I'd help ease her worries. "You don't need to do anything special, Valkyrie. Take your time refamiliarizing yourself with me. You might notice a small difference to what you're used to, but I assure you, we'll enjoy it."

Astrid nodded. Her fingers wrapped around my cock and slowly stroked. I groaned, embracing the feeling of her fingers gliding up and down, tugging my foreskin back and forth. She licked her soft lips as she hesitated again a moment, then pressed them against the exposed head of my cock. She teased, licking up the underside, so feather-light I swore our past teased more than our present. I pulsed at the sensation of her tongue gliding along the sensitive flesh and under my foreskin, making her chuckle as she lifted her gaze to me.

We locked eye contact as she fully pulled back my foreskin, and then eased her warm, wet lips slowly around my cock. Just the exposed head at first, sucking and licking with such practiced ease. I groaned, my grip in her hair tightening. My pulse thrummed in my veins.

Astrid swirled her tongue around the head of my cock while she slowly eased me in and out of her mouth, familiarizing herself with my size and feel. Each time she slid me back in, she took me deeper and deeper.

"That's it," I murmured, rocking my hips. "Be a good Valkyrie, and suck your god's cock like the dirty little thing you are."

Astrid obeyed without hesitation, licking and sucking eagerly as I thrust into her as if it were her mission—her purpose as a Valkyrie to serve me. When I was close to release, she palmed my balls while using one hand to massage my shaft.

My body tightened and my breathing grew ragged. She gazed up at me, her eyes gleaming. She knew I was close and had no plans to stop, which was fine by me. The chase and her subsequent punishment was enough of a battle to win me another immediate round with her.

"Valkyrie," I grunted, unable to hold back any longer.

She moaned in rapturous response, the vibration cresting me over the edge. I convulsed, spilling my hot seed into the back of her throat.

Astrid ravenously swallowed all of it, not stopping until every last drop was gone. I withdrew when I had nothing left to give this round and watched her lick me off her lips, hungry for more.

"Is that all?" she purred.

Creation, this woman. What was I going to do with her? Rhetorical question. I knew exactly what to do with a woman like her.

I gripped her shoulder and shoved her onto her back, her gorgeous red hair fanning out around her. Dipping down, I hungrily kissed along her neck, trailing a path of freckles to the beat of my burning desire.

Astrid softly moaned and tilted her head to provide me better access. I feasted on her delicious skin, and ran my hand and wrist along her curves, familiarizing myself with every centimeter of my Valkyrie's soft form, and enjoying the differences this body of hers offered.

I kissed along the curve of her heavy breasts, up to her hardening nipples, the rosy buds begging to be ravished. I lapped at the stiff peak with my tongue, eliciting a sharp inhale from Astrid. Grinning, I licked her again, and then kissed, and licked, and kissed. I did the same for the other, making sure neither side of her was neglected, before pulling one of her taut buds into my mouth and sucking.

Astrid moaned louder this time, arching into me, begging for more. She grabbed my hand and made me play with her other breast. But it wasn't enough for her.

Confident and wanting, she guided my hand down her smooth belly, and between her luscious hips to the radiating heat of her slick pussy. I didn't hesitate to slide my fingers between her dripping folds, finding her sensitive clit. She gasped and rocked her hips into me, urging for more.

I released her nipple with a satisfying *pop*, before murmuring gruffly, "You're dripping all over me, Valkyrie. You're such a little whore for me, aren't you?"

"Yes…" She ground her pussy into my hand. "Always for you, my god of judgment, if you deem me worthy."

I plunged my fingers inside her, still rubbing her sweet, sensitive spot. "You will always be worthy of my attention, Valkyrie."

Her eyes hooded as desire overtook her. My own lust raged through my body, my still-hard cock pulsing with need. When she began to clench around my fingers, I withdrew. Astrid whimpered and reached for me, begging for more.

I kissed her outstretched fingers before pressing them into the moss.

My hand and wrist skated along her smooth, luscious hips. Gripping them, I laid my cock on the apex of her thighs.

"Please," she begged, her eyes hazy with lust.

"Please what, Valkyrie?"

"Fuck me with your huge cock. I need it. I need it so bad. I can take it. Please."

I grinned. Her begs were intoxicating. Her desire was addicting. And I needed her just as desperately. I was all too happy to fulfill her filthiest desires.

Lifting her hips, I teased her by slowly rocking back and forth along her dripping folds, before plunging deep within her warm pussy until I was buried completely. A guttural groan tore from my chest, the sensation of being inside her better than I remembered. She was victory and battle lust and justice rolled into one incredible package.

"Oh, god," Astrid moaned, her back arching and mouth falling open. Pain mixed with pleasure flashed over her face, my size intense but desired and wanted.

I wrapped my hand around her throat, squeezing just a little. Her mouth parted more, and she tipped her head up in the most natural and instinctive way. "No, Valkyrie. You do not pray to a nameless god. You are my Valkyrie. Mine to punish. Mine to pleasure. Mine to claim. You pray only to me."

"You," she gasped breathily. "Only you, Tyr."

"Good girl." I rumbled in approval before pulling out and then surging back into her, making another delighted cry escape from between those beautiful lips.

No longer gentle, I pounded into her—rough and hard, just as she liked it—how she demanded it from the war god I was.

Then in one swift move, I pulled out and flipped her over.

"Warning, next time," she grumbled, even though she assumed the perfect position with her ass high in the air.

"Do I need to warn you about this, too?" I said before ramming my cock inside her.

Astrid moaned, her fingers digging into the moss beneath us. "Is that all?"

The challenge called me. I thrust into her again. And again. Skin slapped skin as I fucked her hard, showing her the strength and power I wielded and controlled to a point of pleasure for her. "Is this what you wanted, Valkyrie? My cock pounding this pussy, showing how much of a filthy little whore you are? Is it?"

"Yes." Astrid moaned and begged, craving everything I gave her. "Give me more. I need more. Please, Tyr. Please."

Desire blazed hot under my skin, threatening to devour us both in a consuming firestorm of passion.

I braced myself over her, and she tipped her head up. Our mouths fused together, and I drank her in, consuming all she was until I lost sense of where she started and I ended.

She clenched around me, and a moment later screamed my name in ecstasy. Her cries flooded through my body as the most potent caress I'd experienced in centuries. I accepted her prayer, craving and relishing the powerful sensation, bolstering my power in ways I'd almost forgotten she could cause.

I didn't stop fucking her, my pulse pounding in my ears. My body tightened and then I roared as I crested over the edge and spilled inside her.

My pace slowed until I stilled, and the only thing to fill the air was our panting breaths. When sensation returned to my limbs, I carefully extracted myself from her and then collected Astrid into my arms. Her languid body molded into me as I cradled her small form, relishing the feel of her softness against me.

Waves of euphoria cascaded through my being. A gentle smile formed on my lips at the sight of the blissful expression on Astrid's beautiful face. It'd been so long since I'd felt this content—this whole. This was how we were supposed to be.

This feeling brought back the lust, and a returning erection. Sooner than I expected, but maybe because it'd been so long since I'd had her. It'd happened before, when we'd hit a rough patch in our previous marriage.

Immortals had great stamina, but we still needed a breather before getting back to fucking like rabbits. Though, the unique battle-and-prayer exchange I could have with Astrid, when we didn't just fall into our passion, made that short refractory period seem like a mortal's agonizingly slow wait time. It made me appreciate and relish that power Astrid had with me, and only me.

Gazing at Astrid's still-languid state, I guessed she still needed more time before I lured her in for more—which was fine. I had her here, so I could be patient.

The trees rustled, and my happy bubble popped. Normally I wouldn't think twice about the wind blowing the canopy leaves, but their shaking didn't match the light breeze. I know, from my time with Ùna under my service, to never ignore the warnings of the forest, even if I couldn't understand it.

Without moving too quickly, as I didn't want to alarm Astrid, I scanned the area and rose to my feet. We were outside Aya's barrier. It'd been reckless for us to come to the lake, but I'd been more focused on enjoying Astrid than caring where we ended up. That was foolish. If the shifter was lurking, it would have been disastrous if he'd attacked while we were tangled up.

I tensed when a dark figure moved in the tree line, my awareness ready to pull my weapon from its magical storage if I needed it. Sean walked out into the moonlight, his eyes glowing with magic.

"Good, you're already moving," he said. "Something has the forest upset. It would be wise not to be outside the barrier."

I nodded and held Astrid closer. She sucked in a deep breath, an incredibly cute sound squeaking out of her. I stared down at her while Sean chuckled. He didn't look her way. Not even a reflexive glance, as if our nakedness didn't interest him in the least.

"Tyr?" Astrid murmured, her voice sleepy. Had she fallen asleep? "Where are we going?"

"My cabin," I said.

She snuggled into me more. "That sounds nice."

Good. I wasn't letting her leave my side tonight. I'd waited too long to let her slip through my fingers again just yet.

DIEGO

Breathe in.
Breathe out.
Breathe in.
Breathe out.

I repeated the exercise two more times, each time no easier than the first. My head swam, and the only thing keeping me upright was this wall. *The hell did I just experience?*

I shook my head, trying desperately to clear my mind, but the lingering images remained. Tyr swinging his axe. A giant black wolf lunging for him. Blood.

My hand pressed against my face. I was desperate to forget these feelings that came with those images.

"Diego?" Astrid's hushed voice called.

I jerked my head up. Illuminated from behind in the dark house, Astrid stood in her bedroom doorway. Even in the darkness, I somehow could see the concern pulling at her brow.

I ran my fingers through my hair. *Shit.* This was not a good time. It wasn't horrible for Astrid to see me like this, but she'd ask questions, and I wasn't sure how to explain to her what was going on.

"What are you doing up?" I blurted out.

"I couldn't sleep, so I decided to study for my class."

That was right. Not only was Astrid having to balance all the supernatural shit in our lives, she had enrolled in an online summer anatomy class. At the time, it'd seemed like a strange choice for her, but now, with her learning healing magic, it would come in handy.

She padded across the loft and came up to me, placing a gentle hand on my arm while I braced myself against the wall. Her brow furrowed, and she moved her hand to my chest and then touched my neck.

"You're drenched in sweat." She brushed my forehead with the back of her hand. "And you're hot."

I smirked, chuckling. "I'm glad you noticed."

Her mouth twitched, and she shook her head. "That's not what I mean, and you know it. Are you feeling unwell?"

I opened my mouth, and then closed it, running my fingers through my hair again. "No, I'm not sick… I think. I don't know…"

Astrid cocked her head, and then her hand wrapped around mine. She tugged. "Come, sit down."

She tugged again when I didn't immediately comply, jolting me into motion. My gaze fell to our entwined hands, her warmth seeping through the touch, calming the frenzy in my mind.

The sway of her wide hips snagged my attention. The hypnotic motion, and the way her underwear cut high along them and shaped around her firm ass stirred desire in me. How I saw her so clearly in the darkness, I didn't care.

Fuck her. Claim her. Make her mine. The intense urge to bend her over the back of the couch consumed my thoughts so suddenly, I wondered if I really was unwell. The nagging, questioning thought didn't linger, as I enjoyed the view she presented.

Astrid sat us down on the couch, her bare leg pressing against mine. "Talk to me."

Her words snapped me back to my senses, and I met her gaze. Even in the limited light, I could see the way her green eyes sparkled with mirth. She knew exactly what I'd been doing, and she liked it.

I raked my hand through my hair. "I... don't know how to put it into words. It doesn't... it's so bizarre."

She brushed my cheek with a soft hand. "Say it however you can. We can piece it together from there. After everything I've gone through, I'm not sure if anything can surprise me."

I worked my jaw. "It was so confusing. More like flashes than one straight visual. But I saw Tyr... and he was fighting with this enormous black wolf with gold eyes."

I heard Astrid audibly stop breathing. I pushed on.

"It wasn't as big as Fen, but still bigger than a wolf should be, and it had some sort of scar on his face. And it was... bloody. There was so much blood. But I didn't know where it was coming from, because they weren't bleeding."

I clamped my eyes closed, the visuals threatening to return. "And then, when the wolf came at Tyr—"

I shook my head. "I didn't see how it ended."

Astrid cupped my face. "It was a bad dream, Diego. It's okay. All this talk about wolf shifters coming to get me, and Tyr promising it won't happen again, I'm not surprised you're having nightmares."

I lifted my gaze, holding hers. "That's the thing, Astrid—I wasn't asleep."

Silence spread between us. Astrid's eyes widened as my words sank in. "What do you mean—you were awake?"

I sucked in a deep breath, trying to stay calm as those panicky sensations creeped up, like they had when I experienced... whatever it was. "I got up to get a snack. I was standing where you found me, when all of a sudden, I saw what I told you."

Her brow scrunched. "How... is that even possible?"

I shook my head. "I don't... know. I don't know what's going on. What's wrong with me?"

"Hey, it's okay." She cooed. "It's okay. Nothing is wrong with you. We'll figure it out. We can talk to Aya in the morning."

I nodded slowly, still struggling with the flood of emotions that telling Astrid about this had brought on.

Her thumbs caressed my cheeks, the touch tender and soothing.

I leaned in, craving more of the calmness she offered. Astrid pulled me against her, enveloping me in kindness. I pressed my face into the crook of her neck, wrapping my arms around her waist, and clinging to the sanctuary she was.

All the negative emotions drained away, allowing warmth and contentment to settle inside my chest.

I inhaled deeply, the faded sweet aroma of her lavender and vanilla perfume wafting off her skin. The smell was stronger than I expected, and mixed with something else I couldn't quite identify. I inhaled again, and then again.

With every breath, something deeper stirred within me. It sparked into desire that consumed me like a raging fire until I was aware of nothing else save for Astrid's body pressed against mine, her soft curves molding into me perfectly as if we were two pieces of a puzzle meant to fit together, and how little clothing created a barrier between us. *Claim her.*

Astrid giggled and twitched away from my nose. "That tickles, Diego."

"You smell good," I mumbled, taking in one last deep inhale before reluctantly pulling back. My hand glided along her smooth, bare back, exposed by her crop top, igniting flames of desire under my skin.

She gazed up at me with those stunning green eyes, and even in the low light, I took in her features—the shape of her eyes, and the curve of her small nose. The angles of her heart-shaped face, and the way her freckles banded over her nose. Flecks of different green shades in her eyes I'd never quite noticed before. The curvature of her inviting, pouty lips I wanted to ravish.

"How good?" Astrid whispered, her words almost breathless. Her hand slid along my bare chest, sparking more need with each moment of contact.

I brushed a stray strand of hair out of her face. The pad of my thumb traced along her cheekbone, down to her chin. Her teeth caught on her bottom lip and her chest rose and fell erratically, as if anticipating what was to come.

The heat coursing through my veins grew hotter with each passing second. A strained growl rumbled from my throat as my cock twitched eagerly.

I'd promised myself after that moment on the couch late last week that I'd behave with her—that I wouldn't push unless she gave me signs to, no matter how difficult it'd been the last few days. Our interactions during the festival hadn't helped me. And while she and Tyr had grown closer during that, she still shot me flirtatious looks and engaged in less-than-appropriate banter. She didn't shy away from slightly closer-than-needed contact when I failed to keep myself in check.

That promise was crumbling. My thoughts filled with visions of her sweat-slicked body writhing beneath me, her breath coming in ragged cries as I licked and tortured her clit until she orgasmed over and over again.

"Good enough to eat," I murmured, my voice dipping to her favorite gravelly tones.

Astrid's eyes fluttered, and she leaned closer, her soft lips teasingly ghosting over mine. "Promise?"

My grip tightened, my cock hard and straining with the tense current flowing between us. "Cielo, I will bring you to the heights of paradise no god, dragon, or Valkyrie could ever reach, if that is what you want."

She sucked in a sharp breath. Lust filled her eyes, and I swore I could smell it—the dampness growing between her thighs—rolling off her, like the most enticing perfume.

Astrid's fingers slid into my hair, and her next word came out as a soft caress over every barely controlled nerve. "Please."

That single word snapped every reserve I had. Tangling my fingers into her silky hair, I captured her lips with mine. Astrid groaned, the sound reverberating down to my cock. She pressed into me, her tongue darting out and sliding against my mouth, making enticing attempts to hasten my pace. But I didn't give in, no matter how much I was tempted to.

Fuck her. Claim her now. Despite the strong mental urgings pulsing in my head, I took my time, leisurely kissing her—tasting her—memorizing every contact of our lips. After all the wanting and longing, I would savor this moment with her, in case it was my last.

I nibbled and sucked on her lower lip until she whimpered. I couldn't express the sensation of satisfaction I received from that response alone, and as a reward, I gave her what she asked for.

My tongue glided against her lips, and she eagerly opened for me. I inhaled deeply, my pulse rising as my tongue delved deep inside her mouth. Her tongue wrestled with mine, and she tried to pull me closer, as if she could fuse us together.

My hands roamed down her back and along her firm ass, then I pulled her onto my lap. Astrid rocked her hips, grinding into my erection.

I groaned and gripped her ass in an attempt to still her movements, then broke the kiss. "Patience, Cielo."

She trailed kisses up my jawline toward my ear, trying to rock more than before. "No."

I sucked in a tight breath. *Great, she's a brat.* My voice dipped lower for my next words, the ability to do so coming easier than normal. "I promise, it'll be worth it if you don't rush this."

She groaned into my ear. "You'd better keep talking to me like that."

I chuckled and teasingly ran my fingers along the lace trimming of her panties. "Only if you behave."

She sucked in a tight breath and then ground into me again. "Give me a better reason to behave."

I chuckled again, my fingers gliding over her ass and slipping behind her, teasing the wetness soaking her panties, just enough to gain a quiet whimper. "I can do that."

Astrid's fingers dug into my chest, and she whimpered again, biting her lip. "Please, do that again."

I grinned. "Do what?" I traced again. "Tease your pussy?"

She groaned, her hips tipping to press me tighter against her, begging me with desperate neediness. "Please."

I glided my fingers along the frills of her panties, making her rock her hips, as she begged me again, and then pulled my hand away.

She whimpered in frustration. "Diego."

The way my name came off her lips drove me wild with desire, tempting me to skip the slow, sensual buildup and plunge into her immediately.

"I can do even better, but not here," I promised before turning my head and kissing her again.

Making sure I had a firm grip on her, I lifted us off the couch. I'd done so with unnatural ease, finding her far lighter than I was used to, but I didn't question it. I didn't care. Astrid looped her arms around my neck, kissing me back desperately, while I blindly navigated us to her bedroom, relying on muscle memory alone to guide me there.

Astrid's fingers twitched, and the door shut behind us. I couldn't help but chuckle at the absurdity of her *now* wanting privacy. Of course, I wasn't foolish enough to voice that.

My knees hit her four-poster bed, and I pressed one against the mattress as I laid Astrid on her back. She released her grip on me, and languidly laid her arms above her head, her hair splayed around her, making her look weightless as I gazed down at her.

I raked an appreciative assessment down her body, from the way her crop top titillatingly clung to her tempting large breasts that begged to be caressed and fondled, to the dip of her waist, and the curvature of her wide hips deserving to be kissed and feasted upon, to her athletically honed legs.

"If I didn't know any better, I'd think you wore this just for me."

The sound of my voice, which was almost more growl than words, surprised me. And what were words in that deep gravel got Astrid all out of sorts. It wasn't like anything that'd ever come from my mouth. But with the way her chest rose and fell at the sound, I didn't care about the oddity. If it was what she wanted here, then she'd have it.

"It's as if I intentionally dress this way all the time, hoping it'd finally entice you to stop seeing me as *just* your best friend."

Raw lust surged through me, sending a heat wave through my veins that had my dick throbbing in response. Well, if she wanted to entice me, who was I to deny her?

I climbed onto the bed and leaned over her, teasing her with a quick kiss on the lips before trailing down her neck to the hollow of her throat.

She moaned and arched her back when my hands glided over her heavy breasts, her nipples tauntingly stiff under the scraps of fabric she called a shirt. I rolled my thumbs over them, just long enough to coax another moan from her, and then felt the exposed undersides of her breasts, their softness even more exquisite than I imagined.

"You have no idea how long I've wanted to do this since you first wore this shirt," I rumbled in her ear before pulling away.

My thumbs slid along the hem of the crop top and then flicked the fabric up. She sucked in a sharp breath as cool air hit her sensitive, tantalizingly bare skin.

Taking in her stunning beauty for a moment, I slid the crop top up over her head. I allowed my fingers to glide down Astrid's neck, to her collarbone, and playfully around her nipples. Astrid bit her lower lip as I leisurely played with her for a long moment, never quite giving her more than teasing touches.

My caress ventured along her tattoo, appreciative of the permanent body adornment, and then down her belly. She squirmed as if it tickled, yet she didn't move to stop me. I chuckled and continued, over her navel and to the waistband of her panties. Hooking my index fingers into the band of her underwear, my eyes flicked up.

Astrid's lust-glazed eyes tracked my movements as I slid my fingers along the underside of the band to her hips. I paused there for a moment before giving one strong tug, pulling her panties off and tossing them somewhere.

I leaned back, licking my lips and taking in the delicious display. From dusky-rose peaks, erect and begging to be lavished, contrasting against her milky, freckled skin, to her perfect hips and soft, bare, glistening pussy, my imagination had nothing on reality. She was beyond stunning. "You're ethereal."

Astrid's mouth curved into a sinful smirk as she beckoned me with a finger. "Well? Are you going to finish what you started with this ethereal being, or am I going to have to kick you out and take care of myself?"

Desire pulsed down to my cock at the thought. Never had I seen this enthralling side of her before. Yes, she could be flirtatious when she wanted to be, but this… Wherever this temptress had been hiding all this time, I was all too keen to show her what it'd be like if she let me make her mine.

I dragged my tongue across my lower lip, her eyes following the motion. "I'm just deciding which part of you I'm going to devour first."

Her bottom lip caught between her teeth again and her leg slowly crossed over the other in an attempt to direct me to where to begin.

Grabbing hold of her thigh firmly, I grinned wickedly. "I don't think so, Cielo."

Pulling her leg away, I spread them wide, putting her pussy on display. Leaning forward, I kissed passionately along her inner thigh. Astrid gasped with anticipation.

Kissing further up, my right hand glided up her other leg, rubbing my fingers in teasing circles as I went. Astrid squirmed under my attention, and reached for me.

I pushed her away and nipped her inner thigh before licking the pinched skin. "Patience."

She huffed with frustration, and I chuckled. She wouldn't have long to wait.

I continued to devour her with kisses, drawing closer to the apex of her thighs. The scent of her arousal called me, stirring my cravings to consume her—to claim her.

My finger glided along the slickness of her soft, wet folds. Astrid sucked in a sharp breath, her hips tilting toward my touch, her wordless beg for more. I flicked my gaze up to her, and while holding contact with her intense, needy stare, lifted my finger to my mouth and slowly dragged my tongue along it, tasting her.

I hummed and leaned over her, abandoning my previous path, and pressed my lips to the underside of her jaw. Astrid started to growl in frustration, and was cut off when my finger slid between her wet lips again. She gasped and then moaned, her eyes closing.

I chuckled against her skin, trailing quick kisses down her neck. "I'm a tease, Astrid, but I'm not cruel. I enjoy providing pleasure too much. Enjoy the journey. I promise it will be worth it."

She'd had her share of unsatisfying lovers in the past. I would not be one of them.

"Just… give me a little more," she begged in a strained whisper. "Just a little—"

Her plea turned into a moan of pleasure when my fingers teased her clit. If she wanted more, I'd give her a little more. And then a little more after that, until she was ready.

My mouth traveled down over her collarbone, and my tongue licked large swathes of her skin. My free hand trailed along her body as she fisted the blankets beneath us and arched her back. I kissed closer and closer to her sensitive nipples, but not quite close enough, as I worked slow circles in time with my fingers below.

Astrid squirmed and whimpered, trying desperately to catch the right angle to force me to give her more. When she couldn't take the teasing anymore, she begged. "Please, Diego. Please."

Satisfied, I grinned before flicking my tongue over her hard rosy peak and then pulled her nipple into my mouth while I rubbed her sweet spot. Astrid let out a low, pleased groan, falling into the increased pleasure.

Sucking and rolling my tongue over her captured nipple, my free hand massaged her other breast, pinching and tweaking her sensitive bud until she was impossibly arched and she'd firmly tangled her hands in my hair, aching for more.

My thumb continued playing with her clit, as my fingers glided over her growing wetness before they teased the entrance of her pussy. Astrid sucked in a breath and then moaned when I plunged my fingers deep inside her. Her slick heat wrapped around me, inviting me to give her more. She rocked her hips, grinding against my palm as I slid my fingers in and out, rhythmically fucking her pussy.

I listened to each one of Astrid's gasps, each addictive, carnal moan and held-back beg, until she couldn't restrain her need. Lust coursed through my veins. I needed to hear her screaming.

I released her nipple with a *pop* and leaned close to her ear. My words came out raspy and growling, *"Vengas para mí."*

Astrid's mouth parted, and her fingers twisted in the blankets. Her head rolled back, eyes clamping shut, and her hips bucked as she screamed out the orgasm tearing through her. The sound ignited my smoldering need, and it vanquished any control I had.

I captured her lips, devouring the last of her screams, then kissed down her neck as she descended from her high. She quivered and her breath came in desperate gasps when my fingers ceased to plunge in and out of her slick pussy and my thumb continued to rub her sensitive clit.

I chuckled and continued my trail down between her breasts, licking and sucking them fervently before going back to my downward journey. "I told you to be patient, Cielo. I'll make the wait worth it. And I think three more of those will suffice to bring you to paradise as promised."

She gasped. "Three?"

"At least."

My tongue licked under her navel and then lower toward her apex. I flicked my eyes up, capturing her expectant and needy gaze, then slowly slid my tongue between her silken folds. Astrid groaned and tangled her hands into my hair. She ground her pussy against my face.

I licked and sucked, etching her flavor into my very being. My fingers picked up speed, and a moment later Astrid screamed, "Diego!"

I groaned in satisfaction as she shuddered beneath me, her body quaking from the force of her orgasm. I didn't let up as she came down, wanting her to do that again, plunging her over the crest again almost immediately. She screamed louder and her body bucked more, completely overtaken by her ecstasy.

As she came down, her body twitched away from my attention and this time, I allowed her a reprieve. I watched her chest rise and fall in heavy gasps, admiring how beautiful she looked in that moment—skin flushed, hair disheveled, and eyes filled with the satisfaction only an explosive climax could bring.

"Satisfied?"

"Fuck yes," she mumbled breathlessly, running her fingers through her hair. "Why didn't we do this sooner?"

I smirked, pleased with her enjoyment. "We just have to make up for it now."

She bit her lower lip, eyes transfixed on watching me shove my boxer briefs down my legs and free my cock from its fabric prison.

Astrid's chest rose and fell and her tongue dragged across her bottom lip. Her gaze traveled up and down my body before finally settling on the prize between my legs. She swallowed. "I will admit, I have limited experience with intact men."

"Is that a problem?" In my experience, it made some nervous, since it wasn't as common here in the States.

She shook her head. "Of course not. I just ask you to communicate with me if I need to do anything special."

"I'm more than happy to tell you what I want. And right now, I only want you to enjoy what I give. I promise it'll be an unforgettable experience."

She beckoned with a finger. "Then what are you waiting for?"

I complied, hovering over her and chuckling against her lips. "Someone is eager."

She ran her hands along my chest. "I'm a greedy whore who was promised four or more orgasms would be forced on her."

I slid my fingers teasingly along the wetness between her thighs. "No, you're a good girl, who is being rewarded and worshiped."

I teased her clit, making her gasp. "This swollen clit needs continuous attention."

My fingers slid inside her for a brief moment. Astrid bit her lip and groaned. "And this sweet, tight pussy of yours needs to be worshiped with more than just my fingers. Don't you want that?"

She whimpered, tangling her fingers in my hair. "Please. Please give me more. Give me your cock."

Her beg ignited a new fire in my veins. I reached for her nightstand, hoping she had condoms stored so I wouldn't have to run back to my room, but she grabbed my wrist and kissed my jawline.

"Don't worry about that. Immortality comes with a nice perk of the best birth control in existence."

My brow rose. "Oh really? One-hundred percent, then?"

She chuckled. "Just about. As long as I don't have thoughts of wanting kids or not minding the idea, we won't worry about the proverbial magic condom breaking."

I made a thoughtful sound in my throat and kissed her hungrily.

I'd make this so good for her that one day she'd crave thoughts like those with me.

Her hands grazed my chest and tantalizingly brushed my cock, drawing an aroused groan from me. She grinned against my lips, and for a moment, as she trailed light touches along my hard shaft, I thought she might offer up a little payback after all the teasing I'd done. I wouldn't hold it against her, since I did deserve it. But to my surprise, and satisfaction, she didn't.

She took me in a firm grasp and stroked, the motion gentler and more tentative than I expected. I wrapped my fingers around hers and guided her. Her strokes glided up and down, drawing my foreskin down and freeing my head, then back over. Her thumb brushed my cock head when it was exposed, the sensitive flesh jolting with pleasure. I sucked in a breath, and Astrid paused.

"Was that okay? I don't want to hurt you."

"It's sensitive," I breathed. "But I want you to keep going. Your touch feels amazing."

Her strokes intensified, her teasing caresses driving me mad. "Like this?"

"Mmm," I managed to groan out before I kissed her—hungrily— possessively, desperate for more. I'd waited so long to have her like this, and I didn't want to let her go.

When I couldn't take it anymore, I nudged her legs further apart. I gripped her hips and gazed deeply into her eyes, then eased into her tight, wet pussy.

"Fuck," I groaned as her warmth and tightness closed in around me. She felt perfect—like she was meant for me—like she was—*mine.*

Astrid groaned deeply beneath me and arched her back. "Yes."

I didn't stop or hesitate, rocking my hips slowly, then faster and faster, gliding my cock in and out of her. I tangled my fingers in her hair and captured her lips, drinking in all she was as I fucked her.

Astrid's nails dug into my back, and her moans vibrated against my chest. My pulse quickened until it was pounding in my ears. Need burned hotter and hotter until I thought I would combust.

"Diego," she moaned. "More, please, Diego."

Fuck… My name off her lips like this was intoxicating. It drove me on, thrusting harder and faster.

I gazed into her eyes as her mouth gaped and moved, in an attempt to speak through her heavy breathing and moaning. The connection between us, strong and powerful, was nothing like I'd ever experienced. It drew me closer to the edge.

"That's it, mi amor, you're doing so good for me." I slid my fingers between us, finding her sensitive clit, and stroked. "You deserve even more."

Astrid responded with stronger moans and the rocking of her hips, increasing the pleasurable sensation coursing through us together. Her legs pulled up higher on my back, pulling me deeper inside her.

When she finally found words to speak again, her lips brushed my ear, and a single control-breaking word came out. "Diego."

The tension in my body snapped. I grunted and crested over the edge, spilling inside her with reckless abandon. Astrid's scream of orgasm mixed with my punctuated sounds, until we came down together.

The room grew still, only our heavy breathing filling it. My body shook with exhaustion as I held myself over her, perspiration dripping down my skin. Astrid hummed contentedly while sliding her hand along my chest. I lowered myself to my knees and framed her face with my hands before pressing a firm kiss against her forehead. She sighed happily.

I stumbled off the bed to retrieve a towel and helped her clean up. I tossed the towel somewhere with little care and pulled Astrid into my arms. She snuggled in, laying her head against my chest and listening to my erratic heartbeat. This felt right—perfect. That magnetic pull I always felt with her wrapped and twisted around us, as if it were tying us together, demanding I never let her go. I didn't resist. I could lay like this with Astrid forever. *Mine.*

"Satisfied, mi amor?" I murmured.

She hummed. "Absolutely."

I grinned and settled in to fall asleep with her in my arms.

As my exhaustion drew me closer to sleep, my mind pinged back to earlier with the visions in the hallway, and then some of my new behaviors and thoughts. A small flash of fear soured my blissful mood. *What's going on with me?*

TWENTY-FOUR

TYR

The front door swung open, and I entered the house, running into Carrie. I caught and steadied her with my quick reflexes and then immediately stepped back. She may have been doing well around me these last few weeks, but I wasn't going to push it. "I apologize, Carrie," I said. "Astrid is always telling me to be more careful when opening doors. And something about being a lumbering bear in a wood shop."

Carrie laughed and fixed her hair. "I think the expression you're looking for is a bull in a China shop."

My brow scrunched. *Is that what Astrid said?* I was pretty sure she'd called me a bear. I shrugged it off. Didn't matter in the end. "Are you okay?"

She waved me off. "Of course. It was only a slight bump. And really, I should have been more aware myself. I know better than to linger in the foyer."

Wasn't the expression "linger in doorways?" *These people and their idioms.*

I stepped out of the way so she could leave. "Good luck at work."

"Oh, honey, with my skills, I don't need luck. But thank you."

I chuckled. Her confidence and fire were nice to see.

Raeni rushed out of the house. "Mom, wait up! Don't leave without me."

"I told you I was leaving, with or without you," her mother scolded. "I have a job to get to. You're lucky Tyr stalled me."

Shaking my head, I entered the house and looked around. Ùna busied herself in the kitchen, using the human disguise she'd chosen. She insisted on serving Astrid and me like before, but because we weren't returning to Norway anytime soon, she felt obligated to care for the home here as well. Her presence also had a positive effect on Sean, so that was a bonus Astrid enjoyed, and resulted in her discussing with them various rituals and improvements that could be made to make the retreat a comfortable place for fae.

Diego sat at the island, his attention on Astrid, who stood in the great room staring out the window. She fingered the chain of the necklace she wore, but it was clear she did it absently.

I drew closer, curious about what was going on, and shot Diego a questioning look. He shrugged in response. Ùna gave an acknowledging nod to indicate she, too, didn't know what was up with Astrid.

"Valkyrie," I said.

She didn't respond. I pursed my lips and kept an eye on her while going about rummaging in the kitchen. No sound I made distracted her. *Maybe it was a good idea to let her rest today.*

We'd gone hard with her training, with only the festival giving her a break. Aya let me know earlier this morning she was giving Astrid the day off, before she herself disappeared on me. *We might be doing too much at once.*

She was making amazing progress, especially now that almost all her memories had returned. And I knew we'd pushed this hard so that she'd be able to protect herself, and so we could deal with this shifter issue sooner rather than later.

Unfortunately, she hadn't yet recovered any memories that would help us with the identification of our adversary, and I was beginning to wonder if it had to do with us pushing too hard. We all needed rest, and Astrid was no exception.

Astrid turned away from the window and walked for the front door. She didn't seem to notice any of us.

Concerned, I intercepted her, gingerly grabbing her elbow. "Valkyrie."

She jumped and whipped around. Magic coalesced around her hands. Her wide eyes met mine. I took a step back, my pulse skyrocketing, and my senses picking up the growing aura of battle radiating off her.

It then died as Astrid realized she wasn't being attacked. Her reaction time in such a distracted state impressed me.

Astrid's shoulders slumped. "Sorry. Lost in thought."

I held up a placating hand. "It was my fault for startling you. I was concerned and didn't think about your possible reaction. Are you okay?"

She nodded. "Just thinking about some things. I'm going to go for a walk. Hopefully, it'll help."

She left without another word. Ùna shed her disguise and scurried over to the door. She watched Astrid before disappearing from sight.

I turned to Diego. "Ùna will monitor her. Not much trouble she can get into on the property—"

"But it'll put all our minds at ease," Diego said, nodding.

"What got her in that state?" I asked.

He shrugged. "I don't know. When I woke up, she was already down here, staring out the window. Ùna and Carrie both said she was there before they entered the house. And when I tried to talk to her about us speaking with Aya together about something that happened last night, she hardly acknowledged me."

"And she didn't react to any of you?"

Diego shook his head. "You got the most out of her."

I pulled out a barstool and sat down. "Do you think this is related to whatever you and she were going to talk to Aya about?"

Diego shrugged and gazed at the coffee mug cradled in his hands. "Possible, but given what happened last night, it'd be hard to believe it caused such a delayed reaction."

I waited to see if he'd elaborate, but after a few moments, I saw he had no intention to. "Did you talk to Aya?"

"Yeah, she's off looking into it, I guess."

An awkward silence fell over us. This was the first time I'd been in a room alone with Diego. Not even during the therapy sessions with him was I ever alone. And I was acutely aware of the reason why it was this awkward. But bringing it up…

Diego turned to me. "Looks like I'm going to be the one to initiate this awkward conversation."

I grunted. "At least we're on the same page of what needs to be talked about."

"I'll start by stating the obvious, in that neither of us is planning to concede unless Astrid tells us to."

I nodded. Anyone could see that, but I understood the need to put every fact out in the open.

"And it's obvious Astrid is falling into her self-sacrificing habits to avoid all this."

I frowned. "I had hoped I was imagining that."

Diego shook his head. "Unfortunately, no. Was she prone to this behavior back then?"

"Yes, though, from what I'm seeing, it's worse this time around."

He leaned on the island counter. "How different is she from back then?"

"Not much." I thought about all the points I'd run through my head lately. "She has some traits that are different, but they're minor. And a lot of what's the same is actually more intense. Makes it hard to not fall into behaviors and habits as if she'd never died."

Diego nodded, his fingers drumming. "There's no easy way for me to segue this from that, so I'll just outright say it. I don't think we should make her pick, and the three of us try to make this work."

I watched him, to gauge his conviction over the suggestion. After Astrid became immortal, I'd had this thought on and off. Mostly because of Aya's tease the first week I arrived.

When I took too long to answer, Diego continued. "She loved Baldur, didn't she? The reaction she had when you all told her the truth, even for someone just remembering her past, that was too strong for him to have only been a close friend."

I nodded slowly. "The two hadn't confessed anything before she died, but their relationship was teetering along that close-friends-and-lover line for a long while."

"And you were fine with that." Diego watched me with a calculative gaze. "You didn't put a stop to it when you saw what was happening."

I ran my hand through my hair. "Straightforward here, it's not common for immortals to stick with one partner for long. When you live forever, most don't see a point. But those who do rarely take only one partner."

I worked my jaw. "When I first pursued Astrid, I was… for lack of a better term, territorial."

Diego chuckled.

"She was mortal. Back then, I'd be lucky if I had her until she reached forty winters or so before something took her. Since she was eighteen winters when I first met her, that meant I had very little time with her. I didn't want to share any of that time with anyone. But then she became immortal…"

"And that urge went away."

I looked at him, and he had a knowing look about him. "Yeah. I knew Baldur had interest in her when he first met her. But he respected me not to act on it because he understood my reasoning. When Astrid became immortal, I didn't have to hold onto her so desperately. And I knew he'd treat her right, so I watched to see how the swords would fall."

Diego grunted and sipped his cooling coffee. "And now?"

I leaned on the counter. "It's strange. I felt that same need to have her to myself when I first found her. I hated that I was going to have to compete against you for her attention, especially after how long I'd waited to find her alive. But then… within a day of her becoming a Valkyrie, that feeling disappeared, as if it'd never been there to begin with. I want her to choose me"—I turned my full attention to Diego—"but I could be willing to make this work if she's also choosing someone like you."

An amused smile slid up his face. "Like me?"

"You may not be able to physically protect her like I can, but you sure as hel make up for it. You treat her right—more than right. I'd lay the bodies of her enemies at her feet, while you'd pamper her like a goddess on a level I don't quite comprehend, but wish I did."

"I'll take that as a compliment to both our strengths that we embrace."

I ran my fingers through my hair again. "So, we're really going to do this?"

"I've done it once before," Diego admitted. "I think this time it'll feel a bit more natural."

"Because Astrid's involved?"

Diego chuckled. "I spent far too many years trying to pretend we were just friends, and not realizing the reason my relationships weren't living up to my expectations was because no one compared to her."

"If I had a drink, I'd raise my glass to that."

Diego tipped his coffee mug. Before he could drink from it, however, he paused. His brow furrowed and his attention jerked to the nearby windows.

The muscles in my neck tightened. "What?"

"I don't know…" He set his mug down. "Something doesn't feel right."

"What do you mean?"

He was quiet for a moment. "I have this strong need to go find Astrid."

Buggy and Tuggy jumped up on the breakfast nook table. Their tails lashed and an unusual growling sound came from one of them. Without warning, Diego's attention snapped to Angel, who now stood in the foyer, alert and stiffly staring out the front door Ùna had left open. The hair on her back raised, and a low growl rumbled through the dog.

My senses ticked up, awareness spreading out. *What am I missing?*

Then, Ùna's small figure hobbled inside, her old injuries making it difficult for her to run. "Tyr!"

Diego and I jumped to our feet. The small fae ran past Angel, unfazed by the dog's behavior. Angel didn't react to Ùna either, meaning she recognized the fae wasn't the threat I was now becoming more and more aware of… somewhere.

"Tyr, something is wrong," Ùna cried.

I met her halfway and crouched down, holding her steady. "Easy, Ùna, take it easy. What's going on?"

"I don't know," she said through gasping breaths. "I followed Astrid, and she just kept walking, and walking. She didn't stop to take in the forest, or jump on any logs or rocks, like she usually does when she's in the woods, even when consumed by her thoughts. Then… then she walked past the magic barrier without stopping!"

The muscles in my back grew tighter.

"She didn't hear me when I called to her." The small fae was practically whimpering, which wasn't like her. She usually had more fire, even when worried. "I tried to get her attention, but she didn't listen. And then… the forest was upset."

Diego crouched alongside me. "What do you mean by upset?"

Ùna shook her head. "It's… hard to explain to non-fae. But something has it bothered. Something… someone, is making it upset by being out there."

My unease grew. "Sean said the same thing a few nights ago, after the festival."

Ùna's lip trembled. "Tyr, she's not safe. She's by herself and not acting as she should. I wanted to stay, but I needed you to know, too."

I kept my grip on her gentle, and did my best not to seem like my growing worry was agitation toward her. "You did the right thing, Ùna. I know you're not a fighter. We'll go and get her—"

Everything happened so suddenly. Angel snarled and bolted out the door, Buggy and Tuggy hissed, and then the most horrifying sound came after.

A woman screamed.

Diego and I jerked our gazes to each other. "Astrid!"

TWENTY-FIVE

ASTRID

A warm breeze caressed my skin. A twig snapped under my shoe. I hardly noticed, my mind whirling with too much to process. So much magic to understand. The capabilities and limitations, the power, and the control. I struggled with every aspect, compared to what my memories showed me with how easily it'd come to me in the past.

You're failing with your magic.

Being a Valkyrie… there was so much depth to it. It felt like I wasn't getting the hang of the most basic parts, besides flying.

Why do you even bother trying?

Diego.

Tyr.

Both.

Neither.

Why would they want you?

Quiet, peaceful walks.

Warm, comforting hugs.

Rough, calloused hands that knew all the right ways to touch me.

Soft sensual kisses that claimed me with each touch.

Look at what happened because of you.

Baldur…

It'll happen to them, too.

If I walked away, maybe…

Who are you kidding? You don't have the strength to decide. You run away, like always, instead of facing the decision that has to be made.

I stopped and stared out at the lake. Was that nagging voice in my head right? *Of course, it is… I'm pathetic.*

I'd had so much time to think about what I wanted. I could have figured out what I wanted in my relationship and decided who fit that need best. I could cop out, and tell myself that now that I was immortal, and I'd had a known past with one of them, this choice would be less painful to make. But I also knew it wouldn't be.

Picking up a smooth rock on the shore, I angled myself and skipped the rock three jumps before it sank into the water.

Both Diego and Tyr got me in different ways. I would be happy with either of them.

I skipped another rock, this one jumping three times as well.

You can be happy with both of them.

I closed my eyes and sucked in a deep breath. Aya's suggestion to choose them both plagued me. It was such a tempting… selfish option. My gut clenched as guilt from my past life surfaced.

I'd gone through this before, with Baldur. I tried so hard to ignore how he made me feel because I was married to Tyr. I wanted to stay true to my vow.

And yet, Tyr didn't mind.

He wasn't oblivious to my interactions with Baldur, and yet he never stopped it. He never seemed to mind that I loved him and had eyes for another. *Maybe it wasn't a problem, and neither of us knew how to discuss it then.*

I stared at the new rock in my hand. Maybe it wasn't a problem now. Would they consider the option? Could I handle balancing both of them, and possibly be okay with them eventually seeking companionship elsewhere as well, so it was fair?

"Sister," that quiet voice from the other day said. There was a familiarity about it that send a surprising ache in my chest. *"Sister, you're
in danger."*

A gust of wind blew through the forest, rustling the leaves of the
trees. I lifted my gaze and glanced around. *Why am I at the lake?*

Tension twisted up my spine, my senses screaming. Something
wasn't right. If I learned anything from my training with Kirby, it was
to trust my instincts. It understood things I didn't yet.

And I was outside the magic barrier.

I jerked my attention to the woods when a twig snapped. I gasped
at the sight of the large shadow approaching.

I stepped back.

And another step.

Three more.

The trees shuddered again, as if angry, and the shadow emerged.

My heart raced into my throat and my instincts screamed for me
to run, but also to fight. The conflict frazzled my mind as the black
wolf prowled toward me.

He was huge, but not as large as Fen, maybe half the size, and his
frame was slimmer, less muscular. There was a feeling of emaciation or
sickness about him. A large scar cut across his face, and in my frayed
state, I remembered Tyr telling me he had attacked the wolf shifter
that had killed me. *It's the same mark Diego saw in that vision last night.*

The wolf's golden eyes pinned on me, and his lips pulled back,
showing off his terrifying, toothy maw as he chuckled. *"The pretty
little witch is all alone, with no one to protect her… again."*

His words hit my mind and ears in the same way Fen's did when
he spoke in his wolf shape. The sensation, normally only strange to
experience, grated on my panicking brain.

I scrabbled backward, my breath hitching and pulse racing to the
point of pain in my chest. My throat throbbed as memories and
phantom sensations of my deaths surfaced. *It's him.*

My heel caught on something and I fell backward, crashing to the
ground. My body shook and fought to lock up as I tried to get away.
The wolf prowled closer, chuckling more and taking pleasure in my fear.

Everything I'd trained for these last two weeks, *poof,* gone. I couldn't remember a damned thing. I could only focus on the shifter who had killed me as he prowled closer to repeat the past.

He snarled and lunged. I screamed and threw my hands up, my eyes clamping shut. Power exploded out of me and I heard a *thud.* I peeked through my lashes, finding the shifter recovering from being thrown back.

The wolf shook his head and chuckled again, licking his chops. The sound grated on my senses. *"Looks like you're going to be fun this time."*

I swallowed and desperately tried to consciously draw up my magic—to summon my wings and armor—hell, to remember how to fucking run. Something!

The shifter's paws dug into the earth, and he came at me again. I panted and panicked. A black blur flashed past me and then my brain registered barking and snarling. *Angel?*

I watched Angel lunge at the large wolf, teeth bared, and making the most aggressive sounds I'd ever heard from her in my life. She snapped her teeth at the shifter's face. The shifter snarled and backed up, whipping his head back and forth, trying to follow the smaller dog.

My heart leapt into my throat when he snapped his massive teeth at her. Fen was always gentle when he took on his wolf form to play with Angel, but this wolf was not Fen. He'd kill Angel without a second thought.

My familiar deftly darted under him and went for his feet before lunging for his throat. The wolf howled and thrashed when she latched on. He wrenched free, throwing Angel to the ground—hard.

My lungs seized. *Move, Astrid. Move!* I needed to stop this. I needed to save her.

I lifted a shaky hand and willed—begged—my magic to listen to me. Power welled up, and a single black tendril lashed out from my fingers and struck the wolf shifter across the eyes like a whip. He yelped and shook his head, giving Angel enough time to recover and bolt for the underside of his abdomen. She latched on and shook with all her might against the wolf. *Lower, Angel. Aim for the dick. Fight dirty.*

Dad always told me to fight like my life depended on it, no matter how dirty you had to get in order to win. And fuck if this situation didn't fit that exact need.

Heavy footsteps alerted my senses. A chill shuddered down my spine, surging a new wave of panic through me. I scrambled back, my brain screaming at me that this shifter had an ally.

Tyr burst out of the forest. I froze, watching him throw his axe at the shifter, smacking the wolf in the head. The shifter snarled and thrashed. Without hesitation, Tyr charged the shifter, barreling into him and smashing his fist into his muzzle.

A hand clamped down on my arm. I let out a startled shriek, reflexively ripping away from my assailant, my fight instinct kicking in, but not my magic.

"It's me, Astrid," Diego said, his voice rushed. "Get up. We need to run."

Run? I blinked dazedly at him. What was he doing here? My heart rate kicked up when the wolf shifter snarled. What was Diego doing here?

He wrapped his other arm around my waist and tried to haul me up. "C'mon, get up. Get up."

I tried to get my body in gear, but something wasn't working. *What the fuck is wrong with me?* I wasn't like this. I didn't freeze when I was afraid. I pretended I was stronger than I was and kept going. It was like I didn't know who I was anymore.

The wolf snarled, and Angel let out a bone-chilling *yip.* I jerked my attention from Diego just as she landed several yards away from the shifter. When she didn't move, dread settled deep in my stomach. *No. No. No.* Relief washed over me when Angel finally lifted her head. She eased herself onto her feet, shaking it off.

Tyr kept the shifter occupied, allowing Angel to recover, and to my dismay, she went after the wolf again. This wasn't like her. She never acted this way.

Aya warned me Angel would change as she became a full familiar, but she wasn't there quite yet. She should still be my silly goofball of a dog. *She's a shepherd, Astrid. She will protect you, and as a half-familiar, she'll protect you at any cost.*

My gut twisted at the thought. Here my dog was, taking on a beast four times her size, and Tyr, fighting the beast that had killed me so many times before, at a disadvantage with one less hand because of me. And what was I doing? Standing here, paralyzed with fear, like the pathetic excuse of a Valkyrie I was.

I gasped when the wolf slammed the side of his head into Tyr, sending him flying into the lake. Without missing a beat, he turned and lunged for Diego and me.

Time slowed. The sound of my pounding heart filled my ears as my body seized up. Diego shoved me and I crashed to the ground. My eyes widened when he jumped in front of me, using himself as a shield. *No!*

My head pulsed and then pain split through it, fracturing my vision until I was no longer at a lake, but in a timber home. A beautifully stunning, but also scary redhead woman in a dress similar to what I wore at the festival sat in front of me.

I sighed. "Mother, this isn't working. Why are we even trying this?"

She chuckled. "Why? Because you have to learn your magic."

"I'm already using that to heal," I said. "That has come naturally to me. Why don't we merely focus on that? I know I used other magic when it first manifested, but I'm not grasping its concept to use again."

"This magic within you, Sunshine, comes in two parts. You must learn to harness both. You cannot properly understand your magic, and use it as intended, unless you do."

My shoulders drooped, and my gaze fell away.

"What is it, Astrid? What is truly bothering you?"

"Everyone knows I'm a healer. Jarl Rune saw me once perform the healing magic and now everyone knows. They only see me as a future healer. They've forgotten about the other magic I can harness."

My eyes lifted to meet hers. "I'm not you, Mother. I'll never be feared like you are. So, what is the point of trying to harness a magic that I'm struggling to grasp?"

She cupped my cheek. "Feared and respected are two very different things."

This was a memory, but the way she gazed at me, it was as if she could see the past me, and the present. "There will come a day when you surpass even me, Sunshine. You will be even more fierce than I could ever dream of. Your magic will know no bounds. Others will respect you for everything you can do. One day, you will see this. And when that day comes, it'll be when you find a reason to be that woman. It will be the day you find something, or somethings, worthy to protect. This I believe, because I believe in you."

The warm home rapidly faded away, and my sight of the lake flashed back—just as the wolf shifter's teeth clamped down on Diego's blocking arm.

"No!" I screamed. My hands flew out, power drawing up at my command. Golden light sprang from the ground like spikes, spearing the wolf. A black spike mixed within the gold pierced the shifter's eye. Blood sprayed everywhere as he threw Diego to the side and reared back, howling in agony and rage.

I sprung up, the weight of my wings manifesting on my back and propelling me forward. My axe summoning in one hand, and my sword in the other, I launched at the shifter, my fear forgotten, replaced with steely determination. "You will not harm them, you filthy mongrel!"

Years of magical knowledge returned to me, mixing with my modern understanding. My power pulsed and swelled, ready to be used in endless capacity. *My limit is my imagination. And my imagination is powerful and limitless.*

I had struggled in the past with my magic. I didn't know who I was back then, and yet I'd figured it out. I figured it out again. I knew who I was, and I knew more than I did back then.

I am a healer.

I am a protector.

I am fury and passion and I won't be tamed.

"Angel, protect Diego," I ordered through clenched teeth. I didn't wait to see her react to my command. I didn't need to. I felt it. I felt that tug Aya told me about, and it said she understood and would comply.

My axe came down on the shifter, slicing into his shoulder when he tried to jump away. Blood sprayed and sizzled, the stench of burning hair and flesh filling my nose. The head of my axe, wreathed in golden flame, burned as bright as my soul.

I swung my sword, sparkles of gold and black magic flying off toward the shifter backing away from me, and slamming into him like tiny concussive projectiles.

Water splashed, and Tyr charged out of the lake. My eyes flicked to him, my mind quickly assessing his lack of weaponry. Magic activating again, his wrist glowed, and a magical hand clutching a shield manifested.

Tyr didn't even blink, charging right for the shifter and slamming the shield into his bleeding face, then followed up with a strike with his fist.

The wolf backed up, snarling and snapping in frustration. I attacked him again with magic, focusing on his puny mind. He would not hurt anyone I loved ever again.

The shifter howled and writhed. He turned on his heels and fled. *"This isn't over. I will end you, false Valkyrie."*

Roots sprang out of the ground suddenly, chasing after the shifter and ultimately missing as he disappeared into the underbrush. I jerked my attention toward the property line, finding Sean standing at the clearing edge, face tight with concentration and eyes glowing. I blinked rapidly, struggling to process the pacifist elf attacking anyone.

My wings folded in and the power in me drained. Suddenly, heaviness weighed on my mind as an emptiness set in where the magic had been. I listed to one side, the sounds around me dulling, and then, everything went black.

TWENTY-SIX

ASTRID

Heaviness pressed against my mind and body in all directions. The weight was like thick chains wrapped around my body, but they latched even deeper than that. I didn't like it. I wanted to push it away—to escape, but I couldn't move. Why couldn't I move? I needed to.

"Something's different." Diego's voice drifted into my mind. "She seems restless."

I struggled against these strange chains in my mind. I needed to see him. I needed to make sure he was okay.

"Astrid?" he said. "I think she's finally awake, but something is wrong."

Awake? Am I asleep? I couldn't be. I'd never had such difficulties waking up before.

"Have her take this. She's too drained." *Is that Una?*

"Is it safe for her to?"

"She's as conscious as she's going to be until she recovers enough of her magic. This will speed up the process."

"Cielo, we're giving you some tea," Diego said. "Doesn't smell great."

"You've had this before in the past," Ùna said. "It tastes even worse."

I knew the tea she meant. This was not going to be pleasant.

A pungent scent hit my nose and then the warm taste of grass and refuse assaulted my tongue. If I could gag, I would. My stomach certainly protested as the disgusting liquid slid down my throat.

A wave of warmth flooded through me. The chains snapped. My eyes snapped open. I bolted up, coughing and sputtering, my head pulsing with the sudden movement. Angel's close nose sniffled and poked my cheek, and a large hand I recognized, belonging to Tyr, pressed against my back. It felt warm, like skin touching skin, but that didn't make sense. I'd worn a T-shirt today.

A tea cup hovered in the corner of my vision, and I immediately pushed it away. "Gods, why does it still taste so bad? Couldn't you have improved it in all this time?"

Ùna chuckled. "It's fine the way it is. If it tasted better, more would be reckless with their magic."

She had a point.

My head pulsed. I pressed my forehead into my palm. I tried to focus on my surroundings—my bedroom, from the looks of it—but the pain was too distracting. "I feel like shit."

"Well, that's what happens, dear, when you use all your magic in less than five minutes."

Had I? I supposed I had. I was so overcome with rage, I hadn't paid attention to how much magic I'd used.

I held my hand out for the tea. This wouldn't be pleasant, but it would be the fastest way to recover enough of my magic to be rid of this headache. Magic was great, until you learned about its drawbacks.

It was so intrinsically linked to our being that if we depleted ourselves of it, it was like the worst-ever hangover imaginable, mixed with the body aches of Midgard's worst flu, then multiplied by eleven. At least that was how I'd describe this awful feeling.

Nose scrunching, I downed half of the cup's contents before I choked. I coughed and sputtered, barely keeping myself from retching.

Ùna took the cup. "That should be enough. While a good punishment for being so reckless, I'm not one for torture. And that should be sufficient to restore your magic to a more comfortable level until you do so naturally."

I nodded. "Thank you."

My awareness was already returning, and the headache was subsiding. Angel laid beside me, watching me with great intensity. Blood coated her fur, but she didn't seem to be injured. Diego perched on the edge of my bed, near my legs. Tyr sat on the floor on the other side of the bed, close to me. Neither of them wore their shirts. Ùna stood on Diego's side, looking up at me, and Sean lingered in the doorway.

I briefly glanced down at myself and then took a double-take. I shrieked and pulled my sheet over my exposed chest. "Why am I naked?"

Diego and Tyr had seen me naked before, and I knew fae saw nudity differently, so it probably wasn't a big deal to them, but still, I didn't exactly consent to exposing myself.

"That was my doing," Ùna admitted. "That shifter's blood ruined your clothes, and we needed to regulate your temperature while also giving your body the optimal chance to regain its magic. Clothes risk acting as a barrier to both."

I puffed out my cheeks. I couldn't argue with her reasoning. And no one had been staring, as far as I could tell. Well, if Tyr or Diego stared, I wouldn't have cared.

"Oh, and don't worry, your mother's and Baldur's armor are on your nightstand. I knew you'd panic if you realized you didn't have those."

I nodded my thanks. I'd hardly stopped wearing them since Tyr gave them to me.

"What happened? I remember seeing Sean use some sort of nature magic to go after the shifter, and then everything went dark."

"After you passed out, Tyr and Sean chased after the shifter while I got you back to the house," Diego said. "That was maybe twenty minutes ago."

"He got away?" I guessed.

Tyr grunted. "He didn't just get away, he up and disappeared. Not even the forest could answer Sean on how."

I frowned. That wasn't good. Sounded similar to Fen's description of the shifter leaving his calling card. That almost certainly confirmed magic was involved. So either this shifter could use magic to some degree, or someone was helping him.

I looked to Sean. "Thank you. That must have been difficult for you."

He nodded slowly. "I know I told you I dislike fighting, but I wasn't completely forthright about that. I am tired of fighting. I did it a lot, a long time ago, even before your first lifetime. I chose to walk away from that life."

Sean shook his head. "But I wasn't about to let that shifter take you. You've given me a home—something I haven't had in a long time. You asked nothing of me for this home, and you've respected all my needs. This was all before you knew of my true nature. Once you learned, you've done even more for me."

He lifted his gaze to meet mine. "I don't seek war and violence again, but I will protect our home and everyone who lives here. Especially you, Astrid."

My lip quivered, and tightness wound its way through my chest. I nodded, my throat tight and tears stinging the corners of my eyes. I feared if I tried to speak, my voice would crack and the tears would flow.

"Just... don't be so reckless?"

I laughed. "No promises."

He shook his head. "Ùna, why don't we go check the wards again?"

Ùna blinked and then grinned. "Yes, let's. Come, Angel. We'll clean you up as well."

Angel launched off the bed. I watched Ùna skip off with my dog at her side and then passed Diego and Tyr a perplexed look. "Am I missing something?"

"I'm pretty sure they're just teasing us," Tyr said.

Teasing? I couldn't understand why.

Diego's fingers tangled with mine. "How are you feeling?"

My eyes drifted down to our entwined fingers. Realization flashed in me, and I gasped. "Your arm!"

Diego jerked back from my grabbing hands. "Astrid, what are you doing?"

"That shifter bit you." I wasn't doing well fighting back the panic. "I need to see the—"

Diego chuckled and pushed my hands away. "Cielo, calm down."

"That wolf tried to rip your arm off. Don't you tell me to calm down!"

He held up the arm in question. "I'm fine."

I grabbed his arm and yanked him forward so I could see.

Was I rougher than needed? Yes.

Did I care? No.

I stared at his completely fine arm. Bruises marked his skin where he once had puncture marks, and there was some dried blood, but otherwise, he was in one piece, and wasn't bleeding to death.

"See, I'm not dying."

"Who healed you?"

"Well, that's the thing…"

I glanced between the two men, a muscle in my neck tightening.

Tyr ran his hand through his hair. "He healed on his own."

I blinked. "What?"

Neither of them elaborated. They didn't need to. That was a simple concept to grasp. Diego self-healed. "Like… how immortals heal?"

They both nodded.

I looked at Diego's arm again. That's when I noticed something strange. Small patches of black and silver littered his arm. "Um… are those scales?"

Diego rubbed the back of his neck. "Yeah. We haven't gotten around to talking about this, since you were the main priority."

"Well, I'm fine now. Why the hell do you have scales on your arm? What the fuck is going on?"

He brushed his fingers along my cheek. "Are you sure you're okay?"

I huffed. "Stop trying to make this about me. Your situation is more important, right, Tyr?"

He shrugged. "I'm not sure what we can discuss. Seems like, somehow, Diego has an immortal soul now."

"But how? It doesn't make sense. And why are you acting like it's the most normal thing in Midgard?"

"Because, Valkyrie, people becoming immortal or being born as one isn't all that rare of an occurrence. Sure, it's not happening in the thousands every day, but I'd be willing to bet a few hundred every century isn't that far off. And there's no set reason why."

"But there has to be one." I couldn't let this go. It nagged at something in the back of my mind—something big.

"I can think of two possible explanations, and one is impossible."

I gestured for him to continue. "Well?"

"One of his parents is either secretly a creature of the supernatural or has such ancestry that's now activating in him, or he's a dragon. The scales would make me think the latter, but that's impossible."

Diego and I passed each other a look. "How is that impossible? Dahlia is a dragon."

"Because there's only ever been three dragons. The first three were sisters: Urda—now Urd, Skuld, and Verdandi, now going by the name Artura." His brow furrowed. "Or siblings. Aya told me Skuld had taken the form of a man in more recent centuries, so I'm not sure if sisters is the correct way to describe them anymore."

He repositioned himself. "Kirby came into conflict with Skuld… a year and a half or so ago now, I think from what she told me, and it resulted in Skuld's death. Dahlia is a child of Skuld, from what Aya explained to me, so it's not hard to guess that Fate wants to keep balance by making sure when one dragon falls, another replaces them."

"So, what, dragons just have a bunch of potential dragon kids running around, just in case?" I couldn't hide the slight disgust I felt at the idea.

Tyr shook his head. "I doubt it. The three siblings are considered the oldest beings in all Creation. They shared the first stories, the ones we now know as the world prophecies, with anyone who would listen. I don't know what Skuld was doing when they had Dahlia. Given the dragons were the first to be gifted clairvoyance, it is possible Skuld saw their death and tried to have a new dragon ready to take their place. That's, of course, if all children of dragons are born with dragon souls. Not even gods are guaranteed to have children with immortal or god souls."

"Well, my mom is dead," Diego murmured. "We scattered her ashes, so there's no way I'm some secret dragon child."

I slid my hand into his. This had been insensitive of me. I should have been more careful. "Sorry. Between your vision last night and now this, I just wanted to make sense of everything."

Tyr's brow pulled together. "Vision?"

Diego nodded. "I guess that's what it was. Normally I'd say it was a dream, but I was awake this time."

I tipped my head. "You never told me you'd had similar dreams."

Diego shrugged. "I always figured they were just dreams. Last night was the first time I had one while awake. It's also the only one that was unpleasant."

"What did you see last night?" Tyr asked.

Diego recited what he remembered, and Tyr nodded. "That was too accurate of a depiction of the shifter for it not to be clairvoyance."

"Is it normal for them to happen as dreams?" I asked. "My mother Randi only ever had hers when awake."

Tyr shrugged. "I'm not the one to ask about that. Aya would be more likely to know. Any form of magic that could benefit in war, she made sure to understand."

"I did tell her about it," Diego said. "I'm just waiting for her to come home after she said she'd investigate… however she planned to."

"Then we wait for her to get back to discuss further." Tyr hauled himself onto the bed. The mattress dipped, and I fell into him. He slid his hand along my lower back to my hip. "In the meantime, I can think of something far more fun to pass our time."

Diego leaned closer. "I'm game."

I clutched my blanket tighter to my chest, my eyes flicking between them. "What are you two doing?"

Diego's fingers skated along my shoulder. "While you were lost in your own world and walking off the property to be harassed by a shifter with a small-dick complex, the two of us talked."

"About?" From their hungry gazes and lack of care the other was in the room still, I had a good idea, but I needed to hear the words—that I no longer needed to agonize over this decision.

"Us." Tyr grasped my chin and turned my gaze up to him. My heart skipped a beat. "We both want you, and are willing to give this a hard go, if you are, too."

Heat bloomed in my chest. "You want to? You don't feel like you're forced to make this decision?"

Diego's fingers brushed my cheek. "We make this choice willingly."

I bit my lower lip. While this sounded amazing, I couldn't ignore the small bit of twisting in my gut. "I've been trying to figure out how to handle this, because, yes, I would like to try this, but I'm also feeling… guilty. Making you two accept that you won't have me to yourself means I need to do the same, and—"

Tyr dipped his head and captured my lips with his. My eyes hooded, and I fell into the comfortable warmth spreading through me. "There's no need to think about that right now. My heart still beats for only you, after all this time. I will focus on you alone. If I think that will change, we'll discuss it then."

I blinked slowly at him. I shouldn't be okay with such an avoidance choice, but a selfish part of me was all too willing to do it this once.

Diego tipped my chin toward him. "He stole my line."

I giggled as he kissed me. I couldn't help it. The bubbling warmth in my chest was too much to contain. I didn't have to pick. I didn't have to worry about making the wrong choice. Because, as these two men took turns kissing me—filling my heart until it threatened to burst—I knew this was the right choice.

Tyr yanked my sheet, exposing me to them. They raked ravenous gazes over me, sizzling my skin. I fought the urge to cover myself. Being appreciated by two men was hot, but also intimidating.

I extended my arms languidly above my head in an effort to relax, and the two of them didn't complain. "Well, what are you two waiting for?"

Tyr leaned over me first, pinning my wrists above my head and claiming my mouth. His lips were fervent against mine and I eagerly kissed back. I groaned when Diego's hands glided along my belly. His hot mouth pressed against my soft skin.

Tyr kissed my neck; Diego nipped my hip. Tyr dragged his tongue along my collarbone; Diego kissed a tantalizing path along my thigh. Hot, molten desire pooled through me as they worshiped every inch of my body with their mouths and hands.

I gasped when Diego's fingers teasingly slid over my folds, parting them as he went. Tyr kissed my breast, licking my nipple and being rewarded with another breathy response from me. Diego kissed the inside of my thigh and then dragged his tongue expertly along my wet folds. My breathing hitched with overwhelming anticipation.

As if they shared minds, Diego's tongue licked me into a frenzy—circling around then flicking my clit as he drove me wild. Tyr did the same, worshipping my breasts, licking and teasing my nipples until I moaned out in pleasure.

The dual sensations, unmistakably provided by two people, were tantalizingly maddening. I fell into their attention, sliding my fingers into both their hair and holding them captive as I moaned and writhed in pleasure. The feeling of both their tongues exploring my body was too much for me to handle; it felt like too much but never enough at the same time.

Tension coiled inside me until my body was bursting at the seams. One long flick against my clit and hard suck of my tit and I came undone.

My back arched off the bed, and I screamed, uncaring how far I could be heard. Neither of my men were ready to let up yet, prolonging the high a little longer, until I came back down.

They pulled away, gazing down at my languid, flushed body, overly pleased for men who hadn't orgasmed yet. I needed to fix that.

After taking a moment to collect myself, I sat up and threw my arms around Diego's neck, fervently devouring his mouth. Burning need pooled between my legs again.

Diego pulled me closer, kissing me back, fiercer than I expected from him, to the point I was sure it'd make my lips bruise if I were still mortal. His desire for me electrified me.

I broke the kiss and pressed my lips against Diego's ears as I trailed my hands down his muscular chest and taut abs. "*Quiero chupar tu verga.*"

His breathing hitched and he tangled his fingers in my hair. "Say that again."

I relished the sound of his desire and unbuttoned his shorts, speaking again in Spanish, "*I want to suck your cock.*"

Diego hastily shoved his shorts and boxer briefs off his hips before I had his zipper all the way down, his cock springing free. I wrapped my hand around him and stroked, taking my time feeling his hard length and kissing his neck and down his chest. Diego groaned and leaned back on his knees, his hand gently encouraging me to keep traveling lower.

Not to be ignored, Tyr's hand and wrist glided along my sides. The bed dipped as he repositioned himself behind me. His fingers slid along my ass, massaging and appreciating, all the while I licked and kissed along the velvety flesh of Diego's cock. I moaned against him when Tyr slipped his fingers between my legs, sliding along my wet, needy heat.

Tyr chuckled. "Greedy, Valkyrie. Always greedy and ready."

I tossed a glance over my shoulder and wiggled my ass. "Luckily, you know just what to do with a Valkyrie like me."

I closed my eyes and moaned as he rubbed his large finger against my aching clit and inserted another deep inside me, sending delicious shockwaves through me.

"Yes, I know exactly what to do with a whore like you," Tyr rumbled, desire roughening his voice.

As tempting as it was to fall into his touch, I had someone else who also needed my attention. I licked the head of Diego's cock, relishing his taste along my tongue. His eyes half-lidded, he slid his fingers through my hair, murmuring to me how he liked to be sucked.

I took my time, slowly pushing back his foreskin with long hand strokes and being slightly fascinated with how it wrinkled into a rigid band at the base of his head. My tongue flirted and swirled around his satin-soft head, caressing the underside just enough to elicit sharp inhales from him. I teasingly pulling the tip into my mouth, only to release him just as he thought I'd continue.

Tyr's fingers worked their magic on me, making it difficult to focus, and I nearly gave in to Diego's begging urges too soon, but didn't until I wanted to take more of him in.

And take him I did, slowly sliding him in and out of my mouth, enjoying his texture and feel. I used my tongue in all ways I'd practiced and knew would add to his pleasure. There were perks to having a sex goddess as a best friend.

Diego groaned, his fingers tightening in my hair. "That's it, Cielo. Be good and keep doing that."

I eagerly sucked his cock, rocking my body between him and Tyr's fingers. Tyr pleasured me, not letting up as I drew closer and closer to the edge. I gazed up at Diego and he smirked, holding his grip firm. He knew. He knew I was about to come and relished the thought of me doing so with my mouth wrapped around him.

And I did. My body tensed and then released in one powerful spasm. I screamed, Diego's thick member choking off most of the sound. He didn't allow me to stop sucking him as my orgasm took over. The moment I slowed, falling into the sensation, he rocked his hips, driving deep into my throat.

"You wanted this." His voice was so deep and gravelly, it was like I was listening to someone else, as it always sounded when he used this voice. "So be good, Cielo, and suck me like you promised."

I did want this. I wanted them. Inside me. Using me. Me using them. I wanted to fall into more passion than humanly possible.

Pants hit the floor, and Diego's brow rose. "Clearly I'm doing something right if she still wants me after having that."

Tyr chuckled and teasingly slid his massive cock along my still-wet and desperate pussy. "It takes a lot to satisfy this whore Valkyrie. Isn't that right?"

I moaned, and Diego finally released his grip, allowing me to pull him out of my mouth. "Please. Please, both of you, just fuck me senseless and fill me with your cum."

Both of them grinned. My eyes popped wide, and I moaned when they both surged into me at the same time. Pain and pleasure crashed through me, flooding my senses. Tyr slid his hand between my legs, caressing my throbbing clit, intensifying everything.

I rocked back and forth between them, losing all sense of myself and falling into the pleasure as they stretched and teased, and fucked me with their hard cocks.

Orgasm burst through me all of a sudden in an explosion of euphoria, and both my men released all control, cresting over the edge. Hot, warm cum spilled into the back of my throat, and warmth filled my pussy.

Both of them pulled out, their panting breaths as heavy as mine. But I wasn't done. Or, I didn't feel done. I wanted more of them. And I could tell, by the looks they gave me, they wanted too as well. There was only one issue.

"Fuck, if I'm supposed to be some kind of immortal now, why do I have the same downtime issues?" Diego complained through his breath.

"Because not all of us are lucky, like sex demons," Tyr groused. "Or don't have a free fuck ticket that a particular Valkyrie punches when she prays in a special way to you."

I grinned at him. That was fun.

"Just be patient. We'll bounce back quicker than you're used to, and we'll be able to take our Valkyrie all day."

"All day?" Diego grinned. "Sounds fun."

Yeah, but I was impatient and wanted it now, not in the next five minutes. I pursed my lips, a thought coming to me. *Maybe I can.*

"Cielo, what's with that look?" Diego asked. "I'm not sure if it's a good one or not."

I grinned and prowled toward him. "I'm going to push the limits on the idea that my magic is as infinite as my imagination."

He swallowed, eyes reflecting both his concern and excitement.

I traced a finger against his soft flesh. Magic condensed into my fingertip, following the runic symbols I sketched along his shaft. Diego groaned and twitched under my touch.

A moment later, his foreskin slowly pulled back as his cock came back to life. He sucked in a surprised breath and Tyr groaned his approval of this new-found fun use of magic. I chuckled. "I don't think you need another moment, my dragon."

"We've been over this. It's not possible for me to be—"

I kissed him to shut him up. I didn't care what he technically was. Dragon felt right to call him in this moment, so I was going to.

I slid into his lap and his cock eased into my slick, cum-filled pussy. He and I sucked in pleasured breaths. "Fuck me. Praise me. Degrade me. I don't care. Just treat me like the little cum slut that I am, filling me with so much, it leaks out of me. And then fill me some more."

Diego thrust into me. "With pleasure."

And we fucked. And fucked. And orgasmed. And fucked even more.

And I did the same with Tyr. I passed myself between them, separately, and together. Falling into our intense need and passion, bolstered by my magic. Saying and doing dirty, filthy things to each other.

It wasn't lovemaking. A part of me wanted it to be—desperate to claim them permanently as mine. But I wasn't ready for that, and this was far too filthy to possibly be lovemaking.

So, we fucked, until finally, that need was satiated.

We fell back onto the mattress, our heavy breaths mingling. Perspiration dripped from our skin and dampened our hair. Fatigue and bliss mixed in my mind and body, wrapping around me like the most satisfying blanket. Tyr pulled me against him and Diego intertwined his fingers with mine, pressing his face against the top of my head.

"You're perfect," Tyr said. "Either of us tell you that?"

"Don't forget the most magnificent creature in existence," Diego mumbled.

I smiled and snuggled into them. "You could stand to praise me more. This Valkyries enjoys it. Especially after some filthy, rock-your-world sex like that."

Laying here with these two men, feeling their warmth, gentleness, and protection, I felt more whole than I had in my entire life. A part of me still felt missing, but I suspected that would piece together in time the longer we explored this relationship.

I gazed up at Diego and noticed something I hadn't before with his eyes. Silver flecks broke up the brown depths. "Your eyes have changed."

He brushed the back of his hand along my cheek. "In a bad way?"

"Not at all."

I startled when someone knocked on my door frame and shot up, covering my chest. I relaxed, seeing Aya. We'd seen each other naked on enough occasions I never felt ashamed with her around. Now, awkward being seen naked with two men on my bed? That was another thing entirely. Especially with the shit-eating grin she had.

Even without being caught in this position, she'd know exactly what had transpired in this room. Having a god friend with a domain that crossed into sex was not very convenient.

"What do you want?" I grumbled.

Her grin deepened. "You know I wouldn't interrupt your post-coital time if it wasn't important. Though, you could have done me a solid and sent some power my way in thanks for all I've done for you."

I rolled my eyes. "I'll do a blood ritual. Those are better for you anyway."

She may qualify as a sex and fertility goddess, but she was a war goddess first.

Aya winked. "I knew you loved me."

"Now, what do you want?" I repeated.

She sobered. "I've got those answers for Diego. She's downstairs."

Diego sat up. He was a little more modest in covering himself. "She?"

Aya's attention went to his arm. "I can see there've been some new developments. She'll be better at explaining what's going on."

Her avoidance of who this "she" was didn't sit right with me. "We had a situation earlier."

She nodded. "Una already informed me what happened. I'm sorry I wasn't there to help. Convincing her to come here was more difficult than I had hoped."

"Who is this 'she,' amiga?" Diego asked again.

Aya shook her head. "You'll understand in a moment. I'll leave you all to get dressed."

"What was that about?" I muttered when she disappeared from the doorway.

"I don't know, but I don't like it," Diego said. "I get the feeling she might have known this would happen with me."

I looked at Tyr. "What do you think?"

Tyr pursed his lips. "I don't think this is anything nefarious. That's not her. We both know that. But Aya does have her secrets, and if she was willing to go through the lengths she did to hide you away, I'm sure she's got other things going on in the background as well."

I nodded. That was my feeling as well. Even if Diego was right, and

Aya knew or even just suspected this would happen, she wouldn't have kept the truth from him unless she had to. Not with everything that's been going on lately.

Diego slid off the bed and retrieved me a towel, helping me clean up before throwing on his discarded clothes and slipping out to snag a shirt. Tyr dressed as well, but didn't have a shirt.

"Are you allergic to shirts right now?" I teased as I rummaged through my dresser.

He chuckled. "Una didn't retrieve me one when she fetched me clothes so I could change out of my wet ones."

I paused and then nodded. That was right, he'd been thrown into the lake. "My guess, she did it on purpose."

Tyr laughed. "Of course she did. She was getting impatient about us being together again."

I shook my head and pulled a tank top over my head. "I think she'd about die if you took as long as the last time. I know I had back then."

He blew out a breath. "You were so convinced my attempts to befriend you first meant I didn't want you. I didn't understand that."

I laughed and turned to face him, a cute pair of shorts in my hands. "The ironic thing, past-me would have been happier if you hadn't taken your time, but me now, if I didn't have these memories of us, I'd definitely have expected us to build that longer friendship first."

Tyr scrubbed his face. "You are a complicated woman."

I laughed again and slipped into my bathroom to make my hair more presentable, trying out more of my magic to help me freshen up. This power would make me lazy in no time if I wasn't careful. "You wouldn't have me any other way."

He didn't respond until I came out, hair nice and teased to wavy perfection. Tyr slid his arm around me, pulling me against his side. "I'd never want you any other way than however you want to be."

I smiled up at him, warmth blooming in my chest.

Aya waited at the top landing for us. She seemed… pensive. And the longer we waited for Diego, the more apparent her nervousness was. It made me feel a little justified in not wanting to brush off the new developments with Diego. This was as big a deal as I suspected.

Diego finally showed up in a tank top and apologized. "My clothes are missing. I was lucky to find this shirt in my closet."

I pursed my lips. "I'm betting Ùna's doing. She did say something yesterday about wanting to wash everyone's clothes in better soap. She really has an issue with the products we use. She already replaced all my makeup and hair products."

"Make sure you tell her no if you really don't want her doing something," Tyr said. "You know how she can get."

Oh, I knew that quite well. My memories told me Ùna and I got along well, but we did butt heads a lot on how some things should be done.

"Seems a little convenient my clothes went missing so suddenly," Diego said.

Aya smirked. "She's a fae, of course it was. No clothes means you have to stay in bed with our favorite Valkyrie here."

I rolled my eyes, and Diego nodded. "I guess you ruined that plan."

Aya's mirth sobered. "Do me a favor and please promise you'll hear her out."

His brow furrowed. "Why wouldn't I?"

The uneasiness returned to her. "Just… trust me when I say you need to make this promise."

"Okay, I promise I will." He pushed past her and jogged down the stairs. "You're acting like my mom is back from the dead or something."

I froze, staring wide-eyed at Aya. *She couldn't be…* Aya shot me a sheepish, apologetic look that sent my gut twisting. I bolted after Diego.

His propensity to skip steps regardless if he was going up or down had him wheeling through the foyer long before I could catch up. But when I did, I ran into a solid wall of frozen Diego.

I peeked up at him, taking in his wide-eyed stare and tense jaw. Taking a deep breath, I peered around him.

In the great room, a woman with alabaster skin and pale, almost silver hair sat on one of the couches, her attention fixed on Diego with the palest eyes I'd ever seen.

The woman slowly rose, revealing her impressively tall height, and I swore her skin and hair shimmered with a pearlescent sheen. "Diego."

Diego swallowed. "¿Mamá?"

TWENTY-SEVEN

DIEGO

Numbness tingled my whole body. This couldn't be. She couldn't be here. She was dead.

My eyes took in all her features—her hair, her eyes, her towering height for a woman—*She's taller than I remember.* She had to be nearing seven feet tall.

"Diego," she said, her voice soothing, just like I remembered. But her posture was… wrong. She was more hesitant and unsure than I'd ever seen her. This wasn't the strong and confident woman of my memories.

So much buzzed through my head. Things I wanted to stay. Questions I wanted to voice. Emotions I didn't know how to feel. "¿Mamá?"

She approached, and I had to tip my head up to look at her. Her soft, pale eyes gazed down at me, tears brimming her lids. "Look at you, little treasure. Well, you're not so little anymore. You've grown so much. You got your height from me, but everything else from your father."

Her fingers glided over my cheeks. Something in me snapped out of my frozen state. I grasped her hands, pressing them against my skin, and closed my eyes. Her warmth, her smell, her very presence, it was all here.

I opened my eyes and gazed up at her. "How? You… died. How is this possible?"

"I promise I will explain everything."

"I damned sure hope so," a familiar, gravelly masculine voice said behind me.

Mamá's eyes popped wide, and I didn't need to guess to know the shit-show that was behind me. Nevertheless, I slowly turned, finding Darius and Papá standing in the foyer, coolers in their arms, and home two weeks early from their trip.

"Dad?"

"*¿Papá?*"

Astrid and I spoke in unison.

Neither of them acknowledged us. They both stared at Mamá, Darius' expression stern, while Papá's mirrored my reaction. The cooler in Papá's hand crashed to the floor, lid popping off, and wrapped fish and ice spilling everywhere.

"L—Luna?" he stammered.

Mamá somehow became even paler. "My shield… I… I can explain."

"No… no, you can't be her." He ran his hair through his hair. His accent thickened as his distress took over. "I was there when she died. I confirmed the body. I… I buried her ashes."

Mamá chewed her lip. "It was a fake body."

I stared at her. I couldn't believe I was hearing her admit faking her own death.

"I loved you." Papá's face twisted as rage took over the shock. "*¡Qué coño*! I grieved for you! And you have the audacity to stand here and tell me you faked your death?"

"Xavier, I can explain," she pleaded, taking a step closer.

He held up a hand, his face reddening. He sucked in a hard breath through his nose and then he spun on his heels and left. Mamá's shoulders slumped, and she bowed her head. I noticed her fiddling with a ring. *She still wears her wedding ring.*

Papá did, too. He never got over losing her, saying she was the only moon in his sky, and there'd never be another. I wondered if a part of him knew her death was a lie. I'd learned enough in these last few weeks to not discount it as a possibility.

When Mamá opened her eyes again, her back straightened, and her emotions slipped behind a mask of neutrality. I remembered this look from when I was a kid. I'd told her she looked like a queen and asked her when she was going to be the next monarch. And even now, knowing that mask was just to force her composure around others, she still looked regal.

"It's been some time, Darius," Mamá said. "You look well."

The man nodded, oddly calm given the situation. "That it has, Urd. A shame it's not under better circumstances."

I blinked. They knew each other? *Wait, he said Urd.* Tyr had mentioned that name when talking about the dragons. Was she the same Urd? I didn't actually remember the name Mamá went by. The only one I remembered was the name Dad had always called her: Luna. He'd given her that name because according to him, she was a drop of moonlight made flesh and outshone any star.

Darius stepped around the spilled cooler and set his on the island before slipping into the pantry. He returned a moment later with a bottle I'd never seen before. The liquid inside it swirled and shimmered with color. *What the hell kind of drink is that?*

"Today seems like a good day to break out the good stuff. Especially since I'd like to know the story behind why my household is now playing host to a dragon and a second god."

His eyes flicked to Aya, then darted to Tyr. *What the fuck is going on here?* Even a glance to Astrid showed she was now cautious of the situation.

Aya crossed her arms. "So, you were aware of who I was."

Darius uncorked the bottle and poured himself a glass. "Yes, Freya, I knew exactly who you were when you showed up in D.C., and then here, pretending to be a woman who didn't actually exist. What I expect is for you to fill me in on why."

His attention flicked to me and then to Astrid. His eyes lingered on his daughter, as if he were trying to piece something together. "And I hope it'll explain why my daughter and Diego seem more surprised about my behavior than anything else going on right now."

"I think a round-robin of explanations is in order," Astrid said in the calmest tone I'd ever heard out of her. I wasn't sure what to make of it.

Her dad nodded. "I say Urd first, given the severity of the situation, and the fact Diego doesn't seem like he wants you to be kicked out."

Mamá turned her attention to me, and I saw the mask slip, just enough to see the pleading in her eyes. Even with how fucked-up this situation was, I didn't want her to leave. "I want answers. I'll hold judgment until then."

She touched my shoulder, then took a stiff seat on the couch. I sat next to her. Aya sat on the other couch, and Darius pulled up a chair. Astrid and Tyr cleaned up the mess Papá had left before they joined us. Neither of them spoke while cleaning, and Darius watched them from the corner of his eye, but didn't offer any assistance. I had to guess that he was unsure what to do around his daughter right now.

Astrid sat next to me when she joined us, and Tyr joined Aya. Astrid didn't even look at her father, focusing solely on me. She slid both her hands into mine, her presence helping me stay calm as my nerves skyrocketed.

I squeezed her hand to show her how much I appreciated her support. I couldn't imagine what was going on in her head right now, and yet she was going to stay strong and support me through this.

Mamá took in a long breath. "As Darius said, I am Urd, one of the two remaining oldest dragons in existence."

"Two?" Darius paused mid-lift of his drink. "What happened?"

"My sisters and I have always had a difference in opinion on how to interpret our visions and how they should be handled. Unfortunately, as you know, Darius, Skuld chose the path that would ensure those moments would come true. This included her own death at the hands of the former last Valkyrie."

Darius froze, his eyes briefly flicking to Astrid and then to Aya, but he didn't say anything. He was always good at making sure not to derail a topic too much, and would most likely ask more questions later, when it was also his time to share who the hell he really was.

Mamá turned to me and Astrid. "Have the two of you been told about us dragons?"

Astrid nodded. "Enough to follow along with this so far. We also know Dahlia."

Mamá nodded. "I suspected you three might have been introduced by now, but I wanted to make sure. This will help you understand what I'm about to tell you."

I tried not to fidget.

"I did not intend to harm you or your father, Diego. I had every intention of raising you and living out your and your father's lives parading around as the human I'd led you both to believe I was." Her gaze dropped, grief filling her eyes. "But I had a vision. I saw your father die, and not in any normal way a man should who had no connection or knowledge of the true inner workings of this world."

She licked her lips. "Only once before had I not taken a neutral stance to my visions. I see them as inevitable happenings. But I was too close to this one. I desperately wanted to stop this event, and unfortunately, the best solution I could come up with was to not be near you."

Mamá slowly lifted her gaze to meet mine. "From what I saw, I surmised I was the leading cause of your father's death. I believed if I wasn't around, you two would be safe."

My brow knitted together. "So you pretended to be sick and faked your death?"

She nodded. "There was no easy way to reduce the pain I'd cause by leaving. I refused to just up and leave. I couldn't hurt either of you like that. And so, I thought if I died in both of your eyes, that would give you the closure you needed to live without me."

"Why here, then?" I asked. "Why did you have us move here if you thought leaving us would be the answer to keeping us safe?"

"I was paranoid. I feared my leaving wouldn't be enough protection," she admitted. "I knew Aya was in the process of protecting Astrid here, as I'd had a vision about a beloved witch of the gods dying and being reborn, so I approached her, requesting she also protect you and your father."

"Wait," Astrid said. "You had a vision of my death? Was it the same as my mother's?"

I noticed Darius' attention sharpening on Astrid.

Mamá nodded. "It's quite likely we did. Prophecies tend to repeat themselves to various clairvoyants. It's not always in the same way, but it's always about the same event."

"I see." Astrid tapped her lips with a finger, her eyes going distant as she lost herself in thought.

Mamá grabbed my hand. "I am sorry for hurting you, Treasure. I never would have made that choice, had I known you possessed a dragon soul."

I worked my jaw. I could see the sincerity in her eyes, but that didn't erase the pain twisting and pulling in my chest. "Did you ever feel tempted to come back?"

She nodded. "I thought of you two every day. Everything I did since that choice was to ensure Midgard was safer for you. And many times, I had wondered, if I did achieve that and thwarted that prophecy, if I could be worthy to come back and beg your forgiveness."

My fingers tingled with numbness. I wasn't really sure what to feel right now. "How is it possible I'm a dragon? Tyr told us there was only ever three, and after Skuld died, Dahlia took their place."

Her face grew serious. "Because the claim that there were ever only three dragons… is a lie."

The room stilled. I felt the growing, focused attention of everyone present.

"Why would you lie about that?" Tyr asked.

"Because of the story Ùna told us," Astrid said. Everyone turned to her. She had a calm expression, but there was a knowingness to it. "It's related to Midgard losing full access to magic, isn't it?"

To my surprise, Mamá smiled. "You're a perceptive woman. That will do you well in trials to come."

What does she mean by that?

"Yes, the loss of magic is related." She crossed her legs and pulled her shoulders back. "When Midgard was young, it birthed many great and powerful creatures. My sisters and I, several phoenixes, the fates, the fae, and so much more. We cared for it, protected it, and, as thanks, we were blessed with immortality. My sisters and I, and the phoenixes, specifically, were elected to be the primary guardians."

She shifted. "As time went on, more life came into Midgard, including humans, and all was well. Life went along and humans, of all creatures, learned how to harness the powers of magic in the world. They did not abuse this power, and instead built great civilizations."

My brow furrowed. This didn't make any sense. How could they have made civilizations with magic and it not be so well-known in history?

A bittersweet smile pulled at Mamá's lips. "My sisters and I were fascinated by the other creatures of Midgard—humans, especially. For such fragile and short-lived beings, they could do so much. And they loved our stories, or what we once thought were stories from dreams we had, which we later learned were prophecies. It was this fascination that led us to take them as mates, and the resulting children changed everything."

She turned her attention to me. "We would have children who matched the beings that our mates were, and then some, like you and Dahlia, were dragons."

Air left my lungs. *I have siblings?*

"They weren't the only change to come to Midgard. Humans began to change as well. Their souls took on unique qualities. Some became shifters, others became what we know now as gods. And many of those humans and ordinary humans suddenly became immortal."

"Just like that?" Astrid said, her skepticism unmasked. "Just out of nowhere?"

Mamá worked her jaw. "We thought so at the time. We assumed it was just another change that was intended. It was still peaceful, so we never worried. That was our mistake."

Her face grew grave. "We should have seen the early warnings, but we ignored them, lulled into a false sense of security. We enjoyed what we could make and indulged too much. My sisters and I all received visions of what we now call Ragnarök. It wasn't long after that the peace we'd come to love ended."

She leaned onto her elbows. I felt the gravity of what she witnessed with this movement. She never hunched. She even got on my case so much as a kid, because it was "unbecoming."

"It was a bloodbath. Friends, family, they all turned on each other.

Chaos reigned, and it twisted everyone unlucky enough to be touched. We guardians tried many things to stop it, but nothing seemed to work. We feared we wouldn't succeed, and Midgard would end—until a great sacrifice was offered."

Her eyes clamped shut, her face twisting. "Our children and the phoenixes, who had taken up guardian positions, sacrificed themselves to push back Ragnarök."

Astrid and Aya gasped. My lungs seized.

"The sacrifice wasn't enough to stop it completely, but it bought us time. And the sacrifice wasn't just in life. It also came in the form of memories and magic." She lifted her gaze to meet Tyr's. "Those who assisted, including gods and fae, lost memories and had their magic stunted. Humans lost most of their access to magic and forgot what they had built."

"That's why the older gods remember coming into existence, but not how," Astrid murmured.

"And it explains why gods like Odin forgot how to make Valkyries," Aya said.

Mamá nodded. "That is correct, for both."

"But, why didn't anyone remember, with so much evidence around them?" I asked. "They may have lost everything, but shouldn't there have been an entire civilization and written records explaining what they forgot?"

She shook her head. "Because of the severity of the loss, and our fear that Ragnarök would return faster if the knowledge was discovered too soon, we used our magic to erase any evidence we could. Only the oldest of us remembered in the end, and we've held it close to our chests ever since."

So, our history as we knew it, was the restart. It explained a bit more about some discrepancies that conspiracy theorists and even some historians poked at. "How many dragons survived this event?"

Mom frowned. "Just my sisters and me."

Muscles in my neck tightened. *All their children died?*

Of course. That explained why the world only thought there were three dragons.

"And after that, there were no more," she said. "No matter how many children we had after, they were never dragons. It was why I never expected you to have a dragon soul. When Dahlia's dragon soul came to be, it was after Skuld's death. Artura and I assumed this was Creation's way of replacing our sister. But when Zeke came into his nature more recently, I grew concerned, and then Freya came to me with her news."

Zeke… Astrid and I had a friend with that name. It wasn't all that unique of a name, but it still pinged something in my mind. *Why?*

"Who is Zeke?" Astrid asked.

"One of Skuld's other living children," Mamá said. "He is Dahlia's half-brother."

"Makes them both my cousins," I murmured, my mind circling around this for some reason. It was nice knowing I had more family, regardless of how strange of a situation it was for them to be said family. But there was more to this situation that wouldn't leave me alone. "I'd like to meet him."

"I doubt that'll be an issue, since he's also one of Azzie's companions," Aya said. "Kirby mentioned wanting to get Astrid and Azzie together soon, so maybe we can coordinate a dual meet-up."

"Azzie," Tyr murmured. "That's Davyn's woman."

"You know her?" Astrid said.

He nodded. "Not personally, but she prays to me. It was a recent prayer of hers that got Davyn to tell me to head this way to look for you. Something about a guy name Zeke…"

He trailed off. Astrid slowly turned to me. "We know a Zeke."

"And I'm pretty sure he's mentioned an Azzie," I said slowly, my brain now catching up. "Does anyone have a photo of this guy?"

"I do." Mom held up a hand and twitched a finger. A photograph appeared out of thin air. *Neat trick.*

I took the photo and froze. Staring up at me was a familiar rugged, brown-haired, brown-eyed man. *It can't be.*

But it was. Zeke. Astrid's and my friend. The guy we spent time with since we were teens—since we rekindled our friendship after he'd hit rock bottom and pulled away.

We were close now. Like family. *Like cousins.*

That was the face of the man in this photo.

The friend who joined us for holidays sometimes. The friend that'd come up this way to hang out just before all this shit hit the fan. Hell, I talked to him over the phone not long after that visit when he'd called me all distressed over something. *Come to think of it, he was acting squirrelly when he called. Something about a spear...*

Astrid sucked in a shocked breath. "That's Doomsday."

I turned to look at her. "Seriously, why the hell do you call him that?"

"Because the only thing that kept him from totally ruining our trip the first time we met him was the pronghorn I snagged. And his mom was totally a doomsday prepper. You can't convince me otherwise." She shrugged. "Besides, he doesn't mind the nickname. And it's only fair, with the one he gave me."

Darius made a motion to see the photo. I handed it over to him. He nodded. "Yeah, that's the Zeke kid you've hung out with ever since meeting him on that first hunting trip."

"So, you already know him?" Mamá asked.

"Yeah, we're amigos," I said. "We went on a fishing and hunting trip to Wyoming in August, before our junior year. That's where we met him and his mom for the first time. I spent a lot of time with him. Astrid hated his guts for some reason."

"You had so much fun with your new boyfriend you all but forgot I existed until the trip was nearly over," she muttered.

I didn't remember this. I could have sworn I spent a lot of time with her, but with the way Darius was laughing, Astrid and I clearly remembered having different experiences.

I took the photo back from Darius and gave it a good look again. "Either way, this is definitely the Zeke we know."

"Fate has its reasons, even if we don't understand at the time," Mom said.

"Well, our reunion will be interesting." *Actually...*

I whipped out my phone and pulled up my messaging app. Scrolling, I found his name and typed out a text.

Hey, we need to talk about something I just learned that concerns the two of us. Preferably in person. Tell me a time you're free and where, and I'll be there in… a blink.

It took a moment to get a response, but I did.

Zeke
Are you insinuating a very particular form of travel?

Well, it all depends on if the dragon-lady who taught you revealed this ability yet, Cousin.

He came back with a response that made me laugh.

Zeke
Well, fuck me sideways.

Yeah, so I think it would be best we find a time to talk. Probably with Dahlia too. Actually, make that mandatory with her too. All three of us need to talk.

Astrid rested her chin on my shoulder. "Tell him I say hi."

Astrid also says, hi Doomsday.

Zeke
Do you want to talk now? And hi Red.

Astrid smiled at his response. She may have had a jealous-girlfriend reaction to him the first time we met, but they were in-fact friends now.

Today isn't good for me. Too much going on. We'll work something out.

I set my phone on the coffee table. "Well, that just happened. Guess I'm meeting up with my new cousins at some point."

I turned to Mamá. "Do I have any living siblings?"

She shook her head. "No. Of my sisters, I had the fewest children after the sacrifice. It was too painful to watch my children grow old and die, but I refused to have someone else raise them like my siblings chose to do. I raised each and every one with all the love I could offer, even knowing their lives would be short. That was my intention for you as well."

"And you haven't had any since leaving Papá and me?"

She shook her head again. "It was some time between my last mate and me meeting your father. And I have not been with anyone since."

Was that because she took her vow to Papá that seriously? Maybe that would help mend the rift between them… if that was what they wanted. But that was on them. Whatever they did, it didn't change what I wanted to do.

"If I have a dragon soul, does that make me a human shifter or a dragon?"

"Just as Astrid is no longer human, you are not, either," she said. "There are no dragon shifters, like fictional tales would say, just dragons who have the ability to shift into anything they wish."

"But there are shifters and they're human?"

She nodded. "It is a nuance that you will understand more as you immerse yourself in the truth."

"How long will it take for this whole, 'You're a dragon, my son,' bit to seem more real?" I asked. It all was a lot to take in. And I now understood better what Astrid was going through these last few weeks.

"However long it takes for you to accept you're a dragon," Mamá said. "And I mean, accept it at your core. A surface-level acceptance won't work."

"Will this help me protect Astrid?" I'd wanted a way to be better involved. I was doing my best, and I knew she appreciated everything I offered within my power, but if this gave me more ways to help, I would. At this point, I didn't care what that asked of me. I was growing used to the idea of Astrid needing to fight. I'd get used to it for myself if it meant she was safe.

"We dragons are both feared and respected. You may be young, but what you are carries weight and it will not hinder what you are capable of."

"What are we capable of?"

She grinned in a way only an apex predator could. "More than anyone realizes."

It may have been a vague response, but it was enough for me. "Then that's what I am, and I need you to teach me everything I need to know."

She reached out and touched my cheek, her eyes soft. "You want that? You don't hate me?"

I grasped her hand with mine, relishing the familiar touch. "I'm still upset, but I understand why you did it. It's going to take me some time to get past it, but I want to try. I've lost enough time with you. I don't want to lose any more."

Mamá pulled me into a tight hug. "I love you. I made mistakes with my approach to Dahlia when her nature manifested. She doesn't trust me, and as a result, I don't believe Zeke does either, since she took on the task of teaching him. It is a regret I have. I won't make that mistake with you. I promise I will make you into a proper dragon your mate will love."

My lungs seized, and Darius choked on his drink. "His what?"

TWENTY-EIGHT

ASTRID

Heat burned my cheeks. *She didn't just say that.* She had not just said it in front of my dad, no less.

From her confused look, with the way Diego and I now stared at her… *Oh, gods, she did.*

"I don't have a… mate." The word sounded just as strange coming from him as it seemed for him to say.

Urd cocked her head. "Her scent is all over you, so I assumed…"

My scent? *Shit, I forgot some immortals have that good of a nose.* Oh gods, was it getting hotter in here? "It's not that serious, yet."

My words came out as a pathetic, rushed squeak, but I couldn't help it. The way Dad stared did not make this any better.

"Oh, I apologize. By the strength of her scent, I thought you'd engaged in a mate claim. I"—she shook her head—"I didn't mean to offend."

I tugged on a lock of hair. "I'm not offended…"

I didn't particularly want to get into my recent sexcapade with Diego's mom, of all people, and not in front of my dad.

Dad held up his glass. "Well, all I can say about this is, it's about damned time."

Laughter bubbled up and I couldn't hold it back. I shook my head. He knew how to cut the tension, that much I could count on.

Urd's attention unfocused, and then she came back. "I have to attend to something urgent. I'll return as soon as I can so we can begin your lessons."

Diego agreed, and the woman disappeared. He slumped and scrubbed his face. I brushed a tousled lock of hair from his face. He lifted his head and smiled, snagging my fingers and pressing them to his lips. "Thank you."

I opened my mouth to say something, but Dad interrupted when he stood and waltzed over. "You two can hold off on the mushy stuff 'til later. I'm sitting next to my daughter while we talk."

Diego jumped away, and I let out a silly squeak when Dad plopped down without waiting for us. He still had his liquor and its bottle, which had a rather sweet smell to it. The swirling nature, though, was what really got my attention.

I plucked the glass from his hand and swirled the contents before taking a sip. The sweet nectar tingled against my tongue, and went down smoother than anything I'd ever had. It also packed a surprising punch after. "Is this the fabled Olympian wine?"

"Good guess, Ace," Dad praised. Ace, the loving nickname he always called me since as far as I could remember. Because I was his *Ace of Hearts*.

"You've got your hands on some Olympian wine? How'd you manage that?" Tyr said.

"Someone owed me a favor," Dad said. "It's the last of the batch that's lasted me a long while."

So when he meant the good stuff, he really meant it.

Dad set the bottle down on the coffee table. "I've missed a lot on my trip, haven't I?"

My brow lifted. "I think I can say that about my entire life right now."

He chuckled and took his glass back. "I hope you're not mad at me."

I shook my head. One thing I wasn't was mad. "With everything going on, I've had my suspicions, and I have a feeling that what you'll explain to me mirrors a lot of Urd's reasoning to Diego."

He took a deep breath and nodded. "I've been around a few centuries. I know Urd because I used to work for her. As a result, I've gained a number of enemies. I never thought about that as a consequence for the future."

He removed his glasses and looked at them. "I was used to changing my identity and moving on to the next job."

Knowing what I did now about the immortals and how healthy and in peak performance we became, outside of rare instances, I knew now the glasses were some sort of Clark Kent-esque disguise he took.

"What were those jobs?" I asked.

"Protecting people from Skuld's antics." He shook his head. "Urd was suspicious of her sister's activities. She'd run many organizations over the centuries, and their activities always seemed too perfectly aligned with prophecies the dragons had. So Urd recruited me to infiltrate Skuld's operation and report back to her. If I ever screwed up, I'd change my identity and get back in."

He took a sip of his drink. "Then I met your mother, when I infiltrated Skuld's—now going by the identity Lance—more recent organization that made a mockery of Urd, The Followers of Urd, and everything in my life changed."

I watched him closely. There was a torrent of emotions raging in his eyes, but I also felt something calling deeper—from his soul. Kirby hadn't had much time to talk to me about Valkyrie-specific abilities, but she said I'd know them by instinct, even if I didn't understand them yet. And conversations about my mother always hurt him.

"I'd gone centuries avoiding romantic attachments," he said. "My work was just too dangerous for that. I already took enough risks with making allies and friends. But Ingrid was not a force I was prepared for. And before I knew it, she was telling me she was pregnant with you."

He shook his head. "The life we were living wasn't good to raise a family, so I convinced her to get out of it with me. Urd already had a new life for us when I went to her. That's when I started going by this alias."

"And then Mother betrayed us years later."

Dad ran his fingers through his hair. "I don't know what happened there, Ace. Ingrid was the perfect wife and mother. But maybe that's where the red flag was. She was a little too perfect at it all. It could have been because of the training, or maybe I was a love-sick fool and didn't see that she'd never really left FU. But if that was the case, I don't know what you had to do with it for her to turn on us like that."

Tyr, Aya, and I passed each other a knowing look. "We might, but we'll get to that in a minute. I need to understand more why you kept the truth from me. I can understand wanting me to not know your past, but being an immortal… while also trying to connect me in ways like saying you practiced heathenism… I just…"

Dad took my hand in his. "I planned to, Ace. I wanted you to grow up understanding Midgard to its fullest, but your mother asked me not to. She said she was afraid if you knew too much, you might become a target. So I struck a deal with her. I'd keep quiet, but when you came of age, or if your magic manifested before then, I wouldn't keep things from you anymore."

My back straightened. "What do you mean, my magic?"

He held up his hand and wiggled his fingers. Sparkles of light I remembered from my childhood shimmered around his hand. My eyes widened. "That was real magic. You've been using real magic around me this whole time?"

He rocked his head. "Not since the incident. That's why I went strictly to card tricks." He made a disgruntled face. "Which, annoyingly, were your favorite of all my tricks, anyway."

I laughed, taking me a moment to calm. "I just need to know, Dad, why didn't you tell me the whole truth when I came of age? You told me some of it, all coded under the disguise of heathenism, so why not go the whole way?"

He frowned. "Because of everything that happened. After losing your mother and nearly losing your life, I couldn't add something else that would bring you pain and disappointment."

Because I would have been a regular human. Not special. Broken. Unworthy. "So the only way you would have told me, was when my magic manifested."

"If, Ace—if. It was why I was less secretive of my practices. Without your mother telling me to hide my beliefs in our gods, I thought I could entice you to try things out. I wanted to see if you performed the same völva rituals, then it might spark your magic. But the older you got, the more that likelihood faded."

I smirked. "Here's the thing about the world that I've learned—it likes to surprise us when we least expect it. And I really love that I now understand where my magic comes from, since that's been quite the conundrum for the last few weeks."

Dad's attention sharpened. "Ace?"

I held up my hand and made the same shimmer of sparkles he had. "Surprise, late bloomer."

Diego and the gods choked on laughter. Dad, however, stared at me. Both pride and sadness flickered across his face.

"You… learned it without me."

I frowned. "Dad…"

He grabbed my hand and shook his head. "Don't, Ace. I don't want you apologizing. We don't control when our magic manifests. Even if our family is known for much earlier manifestations. I just had hoped, when it did manifest, I would be the one to teach you."

I squeezed his hand. "You still can. There's so much more I can learn. Even if Aya is teaching me, I'm sure you've got a few tricks I can snag."

He smiled. "You're right. I'd be a shit father if I didn't continue the family tradition, even if you've had a head start."

"You'd never be 'shit dad,'" I said. "Well, unless you don't explain to me what you mean by family tradition."

He refilled his glass with wine, allowing me to take a sip. "Our family is one of the few that has a long-standing blessing of magic users every generation. Until me, they were all the firstborn daughters, and sometimes, if that generation was lucky, their other daughters would be as well. Of course, magic is subjective. It wasn't always like ours. Some could heal, others saw—"

"Visions." A strange feeling fell over me. "You made sure I understand we had proud Scandinavian heritage. Are you saying you're from a family line of völva?"

His brow pinched together. "Yes, that's right."

"Did you have a sister?" I asked. "Named Randi?"

He watched me for a moment, his eyes only flicking to Aya briefly, who sat much straighter with this topic of conversation. "Randi is a namesake in the family. The only time anyone deviated from naming their firstborn Randi was when they named her—"

"Astrid." *No fucking way.* The exchange I made with Aya confirmed the exact conclusions I was coming to. "Your sister was your twin, and you were the first and only male inheritor of the magic gift of our family."

Dad's eyes shifted between us. "What is going on? How do you know this?"

"How many Astrids were born into the family after the death of Völva Astrid, daughter of Völva Randi, the reason for the namesake, after her death in battle?"

"Astrid, how do you know that?"

"Answer the question, Dad."

"Nine, including you. It became seen as a family curse because—"

"They all died as children in an animal attack," Tyr finished, catching on. "But regardless of all that, you still felt compelled, possibly unnaturally so, to name your daughter Astrid."

"What the fuck is going on?" Dad sat straighter, though he looked more defensive than interested. "Urd said you were no longer human, Astrid. What did she mean by that? It's time I get some answers instead of providing them."

"You are the descendent of Leif, son of Bjǫrn and Völva Randi." I placed a hand on my chest. "Brother of Völva Astrid, chosen wife of the Norse god Tyr, who ascended to immortality and died in the war of the Norse gods. And through complicated magical means, was reincarnated into the family over and over again, as her former enemy found and killed her, until Freya finally found her first, and made sure she was protected this time."

Dad almost tossed his drink on the coffee table as he surged for me. His hands framed my face, his calloused hands rough, but his grip the opposite, gentle and fatherly. We stared into each other's eyes. "You... you're our lost wingless Valkyrie?"

I smiled and slowly stood, my wings growing out of my back. "Yes, though I'm not so wingless anymore."

Dad stared, mouth agape and eyes wide as a shield. Then his shock morphed into pride. He shot to his feet and gathered me in his arms for a tight hug. I wrapped my arms around his neck, hugging him back, my chest swelling.

When he was finally ready, he set me back down. I pulled my wings back in and then sat on the couch. Dad grabbed his glass and then used his magic to get more. He handed everyone a full glass. "Today is a good day to use this bottle up, I say."

Aya happily took a glass. "And we can fill you in while we enjoy it."

And that's what we did, bringing Dad up to speed about everything. I also learned just how convoluted the situation between him and Aya was. While gods didn't usually hear the name of their followers in the chorus of voices, except for very specific circumstances, if the god met them, they could identify their follower easily.

Despite Dad changing his name many times—originally beginning as Bjørn—his prayers kept the same identifying aura. Aya recognized Dad immediately. Dad, being a more enlightened heathen, knew who Aya was the moment they met. And the two had danced around each other ever since, because Dad understood Aya was protecting me for some reason, but was afraid that if he approached her, she'd stop, while Aya feared Dad would try to run with me if he learned the truth. *My life would have been a hell of a lot simpler if my family just learned to communicate.*

Dad scowled. "So a shifter is still after her?"

Aya nodded. "We had an encounter with him today just outside my ward."

He looked to Tyr. "And you're here now because?"

Tyr's brow lifted. "Isn't it obvious?"

Dad pursed his lips, looked to me, then to Diego, then back to Tyr, and grinned. "Excellent. Double the chance for someone to convince her to give me grandchildren, especially now that I can't pretend the excuse is that I'm not getting younger, and neither is she."

"Dad!" I shrieked, my face growing hot. "Can you not? We're still working on seeing how this goes. There are no plans for grandchildren any time soon."

Tyr and Diego laughed. *Honestly, I should have expected this.*

"You keep saying that." He waved a hand dismissively. "How you see your relationships is your business."

His expression grew serious. "What is mine… is this shifter bullshit. You said he's still after her, and there was even an encounter earlier today?"

Tyr nodded. "He got away, but he showed more of his hand than we did."

Dad looked to me. "You also said earlier that you had a feeling you knew what might be the reason Ingrid turned on us. What was that about?"

"It's also because of Astrid," Aya said. "If someone, say the shifter that's been hunting her every reincarnation, told Ingrid of Astrid's true identity, then if she were more devoted to FU than her own family, she'd do what was needed to be done."

"But why?" Dad asked. "What does Astrid have to do with the prophecies Skuld was trying to bring to fruition?"

Her eyes darted to Tyr. "Because, as we said, Astrid is the same Astrid that Tyr loved. And… there is a prophecy out there about Tyr."

Tyr shook his head. "There are two. They both were told long before Astrid existed, and they were so vague they could have been applied to a number of gods—until I lost Astrid."

When his Valkyrie falls
The god of war will crumble

"Many assumed that one was about Odin," Aya said. "Seeing as his domain touches many, and he was the only one with Valkyries at the time. But I started to fear it actually meant Tyr when Astrid gained her Wingless Valkyrie name. Unfortunately, I had only come to that conclusion shortly before Astrid died."

I chewed my bottom lip. Tyr had become a shell of a god after I died. He admitted that to me. *If that one came true, and others have as well, can you actually thwart them?*

"What was the second prophecy?" I asked.

"This one we thought was about Tyr and Fen, but we're now sure it's about the shifter," Aya said before speaking the prophecy.

So wolf and god shall battle
And—

Neither shall prevail

Everyone looked to Diego when he finished the prophecy for her. "That's the vision I saw, Astrid. I saw Tyr and that wolf shifter battling. I didn't see the ending, but I got this feeling death was the outcome."

A shiver ran down my spine. "That can be stopped, can't it? We're not going to lose you."

Dad grabbed my knee. "Easy there, Ace. Prophecies are never exactly as they seem. They're open to interpretation. That's why Urd rarely believes they can be thwarted, but also why she took issue with her sister's activities. Not prevailing in this prophecy's case could mean many things other than death."

"Death is death," Tyr said.

Dad shook his head. "There are many ways something can die without dying."

My brow furrowed. Was he right? Was there more to this? Then something else came to me. "Wait, isn't there a human myth around that prophecy?"

I pulled out my phone and did a quick internet search. Before I found what I was looking for, Aya spoke up.

"Yes, the humans turned the prophecy into their myth for Ragnarök. They also gave a name to the wolf, though it couldn't be true, because that name belonged to a shifter who wasn't immortal."

"Who was the shifter?" Diego asked.

"Garmr," I said, my voice grave. I stared at my phone, the myth of Ragnarök displaying Tyr's predicted death. My hand shook, my mind flashing with memories of a celebration long ago. "It's him."

"Astrid, it can't be," Aya protested.

I jerked my head up. "It's him. He's definitely immortal. I remember him."

Tension filled the air, and Tyr leaned forward. "Keep talking."

"Do you remember the celebration where Odin asked me to heal Muninn?"

They both nodded.

"Remember, Garmr was with Odin, and he wouldn't stop watching me."

I turned to Dad. "And do you remember the dog Mother brought home? It was sickly but large, and it had a scar on its face."

"Yes, though it wasn't as large as typical wolf shifters."

"But magic can make a shifter smaller. He told Mother about me. His entire goal is to kill me." I shifted my gaze to Tyr. "To weaken you because he can't kill you otherwise. He's using the knowledge of the first prophecy to ensure the second comes to pass."

Tyr set his jaw, his fist clenching.

"That wolf that attacked us earlier today looked exactly like the one my mother brought home, just larger," I said. "And… and I saw Garmr at the festival."

"What?" Tyr and Aya said in unison.

I held up a placating hand. "I didn't realize it was him. I ran into a man who looked unwell, and he gave me unsettling vibes, so I got away from him as fast as I could. It wasn't until now could I place his face. Garmr is definitely immortal."

"But why would he do this?" Aya murmured. "We could assume he was after you and Tyr on Odin's orders during that battle. Odin believed the rumors that Tyr made you into a Valkyrie and was furious. He couldn't accept any god, especially not Tyr, who challenged him at every turn, could have made a new Valkyrie, wingless or not, when he couldn't remember how to do it himself."

"But why kill Astrid?" Diego asked. "You said Odin was a possessive bastard. Why not force her into his service?"

"Probably because he thought I was tainted." I made a face. "Or he didn't think I was perfect enough, so he needed me to disappear so I'd be forgotten about, and he'd be the only god remembered as having Valkyries. Regardless of his reasons, he sent Garmr after me, and the wolf made the active choice to kill me. And then, after Odin died, he's continued to do so, most likely out of loyalty to Odin. But that also means he'd have to go to great lengths to even find out I was reincarnated, let alone seek me out. And the fact he was able to do so better than either of you is…"

"Disturbing," Diego finished for me. "Which means there's more going on than we know."

I chewed my lower lip and looked to Dad. "There's something else… I think… I think Mother is back."

The glass in his hand cracked. "What?"

"When I was at the festival, I passed a woman with red hair." I licked my lips. "I didn't get a good look at her, but the same overwhelming sensation of panic as when I ran across Garmr hit me. I've never had that experience with random redheads I've encountered on the street. I think… I think it was her."

"It would make sense, if the two are working together," Tyr said.

Dad sucked in a tight breath through his nose. "I should have known that jail sentence wouldn't be long enough. And I was foolish to think she'd leave us alone after that."

"Do you think she's the reason Garmr found me again here?" I asked. "Aya has been protecting me since that near-deadly day, so I can't see how he'd be able to find us without help."

He nodded. "Safe to assume that's correct. She has connections like I do. It's why I didn't bother changing our names or keeping you away from anything that tracked our identities. She'd be able to find us regardless, so there wasn't a point in causing you more problems."

"And if they realized it was me there that day, then all they'd have to do is find someone with the ability to sense wards," Aya said. "All wards carry the signature of their caster. It's how we make territory markers for our homes."

"But because you never left Astrid's side, she stayed protected," Diego added. "This shifter is damned determined if he's going to wait over two decades to find a weak point in her protection."

"And cocky if he didn't try to kill her at the festival," Tyr grumbled.

I shook my head. "I have a feeling he didn't think he'd be able to get away with it. There were too many allies moving about for him to attack me unnoticed. That's why he waited for me to leave the barrier alone."

Dad leaned back. "We're going to need a good plan, on top of the training. I'll talk with Urd about what contacts and supplies we can utilize. And I'm going to have to pull my gear out of storage, it seems. Never thought I'd do that, at least not for some time."

I smirked. "Badass dad, incoming."

He roared with laughter.

"I think I'm a little done with doom and gloom," I said. "I want to know about your trip."

Diego stood. "I'm going to go check on Dad. Hopefully, he's calmed down enough to want to be around me."

I wished him luck and let him know I could feel that Angel was with him. My bond with her was definitely stronger now. I also took his glass to finish off the wine he wasn't interested in anymore.

Dad grabbed the bottle of wine off the coffee table. "Arran and Hurrit send their regards."

"I have to ask, are they immortals, too?"

He smirked. "Water horses. Well, Arran will fight you to call him a kelpie, but they're the same thing, just different regional origins."

I rolled my eyes. *Of course.* "I guess now I really have to go with you on the next trip."

Dad pressed a hand to his chest. "I'm hurt, Ace. Sounds like you don't enjoy those trips."

"Oh, I love the hunting and fishing trips. I just don't love being replaced." I raised my voice enough for Diego to hear me as he exited the house.

"I didn't replace you, Cielo!"

Dad laughed and then regaled me with his and Xavier's adventure in the Canadian wilderness.

TWENTY-NINE

DIEGO

Slow, steady breaths.

Focus.

Concentrate.

Find it.

Each step Mamá had instructed swirled through my head. I tried to follow them as she gave them, keeping my eyes closed to block out distracting stimuli.

I let out a frustrated breath and opened my eyes when nothing happened. "It's not working."

Mamá frowned. She sat in front of me, and to my right, Astrid's friend, Bjarke, watched with almost intimidating intensity. He was a little taller than average height, but it was his bulk that added to his grizzly visage.

Dahlia and Zeke were both busy and couldn't get away, preventing any sort of reunion or additional dragon assistance, so Astrid thought Bjarke would be a good stand-in, since he was a born Berserker, rather than made by Odin. That made some sort of difference, though I still wasn't clued in as to how.

Bjarke had yet to give any help, but that was more because Mamá hadn't been too pleased by the intrusion. Of course, Bjarke was more afraid of Astrid than he was of Mamá—not that I blamed him—so she couldn't quite scare him off.

"This shouldn't be so difficult for you," Mamá said. "You've already touched your dragon. You should be able to touch it easier now. Dahlia and Zeke didn't have these connection issues, according to Artura."

I rubbed the back of my neck, fighting the urge to be ashamed. Even though I knew she wasn't chastising me, after two hours of struggling with no progress to show for it, it made me feel like I was being reprimanded. "I don't know. I really can't feel anything. It's just the same old powerless me in there."

I wanted to feel something—desperately. I wanted to be able to protect Astrid. I wanted to be able to do all the cool shit Mamá showed off that she could do, and then more that she hadn't yet.

"I suspect it's because of the different life he's lived compared to them," Bjarke said. "Diego has lived a fairly normal human life. My understanding of Dahlia is that she was raised a soldier."

"Astrid's description of Zeke and his mom being doomsday preppers wasn't that far off, I think," I said.

He nodded. "Then I'd say I'm not far from the mark. They lived a life that was more in line to accept their true nature. You're going to struggle doing the same."

"But I do accept it."

"Your dragon disagrees." Bjarke shook his head. "My bear accepts me and I accept him, but it wasn't always that way. While I was born with my bear, I had to work on that cohesion and prove myself worthy. Your dragon is making you work now that you know it's there."

I didn't quite understand why this was a test. "It showed enough of itself to push me harder to pursue Astrid after she became a Valkyrie. And it showed itself the other day. Why would it hide now?"

"It didn't come out for you. It came out for your mate."

I threw my hands up. "Why is everyone calling Astrid my mate?"

Bjarke smirked. "Because I know if I tease you or Astrid, I'll get a reaction, with how new your romantic relationship is."

I scowled. "No wonder you're her friend. You both enjoy being a pain in the ass."

He laughed. "Life is more fun that way."

I regarded him for a moment. "You're not uncomfortable with that term, are you?"

He shook his head. "I call Alecia my mate, because it makes my bear happy. And I'm pretty sure dragons use the term, too."

I turned to Mamá, who was quiet. "You did think Astrid was my mate because her scent was strong on me, most likely because we'd just been intimate prior to you showing up. What's that about?"

She worked her jaw, her eyes flicking cautiously at Bjarke. "Well, since this one here accepts his bear's desires, I suppose I can talk about it. We dragons are capable of creating a strong bond with our partners that we call a mate-bond. It has a powerful presence, so I misinterpreted your recent intimacy as that bond."

"What does this bond feel like?" If I was going to be able to make it, I should know the signs and what to expect.

"It's a sensation I'm not sure I'm capable of describing, but it's a consuming need, such that if we give into it, it creates an intense and unbreakable bond. Nothing can tear it apart."

My pulse fluttered. *A consuming need? Is that similar to the pull I feel with Astrid?* I thought it'd go away after we agreed to make our relationship official. But these last few days, I swore it was getting more intense. Had this dragon part of me made that decision already and expected me to give in at some point?

Mamá's expression dropped. "Except for death. And the loss of a mate-bond is an indescribable pain. It's why we're thankful the urge to do so doesn't hit us often when we take longer-term partners."

My gut twisted, a visceral reaction, as if the very thought of losing such a bond pained my dragon. "Did you make this bond with Papá?"

The two of them hadn't talked since he found out she was alive. He always went somewhere else when she was going to be stopping by— even talking about her shut him down. It'd put a bit of a strain on his and my relationship, since I wanted to rebuild something with Mamá.

She shook her head. "No. I felt the pull to, and had been tempted, but I resisted. I didn't… think I could handle it. And then when I received my vision, I used that as self-justification to bury the guilt and any more urges that reared up."

I smiled. Mamá really loved him. I could see on her face that resisting wasn't something she really wanted to do. And I could also understand her not wanting to experience that excruciating pain. Losing him to age would have been hard enough without an added, intense bond on top.

Bjarke ran his fingers through his hair. "Damn, my bear is grumpy we don't get that."

Mamá surprised me by smiling kindly at him. "Your mate is that special to you?"

He nodded. "I've had a few wives in my time, and there has been no one like Alecia. She's a force to be reckoned with. Fighting my bear's desire to rut is near impossible with her, not that I ever really want to. She's the first wife I've had who wasn't afraid of my nature. Even my first wife, Ingrid, who was no stranger to the existence of Berserkers, was terrified of my bear. Alecia's acceptance… I'd bond with her in a heartbeat if I could, her mortal status be damned."

Mom's smile turned mysterious. "Fate may yet have something in store for you."

He regarded her for a moment and then turned to me. "Let's get back to your inner-dragon-finding issue."

I ran my fingers through my hair. Yeah, that was a bit more pressing, if not still aggravating.

"Tell me, do you understand what you're looking for?" Bjarke asked. "And I mean *really* understand?"

Of course I did. I was looking for a dragon's presence. *But what does that feel like?* I worked my jaw. Maybe I didn't know what I was looking for. It seemed so simple. A powerful creature shouldn't be that hard to imagine. *But imagining and feeling are different, aren't they?*

Bjarke nodded. "That's what I thought. I was there once, too. I was a child, but it was still the same. I didn't understand what it meant to be a bear Berserker. I saw how my father acted, and I tried to emulate. That didn't work. I struggled to understand why I couldn't get my bear under control. No matter how hard I tried, I failed to prove myself to my bear. Then my father sat me down and told me what I was failing to see."

"What was it?"

Bjarke tapped his chest. "It's me. A deeper, more primal version of me made form."

I stared at him, incredulous. *It can't be that simple.*

He laughed, as if knowing my thoughts. "I know, I thought it couldn't be that simple, either. But it is. Because my bear is this presence within me, I was seeing us as two separate entities in one body. I certainly looked it most of the time, with the half-beast, half-boy appearance I had like all Berserker and shifter children. The moment I shifted my understanding, everything fell into place. Though, let's be honest here, accepting the more primal side of you is not as easy as it sounds."

"What should I expect when seeking a primal side of myself?" I asked.

"It'll be startling. Not sure how else to explain the sensation. You'll know when you find it, though."

Oddly, that was reassuring.

Taking a deep breath, I closed my eyes and turned my attention inward. At first, I experienced much of the same as my last attempt. But I didn't give up. I reached deeper, opening myself to everything I was. And then I felt it.

Something young but ancient.

Something powerful.

Energy rushed through me, and I swore I heard something growl in my ear.

My eyes snapped open. I gasped, my breathing puffing out at the beat of my racing heart. *Shit, was that—*

Bjarke smacked me hard on the back, making me wince. "That's it! Nice job."

Clearly, he saw something. Even Mamá's face beamed with pride. I glanced down at my hands and jerked back. My fingers had elongated into black talons, and black and silver scales patched my arms. The motion of moving messed with my head, and I blinked several times before I realized it was my eyes themselves causing the issue.

Everything was sharper and more vibrant. I'd never seen this clearly before. It was disorienting.

Breathing in deep to calm my racing heart, I instantly regretted it when intense smells assaulted my nose. I complained and rubbed my nose with the back of my hand.

Bjarke barked out a laugh. "First whiff is always the worst."

I made a face. "Is this permanent?"

"Yes," Mamá said. "Your senses will stay sharpened, even if you stick to a human form. You'll get used to it soon enough."

I sure as hell hoped so. I did not like it.

My hearing had also improved. Their words sounded sharper and clearer.

Something shifted behind me and I realized there was now weight on my back and spine. Glancing behind me, I blinked. "I have wings and a tail."

Sure enough, large, bat-like wings grew from my back, and a long silver-and-black-scaled tail lazily swished behind me on its own. *I'll have to figure out how to control that, or it could be a problem.*

"You also have horns," Bjarke said.

I reached above my head, feeling the new sharp protrusions growing from my head. Sensation sparked down my spine when I touched them. *Okay, note to self, they have nerves.*

Mamá kept smiling at me. "Artura would be having a fit right now if she saw you like this. She always hated it when our children took these in-between forms, insisting it wasn't dignified."

"Do you hate them?" I asked.

She shook her head. "Not at all. I understood it as a way for our children to find a middle ground between their heritages. And hearing the way Bjarke explained things to you, I better understand that."

"Do you and Artura not get along?" I asked. "Any time she comes up in a conversation we've had, you haven't had much in the way of nice things to say."

She sighed. "My siblings and I used to be close. But over time, we grew and changed in different ways. Artura and I stopped seeing eye-to-eye on most things a long time ago."

I grabbed her hands and squeezed. She must have been so lonely these past two decades. It really showed how much of a sacrifice she was willing to make for Papá and me.

Mamá turned to Bjarke and smiled. "I want to thank you. I had been selfish in wanting this to be something between my son and me. I was too arrogant, thinking I could do this with my kind of experience."

Bjarke shrugged. "You're his mom. I wouldn't have intervened if Astrid hadn't asked. If she was asking, I figured she knew a nudge was needed."

He wasn't wrong. Today hadn't been my first day of attempts at this. Just the only successful one. It gave me a greater appreciation for what Astrid had been going through on her own journey.

I tipped my head when I heard something come from the house. "I think everyone is back."

Mamá nodded. "Sounds like it. Let's get you in control of your body, and then we'll stop for the day."

Fifteen minutes later, I was mostly back to how I was used to looking. My horns and arm scales were being a bit stubborn, but I could deal with those being out. If Carrie and Raeni came home before I sorted it out, I'd just play it off as costuming for something.

Just as I stood, my vision flashed on me. Images and sounds, quick and confusing. A wolf snarling. A closeup of a woman with deep red lips in shadow smiling maliciously. Someone screaming. Gunshots. A woman cackling.

I gasped when my vision returned to normal. Mamá placed her hand on my shoulder, her brow creased with her concern.

"What did you see, Treasure?"

I shook my head. "I'm… not sure. It was just flashes of things. They felt related, but I can't fathom how."

She nodded and brushed some hair away from my eyes. "That's normal. Our visions aren't always clear. You might gain another to give more clarity, you might not."

I nodded. Of all the things I'd have to get used to, visions were not the ones I wanted. But, we didn't get to decide what powers Creation gave us.

When we entered the house, the kitchen held a comical sight. Astrid's short, sexy ass stood barefoot on the counter, rummaging through the cupboards. Una was below her, scolding her about putting "dirty feet" on the counters she just finished washing, even though the fae usually used magic now to clean things in an instant. Darius, Aya, and Tyr were in the great room, cleaning guns and affixing equipment to some bows and crossbows, while watching Fen as he said, "Just give it up, Astrid. You don't need your smelly, dirty leaf-water."

Oh boy. These two were at it again. They really did have an entertaining family bond.

"It's wonderful that we can compromise, and I can have my tea, and you'll try it, because otherwise you'll be sipping it through a straw up your butthole."

Bjarke and I choked on a laugh. Mamá stared in shock. Proper and refined people we were not, which was something she was still getting used to.

Fen snorted. "Like you could disarm me like that."

Astrid smirked. *And here we go.* She grabbed a fistful of tea bags and suddenly disappeared from the counter. She reappeared in the air behind Fen and dropped down on him, wrapping her arms and legs around him. She shoved the pungent tea bags into his face.

Fen snarled and thrashed, scrabbling at her to pull her off. The house filled with roaring laughter. He finally got a good hold on Astrid and yanked her off his shoulders. Restraining her with one arm, he pawed at his nose. "Shit, that smells awful up close. I'm not going to be able to smell properly for a week, you bitch."

She stuck her tongue out at him. "That's for calling it smelly."

Fen complained some more. I only felt a slight twinge of sympathy for him, since I now, too, had to adjust to a far more sensitive nose.

"You need to be put on a leash until you learn to behave," Fen said.

Astrid grinned wickedly. "It's you, Fluffy, that needs a leash."

A peculiar gold ribbon appeared in her hands. *I wonder what that is.* Whatever it was, it had Fen's eyes bugging out. "No. No, you did not remember how to use that spell."

Her grin didn't waver. "Sure did. And I'm thinking it's finally time I teach someone else how to make this."

Fen's eyes narrowed. "Don't you dare."

"I'm thinking Dahlia or Frey would be *very* interested in learning."

Fen paused, thinking about it. Actually thinking about it. "No."

"Too bad. You don't get a say." Astrid then noticed us standing in the foyer and her eyes lit up. "Hey! How did magical-girl training go?"

Bjarke laughed, and my brow raised. "What?"

She held up a hand, as best as she could with Fen still restraining her. "Azzie compared Berserkers to magical girls, so I say your transformation into a dragon is similar."

Fen looked at Bjarke. "Are you really okay with this comparison? If you know what a magical girl is."

Bjarke snorted. "Alecia is obsessed with magical girls."

Astrid's eyebrow quirked up. "I'm surprised a bajillion-year-old wolf like yourself, Fluffy, knows that kind of pop-culture reference."

"I'm not *that* old," Fen grumbled, pulling on Astrid's ear. "And I know, because Dahlia is a walking pop-culture computer. Though, knowing what I do of that reference, there's no way someone like him is going to agree with what you said."

"I demand a magical butterfly wand," Bjarke said.

"Only if you wear a schoolgirl uniform," Astrid said.

"In bear form."

"Wearing knee-high boots."

Bjarke grinned. "Deal."

The room filled with laughter, while Fen just blinked stupidly.

"You don't think that image is funny, Diego?" Astrid said when she noticed I hadn't joined in.

I pursed my lips. "I mean, him as he is does create an entertaining image, but he mentioned bear form, and I haven't seen a transformed Berserker, so I'm not sure what that adds."

Bjarke whipped off his shirt. "Well, let's fix that. But first, making sure my wife doesn't get pissed I ruined another shirt."

He dropped the clothing on the floor along with a watch he removed from his wrist. His face twisted into a snarl as he sucked in a deep breath. He actually snarled before his body grew hairy and larger before my eyes. A moment later, a huge bi-pedal brown bear stared me down.

Astrid being Astrid, she wiggled her fingers, and a magical-girl outfit illusioned onto his body. Bjarke struck a classic pose.

The wall became my support as I held my sides and laughed harder than I had in a while. Astrid snapped a photo of Bjarke before dropping the illusion, and he transformed back.

"Did you get a photo of Davyn seeing you for the first time?" Bjarke asked.

"Duh." Astrid wormed her way out of Fen's grip, who seemed still a little too perplexed to keep her restrained, having been thrown off by Bjarke's willingness to be so goofy. She held up her phone to Bjarke after he'd thrown his shirt back on.

Bjarke guffawed. "That's perfect. I want a copy."

"One copy of a surprised grumpy bear and magical girl bear, coming right up."

I shook my head. This was one reason I loved this woman.

Bjarke looked at his watch. "It's almost twenty past nine back home. I should get back before Alecia gets mad. Aya, would you mind?"

She smiled. "Not at all. Fen, do you want to head back to my brother and Dahlia?"

He nodded. "I should before I get too caught up in things here and miss Frey's dinner plans."

They said their goodbyes and then disappeared.

"I should be going as well," Mamá said to me.

I nodded, trying to smile, though it was hard. I knew the only reason she was leaving was to allow Papá to feel like he didn't have to seclude himself. He'd taken the news well about all the supernatural crap once he was in a good headspace to listen to Darius, so we never had to hide what we were all doing. It was just her.

We hugged. She told me she loved me and then disappeared. My pulse kicked up a moment before I managed to settle it. Seeing Aya teleport was easy. Seeing Mamá do it made me fear I'd imagined her. I knew that was the trauma, and I'd overcome it. It'd just take time.

I wasn't alone in my thoughts for long. Astrid came up to me, and her cute face took in the still-visible changes about me with a big smile on said adorable face. I also took her in, relishing in all the extra detail I could see. She was somehow more stunning, and I wasn't sure if I could take it.

Astrid reached up and touched my horns. I sucked in a tight breath and resisted the urge to groan. The sensation her touch sent through me was indescribable—in the best way possible. It was like she just touched the most intimate erogenous zone imaginable, turning me on to the highest level possible. *Will my full dragon form have such sensitivity, or is just this form?*

I grabbed her wrists to pull her hands away. She blinked, confused. "They're incredibly sensitive."

"Oh." Her bottom lip caught between her teeth when I gazed at her, conveying what I meant. "Oh…"

My nostrils flared, picking up a spike of arousal in her, mixing with her enticing scent. My cock twitched.

I flicked my gaze to Darius. He grinned. "Yup, still here."

I blew out a breath. *That's what I thought.* That was one way to kill my boner.

Astrid stepped back and cleared her throat. "So, how was training? Successfully turn into a dragon?"

I shook my head. "Only as far as that one form Dahlia made, but definitely better than the last few days. Bjarke was incredibly helpful."

She beamed. "I knew he would be. I watched him teach so many new Berserkers, I figured he'd have a way to figure out what was blocking your progress."

"And what about you?" I asked. "I see you picked up a new skill or two."

While I'd been training with Mamá and Bjarke, Astrid and the others met up with Kirby, Azzie, and Davyn for introductions, reunions, and training.

Astrid grinned. "I learned how to make magical massages again."

My brow quirked. That sounded interesting. "And what exactly are those?"

"It's the best thing besides sex you'll ever experience," Tyr said.

That wasn't helpful, but also intrigued me at the same time, especially if a war god thought it was even better than the call for battle. "What does it do?"

She smiled. "It's a form of healing. With the way immortals heal so quickly, their bodies sometimes don't heal back exactly as they should. Apparently, I figured out a healing technique that got deep into the body and fixed those problems. Even Baldur had felt the effect back then."

That did sound amazing. "I'd like one."

She smiled. "After I get my tea?"

Astrid disappeared and reappeared in the kitchen. I shook my head. "That's also new."

She smirked. "I actually remembered how to do this the night of the festival, but I've now got actual practice, and I didn't land my ass in any trees by accident."

She seemed so proud, and the context of that feat was lost on me.

Tyr snickered. "No, you just ended up in the rafters of a house three kilometers away."

My brows shot up, and Astrid pointed at him with narrowed eyes. "Hey! Still wasn't a tree."

Ùna offered Astrid a mug of brewed tea, perfectly sweetened with honey, according to Astrid, which was a feat in my book, since she had her special ratio: insane amounts of honey more than actual tea. While she enjoyed her tea, Tyr filled Darius and me in about Astrid's first time trying to teleport in her first life.

I was roaring with laughter before he even got to the part about Kirby having to come to her rescue. Darius teased her and Astrid stuck her tongue out.

"So, what was that gold ribbon spell that freaked Fen out?" I asked.

Astrid blinked and then summoned the ribbon. "Oh, this? Just a little thing I made on a whim once to mess with Fen and Tyr."

Darius leaned back on the couch. "Ah, so the family stories are true. You did make that, unlike the reinvented myth."

Astrid made a face. "Yeah, jerks stealing my credit."

I was so confused. But before I could find out more, Astrid's phone rang.

She pulled it out of her back pocket and read the screen. Smiling, she answered the call. "Carrie, what—"

A low, raspy chuckle answered her. My spine straightened, dread shivering through me.

Astrid's face grew serious. "Who is this?"

"Oh, you know who this is." I sharpened my senses to hear better. This was not good.

"Garmr, what the fuck do you want?" Astrid snarled. "And what have you done with Carrie?"

Tyr and Darius jumped up off the couch, their attention intense.

He chuckled again and then someone else spoke on the line. A feminine, alto voice that sounded too similar to Astrid. "She's safe for now, dear. As are all your other friends. But I can't promise they will be if you don't cooperate."

Astrid's face twisted in a silent snarl. "What do you want?"

"Meet us at the town square. Alone. You have five minutes, darling." The line went dead.

I was already moving to Astrid. "Astrid, don't—"

Her mug smashed on the floor.

She was gone.

THIRTY

ASTRID

Silence was all that greeted me in the usually active Saturday afternoon of this small town.

No people.

No cars.

Not even a dog or cat.

It was as if everyone had vanished.

A lone raven croaked nearby, its call ominous. A sense of familiarity and warning shivered down my spine.

Every muscle in my body coiled and my senses stretched as I walked down Main Street toward the center of town. Valkyrie instinct said I wasn't alone.

I halted, a chill running down my spine. Movement on the roof flashed in my periphery, but when I jerked my attention up, nothing was there. I was told to come alone, but I'd be naïve to believe Mother and Garmr were unaccompanied. I continued my path.

It was foolish of me to react so quickly and come alone. Without Aya, the others couldn't follow. Even though Urd said Diego would teleport yet.

But lives were at stake. Garmr had no issue with killing me. He'd have no problem killing innocent people. And I knew my mother wouldn't be much different. Not if she had no qualms murdering her own daughter.

My fists clenched and unclenched. *What am I going to do?* I didn't have a plan. I didn't know the situation enough to even make one.

Kill them? Could I?

I could say I was capable of it all I wanted, but when faced with that reality, did I have it in me to do so?

My past said I could. My Valkyrie spirit said I had it within me to do what needed to be done.

I could feel them with me, wrapping around me the calmness and strength I needed.

Breathe.

Shut down the emotions.

Don't be rash.

They encouraged me in ways they knew and experienced. Their experience was my advantage neither of my enemies would see coming.

My mind emptied.

My heart steeled.

My breathing steadied.

Each step I took, power built in me. My magic tingled my fingers and Valkyrie power licked at my mind.

The center square came into view. People stood there. My mother. Garmr. Other people dressed in strange fatigues with their faces covered. My Valkyrie spirit coiled the longer I looked at these unidentifiable enemies. There was something wrong about them. Something about their spirits set me on edge.

People kneeled in front of them. Fury flared in my chest seeing the four people on the ground.

Carrie.

Officer Rory.

Felicity, the sweet cashier at the hardware store.

Ben, the asshole who, even for all his offenses, still wasn't terrible enough to deserve this.

Prisoners.

Hostages.

They were hostages.

They all were forced to hold their hands up behind their head while someone stood behind them, a gun poised to be used. Rory appeared the calmest of them, which came as no surprise. He was a former soldier, turned cop. He knew how to stay calm. The person who did surprise me was Carrie.

Instead of shaking and barely holding herself together, like poor Felicity, she remained calm. Her eyes tracked the movement of those around her, and her mouth twitched as if she wanted to spew off insults. I didn't doubt she wanted to. She'd grown back into herself these past few weeks, and she was a force to be reckoned with, mortal or not.

My eyes tracked Garmr. He paced behind the hostages, his face twisted in what I presumed was frustration. A tall, middle-aged woman with red hair watched him, her gray eyes cold. Were they always that color? I didn't care. I didn't care about anything with her. She betrayed Dad. She betrayed me.

"She's late," Garmr snarled. "I knew she wouldn't have the guts. We should have just sent her a bloody message. That would have worked better."

"Patience. This is the only way to get her away from the gods," my mother said. "And she will come. Her loyalties are her weakness."

I hated that she and I sounded so similar. I hated we shared the same hair. I was only grateful that fate took pity on my height.

I used to lament that I never grew as tall as either of my parents. Now I was glad fate made me the same height as my past. It made me different from her. I didn't want another reminder of her plaguing me. I wanted reminders of Randi, my real mother.

"I don't know," I said, announcing my presence. "I think it makes me that much stronger."

Eyes turned to me. I refused to wilt under the hard attention. My senses sharpened, awareness pushing out. There were people in the nearby buildings. There were people skulking around in the shadows.

Were they people? I couldn't tell. The way they moved, and their presence licking the corners of my magic, didn't feel quite right.

"Well, hello darling," Ingrid said, a false, toothy, too-white smile on her face. "It's so good to see you again."

"The feeling isn't mutual." I leaned heavily on my past to keep my emotions in check.

I wanted so much to run from these two. I wanted to hide and pretend they didn't exist. They weren't the bogeyman living under my bed that could be thwarted off with "monster-be-gone" water made special by Dad. These were real life monsters I had to face. And running away wouldn't make them disappear.

Ingrid frowned. "Is that really how you'd greet your own mother?"

"You only wish you were good enough to be a mom."

I had to bite back a smirk when she scowled. "You were always such a wretched daughter."

"That's cute, coming from someone who tried to kill her own daughter." The words came out, so devoid of emotion.

How recent was it that I'd struggled to come to terms with that fact? When had the tears stopped flowing every time I thought about her rejection and hatred toward me, an innocent little girl who had only wanted to be loved by her?

When a god and a dragon told me I was worthy of their affection. When a dad revealed his immortality and showed me the magnitude of his love—one stronger and fuller than any other child could ask for from a parent.

She held her arms out. "All for the greater good, Astrid. You were to be a sacrifice for something greater. For prophecy. There is no greater honor."

"If you actually believe that bullshit that comes out of your mouth, that'll be the most surprising thing said so far."

Ingrid tsked. "I'm so disappointed. These so-called gods you've been taken by have really done a number on you. How they've weakened you when you had so much potential."

Did she really think she could manipulate me? I knew these tactics. I trained so hard to help people overcome the destruction such attempts created in their lives.

My magic pulsed and my Valkyrie power kicked up. Wings grew from my back, lifting me off the ground. My armor manifested, and my hand gripped my axe, made from the staff of my real mother. "I am far from weak. I am not the scared little girl you think I am, Ingrid. I will not fall for your lies and manipulations. And I won't allow you to harm these innocent people I've sworn to protect. You will let them go."

Ingrid tapped her lips casually. "It seems my magic blockers have, in fact, worn off."

Magic blockers? Was that a thing? Did that explain part of my issues with my magic?

"Well, no matter. We have what we need to deal with… whatever these gods have turned you into."

"Valkyrie," I said, my voice carrying farther and with more weight than I expected. "I am Tyr's Valkyrie, and I deem neither of you worthy of life, or an honorable afterlife."

"Yes, yes, of course," she said in an airy, arrogant way, waving her hands dismissively. "But what about these four innocent people? We'll let them go, of course, seeing as you arrived. But sadly, for how long you took, we can't give you them all. Pick three who live, and one who dies."

It took every ounce of control I could muster not to react. I knew there would be a catch. There was always a catch in hostage negotiations.

My eyes swept over each person whose lives now hung in the balance. They stared back at me. Fear, confusion, awe, desperation, it all played along their faces.

I could see determination and acceptance in Rory. He was a man of honor and served the people. He'd lay down his life if it meant others were free and safe.

Disdain marred Ben's face. He suspected I'd sacrifice him. No doubt this was what Ingrid and Garmr expected. If they did their research, as I suspected they did, they'd know the rocky history between us.

But the thing was, they couldn't make me play by their rules. They didn't own this situation. I did. And they were going to see what folly it was to cross me.

"I have known all of you for a very long time," I said. "Most of you, my whole life. And now I ask you one very important question. Do you trust me?" My eyes flicked to Ben. "Or, do you at least trust my character?"

Each one nodded, ever so slightly, not enough to anger their captors, but enough for me to see. Even Ben didn't hesitate. We may not like each other, but not even he could deny the type of person I was.

"Then I need you to listen to every word I say. I need you to do everything without question—without hesitation. I need you to close your eyes and listen to only my voice."

They obeyed. The tension in their posture eased, and they hung onto everything I said—everything I was. They may be terrified and confused, but they trusted me now. And I would not fail them.

"Aw, how sweet," Ingrid cooed. "You want to spare them from knowing your choice."

"Weak," Garmr snarled. "You always were, false Valkyrie. It's why Odin never wanted you. So pathetically created by an inferior god, that you couldn't even sprout wings until now."

"If I'm weak and pathetic, I wonder what that makes you, Garmr," I said in such a cold tone, I wasn't sure how it was me. "You cling so hard to the machinations of a dead god, you spent your whole life of immortality chasing down her reincarnations. And for what? There's no god left to go back to who will pat you on the head and call you a good boy."

Garmr snarled, his face twisting with his rage, and his body jerked, desiring to shift.

Ingrid held up a hand to him. "Don't. She is trying to rile you up while simultaneously stalling. Pick, child, who will live."

My grip on my axe tightened. She was right, I had been stalling. But it was clear they couldn't see why. Even though my magic senses told me there was a strange, twisting magic about her, she wasn't aware of the magic I'd pushed out, wrapping around buildings and people.

"Choose," Garmr barked.

"I choose… all of them."

In a blink, I was no longer in front of them, but behind the hostages, with my axe raised high. I swung it down on the closest person, slamming it into their neck with a sickening crunch of cartilage and bone. My past life steeled me from the sheer horror that I was taking a life. She urged me not to hesitate. To fight. To protect.

I did.

My magic flared and weapons materialized, slicing into the other enemies holding my people hostage. The scent of blood filled the air as bodies dropped.

"Run!" I shouted.

My feet dug into the ground and I launched for Garmr, whose honed battle instincts already had him shifting and coming at me. My axe slammed into his muzzle, guns fired, and someone screamed in one of the buildings.

My magic flared, protecting everyone I'd shielded. I prayed Carrie and the others found shelter soon. I felt their retreating bodies, my magic coating them in protection and allowing me to keep tabs on them. It was a sense in the back of my mind, not something I had to actively keep up.

Dad knew magic, but he had excelled in defensive and support-style magic. And I'd taken to it like a Berserker to war. Which was good, because I soon found myself overwhelmed with protecting myself.

Guns fired, and I summed all the magic I could, taking out anyone nearby. Longer-range was more difficult, especially with Garmr coming at me. My mother had retreated, but a twisted, gleeful look plastered her face. There was something very wrong about that woman, and I'd deal with her in a moment.

Garmr snapped his jaws, and I deftly dodged, leaning on all the practice with Kirby and Fen to fight a wolf shifter with everything I was as a Valkyrie. I struck him with my axe, wreathed in golden fire, burning him as much as I sliced up his flesh.

I made sure my strikes counted, not worrying about his immortal healing. My axe, my weapon forged from Randi's magical staff, carried the properties I needed to hamper or even sever an immortal's connection to their healing abilities. Even if I didn't kill them in battle, and their healing finally returned, it would be too late to prevent the scarring.

"False Valkyrie!" Garmr roared. *"I will end you! I vowed to see to it Odin's will be done. I refused to allow such a mockery like yourself to exist. I swore, as long as you drew breath, I couldn't succumb to my illness."*

He lunged for me again. *"I suffered for centuries, plotting your demise. And you had to ruin it all by playing with ancient, forbidden magics. When I learned of your sacrilegious rebirth, I had to end you. I didn't care how long it took. I'd destroy you, and weaken that pitiful excuse of a god Tyr had become because of you."*

I slammed Garmr with magical projectiles. "Tyr was stronger because of me. I pity you for never knowing such devotion and love."

Garmr snarled and snapped his teeth, snagging and ripping some of my feathers as I dodged away. Unfortunately, I wasn't quick enough, or maybe paying enough attention, and a black tendril of magic lashed out at me, striking me hard against my back and wings.

I cried out and whirled around; my eyes widened. Black magic leaked out of Ingrid. The way it moved was all too familiar. It looked too much like the black tendrils of magic I'd seen mixing with my own golden magic.

Blackness veined from Ingrid's eyes, and an inkiness seeped into her white sclera. It reminded me so much of Randi, it hurt.

No... it can't be. She couldn't have magic, too. I couldn't have inherited some of her magic.

My mother cackled, her eyes wild and expression crazed. "Surprised? My goddess is powerful, Astrid."

Her goddess? What the hell was this crazy bitch going on about?

"You could have had this too, had we not been told of your greater importance to ascend to death for the sake of our purpose. She would have welcomed you with open arms. But now, you are too tainted to see her grace, her vision, her glory." She spoke with all the reverence of a cultist—and the practice of a cult leader. An unpleasant shiver ran down my spine.

Garmr came for me again, and I wasn't having it. This was getting to be too much, and he was less of a threat than her now.

With a wave of my hand, gold ribbons shot out and wrapped themselves around the wolf shifter. He snarled and struggled against his bindings, but they didn't give. *"What is this?"*

"What, you don't remember this magic from that celebration? I'll remind you." I pulled the ribbons tighter, and he yelped. "You've been honorably chosen to be bound by Gleipnir, as you should have been, instead of the false stories you twisted about Fenrir."

I'd created this spell for fun in my drunkenness. It was silly, and not meant to be anything more. But now, it had a stronger purpose. It held strong as long as my will and concentration did. I was risking much with my magic stretched so thin, but I had to try. Even if just enough to give me the reprieve I needed.

Why haven't the others gotten here? Aya should have been back by now. She should have been able to get them here in a snap.

A large presence loomed over me. I whirled around and stared up at the hulking bi-pedal bear towering over me.

But something wasn't right. There was no life in his snarling face. His eyes were dull and milky. His body twitched and black tendrils leaked out of him in unnatural ways.

The Berserker roared and swiped an enormous paw at me.

THIRTY-ONE

TYR

We all stared at the broken mug of tea on the floor for a moment. She hadn't just... Astrid hadn't just teleported.

I snapped my attention to Diego. "What did you hear?" He'd have heard every moment from the way he reacted. That dragon hearing of his put him at an advantage, but not enough to have stopped Astrid.

"Garmr had Carrie's phone," Diego said, his breathing hitched as he tried not to panic. "And then a woman, who sounded too much like Astrid, spoke to her."

"Ingrid," Darius said, his voice dark. "They have hostages, then."

Diego nodded. "Probably. They told Astrid to come alone."

That explained it. Even in a split-second decision like that, she'd have thought about hostages and if she hadn't listened, there'd be casualties. *Of all the people they could have gotten...*

"What do we do?" Diego asked. "I can't yet do the teleporting thing."

"If Astrid builds enough of a battle aura like Aya has taught her, I can get us there," I said. "But I need that aura to do it."

It was why I couldn't get to Astrid sooner when Garmr attacked her the first time. She had been overcome with fear, not battle. But now, she wasn't surprised. Now Astrid had experience. She wouldn't fail this time.

Diego's phone rang, and he only took a moment to look at the name before answering it on speakerphone. "Aya, we—"

"What's going on over there?" she demanded. "I can't teleport back."

My spine went rigid. "What do you mean?"

"I mean exactly as I said. I can't teleport to the house. It's like it doesn't exist."

"Someone must have erected a barrier without us noticing," Darius said. "And that's some serious magic, if that's the case."

"What are you talking about? What's going on?"

Diego quickly rattled off what he'd just told us.

Aya swore. "That means Tyr can't get to her, either."

My pulse elevated. "Fuck, you're right."

"Why not? He's here in the supposed bubble," Diego said. "Why can't we do anything?"

"If any of us try to teleport here, then the magic will kick us out," Darius said. "It's hard to explain right now, but just believe me when I tell you, if Tyr feels that aura he mentioned, and tries, we're without gods to help us."

Diego's face twisted, his dragon rage boiling up. I understood. Astrid was alone with our enemies in a clear trap, and we had no quick way to get to her. "Then we run there."

My head jerked in surprise. "What?"

Diego pointed toward the woods. "We run. It's the only option we have. Using vehicles means sticking to the roads and alerting them to our arrival. The forest is a straight path down."

"You can't go," I said. "You're not trained."

He grabbed a gun off the coffee table. "Watch me. Bedsides, I don't think I'm going to have trouble shifting this time. I just don't think I can fly us there."

Darius grabbed a grenade launcher and handed it to Diego, along with a belt containing ammunition. "Just in case your shifting fails.

These release a noxious gas that will stun anyone with a sensitive nose. Don't get too close yourself."

"I'll round up Bjarke and the other Berserkers," Aya said. "I'll get us as close as I can, and we'll try to get there as soon as we can."

The last thing we heard from her was Aya scolding Fen about patience—and then the line went dead.

Angel barked frantically outside. When Astrid's familiar knew something was wrong, that was our cue to quit stalling.

Darius and I snagged a few weapons from the coffee table, and the three of us bolted outside.

"Amigos, what is going on?" Xavier asked as we rushed past him.

"Astrid and the town are in trouble," Darius called back. "Stay here."

Angel charged into the forest, leading us through the easiest path possible in the hilly terrain. This dog ran these woods all day long, and her familiar intelligence allowed her to guide us effortlessly.

As we drew closer to the protective barrier Darius had helped Aya push out further, my instinct kicked in. War cloaked me like a second skin; I recognized the sensation of an ambush. I made a motion to alert Diego and Darius in warning, when Diego raised his gun and fired, his impeccable dragon sight showing itself.

The bullets whizzed through the barrier, and his target cried out. The ambush reacted, opening fire on the barrier that soon would no longer protect us.

Darius' magic flared to life, and a shield coalesced around my skin, locking down my senses. The sensation sent a shiver down my spine. I'd never been shielded like this until Darius began teaching Astrid. The feeling of protection it brought was so foreign to me as a warrior. I'd never felt more invincible as a god. *Is this how Baldur felt?*

I barreled through the barrier and didn't hesitate to attack any enemy foolish enough to show themselves. Angel went for the throat of one unlucky individual who popped up in my blind spot. The scent of blood filled the air, and with it came the smell of decay. I didn't have time to process.

The earth beneath us quaked and roots shot out of the ground, wrapping our enemies into a bone-crushing hold. We didn't stop to see which fae came to assist. We didn't tell them to keep home safe. We trusted they would and kept going.

"Good call, Diego, about using the woods," Darius said. There was no sarcasm in his voice.

"Really, because it feels like I made a mistake."

"Trust me. Ingrid specialized in laying traps. That ambush was weak. She expected us to use the road, but she had a small backup just in case."

"What the hell were those things?" Diego asked. "They didn't move like any human I know, but they looked it."

There was something off about them? I must have been too focused to have paid attention.

"Don't know," Darius puffed out. "We can figure it out after we deal with the pressing issue."

The forest flew by. A raven called in the distance, its call insistent and filled with warning. The muscles in my neck twisted. *That sound…* It was all too close to Muninn. But that was impossible.

Darius used his magic to hasten our steps. And before we knew it, our feet pounded on asphalt instead of soft earth. Astrid's voice rang out in the still air, and then gunfire erupted. *Shit!*

I pushed harder. I needed to get to her. I needed to protect her. *I can't fail her again.*

Bullets slammed into our shields. Enemies appeared on rooftops and emerged from alleys and from behind parked cars. Most wore fatigues that hid their identities, though they seemed human. They would be the easiest to deal with. The shocking enemies were the Berserkers and other less-human creatures barring our paths.

Why would Berserkers—

One of the wolf Berserkers twitched, and a black tendril lashed out of its body. He gazed at us with dead eyes. He snarled, a black ichor substance spitting from his toothy maw. A dark aura surrounded the man—no, no longer man, but creature.

No, it can't be.

It'd been so long since I'd seen this possession. Centuries, maybe. I'd thought with Midgard changing, whatever had caused this affliction in desperate and dying men had finally been eradicated. But no, it seemed they were still around. And there were a lot of them.

Every creature here seemed to have been a living being once, but now was this husk of darkness. *What are they?*

There wasn't time to think. Only fight.

"Don't let the cursed ones touch you," I ordered. "They'll infect you."

At least, I thought they would. I couldn't be sure how these things worked anymore.

Darius shot some of the enemies on the roofs. "Push through to Astrid, I'll deal with these."

"*We* will deal with them," Diego corrected, aiming for one of the corrupted creatures. "Just get to Astrid."

I nodded and charged the closest enemy, summoning my axe and slamming it into him. I didn't take the time to kill, only slow them down to become prey for the other two men.

Angel ran with me, avoiding the corrupted creatures, either because she understood me, or she sensed the wrongness about them. Non-corrupted beings, though, were another story. She went after them like any battle-trained dog.

I didn't know where this behavior came from, as I'd never gotten around to asking about it after the first encounter with Garmr. The war god in me approved. The man, however, was concerned, given her primary profession as an emotion guide for the lost. *I suppose it's no different from Astrid.*

The parallels were unnerving when I thought about it. But maybe that was what a familiar bond did.

We pushed through enemy lines. The longer it took, the more my fear for Astrid grew. If this was what we faced, what was she fighting against all alone?

Rounding the corner, we came to Main Street, and the destruction was nothing like the other road. Cars were on fire, buildings had holes in them. I noticed the people huddling in the ones without damage, but enemies crawled around them, trying to get in.

Magic was so thick in the air I could taste it. *Astrid.* I scowled. There was other magic here, too. Something dark and chaotic.

A flash caught my attention. At the center of the square, Astrid fought. Both wolf and… *A witch?*

Her orange locks were all I could make out from this distance. But the dark magic she threw at Astrid made my stomach drop. It was too similar to my memories of Randi—and too similar to the conversations I'd recently had with Aya when I noticed that same color mixed into Astrid's magic.

Aya hadn't been concerned, thinking it was something unique to Astrid because of the reincarnation. Now I worried, if this woman Astrid fought was her mother, had she inherited magic from both parents?

I could think about that later. Astrid was holding her own, but for only so long with the way she sloppily dodged Garmr's attack. Gold ribbons sprung from Astrid's hands, binding the wolf shifter. I grinned. *Poetic that she'd use Gleipnir on him.*

Garmr snarled and said something. Astrid seemed to taunt him back, which was a mistake. She focused too much on him. My heart stalled when she missed the Berserker charging her from behind.

Before I could call out a warning, she noticed the new enemy, but it was too late. He swiped his claws and sent her flying into a police cruiser. *No!*

The car's alarm blared, and there was no movement from Astrid for far too long.

The Berserker roared in victory, but was cut off. I blinked, watching his head fly from his shoulders, black ichor spraying everywhere. Astrid, my Valkyrie, hovered in the air behind the Berserker, her hair a mess, and wounds healing quickly.

Pride swelled in my chest. She'd come so far in these weeks of training. Not even I had predicted that maneuver.

Unfortunately, the attack from the Berserker had weakened her hold on Garmr, and he broke free of his bindings. What no one expected was the bullet that Angel was. She came out of nowhere and attacked Garmr as a bundle of black snarling and snapping teeth. This made everything in the vicinity aware of my presence as well. *No more stalling.*

I rushed in, using the gun I'd borrowed to push Garmr and Ingrid back from a distance. These bullets wouldn't do much to an immortal—they weren't the immortal-killing rounds Aya and Fen told me about from TOM's arsenal, but they'd do something—if they made contact.

The witch managed to keep herself safe, though did nothing for her wolf ally. When I emptied the magazine, I used the gun as a blunt weapon for anything that tried to keep me from my Valkyrie.

Astrid split her focus between Garmr and Ingrid and the enemies going after me, as well as bolstering me. She used her magic in ways I'd never seen from her before. It allowed me to close the distance and focus on Garmr. I wouldn't be able to fight a witch, so I'd have to leave Ingrid to Astrid.

Garmr wasn't interested in agreeing with such an arrangement. He turned for Astrid, snapping at her beautiful wings. *No, you don't!* I swung my arm at him, the one without a hand, not caring if this would hurt or not. I would protect Astrid from this beast.

A strange and powerful sensation ran through my arm. And just before I made contact with Garmr's face, my hand appeared, slamming into the wolf's eye. He yelped and stumbled back. *Thank Creation for Astrid's magic.*

But it wasn't enough. The two of us weren't enough for all the enemies we faced. No matter how much blood I drew from Garmr with my axe, no matter how many times they threw Astrid and me into something and we came back for more, neither of us could break through any weak points in our enemy's defenses.

My senses sharpened when a wolf howled, and then my warrior spirit soared when I recognized it.

Fen charged into the street and barreled right into Garmr. The two wolves tangled in a powerful bundle of snapping teeth.

He wasn't the only one here. Berserkers charged into the fray, Bjarke and the others, attacking creatures still after the hiding townsfolk. Aya appeared, going for Ingrid, her face twisted with fury and battle-rage. She and Astrid focused on Ingrid, pushing the woman back.

Though, oddly, Astrid's mother didn't seem all that worried with our reinforcements. In fact, she appeared quite smug, as if this was fun for her or something.

Garmr was a surprisingly hearty shifter. All the Norse gods knew he'd been struck by some mysterious degenerative illness, but like the warrior he was, he put in his all for Odin. And while it appeared immortality hadn't cured him of that affliction, like it usually did for other conditions, he still showed that same tenacity I was used to. *I wonder how much he's being bolstered unnaturally.* I didn't know what other benefits he received from working with Ingrid.

Garmr untangled from Fen and came at me. But before I needed to put up my defenses, a chilling snarl filled the air. Garmr scrambled back, his wolf eyes going wide. But he wasn't fast enough.

Diego, in his full dragon form, snatched the wolf shifter in his massive jaws and bit down. The squelching sound of tearing flesh and crunching bones echoed through the street, pausing much of the skirmishes. Blood splattered everywhere. Diego slammed Garmr's body on the ground, and it hit with a hard *thud*. Diego roared, the sound shaking windows.

Garmr's breaths came out in a wheeze, and his limbs twitched. *"You think... you have won..."* He chuckled. *"But you haven't. He is coming... for you. He'll kill your... precious Valkyrie... or enslave her."*

He gurgled out another chuckle before Diego gored the shifter.

Garmr breathed no more.

I stood there, staring at the dead wolf, my breathing coming in panting puffs. He was dead. The shifter who'd caused us so much pain was finally dead. And I was alive.

The prophecy I'd heard so long ago flitted through my mind. It'd come true, but not how we expected.

Garmr was dead, never prevailing in his ultimate quest to kill me. And Diego struck the killing blow, stealing that honor I desired in revenge for what he'd done to my Valkyrie.

Ingrid put on the most forced act of concern I'd ever witnessed. "Oh no. You've broken one of his toys. He's not going to like that."

Damn. Some ally she was. *And what did she mean by that last comment?* What had Garmr meant with his final words?

The woman grinned. "Oh well. More fun for us."

I took a step back when she threw out her hand and dark magic sprang from her fingertips. It shot for Garmr's body and sank beneath his bleeding flesh.

He twitched.

He writhed.

He jerked his head up, eyes devoid of life.

I couldn't believe what I was seeing. Ingrid was making these corrupted creatures. Was that how they were always made, even when the host was alive?

It didn't matter. I summoned my sword and swung for the corrupted shifter. I wouldn't allow this thing to so much as move.

The blade sunk deep into Garmr's neck. With what should have been an easy head sever, my sword met with magical resistance. I yanked my weapon free, the body jerking and struggling. Aya jumped in, swinging her weapon into the slice I'd made, severing Garmr's head from his shoulders. The wolf body dropped and his head rolled.

Ingrid scowled. "Well, that was no fun." Her mood switched to flippant and uncaring. "Oh well. This won't save any of you. You will die, no matter how hard you—"

A gun fired three times.

The woman blinked and stumbled back. She looked down at her chest, where a mix of blood and black ichor oozed from three bullet wounds. Her livid eyes snapped up, and we all jerked our attention to Officer Rory.

"You fool!" I shouted. *Why the hel is he out here?*

He didn't respond. Instead, Rory fired his gun again. Except, Ingrid wasn't caught off guard this time. She stopped the bullets and shot them back at Rory. Astrid screamed and flew to him.

Ingrid cackled. "Foolish."

"You bitch," Aya snarled, readying her blade.

Angel snarled out of nowhere. I'd lost track of her in all the fighting. The dog barreled into Ingrid, clamping down on her arm and shaking. Ingrid howled in agony and raised her hand to strike the dog when Fen lunged and snapped his jaws around her other arm.

Ingrid screamed, and power exploded out of her. I braced myself, but the magic was stronger, blasting me back. I landed in a practiced roll and jerked my head up. Ingrid wailed, her arms gushing red blood and black ichor where they'd been ripped off at the elbow for one, and broken and severed mid-bicep for the other, where Fen had crushed it with his overpowering bite force.

"Heathens!" she screamed. "How dare you! You will rue the day you crossed my mistress. When she comes to take what is hers, we will not spare you."

Ingrid's eyes went black, the ichor dripping from her body coming to life. It swirled around her and shot out to her living allies and corrupted creatures. The black liquid consumed them, and then they were gone.

"Fuck, that's disturbing," Bjarke grumbled, his words coming out as growls in the ear but proper words in the mind in the same way Fen's did.

"Fen, take the Berserkers and scout the area," Aya ordered. "Just in case there are more lingering about. We especially don't need those corrupted creatures skulking around."

I spun on my heels and rushed over to Astrid and Rory. She was scolding him.

"I don't know how many times we have to tell you to wear your ballistic vest," she said. Her hands glowed with her golden healing magic, which floated around him and seeped into his wounds.

Rory chuckled. "Well, if I had, then I wouldn't have gotten so close to our guardian angel."

Despite shaking her head, she had a soft smile on her lips. "I'm not an angel."

"Then what are you?"

"A Valkyrie."

He smiled. "Then if I died in the line of duty protecting the people of this town, I'm glad it would be you shepherding my soul."

"Well, I'm sorry to say, Officer, but you're going to live."

The two laughed. It was good to see the man in good spirits, considering what he'd experienced today.

More people ventured out of the nearby buildings, hesitant and wary. That was to be expected. Though, their experience did pose a problem. How would they react? Would this force Astrid and the rest to leave? Runavík was an option, as was our original home together, though I'd need to modernize it before she moved in. But this place was Astrid's home.

Astrid's magic dissipated, and she patted him on the shoulder. "There, good as new. You're lucky those magic coins were in your chest pocket."

The older man's brow furrowed, and he pulled several coins out of the front pocket of his uniform. "Magic coins?"

Astrid tapped them. "I can feel the magic on them. Some sort of protection enchantment. I don't know how you got them, but they saved your life."

He gazed lovingly at the coins. "My son sent these to me on his last tour. Said he found them in a quaint bazaar where the vendor said they were ancient and special. You gift them to those you love to keep them safe. I've carried them with me ever since. And when Edna died, I made sure to carry hers, for the sake of his memory."

I felt a strange pull to this conversation. I held out my hand. "May I?"

Rory handed them over. I inspected the coins. "These are, in fact, ancient. I remember the fae using these coins at one time. How your son got his hands on them, I don't know. They are protective of their artifacts."

I handed them back to him. "But, I believe they're in safe hands with you."

The officer blinked, as if trying to process my mention of fae, and then smiled. "Ethan was always finding strange things in his travels. He had a knack for it."

Something *pinged* in the back of my mind. It felt related to why I was drawn to this man. "Do you happen to have a photograph of your son?"

Though perplexed by my question, Rory nodded and pulled out a photo from his wallet. Numbness fell over me when I got a look at the young man in military fatigues.

"Ethan went MIA in—"

"Desert Storm," I finished.

Astrid tipped her head. "Tyr?"

I summoned my axe, making Rory jump, and tugged on the leather wrapping on the haft. It came loose with ease and upon unraveling the material, I revealed tightly bound and protected dog tags.

Rory sat up straighter, his eyes wide.

I removed the dog tags and offered them to the man. "I met your son. I couldn't get him out of the place that would become his body's tomb, but I made a promise to return these to his family should I ever find them. Know, he died with honor worthy of any warrior."

Tears welled in Rory's eyes. He reached for his son's tags, but just before he could take them, Astrid touched them with her finger. I looked at her, to find her eyes unfocused.

"There's a soul in these," she mumbled.

Magic sparked from her fingertips, and I jerked back when it formed into a translucent man. Gasps filled the air.

"E—Ethan?" Rory managed.

The spirit, or projection of a spirit—I wasn't sure what was going on, as I'd never seen this before—smiled at his father. They reached each other, and on upon contact, golden magic tendrils curled up Rory's arm. His eyes widened and tears broke free, trickling down his cheeks.

"Your mother and I are so proud of you," he said.

"I know." Ethan's words came out distorted, the magic struggling to simulate them.

They exchanged a few more words before Astrid spoke up. "Are you ready, Ethan?"

He saluted her, and she smiled before touching his form. "To Fólkvangr you go, then."

His spirit faded into sparkles that lifted high into the heavens. This choice didn't surprise me. Astrid and Aya had talked about it after she became a Valkyrie. Astrid wasn't comfortable sending souls to Valhalla, even if Odin was gone. So they agreed she'd send them to Aya.

"Fólkvangr?" Officer Rory said. "Not Valhalla?"

Astrid shook her head. "He deserves a more prestigious place of rest."

Rory broke down, holding the dog tags close to his chest. Astrid comforted him, guiding him through his final stage of healing that her Valkyrie soul called her to do.

When he calmed, we helped Officer Rory up. He stood taller, and seemed a little younger, as if the weight of his burdens had aged him prematurely.

This now only left the inevitable discussion. Darius had joined us during our moment with Rory, and Diego had returned to his human form, though it appeared as though Raeni was pestering him. Aya found it funny, whatever the teen was doing.

"I'm really sorry, everyone," Astrid said. "We never meant for this to happen. I didn't think they'd go so far as to attack innocent people. We—"

"Oh no, don't you dare." Carrie pushed herself to the front. "Don't you dare tell us you're going to leave, girl."

Astrid held up a placating hand. "Things are only going to get worse. And we—"

"And you what? Want us to pretend we didn't see any of this?" Carrie challenged. "Pretend that the fairy tales we tell our children aren't actually true? That things that go bump in the night aren't real?"

She vehemently shook her head. "No. Absolutely not. If things like that are out there, you ain't going anywhere, Astrid."

Officer Rory placed a hand on Astrid's shoulder. "Your family has been here for a long time. You grew up here. I don't know how a Valkyrie can grow up, but I think we're all willing to hear you out. We can't forget what we've seen. So, if we know more, maybe we can all agree on how to move forward."

Most of the townsfolk nodded. Some were unsure, but they were by far the minority. It didn't surprise me. Darius and Astrid had built a strong foundation here. These people would trust her with their lives because of that.

Astrid nodded. "Okay. I think we can do that."

I noticed the weariness in her eyes. Her adrenaline was wearing off, and she'd used a lot of magic today. This had been more than a test. This had been everything she'd been training for, and she'd done incredibly.

Raeni raised her hand. "Can I start by asking why Diego gets to be a dragon and I can't?"

Laughter erupted. Fearless, as always. The teen never ceased to amaze me. But I supposed I shouldn't have been surprised. She took after her mother, after all.

"I think the better question to focus on is, what were those things?" Officer Rory asked. "And was that crazy lunatic really your mother?"

Astrid frowned. "Unfortunately, yes. Though, I don't know the answer to your other question." She glanced at me. "It's been centuries since I last saw one of them, and we didn't really know what they were then."

The mention of centuries got the people's attention, especially since they knew Astrid grew up here.

"I can answer that," Aya said. All eyes fell on her. "They're amalgamations created by the goddess Malsumis."

I scowled. I knew little about that deity, but I'd heard she had some relation to Azzie, and something about corruption.

"Malsumis is a deity from these lands. However, her power was so vast, it was capable of occasionally affecting other continents. It corrupted souls and turned them into the creatures you saw today. When other gods and I sealed Malsumis, it locked up that power, and greatly reduced how often those cursed creatures were created."

"So... Ingrid is aligned with this Malsumis?" Astrid said. I found her choice to call the woman by her name and not the title of mother very interesting. Hopefully, it would stay that way. That woman didn't deserve to be called a mother.

Darius tapped the car he leaned on. "Meaning she was either always aligned with this deity, or they converted her after I met her."

I had a sinking suspicion that woman was already worshiping the goddess and infiltrated FU.

Aya continued to talk to the townsfolk, filling them in on various things they needed to know right now to decide what they wanted. I found myself distracted.

Two ravens perched on a light pole, their focus on us unnatural. A ripple of unease worked its way down my spine. *These ravens...*

Astrid noticed them, too, and wandered closer. She cocked her head. "Huginn? Muninn?"

Aya stopped her lesson. "That's not possible. With Odin's death, that should have severed his familiar bonds, and they would have become regular ravens."

We all stared up at the birds, until Astrid spoke up. "Hey, pretty bird. What are you doing?"

I shivered at her familiar greeting to Muninn. After the celebration that resulted in her healing him, the raven would visit with her on the regular. She'd feed him and talk as if he were a friend. I'd tried to warn her not to, as he and Huginn were Odin's favorite spies, but she brushed off that concern, always promising she never told the bird anything Odin would find worthwhile.

One raven croaked and flew off. The other stayed, watching her intently. He then swooped down and landed on her shoulder. Astrid giggled as he excitedly nuzzled her face and played with her hair, the exact way he always had.

"Muninn!" She nuzzled him back. "I missed you too. But how? I don't understand."

She listened as he talked privately with her. Her brow furrowed. "What? What do you mean I need to be careful? Who is lurking? Muninn, how are you and your brother still alive?"

He touched her cheek affectionately once more and then flew off.

Astrid clutched her necklace pendant, chewing her lip. "I don't like the warning he gave me."

"That shouldn't be possible," Aya said. "Not unless someone else took over their familiar bond, but no one could find them after the battle. Baldur spent so long desperately searching for them."

Astrid turned to look at us. "Garmr and Ingrid both said some peculiar things that made it sound like they were talking about Odin in the present tense. Did anyone ever confirm Odin's dead body after the war?"

Aya and I passed each other a look, concern setting in. Neither of us had.

"I think it might be best to look into this," Astrid said. "Just to be sure."

I didn't like this one bit. There was no way Odin was still alive. But a part of me also didn't believe that, either.

"We don't tell Fen," Aya warned. "Or Starkad. Not until we're sure. Both will go off the deep end if we tell them about these speculations."

Astrid and I agreed, and Astrid suggested we inform Kirby in private so we could decide how to proceed.

In the middle of her talking, Astrid yawned so widely that her jaw popped. Diego chuckled as he walked over. "Why don't we get you back home? You've earned a rest."

"But we have to keep explaining stuff to everyone," Astrid said. "And Fen and the others aren't back yet."

"We'll take care of all of it," Darius said. "Don't worry, Ace. Even Angel is doing her job, going between people to give them the comfort they need after all this."

"After she pissed on Garmr's corpse," Aya added, rather proudly.

Astrid laughed. "Okay. Okay. We can go back. I don't have the energy to teleport, though."

Aya placed her hands on her hips. "What am I, chopped liver? I'm perfectly capable of teleporting you without needing to travel with you."

Then suddenly, we were no longer in the town, but in Astrid's room. The remaining adrenaline keeping Astrid up drained quickly, and she listed into Diego.

He steadied her. "Let's get you relaxed. You've been through—"

"I killed people…" she murmured, her eyes unfocused. She lifted her hand up to her mouth, and her body convulsed. "Oh gods, I killed someone."

She shoved away from Diego and bolted into the bathroom. I winced when she puked. That was to be expected. She was lucky she hadn't lost it during the fight.

Diego and I followed her in. He knelt next to her and pulled her hair back.

"Why aren't you a mess?" she complained.

"Because I shot most of my enemies, and, well, Garmr was a wolf, so I didn't really feel like I was killing a person. More like hunting as a dragon. And I… kinda liked it."

She frowned. "At least one of us did."

Astrid puked again.

Diego looked to me. He didn't know how to help. I did.

I nodded for him to leave the room, and he did. She'd want something to drink after she emptied her stomach. Maybe something to eat from all the energy she expended.

I held back Astrid's hair and rubbed her back while waiting for her to stop retching. When she did, she continued to hug the toilet, and hung her head while breathing hard, as if expecting the compulsion to expel everything in her stomach to return.

"I don't understand," she mumbled. "My past-self and my Valkyrie helped me shut down my emotions. Those… things weren't human anymore… I was basically putting them out of their misery. Why do I feel this way?"

She was talking about those parts of her like they were separate entities. Maybe that's how she was processing what she went through. I hoped that was the case, at least. "Because killing with your own hands for the first time is always the hardest," I said. "And because you're a healer."

"I killed in the past."

"But not in the present." I rubbed her back more. "You're a gentle soul, Astrid. Remember what we talked about? You are fierce and bold, but you still balance that with a gentle core. The world we lived in back then didn't allow for you to be that gentle soul. It forced you to be hardy, otherwise you'd be killed yourself. That's not how it is now."

"I'm a Valkyrie, Tyr. I agreed to help Kirby. I swore I'd avenge Baldur. I'm going to have to kill again."

I nodded. "You probably will. I can't say if you'll get used to the feeling or not. If not, that's okay."

I brushed a loose hair away from her eyes. "You did amazing, keeping everyone safe. And even after all the magic you used today, you still saved Officer Rory's life. Maybe you won't be a battle-hardened Valkyrie. Maybe you'll be a support Valkyrie. Someone who heals and protects us with magic."

She squinted. "A battle-medic Valkyrie? Can't say I've ever heard of one of those before."

I chuckled. "A first of her kind. Or you're supposed to be our winged witch. Don't get too close with your weapons if you don't have to, and rely on that offensive magic. Who knows?"

She nodded slowly, her eyes contemplative.

Diego returned, water in hand. "Filled Dad in, reassured him everyone, especially us, is okay, and now he's making food."

"I'm not hungry," Astrid muttered. "I don't think I'll be able to eat for a while."

Diego shrugged. "I'm starved, and from the text I got from Aya, all the Berserkers coming here for a feast are, too. Dad's pretty stoked, especially since Aya promised to get him whatever ingredients he wanted."

I was hungry as well, but for something other than food. Astrid noticed my gaze and rolled her eyes. "Really? You have shit timing."

I rubbed her cheek where blood had dried. "You had that sexy-assin deadly look on your face throughout that fight, I feel the rage of battle victory in my veins, you're covered in the blood of our enemies, and you were just vulnerable with me. How am I not supposed to feel like indulging in a different kind of feast?"

She flushed the toilet and stood. "Because all I can taste is vomit, I feel like a herd of Berserkers ran over me and then backed up for good measure, and I'm sure if I look in that mirror I'm going to look like I belong in a zombie apocalypse movie, and that's not very sexy."

I chuckled. I begged to differ. She was radiant in this moment.

Diego set the glass of water down for her after she finished brushing her teeth, and turned on the tub faucet.

"What are you doing?" Astrid mumbled around the toothbrush in her mouth.

Diego grabbed a jar from a cupboard and poured the white granular contents into the bath. "You said you feel like you've been run over. So, you get to relax."

She let out a relieved sigh. "Thank you."

She then squeaked when our clothes disappeared suddenly. "Una!"

The fae was nowhere to be seen, but I suspected she was scurrying away, invisible.

"Damned fae," Astrid muttered before spitting out her toothpaste.

My eyes raked over her luscious curves. "Well, we need to be naked to bathe."

"It's called consent."

The corner of my lip quirked up. "Would you rather I'd ripped your clothes off?"

"No." Though she said it, her cheeks pinked a little. As much as she hated her clothes being ruined, she did also enjoy my rougher ways.

I motioned for her to lean down, and she complied. I kissed her, enjoying the taste of her mixed with the mint from her toothpaste.

She squeaked when I wrapped my arms around her and pulled her against me, my mouth releasing hers and claiming her body. Astrid moaned, and it sounded like she was about to say something, when Diego came up behind her and claimed her mouth.

I lifted her up and eagerly devoured her pussy, relishing her taste on my tongue, and taking her as my reward for a well-fought battle.

Astrid writhed under our attention and was unable to last long, falling quickly into our pleasure, and she screamed as orgasm took over her.

"You're both evil," she murmured when she came down. "Absolute devils."

"No, just a dragon and a god who enjoy our Valkyrie." Diego swept her up into his arms and carried her to the bath, where he sank into the water with her. "Including pampering her whenever she wants."

She let out a breathy sigh as the warm water soothed her aches.

I pulled myself closer, trying to ignore my hard cock begging for release right now, and grabbed a washcloth. This tub wasn't large enough for me, let alone all three of us, so this would have to do.

Diego ran his hands along Astrid's back, working them into her tight and sore muscles. She moaned quietly, the sound wreaking havoc on my senses. I really wanted to continue indulging in her.

I dipped the washcloth into the water and lightly scrubbed her arm. She made me stop. "Tyr, your hand."

I looked down at them both.

"I'm not using my magic," she said. "How…"

"At first, I thought you might still be," I said. "Because I don't have any feeling in this one. But now I'm realizing a bit more why I didn't regrow my hand."

Astrid frowned and took my new hand into hers. She could tell I felt nothing by my lack of response to her delicate touch. "Is it because of my magic? Did I do something to make it permanent? Maybe there's a way for me to give you back your—"

I pressed a finger to her lips. "It's not you, Valkyrie. Not entirely. I realized, when I made that vow to find you, I put my god power into it. Our words have weight. We have to be careful about our vows and decrees. And as not only a god of war, but order and justice, I ended up making a decree."

Her eyes widened. "You judged yourself?"

I nodded. "I felt responsible for your death. I deemed myself unworthy, and vowing to find you would be my redemption. Then, and only then, would I be deemed worthy enough to be whole again."

She frowned. "But you did find me."

I brushed my new hand along her cheek, wishing I could feel with this one. "Physically, yes—I have—but the vow is more than just the physical. Today, we freed you from the shifter that haunted you through this endless cycle. It freed you from *that* burden. But you're not free, not while Ingrid still lives. So, until we deal with her, I'm still expected to serve my sentence."

She turned her face into my hand and kissed me. "We'll do it together."

I leaned in and brushed my lips against hers. "Always."

I claimed her mouth, and water sloshed out of the tub as Diego moved to entangle himself with her as well. By the time we were done and satisfied after enjoying Astrid, and she us, most of this water would be on the floor.

THIRTY-TWO

ASTRID

My discarded utensil clattered in the sink. I swayed along to the music playing from the speaker on the kitchen island. Xavier cooked something elaborate, refusing to tell anyone what he was up to. It wasn't time for dinner yet, and it was obvious the portion size wasn't for the whole house.

The front door opened, and Angel charged into the house. Dad walked in after her with a grocery bag in one hand, a redheaded baby strapped to his chest, and a dark-haired one snugly secured on his back. I squealed and ran over to him, taking the shopping bag before he could offer it, and ran back into the kitchen.

"Thanks, Dad, I really appreciate you stopping at the store to grab baking supplies I didn't check to make sure I had before I started baking," Dad said in a mocking voice that was supposed to be mine.

Xavier laughed; I rolled my eyes. "Sounds like Grandpa doesn't want a cookie pie all to himself as a thank you."

"No, I never said that!"

I chuckled and pulled out the bag of flour and sugar. I may not be the best cook, but I sure could bake. And Dad especially loved my cookie pies.

Dad sat at the island and perused through a pile of photos I'd taken him away from for my baking quest. They were from the solo trip back up to Canada he'd taken a few weeks ago. I'd wanted to go with him so I could see Arran and Hurrit, but my schedule didn't work out this time, especially with us planning a trip in a few weeks for our daughter-father hunting trip.

Dad cooed at his precious cargo between photograph flips. It brought a smile to my face.

The babies, Birdie and Bard, as they were affectionately called by everyone, were Magnus' *very* special twins. The nicknames had started out as a jest from Dahlia, due to their respective fathers, and then, much to Magnus's dismay, caught on with everyone else, so they ended up sticking. I couldn't even recall their actual names at this point. Luckily, Magnus was a good sport, and it didn't harm the relationship she'd been building with us.

Magnus happily used that relationship for her babysitting needs whenever she and her partners needed a break. And Dad was all too keen to take them in as his grandkids, just like I thought he would. Same with taking anyone else in as family if they wanted. It was creating quite the dynamic in this house, on top of the changes around here.

More and more supernaturals, immortals, and even mortals in touch with the magical community showed up in town looking for a place of sanctuary. It was a strange thing to witness over these past months, especially with how well the mortal people of the town had adjusted to the new reality.

We also had more residents, some staying on the property, others preferring to stay in town but needing the therapy Diego and I offered. We were at a point where I was worried we'd need more help, but I had no resources to source therapists with knowledge of supernatural existence. *I should talk to Dahlia and Aya about it. Maybe between a cyberwarfare goddess of war and a dragon with super-soldier-hacker training, they can find someone.*

Aya breezed into the room and immediately went to playing with Bard. He giggled and babbled. The sight of them both with these babies was just too adorable. *Careful, Astrid, we don't want to be picturing things happening between her and Dad.* That was the last thing I wanted to think about.

"How's that search going?" Dad asked her.

"We're getting close to finding a location," Aya said, between croons at Bard. "Dahlia did another tweak to her program, and it's actually getting a few blips for us to analyze."

Dad nodded. "Good. I'll infiltrate any location we need, no matter how small a lead."

After I'd told Dad and Aya what Ingrid had said about the magic blockers, they'd jumped right into researching what she'd done to me, and the risk these posed for everyone should they try to spread its reach. I had no doubt they already had, long before she revealed the truth to me. They'd have wanted all kinds of test subjects, and if you're going to follow a goddess of chaos, one good way to cause it was to kill the magic in the supernatural community.

Between Dahlia's and Magnus' hacker skills, Aya's cyberwarfare prowess, and Dad's resources and experience, they made for an awesome team. I knew they'd get to the source soon enough.

Tyr entered the room while I was in the middle of mixing my dry ingredients. He walked past and slapped my ass; I gasped. He chuckled while smirking before taking Birdie from Dad. He lifted her high in the air. She kicked her little feet and arms, smiling down at him as he spoke softly and lifted her up and down as if he were bench pressing the infant.

Seeing him be so gentle and caring with these two babies when Magnus brought them over, did something intense to my ovaries. I swallowed. *Simmer down, hormones. Not now. We've got plenty of time.*

Dad turned to me, a wicked grin on his lips. "Ace, when are you going to finally give me grandbabies?"

"Oh, for the love of—" I threw my hands into the air and the others laughed. "Really? You have two right here. That's supposed to distract you for a bit."

Dad continued to grin. "Yes, I have two, but what about another?"

I sighed and rolled my eyes.

"You've got two boyfriends, Ace. Wouldn't be too hard." Dad turned to Tyr. "Ain't that right?"

Tyr's eyes flicked to me, and my stomach swooped at their intensity. "When she wants them, we'll have that discussion then."

Dad blew out a breath. "Dammit."

Aya and Tyr laughed.

I smiled. I knew how difficult that had to have been for Tyr to word himself like that. We'd tried in my past life to have a family. It never happened.

With me having a new body, and better fertility and adoption resources in the event I couldn't carry again, that dream would be on his mind. But I needed time. A few years of navigating and enjoying my relationship with him and Diego, it was all I asked. *Hell, I haven't even used the L-word with either of them.*

"What about me?" Xavier hip-checked me. "Unlike the rest of you, I'm not getting any younger, and I also would like little Santos Erikson feet scurrying around calling me abuelo."

I narrowed my eyes in warning, making him laugh. I was glad he took so well to the truth of the world, and the fact he was surrounded by immortals, but that didn't get him a free pass on this topic. "It'd be Santos Astridsdotter or -son if we combined traditions, thank you."

At least, that was how it'd be right now. Should future children come along, I'd be discussing naming conventions privately with their respective father to be sure we agreed on everything. But bringing in some tradition, even if we blended in our own, was appealing to me.

I'd already gone and changed my surname to Bjørnsdotter, reviving the family tradition. Dad had wanted to do it from the start, but because he was going by his current alias, he didn't think he could make it all make sense. *Thank fuck Aya was able to make that transition painless.* The magical community was a lawless world where we got away with a lot, and mortals were none the wiser.

"Where's Diego?" Dad asked. "I need him here to help us."

I rolled my eyes. "He's with Urd. Not that it matters. He'll take the same stance as Tyr, and you know it."

Xavier briefly paused at the mention of Urd, and then resumed cooking. He still wasn't on speaking terms with her. I hoped one of these days he'd at least be willing to sit down and hear her out, but Diego and I wouldn't push.

This was one hell of a complicated situation, and at the very least, Xavier didn't try to hinder Diego from rebuilding his relationship with his mom. He only got a little weird sometimes when she was brought up in conversation, and made himself scarce when Diego invited her over.

A phone pinged and Tyr pulled out his older-than-dinosaurs flip phone. *I really need to convince him to upgrade.* "I got a text from Davyn."

I sputtered a laugh, and he shot me an exasperated look. "Why do you do that every time I mention using a phone?"

"Because it's you, and I'm surprised you're capable of operating one," I said through giggles.

Technology seriously confused Tyr. When someone said they were technology-challenged, they paled in comparison to some of these gods. It made Saturday night D&D games extra hilarious when everyone couldn't meet in person. The game itself didn't click with him, and adding digital game-play didn't help.

Tyr shook his head. "He has a lead on Loki."

The butter in my hand oozed out of the waxed paper wrapper and plopped on the counter when my hand slowly squeezed the life out of the poor dairy product. *Loki.*

"Ace, take a breath," Dad said. "I know this situation is a hard one, but you need to make sure you go into this with a level head."

He's right. I sucked in a deep breath through my nose and then rubbed Baldur's vambrace on my arm. I wore it and Mother Randi's all the time. They brought me comfort, and helped me stay calm and focused whenever I found myself overwhelmed.

"Do you have a plan yet on how to deal with Loki? It's not easy to kill a god, especially a slippery one like him," Dad said. He knew about the vow I made. He didn't like that I walked down a road filled with bloodshed, and a part of me didn't either, but he also understood I couldn't back down now.

I shook my head. "No."

I didn't know how to deal with him or Ingrid. She'd all but

disappeared from the face of the earth. Dahlia couldn't even find her on some supercomputer program that could find people down to their exact location based on their life energy... or something like that. A part of me hoped Ingrid died of her injuries, but I suspected she hadn't. That would have been too easy.

"But I'll figure something out." I stroked the armor again. I had to come up with something. Not just for my oath, but for my soul. It demanded vengeance against Loki. *How dare he take Baldur from me.*

I went about cleaning up my mess and threw my next question to Tyr. "When does Davyn want us to meet up?"

He looked at his phone. "He hasn't said. They're investigating the lead first. We'll pop in to their location if it's proven correct."

That might give me time to still make my cookie pies, and be a good distraction, because the urge to go find Loki and gut him was quite strong. *I need another stick of butter.*

Whipping out my phone, I let Diego know the update, and also teased him a little on his "how to be a *proper* dragon" lessons with his mom. I then rummaged in the fridge.

I found more butter and closed the fridge door. Turning, I did not expect someone to be directly behind me. I shrieked and chucked the butter stick at him.

Diego pulled into himself to defend against the cold projectile. "Cielo!"

I breathed hard, eyes wide, and hand on my chest, where my heart threatened to burst out. The others lost themselves in their laughter.

After taking a moment to process, I punched Diego in the arm several times. "Don't scare me like that!"

He was lucky I'd lobbed the butter at him instead of magic.

Diego laughed and fended me off. "I didn't mean to. It's not like I can tell which way you're facing when I teleport."

I knew that struggle. Teleportation had all kinds of quirks that required experience to overcome—and experience was not something either of us had much of yet. "Why are you here? You said you'd be gone for a few days."

He held up his phone. "I got your text."

I blinked and shook my head. "That wasn't so you'd drop what you were doing and rush back. I only wanted to keep you informed. We're not even leaving right now."

"I'm not about to let you go after a maniac of a god without proper supervision. And Tyr definitely doesn't count as supervision."

I rolled my eyes, Tyr grunted, and Dad laughed.

"Besides, Mom and I weren't doing anything, so you're not dragging me away."

I shook my head and retrieved my thrown butter stick. Xavier tapped Diego on the shoulder and asked him to follow. He carried glass food storage containers in one arm, as well as a bottle of wine. Diego and I passed each other a perplexed look before he followed his dad out of the kitchen toward his father's room.

I used my magic to perfectly soften my butter and mixed up my batter by the time Diego returned, alone. "Where's your dad?"

He rubbed the back of his neck. "With Mom."

The house grew quiet.

I blinked. "What?"

"Yeah, I guess he's finally ready to talk to her."

"That explains the food."

Aya sighed wistfully. "Even when mad, he's a romantic."

"Let's just hope the talk goes well," Dad said. "I don't care how they patch things up, as long as the tension goes away."

I agreed.

Dad went back to sorting through his developed photos. Diego kissed me on the forehead before offering to help me bake, while also getting distracted by the babies, which gained me a few more looks from Dad, and another round of me chastising my hormones. Tyr settled in at the island while playing with his precious drool-bubble-blowing cargo.

"Oops," Dad murmured when one of his photographs got away from him. It slipped across the island counter and onto the floor on my side of the kitchen.

"Got it!" I snatched it before Diego could. I took a look at the picture before handing it to Dad.

The photo was of a woman with pale skin and wavy copper curls. She wore a cobble of leather, and a bustier along with a long skirt. Everything in me froze as I stared into her green eyes. "Dad, who is this?"

"That's Elin. She's a close friend of Arran and Hurrit. Poor girl lost her memory about five years ago in an accident. They've been helping her out ever since she moved to Bifrost. She's the one who makes the holistic lotion I brought back for us to test with the residents."

He paused. "What's wrong, Ace?"

The picture staring back at me seemed to move, and a flash hit my mind, but not of this moment in the photograph. No, a day in a market, a long time ago.

"Valkyrie?" Tyr said.

"I… I know her," I said, hardly able to believe the words were coming out of my mouth.

Dad straightened. "What?"

"I know her." The memory shifted and solidified. "At the market…"

My attention jerked up to Tyr. "It was the day King Geir tried to make me marry him."

"A king wanted to marry you?" Diego said, sounding impressed.

Tyr grunted. "Hard to forget that day. A lot of fucking balls he had, thinking he could take Astrid from me."

"Astrid, what are you saying?" Dad said. "Are you saying you met Elin back during your first life?"

I nodded slowly, taking in the memory. "My mother Randi and I were shopping in the market when we came in contact with a woman with copper hair. My mother… had a vision. She told the woman she'd face a destiny like none have ever seen."

I closed my eyes, desperate to remember what Randi had said. Then it hit me.

A Valkyrie made not like any have ever seen
Not one to a single god she prays
Not to Odinn like those this day
But behold, a great tragedy will befall you first
A curse of the gods, to wander and live but to forget and live anew

Half an eternity the sun shall rise and fall before they free that
which binds you

My gaze snapped to Aya, realization sinking in. "We need to call
Kirby. I think we know where one of our Valkyries is."